D1462810

.45-CALIBER

CUNO MASSEY, GUN ON THE RUN

.45-CALIBER

A WESTERN DUO

PETER BRANDVOLD

FIVE STAR
A part of Gale, a Cengage Company

Farmington Hills, Mich • San Francisco • New York • Waterville, Maine
Meriden, Conn • Mason, Ohio • Chicago

LIBRARY OF CONGRESS CATALOGING-IN-PUBLICATION DATA

Names: Brandvold, Peter, author.
Title: .45 caliber : a western duo / Peter Brandvold.
Description: First edition. | Waterville, Maine : Five Star Publishing, a part of Cengage Learning, Inc., [2017]
Identifiers: LCCN 2017022960 (print) | LCCN 2017027007 (ebook) | ISBN 9781432837082 (ebook) | ISBN 1432837087 (ebook) | ISBN 9781432837099 (ebook) | ISBN 1432837095 (ebook) | ISBN 9781432837310 (hardcover) | ISBN 1432837311 (hardcover)
Subjects: | GSAFD: Western stories.
Classification: LCC PS3552.R3236 (ebook) | LCC PS3552.R3236 A6 2017f (print) | DDC 813/.54—dc23
LC record available at https://lccn.loc.gov/2017022960

First Edition. First Printing: December 2017
Find us on Facebook–https://www.facebook.com/FiveStarCengage
Visit our website–http://www.gale.cengage.com/fivestar/
Contact Five Star™ Publishing at FiveStar@cengage.com

Printed in the United States of America
1 2 3 4 5 6 7 21 20 19 18 17

For the beer-swilling Feral Pig of northwestern Minnesota,
Kent Quamme

TABLE OF CONTENTS

★ ★ ★ ★ ★

.45-CALIBER TOWN UNDER SIEGE

★ ★ ★ ★ ★

CHAPTER ONE

Cuno Massey pulled the old Pittsburg freight wagon off the main trail and onto a rough two-track that curved gently through autumn-yellow aspens to the base of Crow Mountain. When he saw the tumbledown trapper's cabin hunched before the gurgling creek spotted with fallen leaves, the young man grinned.

She was there, just like he'd hoped she would be.

Kate Lord's calico mare stood in the shade of one of the aspens, near a front corner of the trapper's shack, pulling at turkeyfoot and lazily switching its tail. Cuno clucked and flipped his reins over the backs of the two mules in the traces, and the wagon rattled along the trail through the trees and into the grassy yard spotted with rocks and sage. The calico looked back over its left wither at the mules and the stocky, blond young man driving the wagon, and gave a whinny.

Both mules brayed.

"Hello, there, Miss Ida," Cuno said as he hauled back on the reins.

When the wagon had rattled to a stop in front of the cabin, whose moldering shake shingles were green with moss, Cuno set the brake and climbed down, doffing his hat, running a hand through his shoulder-length, sweat-damp hair, and looked around.

"Kate?" he called.

Quickly, he unhitched the team and led the mules through

the brush to a bend in the creek where they could drink and forage.

The breeze whispered in the golden aspens. It was Indian summer here in northern New Mexico Territory, and the air was unseasonably warm though most of the trees had already shed their leaves, and winter would be here soon with its snows and chill northern winds blowing down over the Sangre de Cristos to the north and from the Llano Estacado to the east.

Soon, today's glorious warmth and fair blue skies would be a fond memory. The air sliding against young Massey's face was spiced with the smell of cinnamon and the tang of pines, junipers, and cedars. There was a slight thread of coolness at the edge of the warmth that bespoke the harsh change to come.

Squirrels chittered and chickadees peeped as Cuno strode around in front of the cabin, pivoting at the hips, looking around for his lover, Kate Lord.

"Kate?" he called.

He went over and looked through one of the cabin's front windows, both shutters of which sagged toward the dilapidated front porch. The shack had long been abandoned. It was used now and then by passing saddle tramps and drift riders from area ranches, some of whom would make a minimal effort to seal the place up from the winter cold, clean birds' nests and bat guano out of the chimney pipe, and sweep out the dirt and dung and leaves that blew in regularly.

But mostly, the shack was a derelict. The air sliding through the open windows was rife with the smell of moldy wood and mouse turds. The east wall appeared as though it would collapse inward with the next stiff wind.

"Kate?" Cuno called into the cabin's heavy, purple shadows.

The only reply was the soft, gurgling call of an unseen pigeon.

Cuno walked to the far end of the porch, the rotten boards squawking beneath his boots, and stepped down into the yard.

He walked around behind the cabin and into the mixed aspens and conifers beyond the swaybacked, door-less privy.

The creek lay ahead—cool and blue and deep here in a broad bend cut by spring floodwaters churning down from the high reaches of Crow Mountain in the Sangre de Cristos. It had been a wet summer, and recent rains in the mountains had kept the creek running nearly to the tops of its banks.

"Kate?" Cuno called again, looking around.

The girl must be off gathering wildflowers or foraging for mushrooms, which she often did when she and Cuno met out here, a good two miles away from the prying eyes of the impudent citizens of the little settlement of Nopal, which meant "prickly pear" in Spanish.

He moved closer to the creek, staring into the woods on the far side.

A shadow slid over the decayed leaves and low sage shrubs to his right. A twig snapped. All too accustomed to danger, Cuno wheeled instinctively, heart thudding.

A girl screamed and stepped back, bringing a hand to her mouth and staring down in shock at the .45-caliber Peacemaker that Massey hadn't even realized he'd pulled from the holster thonged low on his stout right thigh. Of course, he'd known the piece, given to him by the old gunfighter, Charlie Dodge, would be there.

It was always there in his hand when his senses told him he might need it. He had an uncanny ability with a six-gun, an ability he'd never known he had until Charlie Dodge had started showing him how to shoot, bringing that natural ability out in him—a young midwesterner who'd spent the first seventeen years of his life driving freight wagons for his father, now dead.

There was no need for the gun here.

Quickly, he lowered the .45 while depressing the hammer with a soft click, his cheeks and ears burning. Kate stood before him, a hand over her mouth, her own cheeks flushed with shock and surprise, her eyes as wide as silver dollars.

She was naked. Not wearing a stitch. Pink and plump, her breasts firm and pointed. Her strawberry blond hair was piled and pinned in rich swirls atop her perfect head.

"Good Lord—you're fast with that thing!" the girl intoned, sliding her gaze up from Cuno's gun to his face.

"I'm sorry, Kate!" Massey dropped the .45 into its holster and snapped the keeper thong into place over the hammer. "I . . . I'm . . . sorry."

He moved to her, placing his hands on her pale, slender arms. She did not seem nearly as frightened as she was surprised. She studied him now with her crystal blue eyes unblinking. "Cuno . . . where . . . how on earth did you get to be so fast with a six-gun . . . ?"

She did not know him as a gunfighter. As far as he knew, no one in Nopal did. At least, if they did, they hadn't let on. They knew him only as the beefy, muscular, ham-handed young man who'd ridden in out of the high desert one day, four months back at the tail end of spring, on the willowy skewbald paint he called Renegade, to inquire about a job with the local Bar L Freighting Company owned by Chester Lord.

Cuno had not known at the time that Mr. Lord had a comely daughter who also served as the company bookkeeper, though he did soon enough, when Lord invited him into his home one night for supper . . .

Not long after meeting the intelligent, brash, sparkly eyed redhead, Cuno and she began trysting here at the old trapper's cabin, which Kate had known about since she'd been a young girl and the cool waters of Crow Creek had beckoned her on hot summer afternoons.

Cuno did not want to talk about his violent past with this girl. He'd hoped he'd never have to. He especially didn't want to talk about it now.

In fact, suddenly, seeing her standing before him naked, the pink nipples of her upthrust breasts jutting as though she were cold or excited, he said, "Why, Kate—look at you. A stiff wind must've blown all your clothes off!"

Kate laughed and stepped up close to him, pressing her breasts against his belly and wrapping her arms around his bull, sun-browned neck. "I thought I'd save you the trouble of undressing me . . . this time."

"I never considered it trouble." Cuno wrapped his arms around her and kissed her. She returned the kiss, flicking her tongue between his lips, entangling it with his own.

Her bosom heaved, swelling against his chest clad in a sweat-soaked buckskin pullover. He groaned, uncomfortable. Kate pulled her face back and glanced down past his belly. "Gotta problem, there, partner?"

"Yeah. Suddenly, my drawers feel a mite on the tight side."

"Hmmm." Staring down past the buckle of his cartridge belt, she pressed a finger to her bee-stung lips and furrowed the skin above the bridge of her nose. "Well, maybe we'd best get you out of them then. I wouldn't want you to damage anything."

Quickly, stumbling around, Cuno started kicking out of his boots and unbuckling his cartridge belt and then unbuttoning his faded blue denims. "Don't mind if I do . . ."

Kate laughed and pulled his buckskin tunic over his head, tossing it to the ground. "Cuno Massey, you smell like your mules. Before you even think of frolicking with this damsel in the tall grass, you must bathe!"

"Ah, heck—all right." Cuno lowered his summer-weight bal-briggans, which dropped to just above his knees, to his ankles and then kicked them away. "But you first, teacher!"

He picked Kate up in his arms, which bulged with muscles developed from his years of mule-skinning and back-and-

15

bellying heavy freight in and out of stout-wheeled Murphy freight wagons. He turned to the cool, deep water of the creek partly shaded by overarching branches.

Kate screamed, "Don't you *dare!*" a half-second before she hit the water.

She went under and came up, spitting water and smoothing her hair back from her eyes. "Oh, bad man! Very bad man!" She widened her eyes as he stood naked atop the bank, grinning down at her.

"Hmmm . . . but I do think I know how you can make it up to me," she said, her eyes smoldering.

Cuno threw himself off the bank, leaping over her, lifting his knees and causing an enormous, booming splash as his brawny frame struck the water several feet beyond her. She turned away and shut her eyes against the splash and then turned and swam toward him.

He grabbed her, and kissed her.

As they kissed, Cuno backed the girl against the bank.

She clung to him, returning his kiss, groaning and wrapping her long legs around his back.

They made frenzied love there in the water and again, more slowly, up on the bank, in the tall grass near Cuno's clothes and not far from where Kate had left her dress and undergarments.

Afterwards, they dozed, Kate with her head resting on Cuno's broad chest.

"How was your run?" she asked him as they both started rousing from their brief slumber, a shaft of midafternoon sunshine fairly glowing in her strawberry hair, which was splayed out, still damp, against his chest and spilling down his side.

"Uneventful," Cuno said. "Just the way I like it."

He'd run a load of mining supplies to a mercantile that served a small camp of ragtag prospectors on the other side of Crow Mountain, a two-day ride from Nopal. He'd left early yesterday morning and overnighted along the trail. Often, if she could slip discreetly out of town on her horse, Kate met him here on his way back into town from a freight run.

She ran her hand lightly across his chest, her blue eyes following it. "You like driving a mule team, don't you?"

"What's not to like? Just you and the mules, mostly."

"Stubborn beasts," she said. "My father curses them endlessly."

"They can seem stubborn, all right," Cuno said. "But that's usually because they're just not understanding what we want out of them, and most men don't know how to communicate. Mules aren't horses. You can't force 'em by crackin' a whip over their backs.

"Mules are very devoted to a good owner or skinner, and they want to please. Sometimes they just don't understand. You gotta sort of gentle 'em into doing something you want them to do. Sometimes you even gotta show 'em—like climbin' down off the wagon and walking across a flooded arroyo yourself. *Show* 'em. They'll watch you, come to an understanding, and do it themselves."

"Boy, you really do like mules. I guess that's why Father has other men besides himself drive the wagons." Kate glanced up at him, rubbing her hand over his left, well-developed pectoral muscle. "He really drew an ace when you came, Cuno."

"Heck, I'm the one who drew the ace when I saw that flier of your old man's. I was just gonna ride through Nopal after stockin' up on trail supplies, and keep ridin'. Now"—Cuno pressed his lips to her temple—"I'm here. And I like it here."

He gave her shoulders a squeeze.

She looked up at him again, and narrowed one eye. "You don't think I've forgotten about the previous topic, do you?"

"What previous topic?"

"The one we started before you seduced me with that smile

of yours, and those boyish eyes." She slid her hand down beneath his belly. "And everything else about you, Cuno Massey."

Cuno frowned up at the sky, feigning befuddlement. "Reckon I still don't understand, Kate."

She fondled him, and kissed his chest. He groaned.

Then she said in a faintly jeering tone, "That fast-draw of yours, Mr. Massey. Where did a mule skinner learn to draw a forty-five like that?"

CHAPTER TWO

Cuno said, "Kate, you ever hear of an old gunfighter named Charlie Dodge?"

Kate lifted her head slightly and looked at Cuno with renewed interest. "Yeah . . . I think I have. I used to hear the old loafers talking about him out on the mercantile's front gallery. I was just a little girl. He was one of the first of the gunslingers who came west after the war, wasn't he?"

She didn't wait for a reply, but lifted her head a little higher and said, "Cuno, how did you ever cross paths with Charlie Dodge?"

"Dodge ran with my old man, back when they were younger. When my pa and step-ma were both killed back in Nebraska, Charlie taught me how to shoot. Taught me how to shoot running and falling backward and from a horse's back. Even with a Winchester carbine. Taught me how to empty that Colt—his own gun, which he gave to me—into a three-inch square from thirty yards. I spent several days with Charlie practicing my fast-draw. And when I left his stage station, I kept on practicing . . . right up until the day I ran down the two men who killed my pa and my step-ma." His cheeks burned and his ears rang at the names. "Rolf Anderson and Sammy Spoon."

"Well, I'll be hanged, Cuno!" Kate said, her lower jaw hanging in shock. "I heard of both of them, too. There's not too many living on the frontier who haven't. *You* killed *Anderson* and *Spoon*?"

19

"That's right." Cuno reached over and slid Dodge's pretty, ivory-gripped Peacemaker from its holster. He twirled it on his finger, clicked the hammer back, and eased it down against the firing pin. "I promised Charlie that after I killed those two, I'd hang this up. Or I'd sell it. Somehow, I'd get rid of it."

He shook his head slowly, gravely. "I didn't do that, and I think that by breaking my promise to Charlie, I jinxed myself."

"How so?"

"I married a pretty girl I met on the Bozeman Trail when I was trailing Anderson and Spoon. Later, after we'd settled down on a farm, we were bushwhacked. July was killed. Our baby died, too—still in July's belly."

Kate placed her hand on his cheek. "Oh, Cuno."

Massey stared at the sky, but what he was seeing was the pretty half-breed girl in his memory, her black hair winnowing back behind her shoulders in a prairie breeze. He blinked the sheen of tears away, brushed at a stray one that managed to start rolling down his cheek, and cleared his throat.

"Ever since then, trouble has dogged me. Men . . . killers . . . bounty hunters have dogged me."

Cuno dropped his chin to stare levelly at Kate. "I spent time in prison for killing two deputy U.S. marshals, though I was justified in killing those men. They were more outlaw than law-men. They'd been about to rape some girls I was trying to save from marauding Indians.

"I was broken out of jail . . . and an old marshal, Spurr Morgan, said he'd try to get the governor of Colorado Territory to grant me amnesty, but . . . I don't know. As far as I know, that hasn't happened yet. Likely, never will. I never stay in one place long enough for anyone to find me, anyways."

He smiled at the memory of old Spurr, the crusty lawman with the weak heart whom he'd ridden with for a while down in Mexico. He drew a deep breath, and let it out slow. "At least,

I've never stayed in one place long until now, Kate. Until your old man gave me this job . . . and I met you."

Cuno caressed her cheek with the back of his hand. "I've never told anyone about any of that. Leastways, not as much of it as I've just told you. I told you because . . . I think I'd like to stay here in Nopal . . . with you, Kate."

He wanted so much to settle down and live a normal life that it was like a living, breathing, yearning animal inside him. He was sick to death of running.

And killing . . .

Kate looked troubled. "Cuno . . . you . . . do . . . realize . . . that I've promised myself . . . to Brett Cavanaugh . . . don't you?"

Cuno pushed up onto his elbows. "Well, yeah, but . . . that was before . . . we started getting together . . . out here . . ."

"I told you about our plans to marry next spring before we started getting together out here, Cuno. That's true. But, Cuno . . ." Deep lines cut into the pretty girl's forehead. "Cuno . . ."

Cuno said, "But our getting together doesn't mean that your plans have changed, Kate? Is that what you're trying to say?" Suddenly, he felt sick to his stomach. He was embarrassed.

"Cuno," Kate said, placing a placating hand on his chest. "Brett's father is the president of the bank. My father runs a lucrative freighting business. They're very good friends, our father's—Brett's and mine. They're business partners. They were two of the very first settlers to establish Nopal."

"So, naturally you would marry Brett."

"Yes. Of course. Cuno, I'm sorry if I gave you the wrong impression."

"Yeah, I reckon I did get the wrong impression, Kate. I figured that . . . well, I reckon I never figured you for a . . ." Cuno tried to come up with the right word but couldn't find anything that didn't sound offensive.

21

Kate arched a brow. "A harlot?"

"Well, I don't reckon I'd go that far," he lied. "But I didn't peg you for a gal who'd say you were going to marry one fella and spend your afternoons . . . well, *rutting* . . . with another!" He didn't like the silly exasperation he was hearing in his own voice.

Kate chuffed sardonically. "Why not? Men do this sort of thing all the time. I could tell you stories about my own father, in fact. Before my mother died. Part of the reason she died so young, only forty, was because her heart was broken. Why shouldn't a girl be able to enjoy herself as much as any man?

"Let's face it. You've seen Brett. He's a bit of a stuffed suit and a dandy. He knows very little about pleasing a woman— only pleasing himself. He prefers to spend his time gambling over making love. But that's all right. He's a good businessman. In time, I'm sure I'll come to love him. I, however, enjoying making love. Especially with you, Cuno. You're a vigorous, handsome young man. You have some bulk to you. I like bulk."

She plied his manhood and smiled devilishly. "Unfortunately, I am not a right and proper girl—though if anyone said anything around town about that, I'd call him a bald-faced liar!"

She laughed, trying to lighten the mood.

Cuno didn't see the humor in it. He felt like a foolish, lovelorn schoolboy. His heart was broken. All the plans he'd quietly made in his head had suddenly drifted away like smoke on the wind.

He'd told her so much about himself. He'd betrayed himself to her.

"This was a dalliance, Cuno," she said, squeezing his forearm and staring into his eyes with maddening sympathy. "Nothing more and nothing less. I've had a wonderful time, and I think you have, too. I'm sorry if I gave you the wrong impression."

"Ah, hell," he said, chuckling now, though there was no

humor in it. "Forget it." He'd been stupid. A girl like Kate Lord wouldn't settle for a freighter. Especially one with a bounty on his head. A wanted man. If he hadn't today, sooner or later he'd have had to tell her about his violent past.

It was all coming clear to him. He'd wanted to change his life so badly that he'd deluded himself into thinking this beautiful girl from a wealthy family would settle down with him. Possibly even become his wife.

He placed his hands on her arms and gazed at her levelly. "I'm sorry, Kate. I'm afraid I've been a fool. I've assumed too much."

"That's all right, Cuno." Kate stood and walked several yards upstream, bending to gather her clothes. "Like you said, let's forget it."

Cuno stood and started pulling on his trail gear. They dressed together in silence, several yards apart.

Kate finished buttoning the cream, cambric Mother Hubbard frock that would have looked dowdy on any other bookkeeper. Not even a flour sack could look dowdy on a girl with such a body.

She pinned her hair atop her head, pinned her small straw hat to her hair, and walked over to Cuno. Pulling on her long, white cotton gloves, she looked up at him. He was hitching his gun belt around his waist and adjusting the holster on his thigh.

A dark mood had befallen him. He knew it was apparent in his eyes, probably in the lines across his forehead.

Suddenly, everything had changed. No, not really changed. It was just that nothing was really as it had seemed only a few minutes ago. Nopal was just another bump on his endless trail.

"Cuno . . . I think that under the circumstances . . ." Kate glanced down, unable to continue, bending a weed with the toe of her leather high-button shoes.

"We should call it quits?" Cuno nodded. "I reckon it wouldn't be near as much fun anymore, would it?" He kissed her cheek. "I'm sorry, Kate."

"Truth be told, Cuno," she said, "I was sort of planning for this to be our last time, anyway. We've met enough times that I'm worried that Father or Brett, possibly Brett's own father, will start to get suspicious. I wouldn't want that to happen."

"I wouldn't, either, Kate. You're right. We'll end it here."

"I'm sorry, Cuno. I hope this won't change anything else. I hope you'll stay on as a skinner. Father would hate to lose you."

Kate placed her hand on his cheek and pressed her firm lips to his. She gave him a sad, parting smile and started walking toward the cabin. She stopped and turned to him. "Will you give me my usual head start, so we don't show up in town too close together?"

"Of course. I'll grease the wheel hubs before I hitch the mules to the wagon." Cuno shrugged. "Save me from having to do it in town."

Kate winked at him and continued walking through the trees toward the cabin.

He watched her go, feeling hollow, silly, frustrated, and angry.

Angry that he'd allowed himself to fall into the girl's trap, though he knew it was as much his own trap as hers. She'd promised him nothing, just as he'd promised her nothing, in exchange for a little carnal entertainment out here under the aspens.

When he saw her ride away from the cabin, galloping the mare out toward the main trail, he tramped back to the wagon. The mules stood near where Cuno had left them, milling around in the brush and bluestem, grazing, occasionally stomping against the buzzing black flies needling them.

Cuno removed the can of wheel dope from where it was strapped to the side of the wagon with the jockey box, and took his time greasing the hubs. He didn't want to get back to town too soon. He didn't want to see Kate in the front office, where she worked occasionally with her father, helping out with the books.

He didn't want to see old Chester Lord, either. He didn't want to see anyone. If he got back late enough, he could put up the wagons and the mules in the freight company's barn without seeing another soul, and he could take the back alleys to Mrs. Totten's boardinghouse.

He'd have a few drinks in his room, and then maybe he'd see the humor in his ridiculous predicament. It was fairly obvious, after all, now that he reflected on it—him, a drifting, no-account gunslinger/freighter falling for a moneyed, small-town princess who'd already promised herself to the banker's son despite how freely she'd been with her comely body.

Which Cuno had thoroughly enjoyed. Hell, maybe that's what he'd miss about Kate Lord most of all. She knew how to please a man, Kate did.

After a few drinks, a few chuckles, maybe he'd feel good enough to head out to his favorite café for supper and then maybe rustle up a poker game in one of the saloons. He was a pretty good bare-knuckle fighter, so maybe he'd let himself get lassoed into a match or two out behind one of the town's watering holes—for a cut of the bettors' pot, of course.

He'd started fighting back in Nebraska, where his old man, Lloyd Massey, had coached him; Lloyd himself had one boxed in the Union Army. Cuno enjoyed the camaraderie of the competitive matches despite the obligatory swollen eyes and battered knuckles. Tonight, however, the physical aches and pains might take his mind off his consternation.

He'd found sport fighting a nice diversion from his troubles. It was a good way to burn off the pine tar.

No, he'd probably just stay in tonight. He felt like hell, and there was no getting around it. He'd keep to himself.

He knew it was silly, but he was afraid someone might read his chagrin in his eyes and become savvy to his and Kate's history, and that wouldn't go well for either of them.

What would he do now? he wondered as he hitched the mules, Mike and Jim, to the wagon. Nopal wasn't near the attraction it had been for him only an hour ago. He hadn't realized how much he'd been banking on Kate's accepting his proposal. They'd been having so much fun out here by Crow Creek, and they'd gotten on so well together, carnally and otherwise, that he'd really come to believe they'd have a future together.

Just one more bitter pill in a whole drawer full of them. All he could do was swallow it.

He'd finish out the year working for Chester Lord. He couldn't leave the old man short-handed. Lord had given a chance to an unknown drifter, and Cuno wouldn't pay him back by running out on him until the busy season had run its course and the first snows came.

Then he'd inform Lord he was leaving well in advance, so the old freighter could replace him if he felt the need, though there would likely be little freight hauling to the mountain mining camps again until spring.

Spring. That was when Kate would marry Brett Cavanaugh.

Cuno didn't want to be around for that.

He put the wagon onto the main trail, and headed toward Nopal. It was early evening, the light soft and dusty, shadows swelling, deepening. The air was still. Too clear for a storm. So why was he suddenly hearing the low roar of thunder?

As the thunder grew steadily louder, he turned to look behind him.

Riders were bearing down on him fast. Twenty, thirty, maybe more. And what appeared a stagecoach was bearing down on him, as well.

The riders were spread out on both sides of the trail, to each side of the wagon, which was hammering straight toward Cuno and the Pittsburg, and they showed no sign of slowing though they had to see him by now.

CHAPTER THREE

Cuno flicked the reins over the mules' backs, urging them into a gallop, though they were in no mood this late in the day as well as in the trip. They'd come to trust him, however, and thus obeyed him.

As they both gave questioning brays and rocked into heavy-footed gallops, Cuno looked around for a place to get them off the trail. The surrounding country here was all sage and prickly pear, gently rolling toward distant bluffs and rimrocks. It wasn't the most rugged country he'd seen, but he could see no open stretch through the sage.

The low hummocks and the tough, woody sage would prove tough going, and likely rattle the old Pittsburg apart at its seams.

He glanced over his shoulder again.

The stage was bearing down on him, the bearded driver cracking his long blacksnake over the backs of his lunging team. Another bearded man rode beside him, holding a shotgun at port arms across his chest.

The riders to each side were keeping pace with the stage. They were fanned out a good fifty yards to each side of the trail. Even if Cuno found a place to swing off the trail, they'd still be on top of him before he could get clear of that broad swath they were cutting.

Beneath his own wagon's heavy, thundering wheels, he could feel the intensifying reverberations of the stage and the riders. He glanced behind once more.

The man riding in the messenger position on the stage beside the driver raised his sawed-off shotgun, aiming it at the sky. Black smoke puffed from one of the barrels. As the thundering boom echoed across the flats, more black smoke puffed from the second barrel.

It was followed by another deep boom.

Cuno could feel both mules lunge with starts and jerk forward in their rigging.

Cuno cast a glare behind him. "What the hell?" he shouted at the top of his lungs. "Hold up there, you sonso'bitches!"

What were they trying to do? *Run him down?*

He assumed the stage was hauling gold, and plenty of it, thus the accompanying riders. But they had no reason to be bearing down on him as fast as they were even if they had a tight timetable to keep.

"Slow down, goddamnit!" Cuno shouted, thrusting an angry arm out toward the coach and the gang of horsebackers now within fifty yards of him and hammering toward him, too quickly swallowing up the gap between him and them. "Slow down! Slow down! *Rein in!*"

One of the men riding to the right of the stage waved an arm and gave a rebel yell. He spurred his horse even faster ahead, crouching low over his mount's pinned-back ears. He swerved in front of the stage, showing his teeth as he slapped his horse's left hip with his hand. He grinned devilishly at Cuno as he put his white-socked black straight toward the Pittsburg.

He drew a pistol from the holster on his right thigh and triggered two shots into the air.

The mules lunged, and swerved. Cuno squeezed the reins, grinding his boots into the planks of the driver's box beneath the seat, as the heavy wagon swerved behind the mules, fishtailing. He felt the right side wheels rise. They slammed back down on the trail, and then the left side rose.

And then more men began whooping and hollering behind him, and the mules, frightened out of their wits, swerved violently once more. They cut off the trail's right side and into the brush.

They made the move so quickly and while Cuno was recovering from the last, violent swerve, that the freighter had no time to try and stop them, though he knew from experience that there was no stopping them now, anyway.

They'd lost their heads, and all he could do was try to stay in the driver's boot, though the wagon was bouncing so wickedly and wildly off low mounds of clay and sand and sagebrush that his ass was spending more time in the air than on the rough pine boards of the seat.

Out of the corners of his eyes he could see several riders peel away from the main group and follow him. They were bellowing and roaring like mad coyotes ahead of a thunderstorm. Their pistols popped in the air.

Cuno gritted his teeth and prayed he didn't hit a rock or take a gopher mound the wrong way, and turn over. At this speed, he'd be ground to jelly.

He had no control over the team. All he could do was hold on to the reins and try to remain seated, though the wagon was bucking and pitching like a bronco mustang beneath him.

Eventually the mules would tire and slow.

He felt a little hope when he saw the five riders who'd been hazing him across the high desert slant away from him and trace a gradual but lightning-fast arc back toward the trail and the stagecoach and the rest of the gang, which was continuing east toward Nopal.

He turned his head forward, and all hope died. A broad, deep wash lay just ahead.

It was opening wider and wider—the jaws of death. His heart turned a somersault in his chest. The two mules were still galloping as though the hounds of hell were nipping at their hocks. There was no stopping them.

"No!" Cuno cried against the inevitable. "No, goddamnit! *Noooo!*"

Now he could see the rocky bottom of the wash. Rocks and sand sheathed in greasewood and sage and clumps of turkey-foot. It had to be a good hundred feet deep.

The mules were closing on it fast . . . twenty feet away from the edge . . . ten feet . . . five . . .

"Shit!" Cuno cried, and dropped the reins.

He threw himself over the left front wheel, landing on the heels of his boots. The ground wanted nothing to do with him. It was like a spring pitching him high and flinging him toward the draw.

He bounced like a ball, and heard the raking chuffs of air being hammered from his lungs.

Suddenly the ground disappeared. He dropped straight down to land on the inside wall of the draw on his left shoulder. He twisted around and rolled wildly through wiry juniper and cedar shrubs, rocks slamming against him, painfully gouging him.

One rock smashed against his head. If he continued to roll after that, he wasn't aware of it. A darkness like that of a starless, moonless night washed over him.

As the stage rocked and clattered into Nopal, Cecil Craig blinked against the dust churning around inside the blood-splattered coach and leaned forward to pluck a long-nine cheroot from the breast pocket of the dead man slumped on the seat across from him.

The dead man's water-blue eyes were open and staring just over Craig's left shoulder. The dead man was young, probably not yet twenty-five. He was—or *had been*—a medical supply salesman from back East—Illinois, Craig thought the kid had mentioned, just before the outlaw leader had killed him with a .44 round drilled from close range through the kid's heart.

He must have just been starting out, because he'd been carrying only twelve dollars in his cracked leather wallet, which had a photograph in it of a pretty young woman in a lacy white dress.

Scrawled on thc back was: "With love to you, William—forever yours, Doris."

As the coach came to a halt, rocking on its leather thoroughbraces, Craig scratched a match to life on one of the kid's front, buck teeth, and touched the flame to the cheroot.

The outlaw leader drew the smoke deep into his lungs. Blowing it back out, he inspected the long, slender brown cigar with one brow arched appreciatively. Cheap, but not bad. Craig would remember that for when otters were scarce, as the old expression went.

Outside, guns cracked. Men whooped and hollered wildly, and hooves thudded as the horses of his gang members—the Boys, they called themselves—galloped up and down the street. Somewhere, a girl screamed, and one of Craig's men shouted, "Christ—Charlie did you see that purty little thing?"

The girl screamed again, and Craig peered out the near coach door to see a young blonde in a green print dress go running off around a street corner, Charlie Sanchez in wild pursuit, swinging his lariat.

Craig chuckled. He was reaching for the coach door when the handle turned and the door swung open, and Victor Bina stood there, grinning through his thick black beard and holding a shotgun in one hand. The double barrels rested on his shoulder.

"Victor, I see you've acquired a new friend," Craig said.

Bina patted the shotgun's breech. "Always wanted one o' these, but they didn't seem practical. I like how they sound and kick against the shoulder. When you shoot one of these old gals, they kick like a fat, old whore!"

Craig laughed. "And seein' as how the former shotgun guard won't be needin' it no more . . ." The killer rolled one brown eye toward the coach roof, where the driver and shotgun messenger were both resting peacefully amongst the U.S. mail pouches and luggage.

Bina extended his gloved hand. "Give you a hand out, Boss?"

"I will accept your generous offer," Craig said, wincing as he rose from between the old, gray-haired lady slumped away from him, bleeding from the hole in her left temple beneath the brim of her cambric poke bonnet. "After six years in a steel cage, my knees are a mite creaky, and riding in this wheeled coffin didn't help matters. But it was a mite easier on my ass than my saddle, even with the pillow."

Sitting so long in that steel cage six feet in the ground and known as the Hell Hole in the federal penitentiary had also contributed to his chronic hemorrhoid problem, not to mention his chilblains and frequent attacks of the ague.

Sometimes, he nearly coughed up both lungs at once, as well.

The federal bastards.

"What in God's name is going on here?" a man shouted.

The stage was pulled up in front of the Nopal town marshal's office. The town marshal himself stood on the broad, street-level front gallery, flanked by two deputies who were looking around warily as the horseback riders dashed up and down the street, shouting and howling like Rebels with the blue-bellies on the run down the north side of a Tennessee ridge.

"Mule, you old dog," Craig intoned, clapping his gloved hands together once in jubilation. "You're still wearin' the tin?"

Dust was still swirling in the street, as was powder smoke from the popping pistols. The old, potbellied, red-nosed marshal squinted and blinked as he studied Cecil Craig, and then slid his exasperated gaze to the small army of men chasing the good citizens of Nopal up and down the street and into shops and alley mouths.

"Stop this!" the marshal demanded, stomping one mule-eared boot down on the boardwalk's rough wooden floor. "Stop this now! I won't stand for this!"

He glanced at the tall, beefy deputy standing beside him. The deputy raised his long-barreled, double-mawed Greener, aimed it at the sky, and tripped both triggers.

The barn blaster kicked violently against the deputy's thick shoulder, causing him to stumble backward from the blow and knocking a wanted poster askew from where it was nailed to a roof support post.

The cannon-like blast rolled out over the town. It didn't diminish the gang's din a bit.

Craig tossed his long, black, gray-streaked hair back behind his stout shoulders, pulled one of his three long-barreled .44's, rocked back the hammer, extended the revolver, and drilled a bullet through the shotgun-wielding deputy's chest.

The deputy grunted, stumbled backward once more, and dropped the shotgun to the boardwalk. The second trigger tripped, blowing a large chunk of wood from a front corner support post, causing the shake-shingled gallery roof to shiver.

The deputy dropped to his knees and looked at the sheriff as though for corroboration that he had indeed been killed. His face went slack as the light of living left his eyes. He brought both his hands to his blood-spewing chest as though to stem the flow, and then fell forward to lie belly down on the boardwalk, rocking slowly from side to side as his spirit fled.

Both the old marshal and the second deputy stared down in shock at the beefy deputy, beneath whom a dark-red blood pool grew.

As both remaining lawmen jerked their enraged glances back

to Craig, the outlaw leader shot the second deputy. The man screamed, fell back, and piled up against the front wall of the marshal's office. He tried to raise the Winchester carbine in his hands, his spurs gouging slivers from the gallery floor.

Craig fired again, and a quarter-sized, puckered, dark-blue hole instantly appeared in the dead center of the deputy's forehead. The deputy's head snapped violently back against the wall, and then he sagged sideways to the gallery floor.

Craig turned to the old marshal, who stood crouched, right hand on the grips of his Remington revolver, which he had half out of its holster. Mule Mulligan stood frozen at the edge of the gallery, glaring at Craig.

The stocky, long-haired outlaw leader, a ginger-colored spade beard drooping from his chin, smiled at the old man.

"My god," Mulligan intoned awfully, his right, heavy-lidded eye twitching. "It's you, isn't it? My god . . . it's *you!*"

CHAPTER FOUR

"It is me, my good man," Craig said in the phony English accent he'd picked up from an Englishman he'd once ridden with—Emory Kibbles, who'd been hanged for rustling and murder up in Wyoming.

Craig, who hailed from Missouri, had always loved how Kibbles had talked, so he'd adopted the accent, though often his Missouri twang could be detected beneath it, especially when he was soused, which was often.

"It is me, indeed, and I bet you're wondering why I'm not still wasting away in that territorial shithole, eh, Mule?"

H.W. "Mule" Mulligan was still staring at the spade-bearded, stocky, bull-chested outlaw leader wearing a long, brown duster, as though Cecil Craig was a demon who'd dropped out of the clouds on black wings.

The old marshal was speechless.

"Indeed you are," Craig said, laughing, his pinched, rat-like face turning red. "Indeed you are. You see, I busted out . . . with the help of a few, easily bribed guards. And then I gathered my old friends and made a few new ones." He spread his arms. "And here I bloody well am!"

He frowned suddenly and glanced around at several of his higher-ranking gang members standing in a ragged semicircle around him and the town marshal. The lower ranking members were still hoorawing the town so that their gunfire sounded as though it were a Fourth of July celebration, though the horrified screaming of several women didn't quite fit.

"Victor?" he said, picking out the black-bearded man with the shotgun for severe scrutiny. He glanced at the horsebackers charging up and down the street and returned his admonishing gaze to Bina. "Have . . . we . . . uh . . . cut the telegraph wires, Victor, or are we too busy entertaining ourselves . . . ?"

"Oh, shit—right, Boss!" Bina said, jerking with a start. He turned to the man standing to his right, and said, "Clell, take some of the boys over to the telegraph office and cut them wires, for cryin' in the Mormon's beer! Jeezus!"

"Oh, right, right!" Clell said, turning to the horse standing jittery-eyed behind him, and swinging up into the saddle.

He yelled for several of the other men to follow him. When he was gone, Craig turned back to Marshal Mulligan, whose face was crimson, his blue eyes watery with rage.

"What the hell you think you're doing, you crazy bastard?" Mulligan barked, taking one angry step toward Craig, clenching his fists at his sides. "You can't cut those wires! Just take what you want and ride the hell out of here!"

Craig punched the old man in the face. Mulligan stumbled backward against the front wall of the marshal's office, his Stetson tumbling off his shoulder.

He brought a hand to his left cheek, blinking. He shook his head as though to clear it, then froze, stunned. He glared at the grinning Craig.

Pushing himself off the wall, he moved toward the short, stocky outlaw leader, raising his clenched fists up around his chin and crouching and weaving like a sparring fighter. He stood a good four inches taller than Craig, and that seemed to buoy his fighting spirit.

The muscles over his jaws bulged with fury.

Craig gave his cigar to Bina, then stepped toward the old marshal, raising his own fists.

"You asked for it, old man," Craig said. "And I'm just the man to give an old man what he asks for."

Craig flung his right fist at Mulligan's jaw. Mulligan stepped back, ducking, and Craig's fist merely grazed the old man's chin. Mulligan grinned devilishly and jabbed once with his right hand and then jabbed his left fist hard against Craig's mouth.

The old man still had some gravel—Craig would give him that. Mulligan's blow rocked Craig back on his spurs. The outlaw leader laughed despite the blood trickling from his split lip.

"Good one, Marshal!" he intoned, recovering. "Bloody damned good—congratulations!"

Mulligan was moving in again, feinting, a satisfied gleam in his rheumy eyes.

He swung a heavy roundhouse that Craig easily dodged before getting both his boots beneath him and punching the old man savagely with a roundhouse of his own. Mulligan grunted and staggered backward, throwing his arms out for balance. His heavy boots thumped on the boardwalk, spurs ringing.

Craig was on him quickly, jabbing the old man's chin with his left fist while smashing the old man's right cheek and jaw and temple with his right.

He got Mulligan trapped against the front of the marshal's office, and he worked him over good. Mulligan couldn't even get his arms raised to fend off the blows. Despite six years in prison—or maybe because of the fighting he had had to do to stay alive there—Craig still had power in his thick shoulders.

Slowly, Mule Mulligan dropped to his knees, blood oozing from the deep cuts on his face. Craig smashed the old man's face once with a careening roundhouse. The loud *smack*, like that of a broad fist hammering a side of raw beef, could have been heard a block away.

Mulligan's head bounced off the door of his office. It wobbled on his shoulders, his gray-brown hair hanging in his eyes. He fell slowly, heavily to the boardwalk on his left shoulder, wheezing.

Both his eyes were already swelling shut.

"Damn, where'd you learn to fight like that, Boss?" asked Victor Bina, laughing as he stared down at the half-conscious marshal.

Standing over Mulligan, Craig rubbed his small but thick right fist with his left hand. Then he took back his cigar and sucked a drag from it. "You learn a lot of things in the territorial pen, Victor."

As he turned to face the street, he saw a man in a white shirt and brown vest march out the front door of the large, sprawling building on the street's other side and half a block east. A large sign stretched over the second story announced LORD'S BAR L FREIGHT COMPANY.

The man with the shotgun was middle-aged. He wore a pencil-thin mustache and a string tie. He came across the high loading dock with an angry scowl, raising the shotgun to his shoulder and yelling, "You murdering bastards—get the hell out of this town!"

"Look out, Jig!" yelled one of Craig's horseback riders.

Too late.

The shotgun-wielding man tripped a trigger of his gut-shredder and blew one of the outlaws out of his saddle and into the street, his horse screaming as it galloped away to the east. The outlaw himself lay screaming and rolling in the dust, bloody from the buckshot that had taken him broadly through the chest, face, and shoulders.

The man who'd shouted the futile warning and another man to his right opened up on the gent with the Greener. The bullets punched through him, one splattering blood from his head. He spun around twice and then fell forward over the rail of the loading dock and into the street.

"*Pa!*" a girl screamed from the freight office's open doorway.

She ran out the door and across the loading dock. Craig could see even from a distance that she was a well-set-up strawberry blonde. Holding the hem of her Mother Hubbard above her ankles, she hurried down the steps and ran over to where the older man lay unmoving by one of the several hitch racks fronting the building.

"Pa!" she screamed, louder. "Pa! Oh, *Paaaaaaah!*"

She lowered her head to the man's chest, shoulders jerking as she bawled. The shooting had dwindled when the beautiful strawberry blonde had run out of the freight office, and now it died altogether as the gang sort of gravitated around the girl crouched over her dead father, sobbing hysterically.

Craig scrutinized her for a time, and then he turned to Victor Bina. He said loudly so that everyone within a block of the marshal's office could hear him.

"Vic, I want the marshal there taken to the west edge of town. I want him hung upside down by his ankles from that cottonwood we saw on our way in. Do not kill him. I want him to hang there and think about his sins of six years ago. He knows what I'm talking about."

Craig turned toward the blonde sobbing over her father. "I want that man, who, I believe is Chester Lord, if memory serves, taken out there, too, and hanged by his neck from the same tree."

"Ooooh—a gruesome display, eh, Boss?" said Bina delightedly.

"Yes, a gruesome display. One that should discourage any visitors to the town—for as long as we're here, anyway."

Craig raised his voice so that the entire gang now sitting their still horses here and there about the street, most clumped before the freight office, could hear him.

"Boys, I want all the town councilmen, including the mayor, hauled out of their shops or houses and shot. I want them hung on the east side of town, near the road, where any would-be visitors to this fair city will be sure to see them and get the message that for the next several days, Nopal is closed to business."

From somewhere to the east, a woman screamed and there was the sharp crack of a door slamming.

Craig smiled like the cat that ate the canary and blinked slowly.

"Why you want all the councilmen killed, Boss?" Bina asked. "Not that I object, you understand. Just call it curious."

"Because this town is foul, and the men who run it are even fouler. I want there to be no mistake how I feel about this town. Those councilmen might not have been in office when I was here last and was so badly mistreated by the old marshal and his posse, but I've little doubt that some were.

"They sanctioned the marshal's actions, and most of those men would hold those positions on the council for life. As for the others, they represent those who were in office before them, and for that they shall be damned right along with the rest of this fucking jerkwater!"

Another outlaw asked, "How're we gonna find out who's on the town council, Boss?"

"Just ask the shopkeepers," Craig said. "Tell 'em if they wanna live, want their families to live, they'd better write down the names and locations of those men sitting on the town council."

As Bina and several others who'd been standing with Craig began heading for the nearest shops to start their queries, Craig strode out into the middle of the street. Suddenly, all the shops appeared closed, curtains drawn over windows, front doors shut.

Some of the windows had been broken by bullets.

A heavy silence had fallen now in the aftermath of the din. Only the sobs of the strawberry blonde could be heard beneath the occasional blowing or stomping of a horse.

Craig raised his voice and turned slowly as he spoke:

"Good people of this fucking jerkwater—I know you can hear me." His voice echoed ominously off the false façades around him. "My name is Cecil Craig, and I'm taking over your town for a few days. As of right now, my boys and I will have the run of the place. That means we must be given whatever we want, or we'll take it from you and shoot you and leave you for the wild dogs and coyotes. Is that understood?"

He paused for emphasis.

The girl sniffed and jerked her head up, glaring at him.

Craig winked at her, and continued. "By 'whatever we want,' I mean food, clothing, guns and ammunition, whiskey, and"—he turned toward the strawberry blonde and smiled—"women."

"Bastard!" the girl cried, heaving herself to her feet. The horseback outlaws followed her with their leering gazes as she began striding purposefully toward Craig, her jaws hard, blue eyes blazing.

"Murderer!" she screamed, leaning forward at the waist. *"Murderer!"*

Craig chuckled and said, "And here's *my* woman right now."

He adjusted the lapels of his duster, brushed the trail dust from his shoulders, hiked his cartridge belts up higher on his broad hips, and adjusted his hat, as though he were going out on the town with the woman of his dreams.

"Murderer!" the girl screamed hoarsely as she approached Craig and swung her fists at him, one after the other.

The outlaw leader ducked both swings. The girl pinwheeled, and Craig grabbed her from behind, clutching her breasts and nuzzling her neck. "Now, that's what I call service—eh, boys?" he said, laughing.

The girl struggled against him, cursing, but to no avail. Craig held her fast against him. He grabbed the collar of her dress with both hands and gave it a savage tug. The girl screamed shrilly as the dress was torn wide. Then her camisole was torn, as well, laying her breasts bare.

Finally, when Craig had pawed and nuzzled the girl long enough that his loins throbbed with desire, he picked her up, threw her over his shoulder like a sack of grain, and, puffing his cigar, headed toward the hotel that stood across the street from the marshal's office.

The door was locked, so he kicked it in and entered.

The girl's screams echoed hollowly from inside, as did the pounding of the outlaw's boots as he climbed the stairs toward a room.

CHAPTER FIVE

When Cuno regained consciousness, he wasn't sure he was really awake, for his surroundings were nearly as dark as the inside of his head only a moment ago.

Then he heard himself groan. His head throbbed.

He was awake, all right.

He raised a hand to his aching temple. The hand took a little more effort than usual to raise. Looking around, he realized why.

He was lying on the side of the ridge, head jutting toward the bottom of the draw, boots pointed toward the top of the ridge. He was fighting gravity to raise his hand. He had a feeling that all the blood that had pooled in his brain from lying in such a fashion was contributing to the hammering ache in his skull.

He touched fingers to a gash on his right temple. It wasn't deep, but it stung like hell when he probed it. It seemed to have stopped bleeding. The blood was of the consistency of dried plum pudding.

He rolled over and groaned as he slid several feet down the steep cliff. He shouldered up against a large boulder, which stopped his descent. He gained his hands and knees, moving slowly, mentally probing his body for broken bones.

He was sore. Every joint ached and his shoulders and the back of his neck were barking fiercely.

But he didn't think anything was broken.

Above the tolling of the bells in his head, he heard what

sounded like animals growling and snarling. There were scuffing sounds, occasional indignant yips.

He lifted his head to peer into the draw. It hadn't been as dark as he'd thought at first. Stars were sprinkled across the sky. The faint light limned brown shadows jostling around on the ravine's floor.

A cold stone dropped in Cuno's belly.

Coyotes, most likely.

They were already feeding on Mike and Jim.

Mike and Jim . . .

Cuno hardened his jaws in fury. A senseless waste of two good mules. What had been the point? Fun? Had that gang of outriders hoorawed his team for fun? Because they were coming up on a town and likely whores and plenty of whiskey, and they'd felt like celebrating?

They'd celebrated a frightened mule team and their more-or-less defenseless driver right into a canyon. They'd been a pack of frenzied wolves running off their leashes.

Just like wolves or dogs, more than two became a pack, and a pack was an ugly thing.

This pack would pay.

But then Cuno remembered how many of them there had been, and the futility of exacting revenge only aggravated his frustration and rage. Well, he'd report the assault to the town marshal, Mule Mulligan, anyway. Mulligan would likely find out who'd employed the gang—likely Wells Fargo on behalf of one of the mines in the Sangre de Cristos—and he'd make sure that Chester Lord was paid for the mules and the wagon.

Money wouldn't bring back two good mules Cuno had been fond of, but what more could he do?

Another bitter pill in that bottomless drawer . . .

At least his .45 still sat in his holster, secured by the keeper thong. He was relieved the weapon hadn't fallen out when he'd

45

flung himself from the wagon and tumbled down the ridge. All he really had of any value were his gun and his horse.

Gritting his teeth against his aches and pains, he scrambled back up the side of the ridge.

Cuno found his hat hung up on a sage shrub and donned it. He looked around, orienting himself. The night wasn't as dark as it had appeared from inside the canyon. There was still a faint lilac glow in the west. There was enough light that he could perceive outlines of rocks and brush around him.

Nopal lay to the east, probably a mile or so away.

Heavily, he tramped through the high-desert scrub and came to the trail. He followed the trail eastward up and over a gradual hill. Ahead now, he could see the dim saffron glow of Nopal beyond another low rise.

His feet ached inside his boots. The boots, which he'd purchased two years ago in an El Paso shop, had been made for toeing stirrups, not walking much farther than half a block in your average-sized town. His knees and all the rest of his joints and his shoulders and neck ached so that he, in his early twenties, could imagine what life would be like as an old man.

He wouldn't like it. Probably wouldn't live that long, anyway. He was lucky he was still alive, after all the bullets and even Indian arrows he'd dodged . . . not to mention rawhiders intent on turning him to jelly in that canyon behind him.

As Cuno walked, he stewed.

His fury over the wagon and the mules, the senseless hazing, was a hot, steady fire inside him. Likely, he'd never again see the men who'd run him into the ravine, but he'd report them to Marshal Mulligan as soon as he reached town. The entire gang could be charged with the destruction of private property if not attempted murder.

As his boots and aching feet chewed up the gently rising and falling trail between him and Nopal, the lights of the town gradually growing before him, he fantasized about what he'd do to that gang if he ever caught up to them.

The fantasy was made muddy by the sheer number of men he'd be dealing with, however, and frustration aggravated the barking in his shoulders and neck. Mine companies had power, too, and they'd likely protect the men who rode for them.

Cuno cursed as he walked, occasionally pausing to kick a rock and watch it tumble in the scrub along the trail. Ahead, Nopal became separate, flickering lights spread out in a hollow amongst low buttes. For a time Cuno could see only the lights, but then he could make out the shadowy outlines of structures spread out in a large, ragged-edged circle. On the quiet, cool night air, the tinkling of a piano grew gradually louder. Then he could hear the shouts of men and the occasional cracks of pistols.

The shots were muffled, as though someone . . . or several men, in fact . . . were shooting indoors.

Cuno topped another rise and as he started down the other side, the main street shone ahead of him, a quarter mile away now and lit with the reddish glow of burning oil pots. Shadows moved in the street. More than usual, Cuno thought. But then he thought it must be Friday night and the ranch hands were in town.

But, no. The freight run he'd made had been a midweek run, and he was due to make another run on Saturday, still three days away . . .

The sporadic shooting grew louder as did the frequent, celebratory whooping and hollering. Cuno had just started to acquire a queasy feeling deep in his gut when he came to the big cottonwood standing tall and broad along the trail to his right, on the outskirts of Nopal. There were old, abandoned stock pens and corrals out here, on both sides of the trail, overgrown with rabbit brush and sage.

Amongst those murky shadows, Cuno spied two shadows that caused him to look twice. They were lean and long, and they seemed to be suspended in the air beneath the large tree that looked spindly now in the fall, having lost most of its leaves.

One of those long shadows moved slightly, sort of jerking and turning first one way and then the other way.

"Help me," came a pinched, croaking male voice out of the darkness. "For chrissakes . . . help me!"

The voice, so unexpected and obviously anguished, nearly literally rocked Cuno back on the heels of his boots. It was like the voice of a ghost. The hair at the back of Cuno's neck pricked, and his heart hammered.

Then, realizing someone was in trouble, he hurried off the trail but slowed cautiously as he approached the two long, lumpy shadows.

The shadows of men hanging from a stout branch of the tree not ten feet from the trail.

One appeared to be hanging by his neck. The other one, the one who was moving, causing the rope to jerk, had been hung by his ankles, arms hanging straight down toward the ground.

"Help me!" he rasped again.

Cuno saw something shiny on the man's pinstriped shirt. A badge. He moved closer. It was Mulligan. The marshal's face, nearly level with Cuno's own, was dark and swollen.

"Christ!" Cuno said, and ran over to the trunk of the tree.

Both ropes had been tied off around the left tine in the trunk's fork, about six feet up from the bottom. Cuno untied the rope holding the marshal and then, holding the rope in both his gloved hands, eased his grip enough that the hemp snaked slowly out of his hands and around the bow of the tree, making rasping sounds.

Bark dribbled down from the branch.

The marshal dropped slowly, his head and shoulders meeting

the ground first, then his legs. Cuno released the rope and untied the other one, lowering the second body of the man, whom he assumed by the way he'd been hanging by his neck, was dead.

Cuno ran over and dropped to one knee beside the marshal. "What the hell happened?"

The old man shook his head, and pushed himself up on his elbows. He was having a hard time, so Cuno grabbed one of his shoulders and helped. Now he could see that both the man's eyes were swollen, as were his lips. They were also bloody, and several other cuts and gashes on his face oozed blood. He was filthy, his clothes torn, as though he'd been dragged.

Beaten and dragged.

The man's chin dipped toward his chest, and he breathed hard.

"What happened?" Cuno repeated.

The old marshal's swollen, bloody lips moved, and he said something too softly for Cuno to hear.

"What?"

"Siege," the old man said, turning his battered face toward Cuno. "Town's . . . under . . . *siege!*"

Cuno knew right away what he was talking about. The gang who'd run him into the canyon hadn't been working for Wells Fargo. They were rawhiders. Outlaws. Desperados. Now he realized why he was still hearing sporadic yelling and shooting from inside the town.

Cuno glanced across Mulligan toward the other man, who lay unmoving eight feet away.

"Who's that over there?"

Mulligan turned his head and said in a clearer voice than before, "Your boss, Kid."

"What?"

Cuno scrambled over to the other man, dropping to a knee

beside him. The man had been shot several times. He was so bloody and his features were so slack, it was hard to tell in the darkness, but now he could see that Mulligan was right. The man who'd been hanged—but who had likely been dead before the gang had played cat's cradle with his head—was old Chester Lord.

Cuno's boss.

Kate's father.

Cuno stared down in shock at the dead man. His aching heart drummed anxiously in his ears.

Vaguely, he could hear men shouting and yowling and shooting the occasional pistol. Just then a woman's scream reached Cuno's ears, and then a man laughed raucously and shouted something.

"Kate," Cuno said under his breath, semiconsciously closing his hand around the ivory grips of his .45.

A hand closed over his shoulder. He jerked with a start, and looked up to see Marshal Mulligan standing over him. The man's big, bony, age-spotted right hand squeezed his shoulder.

"Forget it, Massey," the old lawman said.

He'd been a friend of Chester Lord's—in fact, they'd played chess together every afternoon after lunch, so Cuno was familiar with the old lawman, though he'd tried to steer clear of him as much as possible. The old badge-toter had been in the habit of regarding Lord's newest mule skinner with skeptical, overly thoughtful, vaguely suspicious glances, as though he were trying to place him.

Cuno had always hoped old Mulligan was just naturally critical and that he didn't start pouring too carefully over his stack of federal wanted circulars.

"There ain't nothin' you can do for her tonight," Mulligan said in a low, gravelly rasp, his broad chest rising and falling sharply as he breathed. His gut overhung his cartridge belt. The holster on his right hip was empty. His thin, gray-brown hair was badly mussed.

Cuno stared up at him, his temples pounding with worry.

"I know who you're thinkin' about." Mulligan shook his head. "There ain't nothin' you can do about her tonight."

"Where is she?" Cuno croaked out, rising slowly. "Is she safe?"

Mulligan shook his head once, staggered backward, and dropped to a knee to keep himself from falling. He groaned, shook his head again, and brought both of his hands to his forehead.

"Hell, no one's safe in Nopal tonight. No one." The old marshal looked up. "We need a coupla horses. Then I want you to help me get down to Miss Loretta's place on Sand Creek. I need some tendin' before I'll be worth a damn. I need to get word to the county sheriff, and there'll likely be someone at Loretta's I can send."

"What do they want?"

Mulligan blinked, and scowled impatiently, deep lines cutting across his leathery forehead. "What?"

"What're they here for?" Cuno said, dropping to a knee and wrapping a desperate hand around the old marshal's left arm.

He knew it probably wasn't rational, but he couldn't help feeling miffed that the lawman had let this happen. That he'd let it happen to the town as well as to Kate. That Chester Lord was lying here dead.

There was a dreamlike quality to all this, but beneath the blurry confusion of the dream there was the stark, cold fact that it was not a dream. That it was real.

That the old lawman had given up his town.

"What the hell do they want and why the hell didn't you stop them, for chrissakes? Where're your deputies?"

"My deputies are dead, and I'm useless," Mulligan said, jerking his arm free of Cuno's grip. His eyeballs were mere slits glistening in the starlight between his swollen lids, beneath his bushy, gray-brown eyebrows. "That what you wanted to hear? You satisfied? And as far as what they're here for . . ."

Another girl's scream sounded from Nopal. It seemed to have come from the main street. Both Cuno and Mulligan looked in that direction though all they could see were flickering lamps and oil pots, a few dancing shadows.

". . . revenge," the old marshal finished his sentence. "They're here for revenge. And there's too many of them for either of us or both of us, so what I need you to do, you smart-assed young buck, is to see if you can sneak into town and fetch us a couple of horses. You can do that, can't you, Massey? They're likely all drunk and otherwise involved, and, besides, you've been avoidin' the law long enough that sneakin' into a town and stealin' horses oughta seem like child's play to you—a wild-assed young firebrand with federal paper on his head?"

Mulligan hardened his voice and flared his nostrils. "Ain't that right, *killer*?"

CHAPTER SIX

Cuno stared down in shock at the old town marshal.

So, he knew . . .

Mulligan glared up at him, challenge in his eyes. Or in what Cuno could see of his eyes through the puffy lids under the discolored brows.

The old man had been humiliated. He was rubbed raw and looking for a fight in any quarter despite his condition. Cuno found himself sympathizing with him, admiring him as well as feeling grateful the lawman hadn't exposed him, though Massey knew that giving any indication of such thoughts would only piss-burn the mossyhorn even worse.

Cuno helped the oldster to his feet and draped the marshal's right arm over his shoulders. "Let's get you out of sight."

Moving slowly, the lawman shuffling beside him, Cuno led the burly Mulligan away from the cottonwood. There were several old stables and corrals out here, from what was left of an abandoned ranch and stage relay station. There was a lot of brush—mesquites, greasewood, and cedars—and Cuno led the old man around these and piles of old lumber and stone foundations.

Mulligan could walk a little, but he needed help. He was a large, tall man—a couple of inches taller than Cuno—and he had more than a few extra pounds, mostly around his waist. Cuno grunted under the old man's near-dead weight as he led him into a tumbledown stable with a rusty, corrugated tin roof.

He eased Mulligan down against the back wall, on a thin carpet of strewn, moldy hay. Here the lawman would be out of sight if anyone came snooping.

"Hold on—I'll get you some water," Cuno said, and left the quietly cursing, hard-breathing old lawman there against the wall.

"I don't need no water," Mulligan rasped, angrily. "I need a horse and a rifle!"

Cuno went out and looked around. He knew there was a windmill amongst the abandoned debris and overgrowth. Now he walked past a low-slung log shack that was missing its windows and doors, and saw the windmill standing pale against the starry sky.

He could still hear men's loud voices emanating from the heart of Nopal to the east, but there'd been no pistol shots in the past several minutes.

Maybe the marauders were quieting down. Most were probably good and drunk and shacked up with whores in Nopal's four watering holes.

The stone tank at the base of the windmill was half-filled with cool, relatively fresh water. A small Mexican family who raised goats and a few beeves and chickens lived in a shack nearby, and Cuno had seen them watering their stock from the windmill. A bucket with a rope handle sat on the ground near the stone tank. Cuno half-filled it and carried it back to the stable.

"Here—drown your sorrows."

"I told you—"

"Ah, shut up," Cuno said. "If you don't get that swelling down around your eyes, you won't see for a week. And you better take you a big drink."

On one knee beside Mulligan, he tore off one of the man's shirttails, wadded it up, soaked it in the water, and pressed it to the marshal's face. "Hold that. Dab at your cheeks and eyes till I get back."

There was something about this old man that reminded Cuno of the old deputy U.S. marshal he'd known and begrudgingly admired in Mexico—Spurr Morgan. Maybe it was Mulligan's pluck and sand that, like Spurr's, only partly concealed a sentimental streak.

Not only had the wily old badge-toter not revealed Cuno's past to other folks in Nopal or tried to arrest him, he'd somehow sensed Cuno's feelings for Kate, though Cuno and Mulligan had never had a conversation more than three sentences long.

It was that which reminded him of his father and Spurr, Cuno knew, but also Mulligan's unwillingness to give in to old age despite having the shit kicked out of both ends.

This was a lawman who'd go down shooting—if he lived, that was.

Mulligan didn't say anything as, staring through his swollen lids at Cuno, he reached up awkwardly, took the wet cloth, and pressed it to his right eye.

Cuno walked out of the stable and headed off to retrieve the body of Chester Lord. He didn't have time to bury his boss, but he'd at least try to keep him from the coyotes.

When he had Lord lying in the deep shadows of the stable, he headed for the stable door once more.

The old lawman said behind him, "Don't try to be no hero. You'll only get yourself and her killed, if she ain't dead already—despite how good you might be with that hogleg on your thigh." He chuckled dryly. "Shit, whoever heard of a mule skinner wearin' a tied-down Colt, anyway? A well-kept Colt, at that. You never had me fooled, Kid. Not for a day."

"Anything else?" Cuno asked him from the open door.

"Nope, that's it. Once we get to Loretta's place, I'll send a rider—maybe *you'll* be that rider—to fetch the sheriff from the county seat. He'll come with a posse, and *then* we'll run those devils back to hell. So don't get no heroic ideas."

"So there was something else," Cuno said through a growl, and headed on out of the stable.

He picked his way through the brush and old ranch ruins and into the town, sticking to the shadows of the shacks and stock pens on the south side of the main street. Here there were no lamplit windows, and Cuno sensed the townspeople cowering inside the dark hovels around him, praying that the gang would not come for them.

Or for their women . . .

He was heading generally for the livery barn in which his horse was stabled, on a cross street just off the main one. He could not resist the urge to get a look at the main street, from where wan light was emanating, and found himself crouched in an alley mouth between two buildings, casting his gaze up and down the street.

There were more shadows than light, but there was enough light that he could see several bodies slumped in the dirt.

A saloon lay down the street on his right, on the opposite side of the street, and men's loud voices carried over the saloon doors. There was another saloon to his left, on his own side of the street, and more voices carried over those doors, as well, as did the off-key pattering of a piano keeping tune with the singing of a saloon girl.

The girl's heart didn't seem to be in the song she was crooning, "Carry Me Back to Ole Virginny." Her voice cracked and sputtered.

There was a loud thud, as though of a man hammering a table.

"Goddamnit, you sing it right, me darlin', or I'll slit your bloody throat!" came the man's phonily English-accented remonstration.

The girl squealed and sobbed.

The piano started up again, and the girl resumed singing too loudly, her voice quaking even more than before.

Cuno ground his teeth in anger.

Directly to his right lay the marshal's office. If he could slip inside, he'd likely find a rifle for Mulligan, though he doubted the old man would be able to wield one in the near future. Not after what the gang had done to his face. Cuno sensed while leading the man to the stable that he'd likely bruised or even cracked a few ribs.

Cuno moved forward and turned onto the gallery fronting the marshal's office. He stopped suddenly.

Two dark shapes were slumped on either side of the gallery. Crouching over the nearest one, Cuno saw one of the marshal's two deputies lying sprawled on his side. Something especially dark in the shadows of the dark office lay beneath him. Cuno smelled the coppery odor of blood, and wrinkled his nose against it.

A long double shotgun lay at Cuno's boots. He picked it up and then rummaged around in the deputy's vest pockets, coming up with eight shotgun shells. He'd likely find more inside. As he started to move toward the half-open door, voices grew louder on the other side of the street and east a ways.

Cuno crouched, spun, and froze.

Men were moving out of the Glory Hole Saloon and House of Ill Repute, their voices thundering out into the night as their boots hammered the gallery floor. They were laughing and jabbering, obviously drunk, one man saying, "Smithy, I think she plum liked you—she was just one of them that didn't like to let on!"

As the others laughed, Cuno slipped down off the end of the marshal's office gallery and dropped low behind a rain barrel abutting the building's west wall.

As the group of men stepped out into the street, one said, "Well, let's go see what the New Mexico House has to offer by way of women. Boys, it's been a while for me, so I'm just gettin' started!"

One of the group had stopped while the others were half-stumbling, half-staggering in the direction of the saloon to Cuno's left.

"Hold up a minute," said the man who'd stopped, who was little more than a man-shaped shadow.

"What is it?" asked one of the others.

"I seen somethin' move over there in the mouth of that break."

The others swung their heads toward Cuno, who crouched even lower, slowly reaching up to doff his hat.

"What was it?" asked another man.

"I don't know—but I seen somethin'," said the first man.

"Well, go check it out."

Cuno heard the snick of steel rubbing against leather. At least one of the marauders had drawn a revolver. Slowly, breathing through his mouth and hearing his heart beat slowly but insistently in his ears, Cuno broke open the shotgun.

"Probably a local," said one of the men on the street. "Skulkin' around to see about the noise."

"Shit, everybody in town knows we're here, and none of 'em but the marshal and that old freighter had the *cojones* to try to do anything about it. But go check it out, anyway, Fritz. Me— I'm gonna go and see about another poke over to the New Mexico House. I done heard the sister of that one called Lila from the Glory Hole works over yonder."

"I'm comin' with ya," said one of the others, and then all except for the first man who'd seen Cuno tramped off in the direction of the New Mexico House, in which the piano was still playing but the girl was no longer singing.

Cuno glanced around the side of the rain barrel, through the three-inch gap between the barrel and the marshal's office.

Fritz stared toward him, pistol extended in his right hand. "Hey," he called, not raising his voice much. "Hey, somebody over there? If so, you'd best come out or I'm gonna start triggerin' lead."

Cuno had filled both the shotgun's barrels. Now he quietly closed the gun, wincing when he heard the soft click as it locked. Thumbs on the hammers, he looked around the rain barrel again.

Fritz was moving slowly toward him, hatted head canted to one side, pistol extended half out from his right shoulder. His duster winnowed out behind him as he came. He was a solid-looking man of average height wearing a mustache and a battered Stetson. Double cartridge belts sagged low on his hips. A bowie knife dangled from a sheath looped around his neck.

"Hey," he called, slightly louder this time, "come out or I'll start shootin'. I don't care if you're a kid or a girl or nothin' about that. If I catch you skulkin' around out here, tryin' to hide, I'm gonna gun you." He grinned, showing his teeth beneath his thick mustache. "Cause that's what I do, ya see. I'm one of the Boys!"

As Fritz came within ten feet of the rain barrel, Cuno drew his head back out of sight. He could hear the faint trilling of Fritz's spurs and the crunch of his boots in the finely ground dirt and horse manure. He could smell the liquor stench of the man as well—a sour, eye-watering stink. Cuno hoped that whatever girl had lain with him had a strong nose.

Then he thought about Kate. He thought about the wagon and the mules, and his rage flamed anew.

"Come on, now, blast it—I seen you." Fritz stopped just beyond the rain barrel and slightly to the left of it. Cuno couldn't see him, but he could smell him. He knew the man was staring into the dark break between the buildings. "Come on out before I start shootin'."

He took a couple more footsteps. Now his shadow moved to Cuno's left. The stench was stronger. He must have sensed Cuno, because suddenly he wheeled toward him.

"Hey!" Fritz said.

"Hey, nothin'."

Cuno squeezed the shotgun's left trigger.

In the flash of flames lapping from the left barrel, he watched the buckshot take Fritz dead center and lift him up and hammer him so hard against the building behind him that a couple of clapboards cracked and tumbled to the ground with Fritz's bloody corpse.

CHAPTER SEVEN

"Holy moly, Fritz," Cuno muttered through clenched teeth. "That had to hurt."

He turned toward the main street and then stepped back into the darkness of the alley mouth when man-shaped shadows pushed through the batwings of the Glory Hole and a man said, "Now, what in hell was *that*?" He raised his voice. "Who's firin' a barn blaster out here? Bina—that you?"

"How could it be me?" shouted a voice from the direction of the New Mexico House, along the street to Cuno's left. "I'm over here with a whore on each arm!"

Another man shouted from Cuno's left, "Fritz? You over there, Fritz?" There were the quick thuds and spur chimes of men running toward the alley.

Cuno stepped farther back into the darkness, replaced the spent wad in the shotgun's right barrel with fresh, and then snapped the gut-shredder closed, turned, and jogged off down the gap between the buildings. He resisted the urge to hold his ground and blast the next man who entered the alley from the main street.

As enticing as killing more of the gang was, it would likely be suicide. He might be able to take one, maybe two or three others down this evening, but there were too many more. They'd finally run him down. Best to live out the night and come back to fight when the odds weren't stacked so high against him.

As he jogged around the rear of the marshal's office, men

shouted loudly, angrily, behind him. They'd found Fritz.

Cuno kept jogging, making his way through the darkness around warehouses, stock pens, and shacks, heading for the cross street called Fourth Avenue, on which sat the livery barn in which he'd stabled Renegade. The shouts grew faint behind him. The gang members were likely trying to find the man who'd shotgunned Fritz, but they'd be moving with great caution, not wanting fates similar to Fritz's.

Cuno came to Fourth Avenue. Standing between a barbershop and a drugstore run by a Chinaman, both buildings ominously dark and silent, Cuno looked both ways along the street, narrower than the main one. The livery barn sat directly across the street from him—as dark and silent as the whole rest of the town off the main drag. Cuno could sense the townsfolks' fear.

Somewhere off to his right, a dog barked incessantly and angrily. Farther off to his left, coyotes were yammering in the foothills rising toward the mountains, as though they could smell the growing carnage here in Nopal and were looking forward to their furtive investigation in the early hours of the morning.

Spying no movement on the street, he ran across to the front of the barn, and pulled at the double doors.

Locked. Probably barred from inside.

He moved to the smaller door left of the main doors. That, too, was locked. Cuno stepped back and then swung his right boot back and forward, smashing the heel against the steel handle. The door gave easily under the power of his stout leg, splinters flying.

Inside, horses whickered nervously and kicked their stall partitions.

"Easy, easy," he whispered, moving inside, blinking as though to help his eyes adjust to the dense shadows. The air was warm and heavy with the smell of hay and ammonia and the especially fetid-smelling brand of chaw the man who ran the place, Fernando Silva, favored.

Cuno had never been in the barn at night, so it took him a while to feel around for a lantern hanging from a spike driven into a ceiling support post. When he'd lifted the bail and lit the wick, he replaced the lantern on the spike, and jerked back with a start.

A figure stood not six feet away from him, holding a Winchester carbine straight out from her right shoulder. The girl's thick hair hung messily about her shoulders. She wore a calico blouse, cream skirt made of flour sacking, and low-heeled, brown leather lace-up boots. Her head was canted over the carbine, one dark eye squinting at Cuno along the barrel.

With a quietness that did not match the fury of her words, she said in a heavy Spanish accent, "Get the fuck out of here, or I will blow you to kingdom come, *amigo,* and urinate on your foul remains." She'd given the warning, flaring her nostrils and showing her teeth like an enraged cur—albeit a pretty one with full, alluring lips.

Cuno said, "Put the gun down, Ella. It's me—Cuno."

"*Jesucristo!*" the girl said, depressing the carbine's hammer and lowering the gun to her side. "I damn near shot you, Cuno. What the hell are you doing here?"

"I came for Renegade." Cuno brushed past the girl, heading down the broad main alley for his paint's stall. "What are you doing out here, Ella? You oughta be in your cabin with your old man. He oughta have you locked up tight in your root cellar."

He leaned the shotgun against a post.

"What root cellar? We have no root cellar."

"Well, he oughta have you locked up *somewhere.*"

Renegade snorted and bobbed his head at the sight of his rider, rippling his long, cream mane. A long patch of white dropped from just above the stallion's eyes to his nose, and the chocolate eyes peered out from the cinnamon hair on each side of his snout.

"Fernando is drunk," the girl said distastefully.

"Great time for it." Cuno knew Silva, the liveryman who'd adopted the pretty, salty-tongued young Mexican girl when she'd been orphaned at only six years old, as a hard drinker, though he and the girl ran the barn themselves. They'd been doing so for years.

"I came out to check on the horses before turning in."

Ella Silva ran up past Cuno and pressed her back to the door of Renegade's stall. She reached up and placed a quieting hand on the side of the stallion's face. She was a pretty, slender girl with warm, intelligent eyes that often flashed with a coquettish shrewdness that belied her youth. She had a small, pale scar on her chin.

"Cuno, what are you doing? Those rawhiders have warned everyone in town to stay in their *casas*. Anyone seen on a horse will be shot on sight. They don't want anyone leaving town."

"Don't worry—I won't let 'em see me."

"Fool!" she intoned, anger blazing in her eyes as she pressed her back tighter against the stall door. The two pert lumps of her breasts pushed against her blouse, which was unbuttoned far enough to reveal some alluring cleavage. "I will not let you kill yourself! Do you know that they hunted down all the town councilmen and shot them down in the street like dogs? All six, including Reverend Josephson! Like dogs! They hanged them from the trees on the east side of town!"

Tears shone in the girl's eyes. She threw herself against Cuno's chest, wrapping her arms around him. "Oh, Cuno! Please, you must save me from them! Fernando is curled up in bed with a bottle and his old Civil War pistol he couldn't hit the broad side of this very barn with!"

Cuno gave a wry chuff and pushed the girl away from him. "Ella, I don't think you're afraid of any damn thing in the world. If you were, you wouldn't be out here in the barn with a gang of marauders on the prod."

"*Sí*, I am a foolish girl." She curled one side of her mouth, her dark eyes flashing coquettishly, and placed the flat of her hand on his broad chest. "One that needs saving despite herself."

"Stop foolin' around and go saddle the marshal's horse, and be quick about it. We need to get that lamp out *pronto*!"

"The marshal's horse?" Ella said, frowning up at him. "Why? Cuno, what are you up to?"

"I don't have time for palaverin', Ella," Cuno said, giving her a shove toward the marshal's speckled gray standing in a stall three stalls down from Renegade. "I gotta hightail it out of here. I killed one of 'em, and the others are likely headed this way right now."

Ella's eyes widened in shock. "You *killed* one?"

"Ella, move!"

"Okay, okay!"

Ella ran off down the alley.

As Cuno led Renegade out of his stall, the Mexican girl did the same with the marshal's speckle-gray. Cuno tossed his blanket and saddle onto the skewbald paint's back, and then replaced the hackamore with his bridle. He worked quickly. Slight as the girl was, she worked just as quickly, casting several skeptical glances toward Cuno.

"You *killed* one?" she muttered half to herself. "Why would you do that, Cuno? Are you stupid? You drive freight wagons. Why would you get mixed up with those killers?"

She whipped her head toward Cuno once more as she lifted a slender, brown knee, which her skirt hiked up briefly to uncover, and rammed it against the gelding's ribs with a grunt. At the same time, she drew the latigo taut. "Oh, I know why," she said dryly. "You heard about *Señorita* Lord."

Cuno only vaguely wondered who else in town knew about his infatuation with Chester Lord's comely daughter.

He looked at Ella sharply, worriedly. "What'd they do with her, Ella?" He shoved his Winchester, which he'd stored in the barn as he'd had no need for it in his rooming house, down into his saddle scabbard. "Did they hurt Kate?" He walked over to Ella, grabbed her arm, and swung her toward him. "Tell me— did they hurt her? Where is she?"

"Ow!" Ella snarled. "Cuno, you're hurting my—!"

Cuno stopped her by suddenly pressing two fingers to his lips. He'd heard something outside. Distant voices. He ran over to the lamp, lifted the bale, and blew it out, instantly filling the barn with inky darkness.

"What is it?" Ella rasped.

"Shhh!"

Cuno stood in the darkness near the front of the barn, pricking his ears to listen.

Outside were the scuffle of boots and the faint rings of spurs. Men were talking softly but Cuno couldn't hear what they were saying until, coming closer, one said quietly, furtively, "I know I seen lamplight in there. Wasn't very bright, but I seen it. And now there ain't none."

"Someone's inside, then," said another man, even more softly.

They were milling around outside the barn.

Silently, Cuno cursed his foolishness. He'd led the gang, or at least part of the gang, to the barn. Now not only was he in deep trouble, but Ella was, as well.

Very quietly, through a soft, raking sigh, Ella said, *"Ay caramba . . .* those *pendejos* are out *there."*

Cuno's eyes adjusted to the darkness. By the faint lilac glow angling through the barn's windows, he made his way quickly back down the barn alley.

"Stay very quiet."

"It's those *pendejos,* isn't it?"

"Yeah, it's those *pendejos.*"

Cuno grabbed the girl around her narrow waist and heaved her up onto the marshal's saddle. "What are you doing?" she hissed in surprise.

"I led those *pendejos* to the barn, so now I gotta get you out of here."

After a slight silence, the girl said, "Where are you going to take me?"

"You'll find out soon enough." Cuno led both horses toward the front of the barn. He winced against the clomps of the shod hooves on the barn's hard-packed earthen floor.

"Stay very quiet," he told Ella when the horses had stopped.

He stepped forward and canted his head toward the doors, listening. He could hear men moving around out there—more than before, as though the first two had quietly summoned others. They were likely surrounding the barn. Someone gave a low whistle.

Quietly, Cuno removed the wooden locking bar from the steel braces, and leaned the bar against the wall. Holding both sets of reins, he turned out a stirrup and swung up onto Renegade's back. Both horses were whickering softly, nervously, and clomping around.

Cuno leaned toward Ella, who sat her saddle ramrod straight in the darkness beside him, staring straight ahead.

"Ella," Cuno said, "I'm gonna lead your horse out of here. You grab the apple and hold on tight, and for godsakes keep your head down. There's gonna be shootin'. There's no doubt about it. And I don't want you to get your pretty head blown off."

"Really?" Ella whispered, turning to him. "You think I'm pretty, Cuno? You never let on—."

"Shut up, fool girl!" Cuno hissed at her. "This is serious business, and I don't want you gettin' drilled. We're gonna bust out of here like broncs out of a stock car durin' a Texas twister, so you hold on tight to that horn and bury your face in the steeldust's neck!"

"Okay, okay!"

"You ready?"

Ella grabbed the saddle horn with both hands and crouched low over the gelding's neck. "*Sí.* Yes."

CHAPTER EIGHT

Cuno wrapped the steeldust's reins tightly around his right hand. Then he thumbed both hammers of the shotgun back to full cock and rested the double-bore across the pommel of his saddle, aiming away from Ella on his right.

"Okay," he whispered. "Here we *go!*"

He ground his spurs into Renegade's flanks. The horse gave a fierce whinny and lunged forward, ramming his head against the barn's left door.

At the same time, Ella batted the heels of her black leather shoes against the gelding's ribs, and Cuno gave the steeldust's reins a jerk. A quarter-second after the left door flew open with a bang, the gelding blasted the right door open, and both horses lunged forward against their breast straps, hooves hammering the ground.

Cuno caught a glimpse of two figures standing nearly directly in front of him, maybe ten feet away from the barn. They both had two revolvers aimed straight out in front of them.

Apparently they'd expected their quarry's attempt to flee, but they hadn't anticipated the fury with which both horses busted out the barn doors. The man on the left snapped one wayward shot a half-second before Renegade slammed into him. The man screamed and disappeared, as did the man on the right, who also screamed as Ella's gelding slammed him into the ground and then hammered him with its lunging hooves.

Cuno saw the man Renegade had run over roll away beneath

him. As Cuno and Ella galloped straight out away from the barn, guns flashed from both flanks. Men's angry shouts could be heard beneath the thunder of the horse's hooves.

Crouching low, hearing lead screeching through the air around him and between him and Ella, Cuno angled the shotgun back off his left hip, and tripped a trigger.

Men's screams were drowned by the echo of the thundering blast.

Cuno whipped the shotgun out to his right, aimed it at that front corner of the barn, where guns flashed amidst man-shaped shadows, and squeezed the second trigger. More men screamed as the rocketing blast of the Greener hurled a wide spread of buckshot into the jostling shadows.

One man fired his pistol into the ground as he flew back against the barn's front wall.

Cuno turned his head forward and then swung Renegade hard right, jerking the steeldust along behind him. They were on a two-track trail now that angled between shacks and barns of the town's original settlers, most of this area now abandoned and overgrown with sage, bunch grass, and junipers.

Cuno wasn't familiar with this haphazardly laid-out section of town, so he watched for the windmill. When he saw it, he turned Renegade off the trail and into the brush. He had to slow both horses to a walk when the brush and old wooden debris got too thick for hasty negotiation.

The silence that had settled over the town on the lee side of the gunfire was nerve-jangling.

Cuno swung Renegade up to the stable in which he'd left Mule Mulligan, and swung down from the saddle. He ran over to Ella and placed his hand on her thigh. "Are you all right?"

"*Sí,* I think so," the girl said, a frightened trill in her voice.

"You're not hit? They flung a pile of lead at us."

"No, I am not hit." Ella glanced back in the direction from

which they'd ridden. "What about Fernando?"

Cuno didn't know what to say about her adoptive father, who lived in the house they shared on the other side of a wash from the barn. Cuno squeezed the girl's thigh reassuringly, and said, "Sit tight."

He hated leaving old Fernando there, likely drunk and defenseless, but he'd had to get the girl away from the barn *pronto.*

He moved into the stable shrouded in cottonwoods to find the marshal heaving himself heavily to his feet. "Who in the hell was you talkin' to out there?" Mulligan asked.

"Ella Silva."

"What?" Mulligan said, whipping an angry gaze at the young freighter as Cuno helped him hobble out of the stable. "Why in hell'd you bring her? This ain't exactly a Saturday night *baile*— oh, shit, hello, there, Ella . . ."

"No choice," Cuno said. "If I hadn't brought her, the gang would have found her. They followed me to the barn."

Cuno reached up and swung the girl down from the saddle. He led her brusquely over to his own horse and then threw her up onto Renegade's back, behind his saddle and over his bedroll and saddlebags. She didn't weigh much. Her body was slight but supple in his hands, though he tried to ignore it, *had been* trying to ignore it since he'd first met her some months ago. He wasn't sure, but he didn't think she was sixteen.

"What in hell was all that shootin' about?" Grabbing the steeldust's reins, Mulligan stared hard at Cuno. "You wasn't out there pretendin' you was Jesse James, was you?"

"Well, I wasn't robbing any banks," Cuno said, tossing the shotgun to Mulligan, who caught it out of the air. "But I did burn a couple of 'em down with your deputy's Greener."

"Christ!"

"That's four or five fewer than we'll have to—" Cuno stopped suddenly. A shadow was moving out of the stable. Cuno's .45 was instantly in his hand, the hammer clicking back.

A man cried out. Two pale hands rose in the starlight, palms out, and the shadowy figure stumbled backward.

"Hold on, hold on," Mulligan said. "Holster that hogleg before you shoot someone else, ya damn owlhoot!"

"Who the hell's that?" Cuno wanted to know, lowering the Peacemaker but keeping it aimed. He was wound tight as a coiled diamondback. "Come on out of there, goddamnit. Show yourself!"

"Holster the hogleg, Massey!" Mulligan ordered. "It's Cavanaugh. Brett Cavanaugh."

Cuno scowled into the shadows.

A tall, slender man in a three-piece suit and who looked more like a gambler than a banker's son came slowly, tentatively, out into the starlight. He lowered his hands and adjusted the set of his broad-brimmed, tan planter's hat, as though he were getting ready for a debutante's ball. It was so dark inside the corral that Cuno hadn't seen him.

"What the hell are you doing here, Cavanaugh? Where's Ka— Miss Lord?"

"God knows what those savages have done to her," Cavanaugh said. He was dark and angular-faced—some might even say handsome, though Cuno thought he was more pretty and stylish than handsome, with his dimpled chin and carefully trimmed mustache. "I don't even want to think about it."

A dam broke inside Cuno. Time seemed to leap forward two fast seconds, and then he was aware of the banker's son flying away and down from Cuno's clenched right fist.

"Hey!" Cavanaugh cried, and hit the ground hard, losing his hat.

"Goddamnit, Massey!" Mulligan rasped. "What the hell's got into you? Whose side are you on, anyway?"

Cavanaugh rubbed his jaw, scowling up at Cuno. His hair was badly mussed. He grabbed his hat, rose, donned the hat, and stepped up to Cuno, balling his fists at his sides. "I oughta have you whipped for that . . . mule skinner!"

"You oughta try."

Mulligan shuffled weakly up to Cuno and Cavanaugh, and shoved them apart. "We ain't got time for this, goddamnit! Now, mount up—both of you. I'll send word to the sheriff, and he'll bring a posse just as soon as he can."

"No, you two mount up," Cuno said. "We only have two horses, anyway, and there's four of us . . . now."

"What're you gonna do?" Cavanaugh wanted to know.

"Shut up and get on my horse," Cuno said, tossing the man Renegade's reins.

He glanced up at Ella staring down at him incredulously, trying to take it all in—this night, the man Cuno turned out to be in her eyes. "And you make damn sure Ella gets to where you're goin' *safely*, Cavanaugh, or I'll hammer you so deep in the dirt, you'll feel a Chinaman tickle your toes."

Cavanaugh glared at him from beneath the wide brim of his planter's hat. Men's shouts rose in the distance.

Cavanaugh looked around quickly, enervated, and then turned back to Cuno. "You're obviously a man who does not know his place." He toed a stirrup and swung up into the saddle. "Rest assured that if we make it through this night alive, I intend to make sure you are taught that place."

He ground his heels into Renegade's flanks, and the horse galloped away. Mulligan, who'd mounted his steeldust, stared at Massey.

"Don't be a fool, Kid. Even a cold-steel artist of your caliber, pardon the pun, hasn't got a chance against that gang. Cecil Craig is the toughest, poison-meanest outlaw this territory has ever seen, and he rides with only the worst."

"I'll keep that in mind," Cuno said, setting the barrel of his Winchester on his shoulder.

Mulligan shook his head and rode off in the direction of the trail that led south to Loretta's Place, an old stage relay station Loretta Blanchard, a former saloon girl and current madam, had turned into a watering hole and whorehouse that was a frequent destination for area range riders.

It had become somewhat of a legend, in fact.

Fernando Silva woke with a start, grunting.

He lifted his head from beneath his pillow, spilling the pillow and a half-empty tequila bottle onto the floor where the bottle landed with a thud.

"*Mierda!*" Silva cried beneath his breath.

He cocked his head, listening. It came again, five hard, echoing raps on the door downstairs. Each rap was like a lightning bolt to the old man's heart.

"Open up, Silva. We know you're in there!"

"Oh, shit. Oh, shit," Silva said, wheezing, his old heart racing.

His ears rang from terror as well as from the half a bottle of tequila he'd guzzled to help him sleep. Cecil Craig was the worst outlaw the territory had ever seen. He'd run roughshod over this county for several years, murdering any man who tried to stop him from rustling cattle, robbing banks and stagecoaches, and raiding mines and small ranches.

He rode with such fury that some said he was not human but a devil who was even too bad for hell, so he was cast back to earth to raise his own particularly merciless brand of hob here amongst the defenseless mortals.

"Goddamnit, old man!" Craig shouted through the door downstairs. "If you make me break this bloody door down, I'm going to see to it you die very slow. I'm talking *Apache-slow!*"

"*Dios mio!*" Silva cried, and, clutching his old Spencer repeater, crawled out of bed, thumbed his suspenders up his slender, bowed shoulders, swiped his long, thin, gray hair out of his eyes, and made his way down the rickety wooden stairs, running his left hand along the worn ironwood rail.

"I'm gonna give you five more seconds, old man!" came the outlaw leader's wicked voice through the door once more.

Quickly, Silva looked around for Ella. She must be back in her room, hiding behind the old chest of drawers in her closet, which Silva had told her to do if she sensed more trouble this night. They'd already had one visit from Craig, and it had gone relatively well—at least, Silva hadn't been gunned down as he'd heard the town councilmen had been and then hung from trees east of town.

Now what in the hell did Craig want?

"Old man!" the outlaw shouted, in his strangely affected accent. He sounded a little like some Englishmen Silva had known, but also like a few Missourians. Very strange . . . "I will bust this bloody door down, bucko, and then I will—!"

Silva threw the locking bolt and opened the door.

He stepped back, half-heartedly holding the old rifle across his thighs.

A half-dozen men stood in a semicircle around the doorway and Craig, who stood glaring at Silva. His eyes dropped to the rifle in the Mexican's hands, and then flicked back to the old man's craggy face. "What on earth are you doing with that?"

Silva swallowed and stood frozen before the stocky, pinch-faced outlaw.

"Set it on the table, *Señor* Silva, before you shoot yourself or do something silly and cause me to have to shoot you."

Silva set the rifle on the table.

"Now, then," Craig said, waving a pistol in the old man's face. "You've been a bad boy, haven't you, *Señor* Silva?"

"Huh? What are you talking about, *señor*?"

"Someone just busted like a bat out of hell from your stable. Two people, in fact. One being a young lady who appeared, in the short time I had to study her, Mexican." Craig arched a suspicious brow. "Your daughter, perhaps?"

Silva swallowed again. His mouth was dry and his heart was fluttering like a frightened bird in his chest.

"*Señor,*" Silva said, his voice quavering, "but that is impossible. I locked the barn. You told me to do that, and to not allow anyone to ride away on any of my horses, and I did that. As for a daughter . . ." He shook his head, frowning as though puzzled. "I have no daughter."

"No daughter?"

A man standing to Craig's left said, "He has a daughter. A very beautiful one." He raised his hand to his chest, making a lewd gesture. "*Muy deliciosa.*"

Craig canted his head to one side. "Were you lying to me, *Señor* Silva?"

Silva took one more step backward. His heart was racing and his knees were weak. "No, no, no! You see—I do not technically have a daughter. I have an *adopted* daughter. See? She is not really—"

Craig took another step into the small, adobe brick *casa*. "Enough with the lies, Silva! That is twice now you've defied me. You told me you had no daughter and you allowed someone . . . and your *deliciosa* daughter . . . to ride away on two horses when I strictly forbade you to rent or even lend horses to anyone until further notice!" The forbidding, menacing-looking outlaw slammed a gloved fist down on the table, upsetting a small, tin ashtray. "Did I not do that, *Señor* Silva—just a few hours ago this evening?"

"*Sí, sí*—you did. And I locked the barn doors. If someone

rode away on two horses, they did so without my knowledge, *señor!*"

"So your daughter allowed this to happen." It was not a question.

"No, no, *señor*—Ella is in bed. She is a good girl. She does what I tell her. If a girl helped someone make off with two of my horses, I assure you it was not Ella!" Silently, Silva sent up a quick prayer that Craig would not insist on seeing Ella herself.

To no avail. Are there no gods left in heaven? After this terrible night, Silva was seriously beginning to think so. May whatever dark power rules the earth and heavens have mercy on his soul . . .

Craig said, "I would like to speak with your daughter, *Señor* Silva. And for your sake, I bloody well hope she had nothing to do with this."

CHAPTER NINE

Silva said, "But it is late, *señor*. Ella is sleeping. She works very hard. It would not be right to wake her."

Deep down, he knew Ella would not be in her room. If a girl had been seen riding out of the barn, it was likely Ella. Who else? Silva had ordered her to stay in her room and hide in her closet if the outlaws came, but Ella must have been up to her tricks. She must have found a boy, though with her beauty Ella did not have to look very hard for boys.

A headstrong, often mysterious girl was Ella. And blooming into womanhood . . .

Cecil Craig stared hard at Silva, his eyes fairly burrowing into the old man's. Then he glanced at the men behind him, and jerked his head. They all came in as one, and fanned out around the house. Two went upstairs while the others thundered through the three rooms beyond the small parlor and kitchen area.

Dread hung heavy on Silva's shoulders. Now he hoped against hope that the girl galloping out of the barn had indeed been Ella. He hoped she was not here. It was not hard to figure what these men—these lusty, brutish goats—would do to her if they found her, such a pretty girl in first blossom.

When the men returned after clattering around the house, knocking things around, shattering lamps, they shook their heads. They had not found her.

Silva heaved a slow, quiet sigh of relief.

"So, then," Craig said, standing before Silva and tapping the barrel of his pistol against his open left palm, "it *was* her."

Silva slapped his hands down against his thigh as if to say, "What are you going to do about foolhardy young girls?"

Craig lifted a slow smile with one side of his mouth. "Who was the man riding with her? Big, broad-shouldered lad on a paint stallion?"

Silva frowned. He instantly knew whom Craig meant. Silva was stabling only one paint stallion.

Cuno Massey had to be the man the outlaw was referring to. Silva knew that Ella had harbored a flame for the good-looking younger freighter. That had been obvious every time Massey had come to the barn to take the paint for a ride.

Had Massey and Ella been meeting on the sly?

"Who?" Craig asked, raising his voice.

"I do not know, *señor*," Silva said. "A paint horse, did you say?"

Craig thrust his hand forward so quickly that Silva had no time to brace himself. The outlaw stabbed the barrel of the revolver savagely into the old man's belly. The breath left Silva's lungs in one, loud chuff, and then he dropped to the floor on his knees and rolled onto his side, desperately trying to draw air.

Craig and the other men, some grinning delightedly, stared down at him. One had found a mescal bottle and was tipping it back.

"Who?" Craig said.

Silva writhed on the floor, raising and lowering his knees, trying to pump some air into his lungs. Black spots danced in front of his eyes, and his head felt as though it were swelling. He thought he was going to pass out. But then, finally, he managed to rake in half a breath and his eyes started to clear.

His gut ached miserably. He thought the gun barrel must

have gone clean back to his spine.

"Who?" Craig asked again, much louder. "Who, *Señor* Silva, or I will have these men stand you up and I will do it again!"

"Massey," Silva said, grunting, gasping, hating himself but seeing no other option. He couldn't stand another assault like that which he'd just endured. "Cuno Massey. Works for *Señor* Lord. Or . . . he did work for him."

"Who is this Massey?"

"He drives . . . or, drove . . . a freight wagon for *Señor* Lord. New in town. Only . . . he's only been here a few months."

"What do you know about this Massey?"

Lying on his side, knees still drawn up to his waist, Silva said, "Nothing. I know very little about him. He comes to get his horse once in a while, and rides him in the country. That is all I know. He works for *Señor* Lord."

"He killed three of my men tonight—this Massey."

Silva didn't know what to say to that. Beneath his own misery, he felt surprise at Craig's words. But he was too worried about himself and Ella to give much thought to Cuno Massey's motivations.

Maybe Massey and Ella had been meeting secretly in the barn and ridden out to escape the outlaws . . . ?

"Where do you suppose I might be able to find this Cuno Massey?"

"Shit, I don't know. If he ran off with my girl, I have something to talk to him about, too."

Craig kept his eyes on the old man. Those eyes were like having two cocked Colts on Fernando Silva, who looked away, cowering. He wished a hole would open up in the floor beneath him.

"Why do I feel you're lyin'?" Craig asked.

The old man snapped his head up. "No, no, no! I would not lie! Not to you, *señor*. I don't know where he went. He stays over at the boardinghouse, I think, but I don't know where he and my daughter ran off to tonight!"

Craig sighed. "All right, all right. I believe you."

Silva smiled with relief.

"Just the same, your girl's been a cause of great trouble to me—helpin' Massey ride away after killing three of the Boys."

Craig reached around behind him, and when he showed his right hand again, it was filled with a walnut-gripped bowie knife with a small silver profile image of a buxom girl inset in the handle, beneath the silver cap.

"I need to make sure that the other good citizens of Nopal know what will happen to them if they or anyone in their families crosses me."

"Oh, no, *señor*!"

One of the other men laughed. "Ear?"

"Yeah," said Craig. "Two Bears, Patten—hold him down."

Silva clamped both hands over his ears and stared up in shock at Craig holding the knife up close to his chin and giving an ominous half-grin, showing the sharp ends of his eyeteeth beneath his mustache.

"No, *señor*! *Por favor*! In the name of all the saints in heaven, I beseech thee! I told you what you wanted to know!"

The two men each grabbed Silva's arms and drove him, howling and kicking, to the floor.

"Hold his head steady," Craig ordered.

One of the outlaws slapped his hand over the lower left side of the old man's face, and held the right side of his head down hard against the floor, grinding that ear into the rough, splintery wood. Silva kicked and shrieked as Craig crouched over him.

"Have mercy!" Silva cried. "It is not right to inflict such savagery on an old man!"

Then he felt the sharp slice of the knife.

81

It was like a dozen lightning bolts hitting him all at the same time.

Silva's eyes opened wide, as did his mouth. He stopped kicking and stiffened. His scream was so high-pitched as to be nearly silent.

"Thank you," Craig said a few seconds later, rising with the bloody appendage in his hand. "Don't worry, *Señor* Silva—I'll run a string through it and wear it proudly around my neck."

Cuno hunkered down behind a stock trough on the south side of the main street, nearly directly across from the hotel, which was where Mulligan had told him Kate had been taken. She was probably up in a second- or third-story room being forced to do only God knew what.

No, Cuno knew what. He blinked his eyes to rid his brain of the images.

Three horses stood tied to one of the two hitch racks fronting the hotel.

A group of outlaws stood clumped in the street a half a block away on his right. The town and the night were so quiet, Cuno could hear everything they were saying. The outlaw leader was addressing several of his men, some of whom he'd already ordered onto several rooftops to keep a close eye on the town.

Cuno had heard his name mentioned.

Where the outlaw leader had learned Cuno's name, the young gunfighter had no idea. It didn't matter. All that was on Cuno's mind was getting Kate out of the hotel.

He raked a thumb across the sandy beard stubble on his cheek.

Easier thought about than done. At least on this part of the street, which was well-lighted by the lamplit saloons, all of which hunkered together within a block of each other, around the hotel, as though to give the drunks a shorter route to crawl.

The roof squawked above and behind Cuno. He caught a whiff of cigarette smoke.

Quickly, gritting his teeth, he slipped back away from the stock trough, ducked under a hitch rack, and moved off into the break between business buildings. Slowly, quietly, he made his way behind the building atop which must be a night guard. He kept moving west through the darkness punctuated with the tan shapes of privies and piles of stacked wood.

He stopped when he reached the rear of the New Mexico House Saloon.

The saloon's windows were lit, its back door propped open atop a small, roofed stoop. A low roar of voices and the pattering of a piano drifted out the open door.

An oil pot burned on the stoop. A man sat on the stoop's top step, leaning back on his elbows. He wore a short *charro*-style jacket over a pullover shirt and a knotted neckerchief. He also wore a narrowed-brimmed, short-crowned, tan Stetson with a yellow feather poking up from its braided rawhide band.

His pants and underwear were pulled down around his ankles. One of the whores who worked the New Mexico House was now toiling between the outlaw's spread, bare knees, raising and lowering her head, making sucking sounds. She moaned, as well, pretending to be enjoying it.

It was the half-breed whore Cuno had seen before in the New Mexico House, though he'd never had the pleasure. Not that he was above patronizing the line, as it was called, but soon after throwing in with the citizens of Nopal, he and Kate had started trysting out at the old trapper's cabin.

The outlaw grinned as he watched the whore working between his pale knees. He placed his hand atop the girl's head and, gritting his teeth sadistically, forced her head down farther and held it there until she gagged.

The outlaw laughed and let her go.

"Jesus Christ—you tryin' to kill me?" the girl said, gasping.

The man laughed again. Cuno recognized his droopy mustache and red neckerchief. He was one of those who'd hazed Cuno off the trail, wrecked his wagon, and killed his mules. He'd enjoyed himself then as he was now. He was obviously a man who took his pleasure where and when he felt like it.

Cuno saw the man's shell belt coiled around two filled holsters beside the man's left elbow on the stoop. Hunkered low in the shadows behind a business building, Cuno caressed the hammer of his Winchester.

He could kill the man so easily. The desire to ram a bullet into the self-satisfied killer's brain plate burned in him.

The whore was raising and lowering her head rhythmically. The man threw his head back, raising his chin sharply, and grunted, bucking up against the girl, his belt buckle clanking against the wooden step.

So easy . . .

Cuno resisted the urge. *There'll be time later,* he told himself. *First, you have to get Kate out of the hotel . . .*

Moving to his left, he dashed off behind a large woodpile and traced a broad arc south of the New Mexico House, weaving amongst private dwellings and scrub brush and privies. At the far west end of town, almost to the tree from which he'd found the old marshal and Chester Lord hanging, he crossed the main trail that became the main street farther east, and circled around the north side of town until he approached the hotel from its rear.

The hotel, a sprawling, three-story mud-brick and clapboard structure, was lit up as brightly as the saloon. In the light angling out its windows, he could see no men loitering in the yard outside.

Likely, the outlaws thought they'd seen the last of Cuno. That he'd lit out with Ella and was gone, fled. They probably weren't counting on him coming back. Not so soon, anyway. They probably had no idea that he—one man—intended on blowing them all to hell in a fine blood vapor.

Eventually, each and every one.

CHAPTER TEN

Holding his rifle down low across his thighs, Cuno crossed the open area behind the hotel, heading for the hotel's rear door, which sat atop a low, broad dock used for off-loading supplies from wagons into the kitchen.

He stayed as much to the shadows as he could, paused behind a two-hole privy to give the yard a second look, and then, confident no one else was back here or on the roof, he ran crouching to the loading dock. He climbed the steps on the balls of his boots and stepped up to the closed door.

He tried the knob and cursed.

Locked.

He looked around. Then he peered through the door's glass pane, unable to see anything inside but his own reflection. He thought the door opened on a storage room off the kitchen, which worked well for him tonight. When he gently busted out a corner of the glass with his revolver butt, hearing nothing but the soft tinkling of the glass, he was fairly confident no one had heard.

He holstered the gun and then reached inside and unlocked the door.

He gritted his teeth against the squawking of the hinges as he pushed the door open and then slipped inside. He moved through the storage room, which was cluttered with crates and barrels and cured meat hanging from the ceiling—the hotel's dining room did a romping business, because it had two excellent cooks, an Irish couple—to a door at the far end. He slowly opened the door, which let on to a hall by a rear stairs climbing to the second story on his right.

The hall was dimly lit by a colored glass lamp hanging from the ceiling, spreading a watery light over a large oil painting of George Washington on a white horse. Beyond lay the hotel's saloon. A few men were talking inside the saloon, but he couldn't see any more of them than the toe of one worn boot, which appeared to be propped on the boot wearer's knee. The bar was to the left.

Cuno could see only part of that, as well. He could see no one standing behind it.

Boots thudded at the far end of the saloon. Cuno stepped back into the shadows as a man pushed through the batwings—a tall *hombre* with a blond goatee wearing a bowler hat, round, gold-framed spectacles, and with two sawed-off shotguns in custom-made holsters hanging down his thighs.

His long, black canvas coat billowed as he stepped into the saloon, stopped, spread his high-topped, lace-up black boots, and planted his gloved hands on his hips.

"My turn," he said.

"What's your turn?" said one of the men sitting to the right of the saloon's rear door and whom Cuno couldn't see. He believed the voice belonged to the man wearing the boot, because the boot had shifted when the man had spoken.

"My turn with the redhead," said the newcomer in the spectacles and sawed-off shotguns.

"You think so, do you?" said one of the others snidely.

"Yeah, I think so. Which room's she in?"

"Bob Wade and Chet Ingersoll are takin' a turn with her at the moment."

"Ah, shit," said the tall man, turning. "Knowin' them, they're probably up there ignorin' the girl and playin' grabby pants with each other!"

"Take the back stairs," said one of the men in the saloon, his laughing voice echoing around the hall-like room. "Closer. It's nineteen, top right door. Say hey to Bob and Charlie for me, and tell 'em they need to haul their asses outside. Boss wants us to keep ten men on watch all night, in case that *hombre* who killed Spade and the others comes back."

"It would be my privilege," said the tall man, who strode toward the hall where Cuno lurked, his heart quickening.

Moving quickly, he opened the storage room door about three feet, slipped through it, and winced as he quietly closed it.

The newcomer's boot thuds grew louder. Cuno could feel the vibration through the floor. He could tell when the man was in the hall, when he was climbing the stairs, the steps squawking beneath his weight.

Cuno cracked the door. The man was halfway to the top. He stopped and grabbed the handrail as though to steady himself. He was obviously drunk. Cuno could smell the liquor on him.

As the man continued stomping heavily up the stairs, Cuno started climbing up behind him, on the balls of his boots. He moved quickly, taking two steps at a time. Ahead and above him, the man with the shotguns stopped at the top of the stairs, tilting his head to listen through a door on the hall's right side.

The man rapped on the door with the back of his right hand. "Bob, Charlie—that you boys in there?"

"Go away, Deitz!" a man shouted from behind the door.

"Open up, goddamnit—it's my turn!" Deitz rapped on the door once more. Before he could say anything else, Cuno stole up behind him and smashed the Winchester's butt against the back of the outlaw's head so hard, Cuno could hear the man's skull crack.

Deitz flew headlong, running and falling and then hitting the hall floor and rolling.

Cuno turned to the door, stepped back, and flung the heel of his right boot against it. The door crashed open and slammed back against the wall to Cuno's left. Cuno stopped its bounce with his boot, raised his rifle, clicked the hammer back, aimed at the man who was just then getting dressed to the right of the bed, which was directly in front of Cuno, and fired.

The man had his summer underwear half on, and, seeing Cuno, he'd opened his mouth to yell but didn't get more than a first note out before Cuno's .44-40 round punched a hole through his right cheek, just beneath his eye, and sent him flying back against a dresser.

The man lying between Kate's spread legs on the bed whipped his head toward Cuno, rising and reaching for a pistol hanging off a bedpost. He, too, was about to yell before Cuno's Winchester spoke again, turning the man's right eye to blood pudding and painting the wall above the bed with blood and bits of brain.

The man's ruined head bounced off the wall, and, half-dressed, he tumbled onto the floor, quivering.

Cuno hurried around to the side of the bed. Kate lay staring up in bewilderment at Cuno, slowly drawing her knees together. She'd been beaten. Her face was cut up and swollen, her lips cracked and bloody. Her hair hung in a tangled mess about her shoulders.

"Jesus *Christ!*" someone shouted from the saloon downstairs. "What did you boys get into up there?"

Another man laughed.

Another man shouted, "Let's try to be adults and take our turns, fellas!"

Cuno gazed down at Kate. "Christ," he said, sliding a tangled lock of hair back from her cheek.

"Leave me," Kate said wearily, rolling onto her side and bringing her knees to her chest.

"Not a chance." Cuno wrapped her up in a blanket.

"No," Kate said in a barely audible voice, groaning and grinding her head against the pillow. "Leave me." She sobbed.

Cuno picked her up in his arms, holding his rifle in his right hand. She was too weak to fight him. She pressed her face against his neck; he could feel the wetness of her tears dribble down beneath his shirt collar.

"It'll be okay, Kate," Cuno said, walking out of the room with the girl. "Everything's gonna be all right—I promise."

He started for the stairs he'd ascended but stopped when a man shouted from the bottom, "Hey—everything all right up there? You boys work it out?"

"Yeah!" Cuno shouted. "Shut the hell up—we're busy up here!"

He swung around and carried Kate in the opposite direction along the hall. He'd stayed in the hotel his first week in Nopal, and he knew there were two sets of stairs—one from the saloon and one from the lobby. He found the one from the lobby at the other end of the hall, and dropped quickly down the steps carpeted in a red and gold floral pattern.

He heard men loudly climbing the other set of stairs behind him.

Cuno's heart raced. He squeezed the forestock of his Winchester tightly in his right hand.

He dropped into the lobby and was relieved to find it vacant. No one was sitting at the main desk to the right, just off the end of the stairs. As he hurried toward the double doors, he glanced into the saloon, which opened off his right.

Only one marauder was sitting in there now, boot hiked on a knee, staring at the ceiling while sipping whiskey from a shot glass. Cuno could see the bartender now, too. The short, bald man who owned the place stood behind the bar, also staring at the ceiling above his head.

As Cuno hurried past the saloon, the outlaw slammed his glass down on the table and yelled, "Hey!" He must have sucked some of the whiskey down his windpipe, because then he started coughing loudly.

Cuno pushed out the saloon doors, hoping like hell the horses he'd seen earlier were still tethered to the hitch rack. They were. He moved down the steps and heaved Kate up onto the saddle of a sturdy-looking bay.

"Hey, who's shootin' over there?" a man yelled.

Cuno looked around and spied the shadow of the man standing at the top of the saloon's high false façade, holding a rifle up high across his chest. Three more men were walking quickly toward the hotel from Cuno's right.

"Hey, what you got there?" shouted the man atop the saloon.

"I got the girl," Cuno yelled, grabbing his Winchester, which he'd leaned against the stock trough. "And I'm ridin' out of here with her—and you can kiss my ass!"

He jerked the rifle up but not before the man on the saloon's façade snapped off a shot, which screeched into the dirt at Cuno's boots, pluming dust.

Cuno fired three quick rounds.

The man atop the saloon screamed as he fell back against the façade. He dropped his rifle, stumbled forward, and turned a somersault in midair before landing with a crash on the saloon's shake-shingled porch roof.

As he rolled down the roof and dropped into the street, Cuno swung up onto the bay behind Kate, who was sagging forward, both hands gripping the apple. She appeared only half conscious. Cuno turned the bay into the street. As men started shouting behind him and from inside the saloon, and snapping shots at him, he ground his spurs into the bay's flanks.

Lead sizzled and whined through the air around his head, blowing up dust beyond him.

The horse whinnied as it lunged off down the street as though it had been shot out of a cannon. Cuno hunkered low over Kate, gritting his teeth against a bullet burning across his right shoulder. They gained the edge of town, and the darkness of the countryside closed around them.

The cool night air pressed against him, threatening to rip his hat off his head. He pulled the brim lower and glanced back at the pinpricks of light that were the outlaws still shooting at him. The darkness of the town sheathing the dimly lit main street closed gradually, like a black thumb and black index finger moving closer together.

The frightened bay traced a curve in the trail, and the town was gone.

Cuno turned forward and kept the horse moving down the wide wagon trail. He wondered if the outlaws would follow him. Likely Craig would send some after him, but not the whole pack. It was too dark for accurate trailing.

They'd probably wait for morning, and then they'd give chase. There was no doubt about that. Cuno had burned down a good many of them—a half-dozen, at least. They'd come after him for revenge if nothing else.

And because they had to be feeling pretty stupid about now.

He doubted he'd have been able to do what he'd done if they hadn't got careless and, figuring they had the town locked down, got drunk and started taking advantage of Nopal's fineries, namely its whiskey and its women.

After he'd ridden a good quarter mile beyond the outskirts of town, Cuno slowed the bay to a canter, which was easier on both the horse and Kate, who leaned back against him now, groaning and muttering what he thought was "Leave me, leave me," though he could barely hear her above the bay's thudding hooves.

After a little more than a mile, they came to an unmarked

fork in the trail—two tines angling off to the south. One trail, angling south and west, led to Santa Fe, Cuno knew, while the other tine, which was no more than a single-track horse trail, led straight south over low buttes humping darkly against the starry sky. He'd never been to Miss Loretta's roadhouse, but he'd become familiar enough with the country to know that the narrow trail led to the old madam's watering hole.

There was also a more direct trail from town, which was the trail Mule Mulligan, Brett Cavanaugh, and Ella Silva had taken. Cuno hadn't wanted to take that one. Even if he'd had easier access to it from the hotel, which he hadn't, it was better to take a more indirect route and hope for the slim chance the outlaws wouldn't realize where he'd gone, though there was likely a good tracker or two amongst the group, and they'd find him sooner or later.

He couldn't worry about that now. His main concern was getting Kate somewhere relatively safe.

For the time being, anyway.

CHAPTER ELEVEN

A half a mile after he'd turned onto the narrow trail, Cuno slowed the bay to a walk.

He had only another mile or so to go, but he was pushing the horse hard and he didn't want one of its hooves plundering a gopher hole. If he and Kate were stranded afoot out here, they'd likely be finished.

They rode up and over the buttes through piñons and cedars. The trail dropped down into the same ravine that the outlaws had run Cuno and his wagon and mules into, and then it twisted up the other side, over another jog of slightly higher, rockier buttes and shelving dikes.

On the other side of the buttes, Cuno saw a light. As he rode on down the slope along the trail meandering through scrub cedars, the light became several lights—several windows of the roadhouse, which was an inky smudge sitting along the old stage road that was a pale ribbon in the darkness.

He rode on into the yard of the sprawling place flanked by several old stables and sheds and corrals, likely the remnants of the old stage relay station. The main building, window casting umber light into trapezoids on the hard-packed yard, appeared a story-and-a-half tall.

Constructed of vertical pine planks, warped and silvered by time and the harsh northern New Mexico weather, it also looked as though it could fly apart in the next stiff breeze. Ornately painted red, sun-faded letters on a large sign stretched across the second story announced simply MISS LORETTA'S.

Cuno drew the bay to a halt out front, where a half-dozen or so saddle horses lazed at two of the three hitch racks. He swung out of the saddle and then reached up for Kate, gently easing her down to the ground.

"Leave me," she continued to mutter though her eyes were closed, her head wobbling on her shoulders.

Cuno picked her up in his arms, moved to the Z-frame front door, flung it open, and stepped inside.

The place didn't look nearly as bright inside as it did outside, for the lamps were positioned so that they shed light out the windows without casting very much of it inside, which was most likely the owner's strategy. It gave the roadhouse an atmosphere of seedy mystery and intimacy. This was a place, most likely, where sundry nefarious deeds were proposed, negotiated, planned, and maybe even implemented.

Cuno blinked as he cast his gaze around the shadowy figures hunkered over long tables outfitted with benches. There were only five men in the place—at least five he could make out in the dimness. The air pushing against Cuno was a miasma of stale alcohol and human sweat odors that hung around him like a sour, wet blanket.

At the back of the main long room was a horseshoe-shaped bar. A small, pale figure stood behind it, smoking a pipe. Cuno couldn't tell if it was male or female—it was too small and too far away. The bar was lit up like a stage in an opera house after the house lamps had been turned down.

"Well, well, well—what have we here!" came a nasty, nasal, chirping voice from behind the bar. It apparently belonged to the figure standing behind it. It had been a woman's voice, however unattractive.

Cuno moved down the center aisle between the long plank tables, glancing warily at the figures sitting to each side of him, their heads swiveling as they followed the newcomer and the girl with their menacing gazes—at least, the atmosphere was menacing.

It was too dark to make out the eyes beneath broad hat brims. Occasionally there was the fleeting orange glow of a quirley or a cigar being dragged on.

Arranged here and there about the broad room were miniature smoking parlors—at least, they appeared that way, furnished as they were with comfortable, almost fancy-looking armchairs or settees arranged in intimate circles upon ornate rugs, with brass spittoons and small tables for setting drinks on. They must be where the girls entertained prospective jakes before leading said jakes upstairs to get down to their toe-curling business.

It probably didn't matter to anyone on the premises how out of place these little areas looked amidst the rough-hewn tables and the unadorned, bare board walls through the gaps of which the cool night air pushed, mercifully tempering the fetor.

Cuno approached the bar, and the little birdlike woman standing behind it, smoking a reed-stemmed corncob pipe, gazed at Cuno and the girl in his arms with amusement. She was dressed like a man. A tiny dog was sound asleep on an army blanket atop the bar, curled in a tight ball. It appeared a cross between a dachshund and a Chihuahua. An old dog with a gray muzzle, probably accustomed to noise, much more than there was here tonight, a weeknight.

"I need a room for her," Cuno said. "She needs care. A woman's care."

"I ain't a fuckin' hospital," the old woman barked in her nasty, magpie voice, blowing pipe smoke out her withered nostrils.

"Ain't Mulligan here?"

"He's up yonder. But he's been a payin' customer. Who's she?"

Cuno jutted his chin at the old woman. "She's Kate Lord, you old bat. And she's going to get a room here whether you say so or not."

Cuno turned toward the stairs he could make out angling up from the far right side of the room and over the bar, to the second story. He could see only the staircase's outlines in the dimness beyond the sphere of light from the sooty lamps hanging over the bar.

Something whistled through the air over his right shoulder, missing his ear by a hair's breadth and thudding into a roof support post six feet beyond him. The knife handle quivered.

Cuno jerked around, eyes wide with shock. He'd seen no one sitting near the bar. But now he did—a shadowy figure crouched behind a table not ten feet away.

A man in a high-crowned Stetson.

A gravelly voice said, "Don't you dare come in here needin' help and talkin' to Loretta like that, you disrespectful, little tit-chewin' calf. You needin' a hide-tannin', boy? Grow you up some. Shake the gravel down."

Cuno's surprised gaze turned to one of incredulity as he stared at the man in the shadows behind the table. The man was straightening from his crouch—an older gent by the set of him, the withered-looking neck and sloping shoulders.

A voice like a night breeze scratching through cattails. He wore a mustache. That much Cuno could make out as renegade spears of light hit him. There was a bottle and a shot glass on his table. A cigarette smoldered in an ashtray. A rifle sat on the table's right side, within quick reach if needed.

"Holy Christ," Cuno said quietly as he married the familiar voice to the familiar outlines of the old man's craggy, angular face and weathered, potbellied frame. "Spurr Morgan, you cobwebby old saddle—is that you, and has this night just gone from bad to downright unbearable?"

The older man studied the younger one silently from the shadows. Then his gravelly voice rolled out, "Kid Massey?" That's what Spurr had started calling him before they split up in Mexico. He was one of those who liked to give everybody a nickname.

"Shit, Spurr," Cuno said, feeling buoyant relief at seeing the old man.

Old was Spurr Morgan, and he had a logy ticker as well as a profound weakness for liquor and women half his age, but Cuno had known few tougher or more capable frontiersmen, let alone frontier lawmen. The younger man was so happy to see the older man, despite the sundry warrants and bounties on Cuno's head, that a small lump formed in his throat.

"I need help here," he blurted out, lifting Kate a little higher in his arms.

"Well, shit, if you're a friend of ole Spurr Morgan," intoned the woman behind the bar in her tooth-gnashingly nasal voice, "you're no friend of mine." She laughed ironically. "But take that poor critter upstairs, anyway, and I'll give her a lookin' over since my doxies are all knotted around Mule up there—leastways all but the one Spurr left so's she won't be able to walk for the next two weeks! And the one with Cavanaugh . . ."

Cuno glanced at Kate. The girl in his arms did not react to that last comment from Miss Loretta. Maybe she hadn't heard.

The woman flung an arm toward the stairs. "Go on! Go on! I'm right behind ya soon as I fetch a pail of cold water. Put her in any o' them rooms up there. Oh, hell—since she's a fuckin' Lord, an' all, and her daddy's a local musky-muck, you'd better put her in my bed so's she don't get all et up by the bedbugs. Last room on the far end of the hall! Keep in mind I wasn't expectin' visitors—shit, I ain't spread my knobby old knees in twenty years—so don't expect the tidy palace of a friggin' Dutch queen."

Cuno was already on the stairs, which swayed precariously beneath him. Below, Spurr said to Loretta, "What in the hell is goin' on here? Is Mule here?"

"While you was upstairs gettin' your ashes hauled, you old mossyhorn, Mule come staggerin' in here with that Fancy Dan banker's boy, and a Mescin gal . . ."

The voices trailed off behind Cuno, as he and Kate gained the second story.

Vaguely, he wondered about Ella as he tramped down the bare wooden floor of the hall, tripped the latch of the last door at the end, and toed it open. Footsteps sounded in the hall behind him and as he laid Kate down on the broad, canopied, four-poster bed, he glanced over his shoulder to see Brett Cavanaugh step into the room behind him.

"Oh, thank God," the banker's son intoned, "you found her!"

Cuno turned to him, choking back the anger burning like liquor bile in his throat. Cavanaugh had soaked his hair and mustache and combed both, and apparently brushed the trail dust from his suit, as well.

And he'd already had a woman . . .

"Thanks . . . uh . . . What's your name again?" he said.

"Diddle yourself, you worthless bastard," Cuno said, keeping his voice down.

Kate appeared to be unconscious, though hers was a restless unconsciousness. She was clamping her knees together tightly. While Cavanaugh had been hunkered down somewhere, cowering like a dog beneath a boardwalk, his young lady had been ruthlessly savaged. Used like an old flour sack.

He held his glare on Cavanaugh, who returned it. His eyes flickered, his cheeks flushed, and he turned to Kate. "Leave us, mule skinner. I'll settle up with you and your unbridled mouth later."

"Yes, you will." Cuno glanced once more at Kate, his heart breaking for her, his chest burning with rage at her so-called betrothed as well as the savage gang who'd done this to her.

Absently fingering the leather keeper thong over his Peacemaker, he left the room. He met Miss Loretta coming up the stairs with a bucket of water and several towels on her arm.

She stopped before Cuno. "There as many as Mule said?"

"How many did Mule say there were?"

"Thirty, at least. The Boys, they call themselves. Cecil Craig's old gang—or his new one, I should say."

"Well, there *was* thirty. Maybe forty. There's a mite fewer now, but just a mite." Cuno pinched his hat brim to Loretta, and continued on down the stairs.

Spurr stood at the bar now, the bottle, shot glass, and 1866 Winchester Yellowboy repeater on the bar, as well. He'd returned his bowie knife to his belt sheath. He stood with his elbow on the bar.

He blew thick cigarette smoke out his nostrils as Cuno approached. "You've aged since I last seen you, Kid."

Cuno looked the old mossyhorn up and down. He looked like a bag of old bones over which someone had drawn badly weathered rawhide and sewn it tight as a drumhead. The old man's liver-spotted, patch-bearded face made Cuno think of an ancient, falling-down church in Mexico.

"You look as fresh as a dove in the morning, Spurr."

Spurr grinned, showing several gnarled, chipped teeth, and raised his bottle. Cuno nodded. The old federal lawman grabbed a shot glass down off a pyramid and splashed whiskey into it. "How's the girl?"

"Not good. They savaged her, one after a goddamn other."

"Who's the Fancy Dan Loretta was yakkin' about? I musta

been upstairs, ya understand, when they came in."

"Her betrothed."

Spurr sipped his whiskey, frowning at Cuno over the lip of the shot glass. "If *he*'s her betrothed, how . . . ?" He shook his head. "Never mind. I don't even wanna know."

Cuno threw back half his shot. He didn't hold much for drinking, as it dulled the senses, which could be a terminal illness for a hunted man. But under the circumstances, he felt like polishing off Spurr's bottle and popping the cork on another.

He wouldn't. The Boys might very well be trailing him even now. But he wanted to.

"What're doing here, Spurr?" he asked, polishing off the shot and setting the glass down on the bar.

Spurr refilled Cuno's glass. "Shit, Kid—I'm after Craig."

Cuno blinked, scowling. "Well, hell, old man—you're a mite late to the party!"

"Don't get your shorts in a twist. But you're right—I am late to the party. Me and four other federals been trackin' that gang ever since Craig broke out of the very same federal pen you broke out of some time ago. Only he didn't make near the fuss you made about it. He quietly paid off four of the guards with stolen loot, and Craig slipped out undetected . . . until a whole eight days after he'd vamoosed.

"Rode over to Kansas, as far as I can tell, and spent the last three months livin' under an alias and puttin' a gang back together. Some of the *Boys* are from his old gang, some are new. I reckon he and the Boys returned to Nopal to settle up for Mulligan arrestin' him six years ago after shooting and killing two of Craig's brothers. They all grew up around Nopal, you understand.

"Mulligan served 'em with warrants for raping three young ladies in Hollybrook, in western Kansas. They were wanted for various black deeds, but the rapes were fresh evidence, so that's what they tried 'im for, right there in Nopal. They didn't want to risk him escaping if they transported him back to Hollybrook. Shoulda hanged the sonofabitch. I tell you, if it had been me instead of Mulligan, I wouldn't have given him the pleasure of being arrested."

"Under the circumstances, I wish it had been you, Spurr. They got that whole town under siege. They've killed willy-nilly, hanged men from trees. Now they're ridin' roughshod—at least, they were until I sort of distracted 'em."

"Will they be headin' this way, you think?"

"I think."

Just then, the front door opened. Cuno and Spurr both wheeled, Cuno palming his Peacemaker while Spurr loudly racked a cartridge into his Yellowboy's action.

CHAPTER TWELVE

On the far side of the long, mostly dark drinking hall from the bar, a slender figure walked through the front door. Ella opened her mouth in shock at the two guns aimed at her, and she stepped back against the door.

She was holding Cuno's Winchester, which she nearly dropped.

"Easy," Cuno told Spurr. "She's with me."

Spurr depressed his Yellowboy's hammer. "Well, I'll be hanged. Where'd she come from?"

"The barn," Ella said, latching the door and striding forward. "I was tending the horses. I tended Renegade, too."

"Obliged," Cuno said.

As she walked toward the bar, Ella glanced around the room before returning her liquid dark gaze to the bar. "Did you *gringos* frighten all the other customers away?"

She tossed Cuno the Winchester.

He looked around, probing the shadows with his eyes. "What the hell . . . ?" He glanced at Spurr, who was also scowling across the dim room. All the tables now appeared vacant. There were only the leavings of the half-dozen other customers, their tobacco smoke still webbing in the shadowy air.

"I didn't even hear 'em leave." Spurr gave a wry chuckle. "They must've heard the name Craig and 'the Boys,' and that was all it took to clear the room. Decided to do their drinkin' an' fuckin' elsewhere." He looked quickly at Ella. "Good Lord—

listen to my privy mouth in the presence of a lady. I do apologize, *señorita*."

"I work in a livery barn," Ella said.

"Still, it is ungallant to curse in front of a woman. Apparently I wasn't horsewhipped near enough as a shaver." Spurr sipped his whiskey and turned to Cuno. "I was hopin' to get a little help out of a couple of the other customers. I recognized two rather notorious cold-steel artists in that bunch. They was the two playin' checkers. One was drinkin' sarsaparilla." Spurr snorted.

"What does it say for us that they ran with their tails between their legs?"

"Nothin' good."

"You said you were riding with four other federals."

"Yeah, well, one's Cupid itch got to itchin' too bad for him to sit a saddle. Another's a lunger. After he coughed up three-quarters of one lung onto his saddle the other night, I told him to go on back to Denver and get himself fitted for a wooden overcoat. The other two oughta be here in a few days. They circled around to Bridger City, and if they didn't run into the gang, they were going to meet me here early next week."

"Why?"

"According to the federal report, Craig was tried down there."

"That ain't right," Cuno said. "He was captured by Mulligan and tried in Nopal."

"That's federal pencil pushers for you," Spurr said. "Craig has a woman he wrote to there from prison, and that must've been the source of the confusion, though it don't take more than a month with thirty-one days in it to confuse a federal. I speak from experience."

The old marshal raised his glass in salute, and tossed the rest of his whiskey back. "So they're headed here, you say? Well, hell—sorry, honey; there I go again—my time's about up anyway and I ain't havin' nearly the good times I once did. It's you I feel sorry for, Kid.

"You're too damned young to get kicked out with a cold shovel. Why don't you take Miss Ella and that other girl up yonder, if she can ride, and head for the Sangre de Cristos. If you hole up tight enough, the Boys won't find you till they grow bored of lookin'. Outlaws of that caliber are easily bored."

Cuno glanced at Ella, who stared back at him with fear in her eyes.

"Go on," Spurr said, canting his head toward the barn. "Fetch the girl up yonder and go. Loretta'll fix her up good enough she can ride, and hell, beatin' herself up ridin's a whole lot better than what Cecil Craig likely has in mind. Me an' Mulligan'll hold 'em off. Him an' me go back a ways. Mule's a couple years younger than me, so unless they tore him limb from limb, he's still got some bob wire in his spleen. Hell, I could tell you stories of our old buffalo huntin' days—Mule's an' mine. . . ."

"Love to hear 'em."

"Yeah, I know—maybe later."

"No, I think we got time tonight, Spurr. 'Cause I'm not goin' anywhere." Cuno sagged into a chair near the bar. "You don't understand—another long ride would kill Kate."

Spurr sighed and poked his hat brim up off his forehead. "They beat her up that bad, huh?"

"Worse."

Spurr looked at Ella. "What about Little Miss here?"

Cuno looked at the girl, who was turning her mouth corners down at him and wrinkling the skin across her otherwise smooth forehead.

"Stupid kid," Cuno said to her, shaking his head. "What in the hell were you doing out in that barn, anyways? After Fernando told you not to!"

Ella's eyes blazed. She bunched her lips and leaned slightly forward at the waist, giving free rein to her south-of-the-border fury. "I am so sorry to be such an imposition! I am so sorry to have distracted you from the banker's little flower! If you think she would ever marry you, anyway—a man who works for measly wages driving mules—you are a fool. A stupid *gringo* fool!

"And if you think I don't know about you and her riding out to meet each other in the country—ha! You got another think coming, bucko! You think I didn't catch on after you two came for your horses on the same day every week, always about fifteen minutes apart? *Mierda,* the whole town probably saw you riding out in the same direction."

Ella shook her head, glaring at him as though she hated him more than the gnarliest demon in hell's bowels. "Cork-headed *gringo fool!*"

She wheeled and, long dark-brown hair shivering down her back, she strode quickly over to the end of the stairs and began climbing the steps, her black shoes thundering loudly, like pistol shots.

Halfway up, she stopped, leaned over the rail, and lifted her calico blouse, revealing two full, rather splendid brown breasts caressed by the dim lantern light from over the bar. "Do I look like a kid to you *now,* simple *gringo* fool? Ha!"

She dropped her blouse and continued thundering furiously up the stairs.

Her clomping dwindled gradually.

Cheeks as hot as fireplace bricks, Cuno glanced at Spurr, who regarded him with brow arched.

The old marshal raked a thumb through the patchy beard on his jaw and said, "I'm glad you settled down, Kid. Nice to see you livin' a nice, quiet life in a peaceful little town." He snorted, amused. "Hell, Craig and his Boys probably seem like a stroll along a chucklin' creek after all your tanglin' with two she-cats from the same lair."

Cuno rose from his chair, muttering, "You're just jealous." He grabbed his rifle off the bar and started tramping across the drinking hall toward the front door.

"Where you goin'?" Spurr called.

"I'll keep the first watch," Cuno said. "You'd best get some rest after all the whiskey you been drinkin'."

"I don't know if I can sleep with such a purty, buxom, and obviously horny little *señorita* on the premises, but"—Spurr grabbed his rifle, bottle, and shot glass, and started ambling toward the stairs—"I reckon I'll give it a shot."

Cuno's ears burned as he closed the roadhouse door behind him and strode out into the night, looking around carefully, listening, trying to shut out his embarrassment. There was no time for it. But that didn't keep him from feeling like the fool Ella had so venomously informed him he was.

He'd been blinded by his passion for Kate Lord. And Ella had known about it. If she'd known, others must have known. How many others had been snickering behind his back at him and Kate?

Or maybe only Ella knew because she'd stabled both his and Kate's horses, and she'd had a special interest. God knew why. She'd obviously known him to be a fool.

His humiliation was crowded out by his concern for Kate. He still loved her, even after she'd professed her intention of marrying Brett Cavanaugh. He remembered how she'd looked on that bed—her beauty and earthy charm and dignity taken away from her. She'd been beaten senseless and abused horribly, treated as though she'd been no more to those animals than a place to sate themselves.

Which is what she'd been.

Savaged by savages.

Cuno's heart raced. He squeezed his Winchester in both hands as he held it low across his thighs.

He'd circled the yard once and was leaning back against the peeled log rails of the corral flanking the roadhouse. He stared off toward the buttes humping up pale against the starry sky. He found himself grinding his teeth and hoping they'd come. Foolish to think that way, because when they did come, he and Spurr would be outmanned. It was hard to say how much help Mulligan could lend in his condition.

Likely, they'd get no help from Cavanaugh. Cuno doubted that the banker's spoiled and immaculately attired son had ever fired a pistol in his life, much less a rifle.

He'd abandoned the woman he presumably loved. Left her to the brutes giving free rein to their goatish desires.

Cavanaugh was another one Cuno would settle up with. He wasn't worth killing, but Cuno had a mind to beat the man senseless, though the impulse probably had as much to do with raw jealousy as indignation for what Cavanaugh had done . . . or not done . . . in town.

"Settle down," he told himself quietly. "For chrissakes, settle down."

He squeezed his eyes closed and tried to silence the voices in his head. He managed to dull most of them, but not the one ominously muttering "Craig and the Boys."

There was no way he and Spurr could take down the entire gang, but Cuno vowed here and now that he'd kill Craig before he himself was riddled with the gang's lead. He'd cut off the snake's head, at least.

He sat on the top corral rail and rested the rifle across his thighs, staring northward. Gradually, he managed to calm his mind so that he was aware of only what he was seeing—the stars and bluffs and breeze-ruffled sage shrubs, the occasional tumbleweed tumbling slowly across the dark roadhouse yard.

The breeze whispered, and once in a while a lonesome coyote wailed. About two hours after he'd left the roadhouse, an entire chorus of coyotes kicked up a hair-raising cacophony in the buttes to the east. Muffled by distance but somehow off-putting, just the same.

He half-consciously imagined they were the voices of the kill-crazy gang that had savaged Kate Lord and the entire town of Nopal.

About an hour and a half after he'd left the roadhouse, he heard the soft crunch of footsteps. He turned to see a tall, stooped figure in trail-worn clothes and a battered, tan Stetson ambling toward him. Spurr was puffing a quirley. He held his rifle low in his right hand.

"Couldn't sleep," said the lawman. "The affliction of the old and feeble. Why don't you go in and give it a try? Miss Loretta's mannin' the front door with a shotgun. There's two other doors—both locked."

Cuno was sitting down against the well coping near the corral, facing north. He glanced at the sky. By the set of the stars, he could tell it was around four o'clock. It would be getting light soon.

"Miss Loretta say anything about Kate?"

"She's gonna be all right. Like you said, they beat her up some, but she's gonna be all right. Who's the Fancy Dan again? I forget."

"Kate's beau." Cuno heaved himself to his feet. "They're gettin' hitched next spring."

Spurr studied him, shook his head, and sagged down against the top of the well coping. "I'm too old for this shit."

"Yeah—me, too."

CHAPTER THIRTEEN

Cuno walked back around to the front of the roadhouse.

All the lamps had been turned off by Miss Loretta—he'd seen her earlier moving to all the windows, and turning the wicks down—and an eerie, hushed darkness lay over the yard. The stars lit the sky but they didn't send much of their light to earth. Cuno could make out only the dimmest outlines. He stood outside the front door, staring off into the night, listening, wondering if the gang was on the lurk out there, preparing an ambush.

Cuno and Spurr and the others had the advantage of the roadhouse. But Craig had the advantage of numbers. The Boys could be held off for a while, but sooner or later they'd storm the place and take it.

Cuno tapped on the door.

"Who is it?" came Miss Loretta's voice.

"Cuno Massey."

The door opened. Cuno stepped inside. The mannish, bird-like little woman, holding the locking bar in both hands, said, "What kind of a name is that?" A candle burned on a table behind her. There was also a coffee pot, a China cup, and a shotgun.

"The only one I got."

Loretta snugged the locking bar back down into its braces. "Cup of coffee?"

"Think I'll try for forty winks." Cuno watched the old woman sit down on a bench and begin to pack her pipe. "Sorry about the trouble," he said.

She looked up at him, incredulous. "Shit, I've known trouble before. Hell, I moved into this country when the Comanches, Apaches, Kiowas, Utes, and Southern Cheyennes were still runnin' crazy, determined to scour all us whites from the face of the earth."

She struck a match to life on the table and held it over the pipe. "I've known trouble, all right. Trouble country is what this is. Anyone tryin' to come through that door I don't like is gonna get a belly full of double-aught buck for his trouble."

Cuno smiled. "Can I get a room?"

"Take the third one down on the left. Wrong end of the hall from that Fancy Dan. I get the feelin' he don't cotton to you." Loretta chuckled deep in her throat. "And we don't need to start fightin' amongst ourselves."

"I reckon."

Cuno set his rifle on his shoulder and climbed the stairs to the second floor. Lamplight shone through a gap in the door to his right. Voices pushed through the gap as well—girls' voices as well as a man's voice. Cuno glanced through the gap to see old Mule Mulligan stretched out on a bed, head propped on two pillows.

Two pretty girls dressed in very little sat on either side of the bed, and they were giving the old town marshal a sponge bath. They were cooing and giggling, sounding like excited pigeons. Mulligan smiled despite his broad face resembling raw ground meat.

The girl on the far side of the bed from Cuno—a pretty, pale blonde—leaned down over Mulligan's chest. Her wrapper opened, showing her pale breasts slanting down toward the old lawman's bulging belly. She pressed her tongue to Mulligan's fat, hairy belly, and said, "Like that?"

"Ahhhh," Mulligan said, tipping his head back on the pillow and closing his eyes. "Just what the doctor ordered, Miss Cincy!"

Cuno cleared his throat, nudging the door a little wider with his Winchester's barrel. "Forgive me for intrudin'," he said. "I was just wonderin' how the marshal's doing. None the worse for wear, I see."

Mulligan jerked his head up, flushing. He scowled and rested his head back against his pillow. "Yeah, I heard you made it, Massey. They beat that poor girl up pretty badly, I hear."

"Don't get to havin' too much fun. They'll probably track me here."

"Oh, I don't doubt that a bit," Mulligan said as the soiled doves continued to bathe him.

Fortunately, the brunette sitting on Cuno's side of the bed was blocking Cuno's view of the grizzled, old lawman's private parts. The young freighter/gunslinger didn't need that disturbing picture after everything else he'd been through this night.

Mulligan said, "You'd best ride over to the county seat and have the sheriff organize a posse . . . if he can find enough men willin' to go up against Craig and the Boys . . ."

"It's too late for that now. I'm not gonna leave this place short-handed. Spurr's here, and—"

"Spurr?"

"Yeah, Spurr Morgan."

"That old reprobate?" Mulligan glowered at Cuno, feigning distaste. But there was a hopeful twinkle in his eyes. "Well, now we're really done for. I used to hunt buffalo with that old polecat. Me and Spurr and Bat Masterson and several others. He could shoot straight back then, Spurr could, but his eyesight's gone to hell. Same place his ticker went. Oh, shit— we're done for now."

"Mule!" cried the blonde, casting a fearful glance at the old lawman. "Me an' Mattie can shoot, and Loretta's got that big ole shotgun of hers. We'll hold them varmints off. Done held others off plenty of times. Now, you stop scarin' us!"

"I'm sorry, darlin'." Mulligan slid a lock of hair back from her cheek with two sausage-like fingers. "Listen to me go on. I was only foolin', dearies. Spurr—why, that old sinner's got more sand in his craw and blood in his teeth than an old turkey buzzard after dinin' on fresh elk!"

He winked and smiled at the two girls. "And I ain't so bad myself, given half a chance. We'll be fine. Just fine."

"I'm gonna close my eyes for a bit," Cuno said. "Since it doesn't look like you're going to be getting much sleep tonight, wake me if you hear any shooting out there."

Mulligan had already returned his attention to the girls' ministrations. "Lordy, Miss Cincy . . . that's just naughty, dear. Oh, but I ain't sayin' you should stop. Why, I can feel myself healin' by leaps and bounds every time I feel your tongue on my pecker." He chuckled. "Who needs a Yale-educated pill-roller, anyways?"

Cuno rolled his eyes and stepped through the door of his appointed room. He closed the door and had just taken his hat off when the door opened again.

It was dark in the room; he saw only a slender, female-curved silhouette step toward him. With the door closing out the light from the hall, he saw very little but a vague outline as Ella pushed the door shut behind her. He recognized her scent.

Cuno said, "What the hell?"

"Cuno—I'm scared!"

She threw herself against him, wrapping her arms around him and pressing her cheek to his chest. She was warm and soft against him. He could feel her heart beating. She smelled lightly of sage and of a woman's musk mixed with the odors of the livery barn—a curiously arousing blend.

Cuno placed his hand on the back of her head, dragging it

through her long hair. "You didn't seem all that scared in town."

"It all happened so fast. I didn't realize the danger we are in. We may all die soon!"

Cuno's eyes had adjusted to the darkness, so he could see her now gazing up at him, starlight from an unshuttered window glistening blue in her dark eyes.

"We're not gonna die. Now, why don't you leave me alone for a few minutes, so I can get some shut-eye. Going to need it in the morning."

"Who can sleep at such a time?" Ella stepped back away from him.

She pulled her blouse up and over her head, and let it fall to the floor. She loosened her skirt, and dropped it. She hadn't been wearing anything other than the skirt and the blouse.

"Now, hold on," Cuno said, throwing his hands up, palms out.

Ella stepped toward him, took one of his hands and placed it on her round, tender right breast lightly screened by her hair. He felt her nipple pebble against his palm.

Male need surged in him. It had started when he'd seen the whore's camisole flop away from her chest. Now, with a beautiful girl here in this dark room lit only by the feeble stars, standing naked before him, holding his hand against her breast, there was no denying it.

He swept her lithe body up in his thick arms. She gasped, wrapping her arms around his neck, and he kissed her.

Her mouth was sweet, her lips pliant, tongue pressing hungrily against his own. He ran his hand down her long, cool thigh.

He pulled his head away from hers, and frowned down at her. "How old *are* you, anyway?"

"Don't worry," Ella said. "You won't be deflowering a virgin—if that's what you're worried about."

He studied her skeptically. He looked at her body. She obviously wasn't as young as he'd thought. Not only was she filled out and nicely curved, but there'd been a woman's hunger in her kiss.

He dropped her into the bed. She laughed as she bounced and drew the covers back. She crawled under a sheet and lay there on her side, chin resting on the heel of her hand, watching him undress. It took less than a minute. He walked over to her, and she reached out and wrapped a hand around him, smiling up at him demurely as she manipulated him.

He could hear her breathing.

Her hand was small and soft. He sighed.

She lay back against her pillow, and he crawled into bed and lay between her spread knees. She sandwiched his face in her hands. "I have been hungry for you," she said. "But you haven't been able to see past Miss Lord."

Cuno kissed her wrist. "That's because I'm a fool. You got it right. But just so you know, Ella—you're pretty and I'm plumb wore out and in need of a diversion. That's all this is—you understand? I make no promises about anything."

Ella spread her legs wide and squirmed around beneath him, digging her fingers into his biceps. "Cristo—do you always talk this much?"

She hadn't been lying. This was not her first time around the breaking corral. That was obvious less than a minute later, when they really got the bedsprings singing, Ella thrusting her hips up in unison with his, knees flapping like wings. She moaned like a mare in heat.

When the bed and Ella had finally quieted down, and he'd rolled away from her, breathing hard, sweat glistening on his broad chest, he jerked his head up off his pillow with a grunt, and held his breath. He'd heard something.

"What is it?" Ella said, panting beside him.

"Shh." Cuno reached for where he'd hung his revolver on a bedpost.

A light tap on the door. Spurr said through the panel, "Dry your dick and get out here." Soft footsteps faded back down the hall.

"Shit." Cuno threw the sheet back, quickly cleaned his privates at a washbowl, and dressed.

Ella knelt on the bed, sitting back against her heels, cupping her breasts in her hands, watching him.

She said nothing, but her eyes were bright with worry in the gray light now washing through the window behind her. When Cuno had buckled his shell belt around his waist, donned his hat, and picked up his rifle, he bent down and kissed her.

"Stay here. Keep the door locked."

"A lot of good that's going to do."

"It's something."

She wrapped her arms around his neck, clinging to him desperately. "I wish we hadn't done that," she whispered into his ear. "Dying is going to be harder now."

Cuno had to wrestle out of the girl's strong grip. Holding her arms, he said, "You're not gonna die. Neither am I. We'll test this bed out again soon." He kissed her breasts, winked, and left the room.

CHAPTER FOURTEEN

Lying on the kitchen floor of his and Ella's house in Nopal, Fernando Silva opened his eyes.

A burning, throbbing pain instantly hammered through his head. Crying out, he clamped a hand over his ear. Over what remained of his ear, rather. Not much but a crusty blood patch and ragged tissue where the ear had been hacked off by Cecil Craig's bowie knife.

Silva shuddered, tears streaming down his cheeks. He pressed his head against the floor, clamping his hand over the ragged hole. He hardened his jaws until he thought he'd grind what was left of his teeth to a fine powder. His head felt as though it had been doused with coal oil and set on fire.

"Cristo!" the old man bellowed. "Ella—help me!"

Silence was the only response.

Silva looked around. Gray morning light shone in the windows. There was a buttery cast in the east where the sun was beginning to clear the horizon. He'd been lying here unconscious for hours.

Sitting up, Silva called for his adopted daughter once more, and looked down to see a hand-sized pool of blood on the floor where he'd been lying. It was as dry and crusty as that over his ear.

"Ella!" he shouted, but before the echo had died in the otherwise silent house, he remembered that Craig had come here because Ella had ridden away with a young man in the dark of last evening.

She was gone.

Last night, Silva hadn't had time to worry much about Ella, or to even wonder where she'd gone. Craig had been his main concern. After the man had hacked off Silva's ear, the old man had passed out from the pain. From pain and all the tequila he'd consumed before he'd heard that awful knock on his door.

But now, beneath the searing pain in his head where his ear had been, he wondered . . . and worried. Why had she run off with Chester Lord's mule skinner, Cuno Massey? Why? Had they been running from the gang?

Most likely.

The remembered image of Craig crouching over him and lowering that knife to his ear while two other men held him down flashed behind his eyes, and rage burned along with the pain. He could see the outlaw leader's eyes flashing with devilish delight as he'd begun slicing into the ear, the men holding the old man fast to the floor, chuckling and yelling encouragement to their leader.

Keeping his hand clamped over his ear, Silva heaved himself heavily to his feet, drawing air sharply through his clenched teeth. He went over to the cupboards around the dry sink and pulled a half-filled mescal bottle off a shelf. He chewed the cork out of the bottle's mouth, spat it onto the floor, and tipped the bottle high.

He took several deep pulls, the fiery liquid plunging down his throat and into his belly. As the fire abated, so did the burn in his ear. The old man stood staring down at the bottle, pensive.

The pain had diminished somewhat, but not his rage. He kept seeing the outlaw's eyes. His worry over Ella fueled his rage at Craig and the other Boys. He looked at the old gray Spencer repeater on the table, and he scolded himself harshly.

Why had he not used it when he'd had the chance? He'd had

Craig in his sights. All he'd needed to do was pull the trigger. Instead, his old man's fear had compelled him to obey the sadistic killer's order to put the gun down and allow himself to be shamed and mutilated.

Better to have died in a hail of lead than to have allowed those killers to humiliate and disfigure him!

Silva ground his teeth once more. He tipped his head to one side and poured the mescal over his bloody ear. It only added more kerosene to the flames.

The old man cried out, tears once again pouring from his eyes and streaming like rain down his cheeks. His head burned but his body felt cold, as though ice were grinding through his flinty veins.

But that was all right. He enjoyed the pain now. That fire only merged with his rage to fuel an inferno of vengeance-seeking fury inside him. It filed off the years. It made him young again, and sharp, and dangerous as he'd once been before he'd settled down to raise an orphaned Mexican girl and operate a livery barn.

Before he'd become a soft, fearful, weak old man.

Silva took another long pull from the bottle. He poured more of the fiery liquid over the ear, knowing it had to be sterilized to prevent infection, and then he took one more pull and set the bottle on the table.

He took a dish towel from the back of a chair, where Ella had hung it to dry after they'd had supper last night. He ripped the towel in two and wrapped one half of it around his head, covering his ear. The towel was higher on one side than the other, knotted beneath the ruined ear, where the lobe used to be.

That would keep the dust out.

He looked at the Spencer on the table.

He needed more firepower.

Silva went upstairs and came down wearing a straw sombrero

and hitching an old cartridge belt and two Remington conversion revolvers in soft leather holsters around his broad, bony hips. He held a liver-spotted hand over one of the Remington's worn walnut grips, liking the heavy feel of the cold steel on him.

He went outside and stood on the sunken ground just outside his front door, between two rabbitbrush shrubs, and looked around. Lemon sunlight angled over the eastern buttes. The sun had just cleared the horizon, and was rising, swallowing up the shadows it cast.

Everything around him looked as it normally did. The willows lined the dry wash and the cedars and scrub brush and prickly pear patches around his wood shed. The birds sounded happy, flitting here and there about the branches. A robin splashed in the stone birdbath Ella always kept filled, under a large cottonwood at the edge of the arroyo.

Yes, everything looked as it normally did.

But so much had changed after that terrible gang had ridden into town.

Including Fernando Silva.

And Ella was gone.

The stoop-shouldered old man, who looked more like a silverhaired scarecrow than a man in his baggy denims and linsey shirt and suspenders, the crude attire appearing a couple of sizes too large for his spindly frame, ambled bandy-legged across the wash and made his way northeastward. Boots kicking up the fine dust as he walked, he made his way around shacks and cabins to the main street.

He continued eastward along the main street, walking right down the center of the trace, both hands on the grips of his pistols. He walked deliberately, keeping his chin down, eyes hard and grim beneath the brim of his straw sombrero.

He looked around. The street was deserted. It wasn't usually deserted this time of the morning. Shopkeepers were usually opening up their businesses and shuttling some of their wares onto their porches and boardwalks, or they were sweeping away the dust and horseshit, and washing windows.

But not today. Here, little appeared the same as it always did.

Because the gang was here, and everyone in town was scared and cowering inside their homes, afraid to go out for fear of getting shot just to amuse Cecil Craig and the Boys, who fed off the town's terror. Just as they'd fed off Silva's misery and horror when they'd hacked off his ear.

The old man wondered where he'd find Craig. The hotel? Maybe one of the houses of ill repute? Possibly the Glory Hole . . .

The Glory Hole's main doors were open, swung back out of sight behind the batwings. Silva mounted the gallery's steps and pushed through the batwings, blinking as he peered around the dusty shadows.

The owner of the place, Toots Wade, was sweeping the floor with a ragged broom. He had a bandage over his nose, a cut on his swollen bottom lip, and he was walking with a limp. A big, fat man with broad shoulders and thick hands and longish, customarily mussed, dark-yellow hair and a thick mustache one shade lighter than his hair.

There were no other men in the room. Upstairs, a girl sobbed.

Wade stopped sweeping to look grimly at Silva. The barman's eyes drifted down to the two pistols on the old man's hips. "What the hell are you up to, old man?"

"Where are they?"

"Where's who?"

"You know. The Boys."

Wade studied him another couple of seconds. "Most of 'em left. Lit out to chase down whoever's been killin' 'em. Some say it's that young freighter workin' for Chester Lord—Cuno

Massey. Craig left three of the gang in town to keep their thumbs on us, make sure we don't fix the telegraph or ride out for the sheriff."

"Where are they?"

"What happened to your ear?"

The old man just stared at him, waiting.

Toots Wade canted his head slightly. "They're over at the New Mexico House. They killed one of my girls last night— threw her out a third-story window after they'd had their fill of her. They did it just to hear her scream and then see how she looked in the street afterwards. She fell on a stock tank. Broke her up bad, snapped her spine.

"She was still livin' when I found her, but—" Wade blinked quickly, and his upper lip quivered—"I put my hand over her face to suffocate her, so she wouldn't suffer. The other girls got her upstairs now, gettin' her ready to plant."

Silva turned and pushed back through the batwings and dropped down into the street.

"What in the hell are you thinkin' about doin', old man?" Wade called behind him.

Silva said nothing but only kept walking, slanting across the street toward the New Mexico House. It, too, was open. As Silva approached, he could hear a girl moaning inside, and men talking, their voices echoing.

The old man mounted the gallery and pushed through the batwings. He felt amazingly calm. The burning ear seemed to mellow him, steady him, focus him. He felt as though he were a living and breathing, slender, blue flame of calm, self-contained fury.

He looked around the drinking hall. Against the wall to his right was a divan, two chairs, and a coffee table. On the divan, a man was toiling between the spread legs of a girl. She lay back at an awkward position, and the man was half-standing, half-crouching over her, driving his hips against her naked pelvis, his pants bunched around his boots on the floor. The girl's red dress was shoved up over her head, covering her face, and Silva saw her head moving to and fro beneath it as the outlaw raped her.

He was a stocky, broad-shouldered gent in buckskins, and with a gold ring dangling from his left ear. He wore a shabby bowler hat on his head. He was one of those who'd held Silva down last night while Cecil Craig had cut off his ear.

"Hey, old man—ain't you heard the new policy?" This from one of the two men playing cards at a table several yards away from Silva, on the left side of the room. He was a rat-faced kid, and he was poking a finger at Silva. "No one is to wear guns but us—*comprende, amigo?*"

The man he was playing poker with turned to smile mockingly at Silva over his left shoulder. The man raping the girl did not stop thrusting his hips. The girl groaned beneath her dress.

Silva pulled both revolvers, and brought them up.

The man who'd spoken leaped up out of his chair, thrusting his hands palm out. "Hey—*what?*"

Silva fired his left-hand gun. The bullet plunked into the forehead of the man standing, and pushed him back through the window behind him in a screech of shattering glass. The other poker player leaped from his own chair, twisting around toward Silva and wrapping his hand around one of his own revolvers.

Silva fired his right-hand gun.

The second poker player fired his Colt through his open-toed holster and into the floor, grimacing as the old man's bullet punched through his upper right chest, throwing him back onto the table.

"Hey!" screamed the man who'd been raping the whore.

He was leaning forward over the girl, both hands on the back of the divan, his wavy, dirt-colored hair hanging in his eyes. The astonishment in his gaze turned quickly to terror as Silva smiled and turned his smoking Remingtons on him.

"No—please!" the rapist shouted, twisting around and throwing his hands up. "Wait!"

His ankles were caught in his buckskins and underwear. He fell back against the divan and the girl, who was rolling onto her side and raising her knees toward her naked breasts, cowering.

Silva gestured with both his aimed Remingtons and said quietly, "Get away from the girl."

The man stared in horror at him, breathing hard, his member dwindling between the hanging tails of his shirt. The man on the table grunted and groaned, and Silva turned to see him trying to draw another of his pistols. Silva turned his left pistol on him, and drilled a bullet through the man's belly.

The man screamed and lifted his head and his knees and rolled sideways off the table and onto the floor where he lay writhing and mewling and clamping his hands over the blood oozing from the wound in his stomach.

Silva turned back to the rapist, who couldn't make any sudden movements without tripping over his pants. He just leaned there against the divan, half-naked, terrified.

"Please, old man," he said, panting, eyes creased with terror. "Don't kill me."

"If you don't step away from the divan, I am going to blow your pecker off, *señor.*"

That wasn't true. He didn't want to hit the girl. But he hoped the outlaw was too horrified and addled not to obey.

The outlaw swallowed, shoved himself up away from the divan, and then, holding his hands up, palms out, shuffled awkwardly away from the bawling girl. He turned toward Silva, his back to the bar.

Silva smiled and angled the pistols low.

The outlaw stared in horror at the old man's guns. Horror turned to defiant rage as his eyes returned to Silva. "Fuck you, old man!"

Both bullets punched through his dimpled knees.

Howling, the outlaw dropped to the floor and fell onto his side, raising his knees toward his belly.

Silva looked at the girl. She was sitting up on the divan now, her dress hanging down around her ankles. Her black hair was tangled. Silva had never seen her before, for he no longer visited *putas,* but he could tell she was Mexican. She had a red welt on her right cheek.

She gazed down at the howling outlaw with the shattered knees and wrinkled her nose with satisfaction.

Silva ambled forward, reached down, pulled the outlaw's pistols from his holsters, and skidded them across the room. He pulled a Green River knife from a sheath on the belt, and held it handle-out to the girl.

She arched a brow at him in question.

"Go ahead, *señorita. Geld him!*"

The girl's eyes widened in shock. Then her lips slowly lifted a smile.

The second man Silva had shot was still groaning. The old man walked over, drilled a bullet through the back of his head, and left the saloon.

CHAPTER FIFTEEN

Cuno dropped down the stairs and stared across the long drinking hall toward the front.

The front door was open. Spurr stood silhouetted against the dawn sky, his back to Cuno, facing south.

Coyotes chortled in the distance.

Cuno strode through the hall and stepped outside, sidling up to Spurr and casting his gaze into the yard awash with a fine, gray light that was competing with the night's lingering darkness. Cuno listened for a time. The chortling seemed to be coming from a jog of low buttes in the southeast.

Cuno glanced at Spurr. "That's not coyotes, is it?"

Spurr shook his head. "Raises the hair on my ass. Sounds like Injuns. But it ain't Injuns, neither."

"The Boys."

Cuno spied movement across the yard. A shadow slid out from behind a pile of broken boulders and cactus. There was a flash and a pop, and the slug shattered the sashed window to Spurr's left.

"That devil!" Spurr whipped up his Yellowboy.

He and Cuno flung two shots each at the shadow by the rock pile, and then Spurr scurried inside the roadhouse with Cuno close behind him, slamming the door.

"To answer your question," Spurr said as two more slugs hammered the front of the roadhouse, the rifle reports flatting out over the yard, "no—that ain't coyotes!"

126

"I believe you!"

Two more slugs hammered the door, causing it to leap in its frame.

"Shit, this is Adobe Walls all over again!" Spurr said.

Cuno hunkered down beside the window right of the door. "You were at Adobe Walls?"

"First one—with ole Kit, that rascal!"

Cuno edged a look around the window, and raised his rifle. "Seems you've been everywhere, Spurr."

"I've *been* everywhere!" Spurr was smashing out the window with the butt of his Yellowboy. "Hell, boy—I'm old. Don't you know that?"

"Not to sound disrespectful, old man, but I was with you until you told me about holdin' Washington's hat at the signing of the Declaration of Independence."

Cuno chuffed. It was a nervous chuff. Three riders were galloping hell for leather toward the roadhouse.

"Never said no such thing, but my people did come over on the Mayflower, and I did have the honor of getting drunk with U.S. Grant one time!"

Spurr fired twice out his window and then jerked back against the wall beside it as bullets caromed through the opening to plunk into tables and benches and awning support posts. "Christ—what are those three up to, anyway?" he yelled above the cacophony of barking rifles.

Cuno edged another look around his own broken-out window. Two of the riders galloped nearly stirrup-to-stirrup, firing carbines as they rode, approaching the roadhouse quickly. A third rider was right behind and sort of between them. He wasn't firing a gun. He held something from which smoke was issuing.

Not one but two other men were firing from the pile of cracked boulders, hammering the front of the roadhouse, including the door, and sending lead buzzing like angry black flies through the windows, making it impossible for Cuno and the old lawman to return fire without getting pinked.

Somewhere in the second story, Miss Loretta bellowed, "All right, girls—let 'em have it!"

Cuno heard the squawks of hinges as shutters were opened. Several rifles began cracking over Cuno's head. The men approaching the roadhouse shouted. Cuno edged another look around the window frame to see the left front rider tumble backward out of his saddle, knocking whatever the third rider was holding from that rider's hand.

"Goddamnit!" he bellowed before he, too, went flying off his galloping mount, hitting the ground in a swirl of wafting dust.

He'd been carrying a whiskey bottle with a burning rag poking out the top and probably filled with coal oil. They'd been intending on setting fire to the roadhouse.

The other lead rider fired two shots toward the girls, shooting out the second-story windows, then swung his horse around, batted his heels against the gelding's ribs, and hightailed it eastward.

"Hold your fire, girls!" came Miss Loretta's nasal bellow from the second floor.

Cuno looked around carefully. The only movement was wafting dust and the rider galloping off to the east, diminishing quickly in the late dawn shadows. His two pards lay in twisted, bloody heaps in front of the roadhouse, neither one moving.

"Those girls can shoot, Miss Loretta!" Spurr yelled at the ceiling.

"I was the one who shot the bastard with the burnin' bottle," Miss Loretta yelled, "but every girl who's ever worked for me I've taught to shoot, and shoot damn good! I was here when the Kiowy was still runnin' roughshod!"

There were thumping noises in the ceiling, and a man said

something. It was Mule Mulligan's voice.

Miss Loretta replied with, "Oh, Mule, get yourself back into bed. You move around like that, you're liable to tear my catgut loose and poke one of those busted ribs through a lung!"

Mule Mulligan yelled, "They ain't busted—they're just bruised!" He yelled louder. "They're a'comin' fellas—more of 'em this time! Whole heap more!"

Staring out the window before him, Cuno saw the riders galloping toward the roadhouse from the southeast—two long lines of them coming hard and fast from both sides of a low butte. At the edge of the yard they started shooting. One line cut to Cuno's left, circling the roadhouse from the northeast, while the second line cut in the opposite direction, circling around toward the west.

Cuno opened up with his Winchester, quickly firing and levering, the spent brass arcing over his right shoulder to ping onto the wooden floor behind him. Running footsteps rose behind Cuno, and he turned to see Ella striding quickly from the stairs. She had a carbine in her hands.

Cuno aimed out the window, fired, cursed as his lead flew wide of a galloping marauder, and glanced over his shoulder at Ella again. "Where'd you get that?"

"Miss Loretta gave it to me, said I must do my part just like all the other girls." Ella smashed the glass out of a window on the east side of the broad room cluttered with benches, tables, parlor furniture, and room dividers, and started shooting. "Don't worry—Fernando taught me to shoot as well as he can!"

"Fernando can shoot?" Cuno said skeptically as he continued triggering lead.

"Who's Fernando?" Spurr said just before he squeezed off a shot through the window left of the door.

"Her old man," Cuno said.

"He was once a border *bandito*," Ella said, and triggered

another shot, evoking a sharp curse from that side of the roadhouse.

"Damn, girl!" Spurr said. "Did you pink one of 'em?"

"I think I got him in the neck," Ella said before shouting, "Take that, you under-endowed bastard!"

Spurr howled a laugh.

Cuno cursed again, shaking his head. "They're movin' too damn fast for me!"

Spurr triggered a round and cursed as he sat back against the front wall to reload. "Reckon we'd best take lessons from Miss Loretta and the *señorita* there."

"I've always been better at close range," Cuno muttered through a frustrated growl. "And I don't cotton to moving targets."

Bullets were hammering the roadhouse, a few chewing through the gaps between the vertical boards and thumping into tables or clanging off iron woodstoves. One shattered an unlit lamp bracketed to a support post.

"I used to be able to shoot the lash off a hare's eye at two hundred yards," Spurr said, racking a fresh round into his Yellowboy's breech. "These days, I can't even see the hare!"

He fired out the window and then drew his head back, wincing as one of the outlaws' bullets slammed into the window frame, spraying him with wood slivers. Outside, the thudding of hooves could be heard beneath the barking of Winchesters and the mad howling of the Boys.

"Those boys must be half-Apache," the old lawman yelled. "They're circlin' just like Apaches!"

They were not only circling the roadhouse and triggering lead—some with pistols in both hands or a pistol in one hand and a rifle in the other, the reins in their teeth—but they were whooping and yelling like marauding Indians. Like Indians, they were trying to bedevil their quarry—scare the hell out of them and cause wild shooting.

Ella yelped and jerked back away from the window. She brushed a hand across her cheek, and looked at it.

"You all right?" Cuno asked her, reloading his Winchester for the second time.

"*Pendejos!*" Ella bellowed, and, gritting her teeth, fired again through the window.

Upstairs, Miss Loretta yelled, "Mule, you sonofabitch—you got one!"

"Hell—that's the second one I done shot, though I only wounded the first!" came Mulligan's reply.

Cuno spat another frustrated curse through his teeth. He didn't think he'd so much as grazed one yet. Now he winced as another bullet tore into the window frame, and then he snaked his Winchester through the window, aimed carefully, and squeezed the trigger.

One of the outlaws galloping from his right to his left cursed shrilly, dropped his pistol, and clamped his right hand over his left arm. Crouching low in the saddle, he broke away from the pack and gigged his horse to the south.

At the same time, several other outlaws were shouting. Cuno watched one tumble out of his saddle. He hit the ground, rolled, and jerked sharply when the hoof of another rider kicked him in the head. He flopped onto his back, slapping his hands to his forehead.

"Who got him?" Cuno asked.

"Wasn't me, gallblast it!" shouted Spurr.

"They got us in a whipsaw!" one of the outlaws shouted somewhere on the east side of the roadhouse.

"Withdraw!" one of the outlaws now in front of the cabin shouted. "Withdraw! Withdraw!"

Cuno triggered a shot at him. He jerked sharply to one side, grimacing, and then cast an angry glare in Cuno's direction. He was a stocky, spade-bearded, bull-necked outlaw with a pinched face. Cuno hadn't seen Cecil Craig close up, but something told Cuno this was Craig.

Cuno quickly racked another shell into the chamber but pulled his head down when he saw Craig aiming two pistols at him while bellowing curses.

Both bullets screeched through the air where Cuno's head had been a moment before. Cuno thought he heard a grunt behind him but he was too distracted to take a gander. Instead, he looked out the window again.

Craig was galloping away toward the northern trail to town. The rest of the gang was following, snaking guns around behind them to take parting shots at the roadhouse.

A couple rode crouched low over their horses' poles, or held an arm tight against their sides, as though they'd taken a slug or two.

"Come back here, you chicken-hearted dogs!" Spurr shouted through the window, triggering another shot. "Get back here and let's finish this dance!"

"Spurr, is that you down there!" Mule Mulligan called from upstairs.

"Of course it is!"

"Shut up, you old fool!"

Spurr shouted at the ceiling. "Why don't you come down here and make me, you grizzled old rapscallion!"

Cuno remembered hearing a grunt behind him. He turned now quickly, wondering if Ella had been hit.

She was still kneeling by her window, looking out, her carbine smoking in her hands. Cuno rose and strode back into the drinking hall lit now by several shafts of sunlight angling through the broken windows. Many shadows remained.

He saw Brett Cavanaugh writhing on a divan in one of those mini parlors where the girls probably sparked their prospective jakes, working them up both literally and figuratively. Cavanaugh sagged back against the divan, clutching his side and groaning.

A Winchester repeater lay beside him.

Cuno walked over to the man. "You hit?"

Clamping one hand over his bloody right side, Cavanaugh said, "What's it look like? I'm bleeding dry here while you idiots jabber as though you were playing poker on a Saturday night in the Glory Hole. Those savages have killed me!"

Spurr had walked up beside Cuno. "What the hell were you doing down here?"

"I gave him a long gun and told Fancy Dan to get his scrawny ass down here and get to work!" Miss Loretta had soundlessly drifted down into the saloon hall, six working girls in underwear and lacy wraps hovering around behind her, each with a carbine in her hand. All were at least a couple of inches taller than their diminutive madam. They were a mixed bag of Anglos and Mexicans, with one who looked like she had some Indian blood and one black girl with lustrous green eyes.

Cuno had heard that Miss Loretta hired only the prettiest girls she could find. He'd heard right.

"Yes, and thanks to you, good woman," Cavanaugh said, "they have killed me."

"Unfortunately, you can't credit me with that, though one less banker in the world is no loss, to my way of thinkin'." Miss Loretta chuckled and puffed her pipe.

"Yes, well, that will make two less bankers in the world," Cavanaugh said, trying to sit up. "That miserable gang stormed into the bank yesterday and killed my father after he'd done what they'd ordered him to do and opened the vault so they could plunder it."

Cuno said, "What the hell were you doing while all that was going on?"

Cavanaugh looked outraged. "I was—!" He stopped himself,

133

and tried another way of explaining himself. He'd probably been cowering in a closet or beneath his desk. "I was one man— one man against forty or more . . . !"

Miss Loretta gave a violent, disgusted wave of her hand. "Get him upstairs! Now I got more work to do because Fancy Dan couldn't keep his liver out of harm's way!"

Cuno pulled Cavanaugh to his feet. Spurr took the string bean's other arm.

"Easy!" intoned Cavanaugh. "Christ—I'm injured here! I'm bleeding!"

"Looks little worse than a bee sting to me," Spurr grouched as he and Cuno led the young banker up the rickety stairs.

Enough buttery sunshine now streamed through the windows beyond the second story's open room doors that Cuno could see to the end of the hall. Kate Lord sat on the floor at the hall's far end, leaning back against the wall, one knee raised. She had her arms wrapped around the knee; she was resting her chin on it.

Her strawberry hair hung down her back; it had obviously been brushed until it shone. She'd been well tended and bathed by Miss Loretta and some of the girls.

As Cuno and Spurr led Cavanaugh down the hall, Kate watched them. There was a dullness about her, due no doubt to shock.

"What happened?" she asked raspily, slowly pushing herself to her feet.

"He took a bullet," Cuno told her.

"Oh, Brett," Kate said. "Are you all right?"

"What the hell does it look like?" Cavanaugh snapped as Cuno and Spurr helped him through a door on the hall's right side. They eased him onto the bed. Kate came in and stared down at him with concern.

Cavanaugh glared up at her, and slid his angry gaze to Cuno.

"I know," he grated out. "It's written all over the two of you." He glanced at Kate again. "Get the hell away from me—both of you!"

A surge of rage swept through Cuno.

He clenched his fists at his sides. "You hide under a desk in the bank while your father is killed and your girl is hauled off and—!"

He cut himself off, lunging toward Cavanaugh. He cocked his arm to hammer his fist against the banker's dimpled chin.

Chapter Sixteen

Spurr grabbed Cuno from behind just in time. The young man's fist only grazed the banker's jaw.

"Hold on, Kid! Hold on! Hold on!"

Spurr was stronger than he looked. He managed to wrestle Cuno past Kate and into the hall. "Pull your horns in, boy! I don't like that yellow-livered bean counter any more than you do, but we got bigger fish to fry!"

Miss Loretta was coming down the hall, puffing her pipe. A couple of the girls followed her, one holding a steaming water bowl, one toting a black medical kit.

Loretta laughed and said, "So the young bull wants to winnow my patients down, does he? Spurr, I don't see the harm in it!" She strolled into Cavanaugh's room. "I never could trust a banker in a paisley vest!"

One of the girls—a sultry-looking brunette with a mole on her chin—gave Cuno a wink and a lusty smile as she brushed past him, raking her gaze across his chest.

From inside the room, Miss Loretta said, "Come hither, Miss Mattie—I know you like 'em with muscles, but you leave that boy alone. Like Spurr says, he's got bigger fish to fry. Go on downstairs, boys! Keep an eye out for them rawhiders. Help yourself to whiskey, if you've a mind. The good stuff's in that red cabinet—but don't overdo it! I got me a feelin' them desperados will be back, and I think we graveled 'em some!"

Spurr looked at Cuno. "I think she's enjoyin' this."

Cuno was still burning at Cavanaugh. The tinhorn bastard was more worried about having been cheated on than about the marauders who'd murdered his fellow citizens, including his own father, and terrorized his town. He probably took sadistic satisfaction in what they'd done to Kate.

Downstairs, Ella sat at one of the many tables. One of the doves—the black girl with green eyes—was swabbing a cut on Ella's right cheek with a small cloth soaked in whiskey. The dove was pooching her lips out and clucking her distaste at the bullet graze.

"You all right?" Cuno asked Ella.

She looked up at him. "I am worried about Fernando."

Before Cuno could respond, a rifle cracked outside. Cuno and Spurr shared a puzzled glance, and then Cuno ran to the front door while Spurr ran to the same window he'd been shooting from.

They each peered out cautiously and then shared another dubious look as they hurried outside.

Cuno looked around the yard, holding his rifle at port arms, ready for another onslaught. When he saw no riders thundering toward him, he and Spurr walked toward where a man was aiming a rifle at another man trying to run away but was having a devil of a time with his wounded left leg.

The rifle barked, flames lapping from the barrel.

The man trying to flee jerked forward and fell, yelling. "Stop it!" he cried. "Stop it! Stop it! You done already kilt me, you old bean-eater!"

He twisted around to glare at the man—an old, spindly-looking man in baggy denims and loose linsey shirt and suspenders, with a ragged straw sombrero shading his face. The man on the ground had a red, horse-shaped bump on his forehead. He was the marauder who'd been shot and kicked.

He spat a spray of frothy blood at the old Mexican. "You got

137

me through both lungs, you old bastard!" He sobbed and flopped back down against the ground, writhing like a landed fish. He tried to get up and run again but the old man calmly ambled up to him, ramming another round into his old Spencer's breech.

He aimed and fired.

That shot blew the top of the outlaw's head off. He lay prone, his limbs gradually relaxing.

Cuno and Spurr slowly approached the old man, both tentatively aiming their rifles at him. "Do not shoot, *Señor* Massey," the old man said in a belly-deep rasp.

Lowering the old repeater to his side, he turned around and grinned his snaggle-toothed grin at Cuno and Spurr. "It is I— Fernando Silva. I have come to inquire about my daughter, *Señorita* Ella Silva."

"Fernando!" the girl cried as she came running out from the roadhouse.

"Ah, there you are, bad girl," Silva said with a sigh. "You had me worried."

His chin fell. He staggered forward half a step, and his knees buckled. Before Cuno could grab him, he'd fallen.

Ella reached him, yelling, "Fernando!" and dropped to her knees beside him. "Oh, Fernando!" she cried, brushing her fingers across the blood-stained bandage on his head. "What did they do to you?"

"Let's get him inside," Cuno said.

"I was wonderin' who that extra shooter on our side was," Spurr said with a grunt as he and Cuno each took an arm and helped the old man to his feet.

Silva groaned, head wobbling on his shoulders, Sonora hat hanging down his back by its thong, as Cuno and Spurr half-dragged, half-led him back to the roadhouse. They helped him onto a bench at a table near the front. Ella crouched beside him, and peeled the bandage back to reveal the ragged-edged hole crusted with liver-colored blood.

"*Dios mio!*" She sucked a sharp breath through her teeth and cast her shocked, anguished gaze at Cuno. "Those bastards cut off this poor old man's ear!"

Spurr said, "All right—let's get him upstairs."

When Cuno and the old marshal had hoisted the old Mexican up from the bench, Spurr yelled toward the ceiling, "Got another one for ya, Loretta!"

They helped the half-conscious Fernando to the back of the room and up the stairs. Mule Mulligan stood at the top of the stairs, a carbine in his hands. He was fully dressed, but his face still looked like a map of some devil's playground.

"Fernando—Christ! What'd they do to you, old fella?" He moved down the stairs, and shouldered Cuno aside. "Here—let the old men tend their own, Kid. You'd best keep watch." He looked at Spurr. "Jesus Christ, you're an ugly son of a bitch!"

"Yeah, well the Boys oughta send you a bill," Spurr retorted. "They made you a whole lot easier on the eyes, Mule!"

Cuno stepped aside and watched Spurr and Mule Mulligan guide Fernando up to the top of the stairs and out of sight in the second story. Spurr and Mulligan barked at each other like old dogs staking out the same territory.

Cuno knew their barbs belied their pleasure at seeing each other again. Neither one probably had all that many friends remaining on this side of the sod.

Ella had climbed the stairs. She stood now beside Cuno, gazing worriedly toward where the three oldsters had disappeared. Cuno wrapped his arm around the girl's shoulders. "He'll be all right. They're tough—those three. Tougher than whang leather. Tougher than most."

"Tough is Fernando, *si*. Tough and foolish."

"That was some good shootin' out there. I had no idea that

old man had it in him."

"Like I said, he was once a border *bandito*." Ella gave a wan smile. "And, as he likes to boast, a breaker of many young hearts." Tears shone in her eyes. "They must have blamed him for us riding out together."

"We didn't have any choice," Cuno said.

"I know. But they cut his ear off." Ella's nostrils flared, and her jaws hardened. "I will not rest until I can give the ear of the man who did that bit of nastiness to Fernando as a keepsake."

Cuno smiled, liking the girl's gravel. He took her hand in his and led her down the stairs.

He released her hand and then strode to the front of the room, which was littered with glass and wood slivers, and stepped outside. The black whore and the sultry brunette, Mattie, were standing just outside the door, the warm morning breeze jostling their hair and their frilly underclothes and wraps.

Cuno sighed and poked his hat brim up off his forehead. "Sorry for the trouble, ladies."

The sultry brunette curled her lip devilishly. She looked sultry but tough. In fact, none of Miss Loretta's doves looked like hothouse flowers. They'd likely grown up hard, accustomed to trouble. "Maybe you can make it up to us sometime."

The black girl laughed and looked Cuno up and down, "Mmm-*mmmm!* There's a lot of you, ain't there, Mister uh . . ."

"Massey," Cuno said. "But any girl who shoots like you two can call me Cuno."

Ella stepped through the door and draped his left arm around her shoulders. "This one does not need to pay for his love. He is mine."

The smiling doves shared a glance.

"I reckon we all could use some belly-paddin'," said the black girl. "Come on, Mattie," she said to the sultry brunette. "Let's leave these two lovebirds and go whip up some vittles before them desperados come back for another helpin' of our lead."

"Good luck with that one," Mattie said, glancing at Ella. "You got a wildcat there!"

"She better remember that," Ella told Cuno when the doves had gone back inside. "There are too many girls here. I don't like it." She smiled. "To be jealous distracts me from my fear. Fear is good, sometimes."

Cuno looked at two dead men lying sprawled about twenty yards away from the roadhouse, thirty yards away from each other. He walked over and stripped both bodies of their shell belts and holstered revolvers. Both had two guns apiece, and one also had a bowie knife sheathed on it.

"Take these inside," Cuno told Ella, handing her the belts. "If those marauders return, we're gonna need all the guns and ammo we can get our hands on."

"What are you going to do?"

Cuno stared out into the cedar-stippled hills rolling away from the roadhouse. "I'm gonna have a look around."

"What for? There might be some of them out there, keeping an eye on us."

"That's what I aim to find out." Cuno glanced back at her. "Go on inside. You're a target out here."

"So are you!"

Cuno gave her a hard look. She turned her mouth corners down and stepped back inside and closed the door.

Cuno racked a fresh round into his Winchester's breech and then began walking out away from the roadhouse. The sun was high, but there were still shadows stretching out from knolls, boulders, and shrubs, and he probed these carefully with his gaze as he continued walking.

If there were any desperados out here, he wanted to know about it. Otherwise, neither he nor the others could afford to let their guards down, and they likely couldn't risk sending

141

someone for a sheriff's posse. Also, if Craig had not left any of his men behind to keep an eye on the place, he might not be planning on returning.

Cuno left the broad yard and stood inside the V where two trails came into it—one leading toward Nopal in the north, the other angling off to the southeast with another angling off that one toward Santa Fe. The gang had stormed out of the yard heading toward Nopal, where they'd probably returned to gather themselves.

They hadn't expected such a strong response to their attack. Their wounded likely needed a doctor. They might also intend to raid the mercantile and gun shops for ammunition.

If they intended to return, that was.

Cuno glanced back at the roadhouse—a large, weathered-gray, barn-like structure with gaps showing between most of its vertical boards. Only the lower story windows had glass. Or, had *had* glass, rather. The glass had been busted out.

The upper-story windows were all shuttered against another possible attack. The building looked as though it had been used for target practice; nearly every rough cottonwood or pine board bore ragged craters where doggets of wood had been shot out. The place had looked rickety before; now it looked as though only one or two more bullets would send it toppling like a house of cards.

Cuno shook his head slowly, scowling.

His group was lucky that none of them had been shot. Damned lucky. It was highly doubtful that their luck would hold if the Boys returned. They probably would.

A slight breeze rose, lifting dust. The dust ticked against the roadhouse and caused the frame to creak precariously.

Cuno spied movement out of the corner of his right eye. He whipped around, lowering his Winchester from his shoulder and clicking the hammer back.

He eased the tension in his trigger finger. A jackrabbit had bounded out of the sage and junipers on the east side of the trail and was running in a zigzag pattern through the brush toward the rear of the roadhouse, its large ears making it look oddly top heavy.

What had caused the rabbit to run west?

Cuno jerked his gaze toward the west side of the trail. A man stood in the slight notch of a pale stone escarpment, aiming a rifle, which stabbed smoke and flames as Cuno flung himself backward and right, twisting around and hitting the ground on his belly.

He raised his Winchester, aimed, and fired.

The shooter said, "Oh, *fuck!*" as he stumbled back into the notch and then fell backward out of sight.

Cuno racked another round into his Winchester's breech and stared down the barrel, sliding the gun this way and that, searching for another target.

When none showed, he rose slowly and grabbed his hat, which he'd lost in his dodging plunge, and stepped deeper into the rocks and brush.

He strode past the escarpment from which the shooter had shot at him and found himself in a maze of rocks of all shapes and sizes strewn amongst the cedars and piñons, as though they'd been flung by an angry god from the sky.

He walked behind the escarpment from which the desperado had fired. The man lay on the ground, on his back, writhing, blood oozing from both corners of his mouth. He was digging his spurs into the red clay earth and clamping a hand over the bloody hole in his upper right chest.

A long beard hung from his narrow, horse-like face with dark, deep-set eyes. He wore a checked shirt beneath a brown vest, and two cartridge belts on his hips. His hat was off. His thin, dark-brown hair was sweat-matted to his head.

He was reaching up behind him for his carbine. Cuno aimed his Winchester at the fast-dying man, staring down at him grimly. The man stopped his reaching hand and, continuing to ground his spurs into the clay, glared up at Cuno.

"You go to hell," he rasped.

"How many out here?" Cuno asked quietly.

The outlaw lifted his mouth corners briefly. "You go to hell." Then he glowered against the pain, said, "Oh, Jesus!" and died, his body falling slack, his eyes going flat.

A rifle cracked in the northeast.

Cuno jerked with a start, swung around, and began retracing his steps slowly back in the direction of the roadhouse. A rifle cracked—farther away this time. Another report followed from nearer by.

Cuno dropped behind a small boulder and a juniper, and looked to the northeast. Spurr was on one knee atop a knoll on the far side of the trail, on the northeast corner of the roadhouse yard, triggering his old Winchester quickly. Cuno could see the brass arcing over the old lawman's right shoulder.

Cuno tried to see what the man was shooting at, but there were too many rocks and shrubs in his way.

Spurr stopped shooting. The old man lifted his head. He wasn't wearing his hat. "There you go, you devil!" he shouted, his raspy, squawky voice echoing.

He glanced toward Cuno, who rose and waved his rifle. Spurr lifted his hat from the ground, and waved it.

"Come on, Kid," Spurr called. "I'll cover ya!"

Cuno rose and jogged across the trail to the northeast corner of the yard. He climbed the knoll to where Spurr still knelt between a twisted cedar and a square boulder, aiming in the same direction he'd been firing.

"There he is—deader'n Jehoshaphat's cat," the old lawman gritted out.

"Craig left two men behind, then."

"At least two. This one was movin' toward you, crouching, all sneaky-like." Spurr spat and glowered off toward where Cuno could see the dead man lying on his back, one leg bent under him, both arms thrown out as though in supplication.

A magpie sat on a nearby rock, watching the fresh carrion eagerly, likely hoping to fill its gullet before the coyotes or a mountain lion moved in.

"I hate those sonsobitches," Spurr said.

"Why do you hate 'em so bad?"

Spurr snapped an incredulous look at his much younger partner. "What—you think you're the only one who can hate 'em? 'Cause of what they did to your girl? You think I'm too old to get my tail in a knot? Shit, you probably think it's time for me to turn in my badge, too, don't you? Well, the day I turn in this nickel's worth of—"

"All right, all right," Cuno said. "Stop crawlin' my hump, Spurr. I was just askin'."

Spurr spat again and looked off toward the dead man and the magpie savoring a forthcoming meal. "Hell," Spurr said, brushing his sleeve across his cheek, his voice breaking slightly, "did you see what they did to my old friend Mule Mulligan's face?"

CHAPTER SEVENTEEN

Cecil Craig and the rest of the Boys were galloping hell for leather away from the roadhouse, the rotten egg odor of gunsmoke thick in Craig's nostrils, causing his eyes to water.

He looked around him and yelled, "Ike, Billy, Mel—you boys take any lead?"

The three were scattered behind Craig, with the rest of the pack, a few men still triggering their pistols or carbines at the roadhouse.

"Me?" said Billy Killeen. "Nah. Hell, no!"

The other two men—Ike Stillwell and Mel "Cutthroat" Claibourne—shook their heads.

"You fellas hunker down here, then," Craig ordered. "Hold them down in there. Don't let 'em try to skin out on us."

Despite having taken a bullet burn across his right-side ribs, Craig was juiced by the fight until he thought his head and heart would explode. This was the sort of thing for which he'd been waiting for the past six long years he'd been in prison. The outlaw leader fed off the pain in his side and whooped loudly.

"This fandango is only just beginnin'! We're gonna take our time and make a night of it, Boys!"

"Where you fellas headin'?" asked Stillwell.

"We're headin' back to town to pick up Ryerson and them other two we left to keep an eye on things in Nopal. This might be a long affair, if we draw it out right and enjoy it, so we're gonna need us some more ammunition and plenty of whiskey

146

and women! Possibly some dynamite!" He tipped his head back. "Wahh-*hooooooooo!*"

"Bring me that Chinese girl from the New Mexico House— will ya, Boss?" shouted Cutthroat Claibourne, as he swung his buckskin off the trail and into the brush and rocks just east of it.

"*Wah-hoooooooo!*" Craig howled, waving his hat in the air.

Several of the others behind him followed suit.

As he galloped his horse up and over the first hill north of the roadhouse and down the other side, he turned to his first lieutenant, Victor Bina. "How many men we lose back there, Vic?"

"I don't know, Boss—I saw Hector, Frank Wade, and Bonifay go down for sure, when they was trying to throw that whiskey bomb. Might have lost two more." Bina glanced over his shoulder. "One saddled horse galloping along behind us, empty. Looks like Pat Garcia's palomino."

At the bottom of the canyon snaking through the high-desert country north of the roadhouse, Craig raised a hand and brought his sorrel gelding to a halt, blinking against the dust rising around him. He curveted the horse as the others circled him, the horses blowing and snorting and whickering their anxiety at all the shooting. Several of the men were sitting funny in their saddles, one leaning far forward over the arm he had tucked across his belly.

"Let's give the horses a blow and some water," Craig said, swinging down from his sorrel's back.

Dust dripped off his hat. He doffed it and swatted it against his leather chaps. That only made the dust billow more thickly. He coughed against it.

As the others followed his lead, dismounting and grabbing their canteens, Craig pulled his own hide-wrapped flask from around his saddle horn, and looked over at the man crouched low in his saddle. He was making no move to dismount. From what Craig could see of his face, it was ashen.

"Johnny, how bad you hit?" Craig wanted to know, popping the cork from his canteen.

Johnny Leslie, an outlaw from Tennessee and cousin of "Buckskin" Frank Leslie, turned his pinched faced toward Craig. Blood glistened on his lips and on his nose. "Oh, I ain't too bad, Boss. A sawbones in Nopal'll sew me up good as new."

Craig had poured a few inches of water into his hat and set the hat down in front of his horse. Corking his canteen, he moved around through the clumped, sweat-lathered horses toward Johnny Leslie.

"Let me see, John—" He cut himself off when he'd walked around to the horse's other side and saw the blood up high on Johnny's right arm. There was more blood oozing down his side. The arm apparently was useless. It hung like a broken wing.

"Good Lord, Johnny—what did those tinhorns do to you?" Craig said.

"I'll be all right, Cecil. I just need a sawbones and some busthead, and I'll be fine."

"How many times they shoot you?"

"Just once . . . I think."

"Johnny, I'm afraid that bullet shattered your arm and then continued on into your chest. From the labored way you're breathin', I'd say it tore up a lung somethin' awful. I heard such in southern Missouri durin' the war. Oh, damn, Johnny—not *you*!"

"I'll be all right, Cecil. Honest, I will."

Craig jerked his head up as though shuttling his gaze to something beyond Johnny. He smiled. "Look there, Johnny. Isn't that a cardinal?"

Johnny turned to follow the outlaw leader's gaze. "Cardinal?

Out *here*? Oh, I doubt that—"

He was cut off by the rocketing blast of Craig's .44, which punched a bullet through the crown of Johnny's hat and into the back of the wounded man's head.

Johnny Leslie, who loved calling out the names of birds he identified from the books and pamphlets he carried in his saddlebags—when he wasn't pillaging, raping, and murdering, that was—bobbed his head violently, as though adamantly agreeing to something someone had said. His frightened horse lurched forward, whickering.

Johnny sagged back in his saddle and would likely have fallen to the ground if his left boot wasn't hung up in his stirrup.

Blood instantly painted his hat crown around the ragged hole.

Some of the other men grabbed the horse's reins and bridle, stopping it.

"Holy Christ!" someone said.

Someone else gave a nervous laugh.

Craig spun his smoking pistol on his finger and dropped it back into its holster. "Damn, I hated to do that. He was a good kid, Johnny. A genuine nature lover."

Several of the other men had cast Craig incredulous, exasperated looks.

"Mercy sakes alive," one of the men said under his breath. "There goes Johnny . . ."

Bina looked at the others and then cleared his throat and said, "You had to, Boss. He was dyin' hard, Johnny was. I hope you'll show me the same kindness, if it ever comes to that." The big, bearded man—always the diplomat—walked over to Johnny's horse. "Help me here, Glen, Ephraim. Let's get the boy down and bury him proper."

Craig looked around at the gang all staring in shock at Johnny Leslie. All except the one man—Hank T. Waddles—who was laughing behind his gloved hand. Waddles was known far and wide to be two or three cartridges short of a full load. He was so ornery and good with a gun, though, that no one took it personally.

"Anyone else get shot?"

No one said anything. Waddles stopped laughing and lowered his hand from his mouth. He continued to snicker, though, as though he just couldn't help himself.

A couple of men straightened, lowering hands or arms they were favoring, and glanced sheepishly away.

"All right, then," Craig said. "Glen, Ephraim—you boys plant ole Johnny out here, say a few words over him for the rest of us, tell him we'll miss his nature-lovin' ways, and we'll meet you in town later."

Craig donned his wet hat, swung up into the saddle, and reined his sorrel northward. "Come on, Boys!" he called, grinding his spurs into the gelding's flanks. "Let's dedicate the rest of this day to our friend Johnny! For Johnny, *we will exact revenge!*"

He howled as he galloped northeast toward Nopal. The others quickly mounted their own horses and began howling and yipping, as well, as they galloped after their juiced-up leader.

Behind them, Glen Sweney and Ephraim Tidewater blinked and coughed against the billowing dust as they dragged young Johnny into the brush and rocks, looking for a place to plant him.

The two didn't look around long. There was no easy place to dig a grave out here. The ground was too gravelly, too rocky, and covered in cactus.

Besides, they were eager to get back to the women in Nopal. Both men had found the town's schoolteacher, a not-unattractive and buxom woman in her early thirties, and had forced her to do the most wonderful things to them under threat of getting her throat cut.

So, instead of toiling away with shovels in the hot sun, Glen and Ephraim hid Johnny's bloody carcass behind a low, spine-like hump of sandstone and then sat in the shade of a cedar tree, rolling quirleys and passing a bottle, fondly remembering aloud their time with the schoolteacher.

After enough time to bury a body had passed, they took one more slug of whiskey, a last drag from their cigarettes, and mounted up. Howling like moon-crazed coyotes, they spurred their horses hard for town.

A half hour later, Cecil Craig scowled out from beneath the brim of his black hat. He and the others were approaching Nopal. But something was wrong.

Craig, who could smell a thunderstorm two days away, smelled something foul here. Not only could he *smell* something wrong, he could *see* that neither the old marshal nor the freighter, Chester Lord, was hanging out here from the tree he'd told some of the Boys to hang them from.

Raising his left hand, he reined his sorrel to a stop.

"Braddock," he said, "didn't I tell you to hang the marshal and the freighter out here?"

"That's right," said Braddock from somewhere behind him in the pack of snorting and blowing horses. "You did."

Only two ropes remained, strewn across a couple of sage shrubs and the ground. No dead men.

Bina rode up on Craig's right, arching a curious brow.

"Hmmm," said the outlaw leader, staring beyond the tree toward the town.

A stiff breeze had come up, blowing dirt, hay, horseshit, and tumbleweeds. Shingle chains squawked along both sides of the street, moaning like wanton women. There was no one on the street. No one, nothing—not even a dog. There was no sound except the wind.

As silent as a breezy boneyard.

Could the locals still be huddled inside their smelly lairs?

Something told Craig the silence was due to something else.

He clucked the sorrel ahead, looking this way and that as he rode into the town. Nopal had an abandoned feel to it. While the buildings were of course still in good repair—excepting the occasional bullet hole or a broken window or two—they seemed empty. Their windows gazed darkly, blindly out onto the street while miniature dust devils scurried over the boardwalks.

Craig glanced down a side street. Nothing either to the north or the south—not a horse, not a soul using a privy or fetching water from a well. Craig didn't even see a dog.

The outlaw leader angled his horse toward the New Mexico House Saloon, which was the first watering hole he came to and a good place to stock up on whiskey. The others followed him. When he swung down from his saddle, they did, too.

Craig tossed his reins over a hitch rack, cupped his hands around his mouth, and yelled for Ryerson. His voice echoed beneath the moaning breeze and the crinkling of an old newspaper being hurled across the saloon's front gallery.

Those were the only responses.

"Well, I'll be," said Bina. "You don't suppose those three are still over at the Ill Repute, gettin' their ashes hauled, do ya, Cecil?"

"Better not be," said Craig. "They're supposed to be keepin' watch on the town, makin' sure nobody rides out." He glanced at Bina. "Check it out, just in case they're stupid enough to climb my hump—will ya, Vic?"

"Sure thing, Cecil."

As Victor ordered two of the other men to join him, Craig mounted the New Mexico House's gallery. He moved up to stare over the batwings and then glanced darkly over his shoulder.

"Never mind," he said. "Think I found 'em."

CHAPTER EIGHTEEN

Craig stared down at Clyde Two Bears, a half-breed who'd taken his mother's name after he'd killed his father with a spade back on their west Texas farm.

Clyde sat with his back against the bar, head thrown back against the bar, as well, his gritted teeth glistening in the washed-out light angling in through the windows. His gold earring glistened, as well, as did his eyes, with the horror of his death.

What a horror it had been, too. His buckskin pants were bunched down around his boots. Both knees had been shot to bloody pieces. His thick, brown hands were clamped down over the bloody mess at his crotch.

His oysters had been hacked off and left on the floor between his knees.

"Good gawd in Heaven," said Bina, walking into the saloon with several others. "Who in the hell did this to ole Clyde?"

"Someone who obviously didn't like him nearly as much as we did," Craig said.

He walked over to where H.P. Givens lay near a table at which he and probably Ryerson had been playing poker, because cards, gold coins, and greenbacks were still scattered across it. A bottle and two shot glasses lay on the floor.

Blood splatters shone on the floor on the table's other side, in front of a broken-out window. Craig walked over to the window and looked out. The rat-faced Ryerson lay in the alley in a pool of blood and blood-stained glass. He stared up at Craig, his mouth and eyes open as though he'd been cut off in mid-sentence.

Anger burned behind the outlaw leader's eyeballs. He clenched his fists at his sides, and opened them.

Who . . . ?

He swung around to see many of the gang standing just inside the batwings, looking around skeptically. Bina stood nearby, staring down at Givens and slowly sucking air through his teeth.

Craig strode across the drinking hall. He pushed through the crowd of men and moved out through the batwings. He dropped down the gallery steps and walked out into the street, looking around.

His heart beat heavily, furiously.

Who . . . ?

He walked up the street and then angled over to the Glory Hole.

"Anyone here?" he asked, staring over the batwings.

He was answered by only the walls creaking in a breeze that was quickly growing into a wind. No one was here, and there didn't appear to have been anyone here in the last few hours. No drinks or bottles had been left on the bar or on any of the tables.

"Wade?" Craig called. "You here, Wade?"

When he again received no response, he swung around to see the rest of his gang walking slowly along the street, cradling rifles in their arms, looking around warily, peering through shop windows.

He yelled, "Victor—split the men up. Look around."

"What're we looking for, Boss? It appears the town's been abandoned."

That burned right through Craig like a molten steel blade. He was beginning to feel his control slipping through his hands.

He should have left more men in town besides Ryerson, Givens, and Two Bears—to prevent this very thing from happening.

He'd been outsmarted.

Someone had outsmarted him and nearly forty of his gang.

Outsmarted and outshot.

"If you find anyone, bring them to me!" he shouted.

Someone whistled. He turned to see one of the men standing a block and a half away to the east, in the middle of the main street and facing toward the north, down a cross street. The man beckoned.

Craig dropped down off the Glory Hole's gallery and strode eastward. When he reached the man standing at the intersection, Bart Francona tipped his head to indicate north. Craig saw a saddled mule standing out front of a small shack that a crude wooden sign jutting into the street identified as simply the TELEGRAPH OFFICE.

Craig, Francona, Bina, and several others strode up the cross street. The mule turned to look at the newcomers and gave its tail a nervous switch. Craig placed his hand on the animal's neck, soothing it to keep it quiet.

He glanced at the other men, silently ordering them to stay back. He glanced at Bina, canted his head toward the office, and then he and Bina quietly mounted the small front porch.

Craig peered through the glass in the door's top panel, then slowly turned the knob and stepped slowly into the office. There were several desks and filing cabinets, a small iron safe, and rows of pigeonholes containing colored telegraph blanks.

A man sat at a small desk against the wall to Craig's right. He was a narrow-shouldered oldster in a white shirt, suspenders, and green visor. He was crouched over the telegraph key, which Craig's men had shot to pieces when they'd first ridden into town.

The old man was working on the key with a screwdriver and

pliers and several other small tools that Craig couldn't identify. An oilcan and a rag lay nearby.

The oldster was cursing a blue streak under his nervously labored breathing.

Craig glanced at Bina and then stepped into the small office. A floorboard creaked beneath his boot. The old man grunted, and froze.

Craig aimed his Colt out in front of him, and loudly clicked the hammer back. Slowly, the old man turned his head to peer in horror over his left shoulder, showing his chipped, yellow teeth in a grimace.

His round spectacles sat low on his long, broad, age-spotted nose.

"Lean to one side," Craig said softly.

"Wha . . . what?" the oldster croaked.

"Lean to one side."

The old man's throat slid up and down in his turkey neck, and, wincing, he leaned to his right. He poked his fingers in his ears and squeezed his eyes shut. Craig's Colt roared once, twice, three, four, five times, throwing the telegraph key in pieces all about that side of the office. Each time the gun roared, the old man lurched on his swivel stool.

Craig lowered the smoking Colt.

The old man opened his eyes, removing his fingers from his ears.

"Where is everybody?" Craig said.

The old man shook his head. "I can't hear nothin' above the ringin' in my ears. I'm an old man. I think you busted my eardrums!"

Craig glanced over his shoulder at Victor Bina, who laughed, lowered his chin, and shook his bearded head.

"I'm gonna ask you one more time, and if I don't get an honest answer from you, I'm going to drill a bullet in one of your ringing ears," Craig told the oldster. "Where—?"

"They left." The old man glared defiantly at the outlaw leader, lower jaw quivering, glasses hanging low on his freckled nose.

The broad nose looked odd on a face so pale and thin, with such close-set, watery blue eyes.

"Soon as that old Mexican killed your men in the New Mexico House over yonder, everybody in town—even the damn dogs and probably a cat or two—saddled up or hitched up and hightailed it."

"Where?"

"Where?" The old man scowled. "Hell, I don't know where. Anywhere but here, I reckon! I was about to pull out myself, just as soon as . . ." He let his voice trail off as he looked despondently at what was left of the key remaining on the desk behind him.

"What old Mexican?"

"What?"

"You said an old Mexican killed my men over at the New Mexico House, you bloody old fool. What old Mexican was that? What old Mexican killed my . . ." Craig paused, thoughtful. Then he glowered, his face flushing. "You don't mean *Silva*?"

The old telegrapher chuckled with satisfaction as he glared back at Craig.

"Well, I'll be damned," Bina said behind the outlaw leader.

"Goddamnit," Craig said quietly, regretting not killing the old bean-eater. Who would have thought such a spindly, cowardly old man could turn out to be such a devil?

Craig turned back to the old man grinning at him. It looked like a grimace, but it was just how the craggy oldster looked with his yellow teeth that seemed too big for his mouth.

"You like that, do you?" asked Craig.

"Sure," said the telegrapher, spreading his lips farther back from his teeth. He shrugged a fragile shoulder. "Why not? I like it just fine. Why shouldn't I? You're gonna kill me no matter how I feel about it. If I was sad about it—which I'm not—you'd still kick me out.

"Well, go ahead. I used to be worth somethin' around here. I used to be a deputy sheriff. I had mining claims, and I ran a saloon. I was married to a good-lookin' girl. I was the envy of the county. Then I got old and I went broke. Now, I'm nothing but an old key jockey who gets paid twenty dollars a month. I don't have a pot to piss in. Go ahead. Kick me out. I'm ready. At least I'll go out grinnin'."

"Why, you old devil."

"Yep," said the old telegrapher. "That's me, all right. At least I got that."

He laughed, throwing his head back slightly. And then he snapped his right hand against his thigh. "And I got the satisfaction of knowing I'm takin' you with me."

There was a slight click. The old man raised his right fist. Washed-out light from the window glinted on the derringer whose hammer he was thumbing back. Craig crouched, raising his own revolver but not before the old man's pocket pistol popped hollowly.

It sounded only a little louder than a cork being plucked from the lip of a whiskey bottle.

Craig fired his Colt, the .44 slug plunking into the old man's wrinkled forehead and snapping his head back against the table.

The outlaw leader stumbled backward, shocked. He hadn't seen that coming.

For a second, he thought he must have been hit, because the old man had seemingly aimed the derringer right at him. He brushed a hand down his chest, checking for blood. Nothing. He felt no pain, but he knew from having been shot before that sometimes it takes a second or two for the pain to register.

But, no. Nothing.

A gurgling sounded behind him.

He turned to see Victor Bina standing against the wall near the door, holding both hands to his throat. He looked as though he were choking. He *was* choking. On his own blood, which was also issuing out from between the fingers of his hands clamped to his neck.

"Oh, shit," Craig said. "Goddamnit to hell!"

Several other men who'd been waiting outside ran in and stood staring in shock at Bina, who gazed pleadingly at Craig, though there was nothing the outlaw leader could do for the man.

"Goddamnit it to hell!" Craig shouted again, stepping toward his first lieutenant just before Bina's knees buckled and he slid slowly down to the floor.

His choking and breathing grew more liquid-sounding and strained.

Then his writhing dwindled. The light left his eyes. He dropped his bloody hands to his sides, tipped his chin to his left shoulder, made a hiccupping sound, bobbed his head, and died.

Craig hunkered on his haunches and studied his dead friend.

"That there, boys, is one of the fiercest outlaws I ever rode with."

"Shit, Boss," said one of the men standing just inside the shop's open door.

Outside, the wind was starting to howl and moan.

"Yeah, it's too bad." Craig reached out and brushed his hands over Bina's eyes, closing them. "It's too damn bad. A real tragedy. A man to ride the river with is dead. Shot by a lowly old telegrapher."

Rage causing his pulse to throb in his temples, Craig straightened. He holstered his empty Colt and drew one of his other two. He turned, clicked the revolver's hammer back, and emptied the gun into the old man's chest and belly, until the oldster's slack body tumbled slowly, heavily to the floor where it lay amidst the scattered parts of the ruined key.

He wished like hell he could kill the old man all over again.

At least he'd kill the old Mex who'd killed Ryerson, Givens, and Two Bears. He'd kill old Mule Mulligan, too. Once and for all. And the kid known as Cuno Massey would die bloody, of course, as well. He knew where they all were. He wasn't sure the Mex was there, but Craig was betting he was.

He thought he'd seen Mulligan shooting out one of the roadhouse windows, and now he knew it had likely been the old town marshal, sure enough, since Mulligan wasn't still hanging from the cottonwood.

Craig cursed under his breath as he slowly, methodically began reloading the smoking Colt in his hand.

His return to Nopal hadn't been supposed to go this way. He was supposed to have ridden in here and exacted his revenge by laying slow waste to the town, shooting all the men gradually and raping all the women, then burning all the buildings to the ground.

But that hadn't happened.

He ground his back teeth together, his heart burning like a hot coal in his chest.

"So . . . now what do you want us to do, Boss?" asked Bart Francona.

Craig holstered his loaded Colt, tucked the flaps of his duster back behind his gun butts, and turned to the men gathered before him. "Boys, I want you to round up all the ammunition you can find. All the dynamite you can find, too. Women, if there're any left. And whiskey. And then I want you to be ready to ride on fresh mounts. We're gonna douse this town with coal oil and set it on fire. I want that fire large enough that the devil himself will be impressed by its size."

He turned to the slack body of Victor Bina.

"Then," he continued, "we're going to ride back to that whorehouse out there that them pilgrims are all huddled in— where that old Mex and Mulligan and the blond-headed gunslinger and the freighter's daughter are likely all huddled in—and we're gonna clean up this mess!"

CHAPTER NINETEEN

Cuno knocked on Kate's door.

"I'm tired," the girl said.

"I have a plate of food for you. Thought you might be hungry."

"I'm not," came the flat, depressed voice that did not sound at all like the Kate Lord Cuno had known.

Massey stared at the door, troubled. He turned the knob. The door opened, squawking on its dry hinges. He looked in.

Kate lay on the bed, under a single sheet, her head on the pillow, turned away from him. Her hair was splayed across it. The curtains had been drawn across the room's two shuttered windows, blocking out even the sunlight seeping between the shutters' cracks.

A wooden clock ticked on a wall, over an old china cabinet and a brocade-upholstered armchair. Kate's clothes had been neatly folded on the chair.

Cuno moved into the room and closed the door. "You should eat something," he said. "Best keep your strength up."

"What for?" she said in a tired, faraway voice. "So I can die when they storm this place?" She rolled over on her left side, facing Cuno now. "I saw those riders galloping toward the roadhouse with that burning whiskey bottle. They were going to burn us out."

"They didn't."

"I heard them," Kate said. "These walls are thin. I heard them say they'd be back. I heard their leader say that. I know

163

his voice. Believe me, I know it very well."

She squeezed her eyes closed. Tears dribbled from them and onto the pillow. She sobbed once, the pale skin of her forehead wrinkling as she fought back emotion.

Cuno had thought she might order him from the room. Since she had not, he thought she might not really want to be alone. He dragged an armchair closer to the bed and sat in it. He forked up some potatoes and, angry, held it out to her.

"Come on—open wide, little girl. Time for your medicine. Ain't half bad. Miss Loretta's girls know how to cook. Whipped up a fine venison roast."

Kate opened her eyes. He was surprised to see a faint but recognizably familiar humor in them. "Bet that's not all they know how to do."

"Oh, I wouldn't know about that."

"Old Mulligan would. I heard them curlin' his toes down the hall. Miss Loretta's girls are known far and wide." Kate paused, licking her upper lip. "When that animal Craig comes, his men will use them in the worst ways possible, and then he'll kill them. He had plans to kill me after all of his Boys had had their fill. They were going to hang me from the same tree they hung my father from. Said so right in front of me while they were switching off."

She closed her eyes tightly again. More tears dribbled onto the pillow. She scrunched up her eyes, fighting the emotion. It got the better of her, however, and she sobbed twice, loudly, her face flushing, veins forking in her forehead.

"Oh, Poppa!" she cried through another sob.

Cuno lowered the fork back down to the plate.

Kate composed herself, brushed tears from her cheeks, and studied Cuno as though seeing him for the first time.

She looked thoughtful, vaguely befuddled. "Who are you, Cuno?"

"Me?" Cuno hiked a shoulder. "I'm just a fella tryin' to steer clear of trouble."

She laughed sardonically, keeping her gaze on him.

"I didn't say I was always successful."

"Who are you? Really? A gunfighter? An *outlaw*?"

Cuno sat back in his chair. "I reckon you could say I'm a little of both. All right—you could say I'm a lot of both. But not by choice. The only laws I ever broke had to be broken."

He was thinking of the deputy U.S. marshals he'd killed back in Colorado, because they'd intended to rape the girls he was leading down out of the mountains and away from the marauding Utes.

"I ended up in the territorial pen. Got busted out. Went to Mexico. Ended up fighting with old Spurr Morgan down there. He's here."

Kate smiled. "He must be the one I heard howling like an old coyote down there, trading barbs with Mule Mulligan." She placed a hand on Cuno's knee. "Thank you for getting me out of that horrible place."

"I didn't have any choice in the matter, Kate."

"You had every right to leave me."

"Because you're marrying the man you promised yourself to?" Cuno chuckled. "That'd be a pretty harsh punishment. Besides, it'd take a pretty cowardly sonofabitch to leave you there . . . if he knew you were there." His cheeks flamed with anger once more.

Kate glanced away, then glanced back at him. "Don't be too hard on Brett, Cuno. He was pampered as a boy. His mother died when he was young, and his father started taking him to the bank early on and gave him everything he wanted. It's not his fault he has an overly high opinion of himself. He's a good man—deep down."

Cuno leaned over the plate on his knees and took her hand

in both of his. "I don't care about him. I care about you. How are you feeling? Are you sure you won't eat something?"

Kate smiled this time with irony, curling her upper lip. "Brett's supposed to be the one in here asking me that."

Cuno squeezed her hand tighter between both of his. "When this is over, I'll be leaving Nopal. My story's out now, and I'll have to take to the trail again, keep ahead of the law. Spurr's been tryin' to get me an amnesty, but it's all political. All that said, please forget him, Kate. Forget Brett. He's a no-account tinhorn. Besides, he doesn't have anything anymore. That outlaw gang took it all, showed him for what he is."

Kate leaned slightly back away from him, taken aback by his anger. "I guess you could say that about me, then, couldn't you?"

Cuno shook his head. "They gave you something you'd best hold on to, because it will see you through when nothing else will."

"Oh? What's that?"

"A hard, cold look at the world." Cuno kissed her knuckles. "Best teacher I know." He shucked the spare Colt he'd snugged down behind his shell belt, and held it butt forward. "You know how to shoot one of these?"

"No."

"You need to learn. All I got time to tell you now is this— anyone comes through that door you don't want comin' through it, you aim, click this hammer back to full cock, center the sites on the son of a bitch's chest, and squeeze the trigger. Blow his heart out!"

Kate accepted the gun, sitting up a little, taking it in both of her hands.

"Careful," Cuno said. "It's loaded. All six chambers."

Kate studied the heavy chunk of iron in her hands. "A hard, cold look at the world, eh?"

"That's right." Cuno rose from his chair, setting the plate down on it. "I'll leave that, in case you get hungry. You really should try to eat something, Kate."

He kissed her forehead again, and walked to the door.

"Cuno?"

He turned back to her. She frowned as though deeply troubled.

"Despite your saving my life, I think I liked the Cuno Massey I knew down by the creek better than the one I know now."

"Yeah," Cuno said with a grim, lopsided smile. "Me, too."

He opened the door and went out.

As Cuno walked down the hall, he heard a soft click behind him.

He turned to see a door open on the hall's right side. Brett Cavanaugh poked his head out of the room, and stared down the hall at Cuno. Glared at him, more like. Cuno glared back at him, and gave his hat brim an insolent pinch.

Cavanaugh turned his head toward Kate's door. He glanced again at Cuno, his eyes hard, and then stepped back into his room and closed the door.

Cuno went downstairs. Miss Loretta stood in the same spot behind the bar she'd been standing in when Cuno had first seen her. She was even smoking her corncob pipe. All her "girls" were sitting at one long table, playing poker. Each one had a Winchester carbine near at hand.

A couple were smoking cigarettes. The green-eyed black girl was smoking a long, black cheroot. They were wearing more functional clothing than the frilly, delicate boudoir trimmings they'd been wearing before—clothes they could move around in and that offered some protection, though a couple still wore bustiers with their long skirts. One wore a powder blue corset under a plaid flannel shirt.

The sultry brunette, Mattie, wore a tan Stetson, a white bustier, faded blue jeans, and cowboy boots—attire that Cuno found striking. She wore a shell belt and holstered Remington around her lean hips.

Cuno did not see Ella down here. She was probably upstairs with Fernando.

"There he is now, Cincy," Mattie said to the blue-eyed blonde dressed the most conservatively of the group—in a plain white blouse and gray skirt. "Why don't you ask him for yourself?"

The others laughed.

"Oh, hush, Mattie. You're always pokin' your nose in. Either raise or fold!"

Mattie turned to Cuno. "Cincy's actin' all shy about it now, but she was wonderin' just a minute ago about some of your . . . uh . . . personal details." She winked.

"Excuse me, ladies," Cuno said, feeling his cheeks warm as he walked past the doxies' table, heading for the front door.

"Think you're gonna have to ask the little Mex girl, Cincy," said Mattie.

Miss Loretta laughed her nasal, raucous laugh, which echoed around the dingy, cavern-like room.

Cuno stepped outside and rested his Winchester on his shoulder.

The wind had kicked up and was blowing fallen leaves and tumbleweeds around. High, flat clouds screened the west-angling sunlight. It was unseasonably warm and windy; the wind mewled around the yard, blowing scraps of paper. Cuno looked around for Spurr and Mulligan. He could hear them yammering, but he couldn't see them until he walked over to the roadhouse's west front corner.

Both old lawmen stood at a corner of one of the several, dilapidated corrals flanking the roadhouse. They were both staring off toward the cedar-stippled hills rolling away to the north.

Spurr had a pair of field glasses raised to his eyes. The felt-lined leather case had been hung from the top of a corral corner post nearby, and Spurr's old Winchester leaned against the same post.

As Cuno started walking toward the two oldsters, Spurr cursed and lowered the field glasses, letting them hang from his neck. He cupped his hands to his mouth and shouted, "I see you out there, you son of a bitch! Why don't you come a little closer, you chicken-livered devil, so I can blow your fuckin' lights out!"

A rifle cracked distantly. The slug screeched off a rock, blowing up dust and gravel about thirty yards in front of Spurr and Mulligan.

"That's all the closer he can get from there," Mulligan said.

"What the hell's goin' on?" Cuno said.

Both old lawmen whipped around, startled.

"Shit!" said Mulligan. "Boy, ain't you been around graybeards before? You sneak up on us like that, you're either gonna give us both heart strokes or get your ticket punched!"

"Christ, I thought you heard me."

"You'll be old one of these days, Kid," Spurr said. "When you are, I hope you got some shaver just like yourself around to devil you."

He turned and raised the field glasses again to the north. "There must have been three pickets out there. There's one more. Ike Stillwell, if my eyes ain't as bad as my ears." He lowered the glasses again, and shouted, "Ike Stillwell! I say, Ike Still-well—is that you, you hydrophobic old mongrel?"

Mulligan spat a wad of chaw onto a rotting corral rail, wiping his mouth with the back of his gloved hand. "If he does respond, how in the hell are either of us gonna hear him?"

"The Kid'll hear him," Spurr said, canting his head at Cuno.

Massey said, "Can I take a look? Maybe I can actually see

something."

"Disrespectful pup." Spurr handed Cuno the glasses. "If he's got big ears—I mean ears the size of dessert plates—it's Ike Stillwell, a hardcase I arrested for stock thievery as well as using the U.S. mail for sundry nefarious purposes about ten years ago in southern Wyoming."

Cuno looked through the glasses. He adjusted the focus until he brought up the man standing on a low, stone ridge about three hundred yards away. The man was bent forward. Cuno could only see the top of his battered Stetson until he straightened, grinned, and then turned around and bent forward again, this time away from Cuno.

Now Cuno could see only the man's pale, naked butt.

The man was pointing at his butt and yelling something, though Cuno couldn't make it out. The sign language was clear enough, however.

"Hard to tell who he is from that angle," Cuno said, handing the glasses back to Spurr, "unless you've seen Ike Stillwell's naked ass before."

"That bastard," Spurr said, gazing through the glasses.

He handed the glasses to Mulligan, who cursed as he spun the focus wheel. "If I had my Big Fifty, I'd pump one up his glory hole."

Spurr turned to Cuno. "We're gonna have to kill that curly wolf."

"We're gonna have to kill 'em all, Spurr."

"I mean, we're gonna have to kill that curly wolf now. Before it gets too late in the day. I got me a feelin' Craig's gonna be back soon, probably at sundown, and I want that son of a bitch out there dead . . . or the plan me an' ole Mule came up with ain't gonna work."

"What plan did you two codgers cook up?"

Spurr gestured to the roadhouse. "That building ain't gonna

withstand another onslaught. It'll tumble in on us like it's built of matchsticks, which it pret' near is."

"Especially after Craig's been reinforced with ammo from town," Mulligan added, daintily touching his thick index finger to the swelling around his discolored right eye. His face still looked as though it had been shredded by a Greener and sewn back together by a drunk surgeon fresh out of medical school. "He'll be able to hole up in the brush and rocks and pump lead at us all night and probably into tomorrow—if he don't just burn us out right away."

"So what do you two have up your sleeves? We got three wounded in there. Two probably can't be moved without killin' 'em. Besides, they'd just hold us up and make us easy pickings anyways."

"We leave the wounded here," Spurr said. "They'll be as safe as they possibly can be in the roadhouse while me, you, Mulligan, and them purty doxies—all of whom can shoot, as you likely saw—are gonna ride out and cut Craig off in that canyon just north of us, before he can make it to the roadhouse."

Cuno thought about it, and nodded. "I see. All right." He glanced off to where Stillwell or whoever he was stood on the stone ridge, staring toward the roadhouse, mocking them with his presence. He appeared to be cradling a rifle in his arms.

Cuno said, "That's why we need to kill him before the others get here—so we can make it out to the canyon without getting picked off, and before he can warn Craig."

"No—not we." Spurr and Mulligan grinned.

Cuno looked dubious. "Not we?"

"Just you," both old lawmen said together. "Me an' Mule here," Spurr said, "we're just gonna observe."

"You're just gonna observe."

"That's right," Mulligan said. "We're old. You're young."

"Besides," Spurr added, "we gotta stay here and make sure

he don't get around you and storm the roadhouse. He might just do that if he starts gettin' hazed out of the brush like a Brasada maverick."

Cuno snorted. "Bullshit. You two are just lazy."

"We're savin' ourselves . . . and our ammo . . . for the big fight later on," Mulligan said.

"Besides, I'm powerful thirsty." Spurr picked up a bottle that had been sitting on the ground by the corral. "It's time for a libation—ain't that right, Mule?"

"I do believe so," Mulligan said, accepting the bottle from Spurr as Spurr dug his hide-makings pouch from a shirt pocket.

Cuno gave another snort and stared off toward the lone picket staring back at him. "That's fine by me. You two would just get in my way, anyway."

He thought it through quickly. He thought the old mossy-horns had it right. It was best to take the fight to Craig before he and his Boys could make it to the roadhouse and likely lay waste to the place.

Cuno narrowed a steely eye at Spurr. "You just keep workin' on my amnesty, old man."

He didn't wait for a response. He swung around and took off running due north.

CHAPTER TWENTY

As Cuno ran nearly straight into the low, rolling hills and sagebrush, he glanced up at the lone picket standing on the distant stone shelf.

The man held his position until Cuno had run maybe thirty yards. It was as though he wasn't sure what he was seeing. Then, when it became obvious that one of the men from the roadhouse was running toward him, he took his rifle in both hands, dropped to a knee, and raised the rifle to his shoulder.

He popped off a shot, the slug snapping a sage branch just ahead and to Cuno's left. He was still out of range of accurate firing, so Massey continued running straight on for another twenty yards.

The rifle cracked again, blowing up dirt and gravel two feet in front of him.

Cuno swerved to his right, ducking behind a boulder.

The rifle cracked again. The bullet spanged loudly off the top of the rock.

Cuno ran out from behind the boulder and into the brush to the east of it. As the rifleman began firing more quickly, popping off one shot after another, Cuno ran straight north, dodging around rocks, boulders, and cedars, leaping over low hills and dashing up the next one before him. The wind snagged his hat off his head, and he ran with his longish blond hair dancing in his eyes.

When the shooter's slugs began getting too close for comfort,

Cuno swung east again. As another slug drilled the ground two feet from his left boot, he dove behind a low stone escarpment. The shooter fired another round into the top of the escarpment, blowing sand and gravel down on Cuno's bare head.

Massey hunkered low, gritting his teeth, panting.

With his free hand, he swept his hair out of his eyes, throwing it back off his forehead.

Sweat dribbled through the dust on his cheeks. It basted his shirt against his back.

He waited, expecting more fire.

Silence. Likely, the shooter was reloading.

Cuno snapped his head up, raised his Winchester to his shoulder, and aimed at the stone shelf about a hundred yards away from him now. Nothing but sky capped the formation. The shooter was no longer there.

Spurr's shout rose from behind him, muffled by the wind and the scratching branches. "Kid, he's moved off the ledge! Movin' toward you from the northwest!"

Cuno looked that way. There were several low, rocky knolls stippled with wind-jostled junipers and cedars in front of him, blocking his view of the shooter. Cuno ran up and over the escarpment, throwing his arm and rifle out for balance. As he dashed down the escarpment's opposite side, the shooter's rifle cracked, echoing.

The bullet plunked into the escarpment behind and above Massey.

He looked toward where the shot had come from and saw gray smoke tearing on the wind from a tangle of dancing green brush.

Cuno stopped, dropped to a knee, and pumped three shots into the brush. His slugs tore branches and plumed dust.

Cuno racked another shell into the Winchester's breech and took off running toward the tangle, pushing himself hard, wincing against the ache in both ankles as he ran over the uneven ground in boots not made for running, or even for walking, much farther than the width of your average frontier street. As he ran, he shuttled his gaze over the terrain before him, mesquites now pushing up around him, widely spaced about the red gravel and tufts of Spanish bayonet.

Ahead, a hat appeared. A rifle barrel shone beneath one sprawling, quivering mesquite. The barrel moved with Cuno, tracking him.

Cuno swerved hard right just as the rifle cracked, smoke and flames lapping from the barrel.

He dove, landed hard, and rolled as the bullet crashed into the ground beyond him. He crawled into deep brush, belly down.

He crabbed through rocks and more brush, panting, grunting. He slowed, crawled another five feet, and stopped.

He lifted his head slightly, until his chin was two inches off the ground. His sweat-damp hair hung in his eyes. His heart was hammering the ground through his breastbone. Windblown grit peppered his eyes.

Faintly, he could hear footsteps moving toward him—the soft crunch of grass and gravel, the occasional trill of a spur beneath the wind's rustling and sporadic moaning. The man was somewhere to his left. Cuno's only cover was a cedar and a mesquite just beyond the cedar.

Six feet ahead lay a steeply slanting boulder. If he made a sound, the shooter would likely spray his cover with lead. He had to reach the boulder. It was the only good cover around.

Gritting his teeth, he placed his left hand on the ground, and dug his fingertips into the sand and gravel. He set the Winchester down, placed his right hand on the ground, and dug those fingertips into the sand and gravel, as well. He gritted his teeth when he could hear his boot toes grinding into the sand.

Slowly, he eased himself ahead—sliding himself along the ground, leaving the rifle behind. He'd have to rely on his Peacemaker.

He gained a foot, then two feet. Three. He could no longer hear the footsteps moving toward him. The shooter had stopped somewhere to Cuno's left and was probably pricking his ears, listening, watching the brush for movement beyond that which the wind was moving.

Cuno's left boot was grabbed by a spindly cedar branch. It raked the spur, ringing it. The sound was like the discordant twang of a banjo string.

Shit!

Cuno heaved himself up and sprang off the balls of his boots. The shooter's rifle crashed to his left.

Cuno ran straight ahead, pumping his arms and legs. The rifle spoke twice more, loudly, the lead screeching through the air around him. He dove, landed near the boulder, and scrambled around to the end of it, putting his back up hard against it.

Running footsteps sounded somewhere on the far side of the boulder.

They grew quickly louder. Spurs rang.

Cuno threw himself onto his left shoulder, rolled, and hit the ground on his chest. He brought up his Peacemaker, clicked the hammer back, and planted the sites on the chest of the man running toward him—he wore a derby hat with a blue silk band, a long, sheepskin vest, and twin bandoliers crossed on his chest.

Two holsters flapped on his hips. The mule ears of his boots danced around his calves.

The man stopped suddenly, eyes showing surprise.

He raised his rifle, but got it only halfway to his shoulder before Cuno's Peacemaker thundered.

The first shot took the man in his chest after punching a hole through the little hide sack hanging from a string of grizzly claws around his neck. The sack bounced violently against the man's chest as he grunted and staggered one step backward, trying to raise the rifle again.

Again, Cuno's Colt roared.

It roared again, and again, peppery smoke tearing on the wind.

The shooter dropped his rifle as the bullets punched him backward into a patch of Spanish bayonet. He ground his spurs into the sand, arching his back up off the ground, groaning. He panted, his chest and belly rising and falling sharply.

"No!" he screamed, staring at the sky with a look of horror on his blunt-nosed, blue-eyed face. Sandy sideburns ran down the sides of his hollow, leathery cheeks.

"No—*Momma!*" he cried.

He kicked one more time, tensed, and then dropped flat to the ground. His eyes grew as opaque as the windows of an abandoned house. His head slowly turned to one side. Both boots quivered a little.

Then he was gone.

Cuno walked over and stared down at him. He was a tough-looking bastard, but he'd cried out for his mother at the end. Cuno saw no humor in that. He wondered if he'd do the same. He'd never know until he faced it, which could come at any time. It had almost come a few seconds ago.

He felt a little sick and weak in the knees. Though he'd become damned good at it, killing always made him feel that way. He supposed he was glad it did.

A few minutes later, he walked back into the roadhouse yard. The dead man's bandoliers hung from his shoulders. He carried his own Winchester and the shooter's carbine. Spurr and Mulligan were sitting with their backs against the corral fence, passing the bottle.

A couple of whores—the sultry brunette and the blonde—stood near the roadhouse, watching him, their hair blowing. Mattie took a drag from her quirley, snapping her head to the side as she blew the smoke into the wind.

"Did he have big ears?" Spurr asked as Cuno tramped past him and Mulligan.

"Ah, hell," Cuno said through a caustic grunt, continuing on toward the front of the roadhouse. He was still feeling queasy. "Why don't you go out there and see for yourself, you old bastard?"

He stomped past the doxies without looking at them.

"What bee's buzzin' around in your bonnet?" Spurr yelled indignantly behind him.

Soon, horses were saddled.

Those who were riding out to bushwhack the Boys—namely, whores and lawmen—mounted up with plenty of guns and ammunition, and rode out. Cuno remained in the roadhouse, giving a last bit of advice to Ella, who stood with her new lover near the front door.

"If all goes well, you shouldn't need to do anything except sit here and drink coffee."

"I should go with you," Ella said. "I can shoot as well as those other girls."

"I know you can, but we need someone here in case some of the Boys get around us."

"What am I?" Miss Loretta asked, puffing her pipe at a table, cleaning the rifle she'd taken apart and spread out before her. "Chopped liver?"

"This is a big place," Cuno said. "You'll need help. Besides, Ella's gotta keep an eye on Fernando."

Cuno had heard boots clomping down the rickety stairs at the back of the room. Fernando Silva stepped out of the shadows, a fresh bandage wrapped at an angle around his head, covering his ruined ear.

"No one needs to keep an eye on Fernando," said the old man, adjusting his pistols on his lean hips. "I am going with you."

He doffed his straw sombrero, the braided horsehair chin thong dangling down his chest. He paused at a table to take a liberal pull from an open bottle.

"You best stay here, Silva," Cuno said. "You're in a bad way."

"A bad way, uh? You would be in a bad way if I hadn't come to your rescue, *Señor* Massey. If old Fernando hadn't effected a crossfire, they would probably still be here, those wild *javelinas.*" He stopped before Cuno and his adopted daughter. "Or maybe they would have finished their business and left by now . . ."

His wizened old face spread a wry grin. There was a lump in his jaw where he'd tucked a tobacco quid. He leaned down, kissed Ella's cheek, and shouldered his rifle.

"Oh, Fernando!" Ella said, wrapping her arms around his waist. "I wish you would stay here!"

"I am needed with the others, little one." Fernando smiled down at her. "It is nice to feel needed for something more than trimming hooves or hitching the white ladies' buggies."

"Then I am going, too!"

"No, no, no," Fernando chided her, grabbing her arm and shoving her straight backward.

He cowed her with a hard, commanding look. When her eyes flickered submissively, he winked, smiled again, turned, and walked outside. "I will saddle my pony," he told Cuno as he walked around the roadhouse toward the barn flanking it. "Kiss that girl, and let's ride!"

He wheezed out a laugh.

"You heard the man," Cuno said.

He drew Ella to him and kissed her lips. She wrapped her

arms around his neck, and kissed him tenderly, raking her fingertips across his ears and down his neck.

"Be careful," she said. "And please watch out for that old man."

"Now I have three old men to watch out . . ."

Cuno let the sentence trail off. He saw someone else step out of the shadows at the back of the room. It was Kate Lord dressed in a bright yellow frock that one of the doxies must have provided. Her hair was brushed. Her face was still cut and scraped, her eyes swollen, but she looked better. At least, she appeared on the mend.

Ella turned to follow Cuno's gaze. Kate stopped at the back of the room, near the bar, crossed her arms on her chest, and turned her head demurely away.

Cuno leaned toward Ella. "Be good to her, will you?"

"*Sí*," Ella said, nodding. "I will be good. And you come back, *amigo*—all right?"

"All right."

Cuno turned and went out and heard Ella close and bar the door behind him.

CHAPTER TWENTY-ONE

Cuno and Fernando Silva caught up with Spurr, Mulligan, and the doxies as the lead group was cresting the ridge overlooking the canyon.

The whores were pretty, but tonight they were all business. Killing business—armed with shell belts and carbines that they'd been taught to shoot by none other than the old frontierswoman herself, Miss Loretta.

As the larger group stopped to peruse the canyon from the ridge, Cuno and Silva approached from behind. Cuno rode up between Spurr and Mulligan. Both lawmen glanced back to see Fernando Silva sitting his grullo, rifle resting across his saddle pommel.

The girls were studying the old Mexican, as well.

"What have we here?" Spurr said.

"Once the sharpest shooter in the border country," Silva returned with a sly smile. "If I may brag."

"You look a mite familiar, Silva," Spurr said, studying the old Mexican skeptically. "You ever have any federal paper on you?"

"*Señor* Morgan, if you haven't caught me by now, you will never catch me."

Spurr brushed a black fly away from his right ear and turned back to the canyon. "Braggart."

Cuno studied the canyon, which was copper-colored now as the sun sank behind the western ridges. Shadows bled out from fissures, clefts, brush, and rocks. The wind had died, leaving a heavy stillness in its wake.

The road dropped at an easy pitch into the canyon, which it crossed before climbing the opposite ridge, which was about the same pitch as the southern one. The canyon was about a hundred yards wide and littered with spring flood debris—rocks, a few boulders, and sun-bleached branches.

Mesquites and willows grew along its sides, at the bases of both ridges. A good many large boulders lay along the ridge bases, as well.

Hoof and wagon tracks scored the canyon bottom, running straight across it.

Deferring to the old lawman's vast experience, Cuno glanced at Spurr. "Spread out down there in the brush and rocks, on this side of the canyon, then pick them off when they're about halfway across?"

Spurr nodded. "Don't see why not."

He glanced at Mulligan.

The town marshal said, "Let's place some rifles low, some high. We'll have that canyon abuzz with lead so the Boys'll think they're hornets"—he grinned at Spurr—"but with a whole hell of a lot more bite."

Cuno could smell the whiskey on both men. They were half-drunk, but Cuno wasn't worried. They could shoot a tighter bullet pattern pie-eyed than most men could shoot sober as parsons.

Spurr turned to the doxies. "Ladies, any of you want to opt out, now's the time to do it. No hard feelin's. Frankly, this could go either way."

"What's the matter, old lawman?" said the sultry Mattie, letting smoke from her quirley dribble out her nostrils. "Afraid we'll see you squirt down your leg when the bullets start flyin'?" She turned her head slightly sideways, and winked.

"Hell, sweet sister," quipped Mulligan, "old Spurr squirts

down his leg when there ain't no bullets in sight!"

Spurr turned a dull-eyed gaze on his old friend. "Ain't that just like you, Mule, to insult your betters?"

He clucked to his horse and started down the ridge.

"Spurr—hold on." Cuno was staring across the canyon toward the northeast.

Spurr stopped his stallion, Cochise, and followed the younger man's gaze.

"Oh, shit," Mulligan said softly.

A red-orange glow shone amongst the pale buttes about two miles as the crow flies beyond the canyon. While Cuno stared at it, the glow grew brighter as the sun continued to sink, tugging on shadows. Gray clouds of what could only be smoke spread out above the glow, which was growing brighter not only because the sun was going down, but because the fire was gaining intensity.

"What's that?" asked one of the doxies.

"Those bastards," Mulligan said. "They're burnin' the town." He paused, then said even more quietly, "Those bastards."

"I just hope everybody got out," Spurr said. "They'll be headin' this way now. We'd best take our positions."

He started down the trail. Mulligan followed. Cuno waited until the girls and Fernando Silva had ridden past him, heading toward the canyon floor, before he started Renegade down the slope, as well.

They picketed their horses in a small canyon feeding the main one from the southwest. The arroyo was well-sheltered by rocks and brush, and, being on the other side of a deep western bend sixty yards from the crossing, would protect the mounts from stray gunfire.

Soon, they were all lined up along the canyon floor, the doxies hunkered in thick brush or behind rocks and boulders only a few feet up the ridge wall. Cuno, the two old lawmen, and Fernando Silva holed up behind the same sort of cover about twenty feet above the women.

Cuno was between Spurr on his left and Mulligan on his right. Silva was positioned on Spurr's left side. They were spread out to each side of the trail crossing the canyon.

Cuno was maybe five feet away from the trail on his right, on one knee behind a low, flat rock and a gnarled cedar angling up beside it. He hoped he wouldn't need much cover. If all went as planned, they should be able to empty at least half the gang's saddles before the Boys even knew what was happening.

After the first couple of volleys, the other half of the gang should go down relatively easily. A few might escape by fleeing back up the northern ridge, but there was no helping that. They'd be too few to worry about.

If all went as planned . . .

A soft whistle sounded to Cuno's left. He turned to see Silva looking toward him and Spurr, his straw sombrero colored charcoal pink by the last, fast-fading light.

"I would like first shot at the lead rider," said the old Mexican. He pointed to the bandage over what remained of his ear. *"Por favor, señores."*

Spurr glanced at Cuno, who shrugged.

Spurr merely touched two fingers to the brim of his tan Stetson and then turned his head forward again, watching the canyon's opposite wall, which was dark now.

It was quiet for a long time. A couple of wildcats mewled in the distance, and there was the ratcheting cry of a late-hunting hawk. Then the night went as quiet as a grave.

Below him, Cuno could see the girls crouched in their positions, moving around a little to keep blood flowing to their limbs but remaining absolutely quiet. Miss Loretta had taught them well.

A minute after the funereal silence had descended, a very low rumbling sounded. It grew gradually, steadily louder.

"Here they come, kids," Spurr said, his voice sounding inordinately loud in the silence of the canyon. He turned to Silva. "*Señor*, wait until you're sure, and then make that first shot count." He raised his voice slightly. "Ladies, *Señor* Silva's shot will be our lead."

"Noted," one of the girls said quietly from cover.

The rumbling continued to grow.

It grew for the next ten, twelve minutes, and then Cuno spied a couple of jostling shadows at the top of the opposite ridge. More jostling shadows appeared against the lilac sky of early evening. Bridle bits and gun iron and spurs began flashing in the late twilight.

The shadows began disappearing as the men and horses started dropping down beneath the skyline, heading down the ridge toward the canyon. For a time, each rider's shadow merged with that of the ridge. Cuno saw the shadows again as the first riders reached the canyon floor and galloped toward him and the other ambushers.

There was one lone lead rider. The others were spread out behind him—three, sometimes four abreast.

The hammering of the hooves was a wild clattering now. There were several sharp clangs of shod hooves striking rocks. Tack squawked and saddlebags and rifle scabbards slapped the sides of the horses. The collective blowing of the horses sounded like several giant, furiously pumping blacksmith bellows.

The riders themselves spoke among themselves as they rode, one humming. One laughed, and shook his head. A thrown bottle shattered on a rock. They were drunk on the violence they'd left behind them, the violence they were anticipating once they reached the roadhouse.

They were black devils galloping out of hell's gates.

The lead rider was nearly upon the ambushers now, his dark

figure growing in the brown shadows of the canyon. He was thirty yards away and closing.

Cuno turned to Silva. The old Mexican's raised Spencer flashed and roared like a cannon, the thundering report echoing off the canyon walls.

The lead rider screamed, threw his arms out, and leaned back to one side. He dropped down off his horse's left hip, and rolled, his spurs flashing in the last light, ringing as he crashed violently amongst the rocks, only to be trampled by at least one rider galloping behind him.

Cuno picked out a jostling silhouette, and squeezed his Winchester's trigger. The roar of his own rifle was drowned by those of the other rifles opening up around him.

"Yee-*hahhhhhh*!" Spurr cut loose, standing and firing his Yellowboy from his shoulder. "Die you devils! Dieeeeeeeeee!"

"Yeah—die, you devils!" one of the girls screamed somewhere below Cuno. "Dieeeeeeeeee!"

The outlaws and their horses screamed amidst the cacophony. Men and horses went down hard. A full fifteen seconds passed after Silva's first shot before some of the outlaws began triggering shots in return.

One of the bullets spanged off a boulder below Cuno, and he shouted, "Keep your heads down!" as he continued firing until he'd emptied his smoking Winchester.

He dropped to a knee behind his cover and started punching fresh cartridges through his Winchester's loading gate. As he did, he stared along the trail to make sure none of the outlaws dashed past him toward the ridge behind him. He wanted to keep them boxed up down here in the canyon, where it was like shooting rats in a privy.

The other bushwhackers must have emptied their guns around the same time as Cuno emptied his. The shooting around him had died off. The outlaws were shouting and cursing and scrambling around, some still mounted, some running around on the canyon floor and hunkering down behind dead horses.

Their pistols or rifles flashed in the darkness. Bullets pelted the slope around Cuno. One of the girls yelled, *"Shit!"*

"You all right, Jen?" yelled another.

"Bastard damn near drilled me a third eye," said the first girl who'd yelled, and she raised her rifle once more.

When Cuno had reloaded, he scrambled down the slope and stepped up between Cincy and Mattie. "You two all right?" he asked after he'd fired another round at the marauders.

"Doin' just fine," Mattie said. "How 'bout you, good-lookin'?"

"Keep your head down!" Cuno told her.

Too late. There was a dull thump. The girl's head jerked sharply. There was the sound of something wet splattering onto the rocks.

Cuno took his Winchester in his left hand as he grabbed the girl, Mattie, with his right.

Cincy screamed and stumbled backward, falling to her rump, as Cuno eased Mattie to the ground.

"What the hell happened?" Spurr called to Cuno's left.

"Mattie's hit!"

"Ah, shit!" Spurr started moving down the ridge, firing and levering his Winchester from his hip. "You sons of fuckin' bitches!" he bellowed, moving down the ridge and out onto the canyon floor.

Mule Mulligan triggered another round and shouted, "Spurr, what the hell you think you're doin', you addle-pated old codger? Get your ass back up here!"

Cuno looked down at Mattie. The girl's eyes were open and staring blankly up at him. He felt the side of her head. It was oily with blood flecked with sharp bits of bone.

187

"Mattie!" Cincy cried. "Oh, *Mattie!*"

"Goddamnit," Cuno raked out, easing the dead doxie to the ground.

His mind flashed briefly on the face of his young half-breed wife, July, lying dead in his arms so long ago—years ago, now, though the memory of her half-Indian face was as fresh as yesterday. Killed by men no different from Craig and the Boys.

Rage and exasperation exploded inside him. It was time for Craig's black devils to be sent mewling back to hell on the wings of a howling lead storm.

Cuno straightened, thumbing a few more cartridges into his Winchester's breech, making sure the rifle was fully loaded.

"God-*damnit!*" he shouted as hot lead ripped the air around him, thumping into rocks and snapping mesquite branches.

Firing his Winchester at the gun flashes spread out across the canyon, he followed Spurr onto the canyon floor, moving slowly, deliberately, and firing, the Winchester leaping and roaring in his hands.

His empty cartridge casings pinged onto the rocks behind him.

Chapter Twenty-Two

"Hold your fire, ladies!" shouted Mule Mulligan behind Cuno. "Hold your fire, Fernando! Lest we pink those two cork-headed fools in the back!"

Cuno fired at a jostling shadow. The outlaw cursed, dropped, and tried to heave himself to his feet. Cuno fired, watching in satisfaction as the outlaw went flying backwards and twisting around before landing on his belly.

"Stop!" he cried. "You've killed me!"

Cuno walked up to the man, who turned his head to glare up at him, eyes flashing hatefully.

"Not quite." Cuno drilled a round between his eyes. "There. Now I've killed you."

Cuno looked around. Men were moaning and groaning around him.

He could see only the small shadows of fallen men and the larger, humped shadows of a few fallen horses widely spread out in the growing darkness before him. Dim light from the sky flashed off a gun barrel as one of the fallen scrambled to his feet and ran toward a dead horse.

Cuno swung toward him, emptied his Winchester into the outlaw, then lowered the smoking Winchester and drew his Peacemaker. The outlaw crawled away from the humped shadow of the dead horse. He was breathing hard, sobbing. Cuno walked over to him, aimed carefully, and drilled a bullet through his left ear.

The outlaw jerked to one side, quivered violently, and then collapsed with a gurgling sigh.

A rifle barked to Cuno's left. He swung around but held fire. It was Spurr finishing off another wounded desperado.

Gray smoke wafting around him, Spurr turned to Cuno.

The younger man said, "Finish 'em all? Or do you want to take them in for fair, impartial trials?"

"Don't be a smart-ass, Kid!"

Cuno and the old lawman walked around the scattered fallen, and polished them all off. When they were done, Mule Mulligan, Silva, and the doxies came down off the ridge, looking around. One of the "dead" men must have made a sound, because Cincy lowered her carbine's barrel and drew another round through his temple.

He was a quiet dead outlaw then.

"There—that's for Mattie," Cincy said through a snarl.

Mulligan approached Cuno and Spurr. Both were reloading.

"You two related?" Mulligan asked, digging into his shirt pocket for a half-smoked cigar.

Spurr looked at Cuno. "He ain't good lookin' enough to be kin of mine."

Hoofs clattered to the south—a single horse climbing the southern ridge.

"What the hell was that?" Cuno said.

Mulligan said, "Christ, we missed one!"

He pointed his rifle at one of the dead men. "You know, that lead rider who Silva shot is not Cecil Craig. I seen Craig up close—too damn close—and that ain't him!"

"Shit," Cuno said. "That crafty bastard must have anticipated a bushwhack. He gave someone else the lead!"

Cuno wheeled and started running west along the canyon floor.

"Hold on, Kid—we're goin' with ya!" Spurr called.

Cuno wasn't going to wait for anybody. If that rider had been Craig, he was likely heading for the roadhouse to exact whatever revenge he could find. He was likely piss-burned as hell. And he was too much of a devil to ride away from here without first getting a taste of satisfaction.

Cuno ran into the arroyo in which they'd picketed the horses. He came out straddling his skewbald paint and galloped past the old lawmen also rushing toward the horses. Silva and the doxies were staying with Mattie.

Cuno put Renegade up the southern ridge, the sure-footed paint lunging into a ground-eating run.

Fury burning in him so brightly that red spots blossomed before his eyes, Cecil Craig galloped into the roadhouse yard mostly cloaked in darkness. A few of the downstairs windows were lit, shedding wan light onto the ground beneath them.

Someone was here.

Craig grunted, cursed, and pressed his hand over the blood oozing from a hole in his lower left side, just above his shell belt, not far from his previous graze.

He'd hole up here, get his wound tended, and try to hold the bushwhackers at bay.

He could do so with his rifle if he had a hostage or two. Maybe a girl or two . . .

If not—well, then, by god, he'd take a few of those bastards with him when he kicked off. A few girls with him. He'd heard girls yelling down in the canyon. Girls had been part of the small gang that had taken out the Boys.

Girls!

"Christaldamnmighty!" the outlaw leader raked out as he stopped his horse near the roadhouse and half-fell out of the saddle. What was the world coming to?

He grabbed his rifle, cocked it, and strode toward the front door, shouting, "Open it! Open the door, goddamnit! I know someone's in there!"

He cast a quick glance along his backtrail, hoping none of the ambushers was close on his heels. He knew they would follow, but he needed a little time. He was losing blood fast and needed to get the wound bandaged.

"I said open this door, goddamnit!"

Craig raised the rifle and drilled three shots into it. He cocked the rifle again, shouting, "Open the goddamn door!" He strode to the door, and kicked it.

It wouldn't budge. Barred from the inside, most likely.

"Did you hear me in there?" Craig shouted. "I order you to open—!"

He stopped as a scraping sounded on the door's other side. It sounded as though someone were removing the locking bar.

Craig quirked a sweaty, expectant half-smile, and aimed his rifle straight at the door, waiting.

A rifle cracked to his right. He saw the flash out of the corner of his right eye. Something hot tore into his right thigh.

He screamed, staggering to his left.

A rifle cracked from that direction, as well. That bullet tore into his left thigh, sending him staggering back to his right, screaming. The pain was excruciating. His knees turned to burning putty, and he fell to his butt, wailing, trying to lift his rifle again.

"No, you don't!" said a girl's voice.

Two figures were moving toward him—one on his right, one on his left.

The one on his left was a short, pretty, brown-haired girl, her Mexican-dark eyes flashing angrily in the light from the roadhouse. She cocked her carbine and stared down the barrel at him.

"Drop it, *pendejo,* or I will send you to *el diablo!*"

Craig let the rifle sag in his arms. "Ella . . . ?"

The Mexican girl said, "Cecil Craig?"

He just stared at her. The other figure—a pretty blonde—moved up on his left, grabbed the rifle out of his slack hands, and tossed it back behind her. She stood to his left, feet spread wide, aiming another carbine at him.

Craig stared up at her.

A cold brick dropped in his belly.

"Ah, shit," he said.

"Remember me?"

"Ah, shit."

"*Sí*, Ella," said the blonde. "This is Cecil Craig. The one who cut your father's ear off."

Ella stepped toward him, bending down. "What is that hanging around your *neck*?"

She ripped the leather thong from around the killer's neck and held her father's ear up to the lamplight. As she did, the roadhouse door squawked open on its dry steel hinges. Craig smelled the aromatic odor of pipe smoke.

"Well, well—what have we here?" said a nasal voice as the door drew wide and a little, birdlike figure stepped out onto the worn spot in the ground, also holding a carbine.

"What we have here," said the blonde, smiling coldly down at Cecil Craig, "is a man minus an ear."

She glanced at Ella.

Ella reached for the big bowie knife on Craig's hip. He grabbed her wrist, glaring defiantly up at her. She grinned and aimed her carbine at his neck. So did the blonde.

"You're not gonna cut off my ear," Craig said.

"Shut up!" screamed the blonde. "You're not the one calling the shots, you stinking bastard!"

Craig was so taken aback by the blonde's rage that he didn't realize that Ella had taken his knife until she straightened, holding it up in front of him, just out of reach. She chuckled as she stared down at him.

The birdlike figure silhouetted against the roadhouse door laughed raucously, her reed-like voice taunting Craig as it lofted toward the guttering stars.

Then the two girls were on him like two coyotes on a wounded buffalo calf. They wrestled him down and held him fast. He could only scream. The pain in his legs had rendered him too weak to fight but only cower and howl.

The knife was a white-hot pain on the left side of his head. It was a lightning bolt of agony ripping through every nerve and muscle.

It was so overpowering that he stopped screaming and just lay there, paralyzed with misery as the Mexican girl held up his ear and let the blood dribble down over his left cheek.

His blood was warm and oily. It dribbled over his mouth. He spat it away as the scream that had been building in his belly finally broke into his throat and exploded from between his lips.

The birdlike woman laughed insanely.

Craig bawled in his arms and clamped his left hand over the bloody, ragged hole where his ear used to be.

Cuno galloped into the yard and around to the front of the roadhouse.

"Hold it there, you devil!" bellowed Miss Loretta.

She stood with the two girls near the open door, over the crouched figure of a man on the ground. Cuno announced himself, and the two girls and Miss Loretta lowered their rifles.

Cuno put Renegade up close to the small group gathered before the roadhouse. A face appeared in a window to the right of the door. Brett Cavanaugh stared out for a brief time, looking around. He winced when his eyes found the girls and the screaming outlaw. He pulled his head away from the window and closed the curtain.

"What have we here?" Cuno said, returning his gaze to the man on the ground and poking his hat brim up off his forehead with his Winchester.

Craig lay mewling and writhing, cupping one hand to the bloody side of his head.

"What we have here is a good helping of revenge served up cold," said Ella, holding up the outlaw's ear and smiling. Suddenly, her expression turned grave. "Fernando?"

"He'll be along," Cuno said. "You three all right?"

"Don't it look like it?" Miss Loretta glanced at Ella, who tossed the outlaw's ear onto Craig's trembling back. "That one there—she'll do."

Cuno smiled. He looked at Kate, who was leaning against her rifle, one fist on her hip as she glowered down at the writhing soon-to-be-dead man.

"Hell," Cuno said, swinging down from his saddle. "I'd ride the river with either one of 'em." He rubbed the back of his neck as his face gained a dubious expression. "Though, uh . . . probably not at the same time . . ."

Miss Loretta threw her head back and roared.

★ ★ ★ ★ ★

.45-CALIBER LEFT TO DIE

★ ★ ★ ★ ★

CHAPTER ONE

A disembodied voice in the night said, "That sure is one fine-lookin' horse, boyo."

Sitting on a stump near his campfire, Cuno Massey had been about to refill his coffee cup from the pot chugging on a rock beside the low-dancing flames. Now, however, he dropped the cup and slapped his hand down to the Colt Peacemaker holstered low on his right thigh.

"No, no, no!" scolded a voice nearly directly behind him, in the opposite direction from the first voice. "If you draw that big popper of yours, we're gonna have to kill you, see?"

"You heard him," said the first voice, and now Cuno could see a shadow move at the very edge of the flickering umber sphere of light cast by his fire. "Take that hand off the popper, bucko. You got one second, and then I'm gonna drill you where you sit, and that, dear boy, will be the end of you."

The man spoke with an Irish brogue. Now as he stepped farther into the firelight, Cuno could see that the man was short and powerfully built, wearing a bowler hat and thick, pewter muttonchop whiskers. He also held a Winchester carbine straight out from his right side, the barrel aimed at Cuno's midsection.

He gave a smug, sadistic smile.

Cuno slid his hand from the Colt, letting it rest on his knee. He wondered how in the hell his normally keen hearing had missed the approach of these men. Even more, he wondered how his skewbald paint stallion, Renegade, had missed them. Massey had always relied on the paint to keep a close watch when he was camped out along some remote, lonely mountain trail, as he was now, in New Mexico.

Maybe he'd relied *too much* on what he'd thought was the horse's acute hearing and sense of smell.

As if to compensate for his negligence, Renegade suddenly loosed a shrill whinny and then a low nicker. In the corner of his left eye, Cuno could see the horse shake itself where it stood tied to its picket pin about twenty feet away from the camp, at the edge of the firelight.

Cuno turned his head toward the horse. A man stood beside the stallion—a thick, round-faced, bearded man in a fringed buckskin shirt, who just then bit into an apple and chewed exaggeratedly.

"He likes apples," said the bearded man, extending the half-eaten apple toward Renegade, who took the rest in his mouth and crunched it up, glancing sheepishly over at Cuno still sitting on the log with his hands on his knees.

Silently, Cuno cursed. So much for his prized stallion's worth as a sentry.

Reading his mind, the bearded man chuckled.

The bowler-hatted Irishman stepped forward until he stood about six feet away, on the opposite side of the fire from Massey. "That coffee sure smells good," he said.

Cuno felt the burn of chagrin as well as anger. He'd let his guard down, and he should know better by now. No man with a past like his should ever depend solely on his horse to let him know when trouble was near. "I'd offer you a cup, but it's the custom of the country to announce yourself."

"I think we done piss-burned the younker." Cuno could hear the soft crunching of brush as the man behind him moved toward the camp.

Three, Cuno thought. *Only three, or were others remaining hidden out in the darkness?*

"Take his gun, Cole," ordered the man with the Irish accent, slowly moving forward. The third man was moving toward the fire now, as well. They were closing on him from three sides.

No, four sides. Someone was moving up on his right.

He turned to look.

The fourth intruder was a girl. She held a rifle in her hands, though the rifle appeared a little heavy for her. She was a slight girl with gold-blond hair pinned up beneath a cream Stetson. She wore a man's checked shirt under a leather jacket, and a long, dark wool skirt.

On her hands were doeskin riding gloves.

She was a pretty girl with an oval face and even features, but her mouth was compressed in a hard line, and her brows were stitched with menace.

Cuno was still staring at the girl, wondering what her business was out here with these hardcases, when the man behind Cuno stopped, leaned forward, released the keeper thong over the hammer of Massey's Colt, and slid the heavy piece from its holster. Glancing over his shoulder, Cuno saw the man hold the Colt up to scrutinize it, arching his brows in approval.

"Nice weapon."

"I'll be needin' it back . . . as soon as you fellas . . . and lady . . . have had your coffee."

"We don't want any coffee," the pretty blonde said in a none-too-pretty voice. Her jaws were set, and she looked all business this evening. "We want to know what you're doing here."

"Hell, I'd like some coffee, Stacey," said the Irishman as he stopped on the other side of the fire from Cuno. To young Massey's surprise, the Irishman wore a town marshal's badge pinned to his buckskin vest. "We rode a stretch, and that mud sure does smell good."

He squatted down across from Cuno, setting his rifle butt-down in the dirt. "Pour me a cup—will ya, bucko?"

"Pour your own."

The Irishman smiled, though his eyes darkened. He blinked slowly, and glanced at the man flanking Cuno. "Cole, pour me a cup of coffee, will you?"

"Sure, I'll pour ya a cup, Marshal."

Cole stepped wide around Cuno's left side, aiming a Spencer carbine at Cuno's head. His own five-pointed star winked in the firelight. He took a cautious step toward Cuno and leaned in between Cuno and the fire to retrieve the cup Cuno had dropped when the man with the badge had first commented on the quality of his horse.

"Easy, Cole," the girl, Stacey, warned.

Cole held his Spencer with one hand, keeping it aimed at Cuno's face as he bent down and slid his other hand toward the coffee cup. When his hand missed the cup, Cole slid his eyes toward the object of his desire. Cuno took advantage of the man's fleeting distraction to fling his left arm up against the carbine's barrel, knocking the rifle wide, and then bolt to his feet.

He grabbed Cole's left shoulder and the back of his neck, and sent him tumbling into the fire. He hit the flames with a scream and immediately bounded out of them, screaming and run-staggering across the camp, beating at the flames leaping up his trousers with his hat.

"Goddamnit!" Cole cried, beating furiously at the flames, still holding his Spencer with one hand. "Goddamnit, goddamnit, goddamnit—I'm on *fire*!"

As soon as Cole had hit the fire, Cuno had jerked toward the girl, intending to snatch her rifle out of her hands. But she was having none of it. She retreated two steps straight back, stretching her lips in a challenging sneer, and leveled her rifle at Cuno's chest.

He could see her index finger tighten over the Winchester's trigger.

The umber flames shone in her dark eyes.

"Jesus Christ, Cole!" the Irishman said, chuckling. "Now, what kind of a damn fool move was *that*?"

The man to Cuno's left—the bearded gent who'd fed Renegade the apple—laughed delightedly, remaining about ten feet away from Cuno, who stood clenching his fists at his sides in frustration. Cole had kicked several logs out of the fire, and scattered cinders glowed burnt orange against the dark ground.

When Cole had beat out the flames, he hopped around, cursing and gritting his teeth. His pants were smoking. So were his boots. He swung toward Cuno, looking like a very angry attack dog, and raised the Spencer, drawing the hammer back to full cock.

"Hold on," ordered the Irishman.

"I'm gonna kill that smart bastard."

"No, you're not, Cole," the Irishman ordered. "Not yet, anyway. Not until we know who he is and where the rest of his gang is holed up. You pull that trigger, and you're gonna be back ridin' the grubline, maybe working out at the Double Aces again for Chick MacDonald. That what you want?"

"Briggs is right. Think it through, Cole," the girl said in her low, taut voice, keeping her rifle aimed at Cuno. "Go ahead. I know you can do it, bright boy that you are."

Cole opened his mouth as he glared over his Spencer's barrel at Cuno, breathing hard. His hat was smoking on the ground nearby. He was tall and gangly, with coarse, dark-brown hair cropped close above his large, pale ears. "You're gonna wish you hadn't done that."

Again, the bearded man laughed.

"Shut up, McCallister!" Cole fumed.

Chuckling, the man with the badge, Briggs, moved forward. He poked the barrel of his own rifle against Cuno's broad chest sculpted by the years the young man had spent working as a freighter with his father in Nebraska, and shoved Massey straight back two steps. He kept a mild, vaguely menacing grin on his broad, ruddy face framed by the pewter muttonchops.

His eyes were pale blue, Cuno noticed. Like a baby's eyes, only they owned a strange opaqueness, like a doll's eyes.

He picked up the cup Cole had been reaching for, set it on the log Cuno had been sitting on, and filled it from the coffee pot, which had miraculously avoided being kicked over by Cole. He set the pot down, and sipped the coffee.

"Tastes as good as it smells. You make good coffee. Must've had some practice cookin' for yourself."

Cuno stared at him, not saying anything, barely able to control his temper. He didn't like folks stealing into his camp, and he didn't like being pushed around. He also felt like a tinhorn for having allowed it to happen in the first place. He wanted to hurt somebody, but with four guns trained on him, what he'd done to Cole would have to do for now.

He'd been lucky none of the others had shot him for that spontaneous stunt.

"Let's get to it, Briggs," Stacey said, shifting her weight on her hips and hefting the Winchester in her hands.

The Irishman gave her a cold look. "That's *Marshal* Briggs, Miss Ramos."

"All right," the girl said. "Let's get to it, *Marshal* Briggs."

Briggs turned to Cuno. "The lady wants to get to it. What are you doing out here? Where's the rest of your gang?" He glanced around as though he might see other men standing around at the edge of the firelight.

"There's no one else here," Cuno said tightly. "There's just me. And I'm just passin' through. You got no cause to invade my camp."

Not unless they were federal lawmen, Cuno thought. He had several federal warrants on his head for various federal offenses, not the least of which was killing two federal lawmen. That the killings had been justified by the lawmen's intention of raping the young women whom Cuno had been guiding out of the Colorado mountains and away from rampaging Indians didn't seem to matter to the federal government.

However, Cuno's old friend, Deputy U.S. Marshal Spurr Morgan, was trying to get a writ of amnesty signed by the Governor of Colorado Territory. Cuno hadn't heard if old Spurr had been successful.

Probably not.

The federals took it personally when two of their own went down, for whatever reason. And, as the girls who'd been the target of the lawmen's vile intentions so far hadn't been found to give testimony in Cuno's defense, there was only Cuno's word against the hard fact of two dead lawmen.

"Oh, come on, boyo!" raged Briggs, suddenly red-faced. "We know Jack Salmon always sends a scout ahead to sniff out information. Where's he and the others? Save yourself a lot of time and trouble, boy!"

"I don't know any Jack Salmon. And I don't know any of the others. Like I said, I'm just passin' through."

"From where *to* where?" asked the girl in the same loud, belligerent tone as Briggs.

Cuno turned to her, raising his own voice, feeling the blood rush to his face. "None of your damn business! A man's got a right to travel *from* where *to* where whenever the hell he pleases."

"Oh, you think so, do you, bub?" Briggs laughed.

"It's no use," Stacey said. "He's obviously one of Salmon's men. He's Salmon's scout. Look at that pistol. Look at his

Winchester. Look at *him*! If he's not ridin' the long coulees, the sky isn't blue."

She stepped back and raised her rifle higher, aiming at Cuno's face. "Take him down. Just like the others. Take him down. Strip him and tie him, and leave him for either his outlaw boss to find, or the wildcats. Either way, we'll be sending Jack Salmon a clear message!"

CHAPTER TWO

Briggs moved slowly toward Cuno, a wry grin tugging at his mouth corners. He kept his gaze on Cuno, who spread his feet and raised his hands chest high, crouching, curling his hands into loose fists, ready.

Briggs held his rifle firmly and barrel up in both hands.

He stopped three feet away from Cuno and merely gazed into Cuno's eyes for a full five seconds. It was as though he was trying to mesmerize his prey. He was so close, standing sideways to the fire, that Cuno could see a faint, inky wash of red in the whites of the man's pale blue eyes, the dirty pores and the faint pits and creases in the man's ruddy face, the skin drawn taut across the high cheekbones by the merciless western sun.

Every muscle in Cuno's body was tensed, waiting, as he tried to anticipate Briggs's first move.

He knew the man would use the rifle. Still, it came as a surprise when Briggs, suddenly flaring his nostrils and gritting his teeth, rammed the Winchester's butt into Cuno's belly.

Cuno's body had been hardened by tough physical labor and by the blows of many fists. He'd tensed his midsection to withstand just such an attack, and he'd tried to get his hands down in time to ward off the blow, but Briggs had moved too quickly, too suddenly. The air hammered out of Cuno's lungs in a loud grunt, and the younger man lurched forward at the waist. Having been trained as a bare-knuckle fighter by his late father, Cuno recovered quickly, lunging forward and head-butting

Briggs as the man tried to raise the rifle again for another attack.

Briggs grunted and stumbled back, his eyes snapping wide in surprise at the viciousness and power behind Cuno's own move.

Cuno slung his right fist up hard and fast, hammering Briggs's left cheek and sending the man stumbling farther away from the fire. Sensing the others closing on him, Cuno started to pivot at the hips to face the assault, but he'd only started to turn around when a rifle butt slammed into the back of his left knee, and then into the back of his right knee.

Both legs folded, and he dropped hard as another rifle butt was rammed mercilessly into the small of his back, knocking him forward and straight into the butt of the rifle thrust toward him by the grinning bearded gent.

The butt's steel plate connected soundly with Cuno's forehead, and his body filled with agony plunging down from the point of the blow. He dropped into semiconsciousness, only vaguely hearing the men around him cursing and hammering his body with the butts of their rifles, kicking him. He registered a few punches to his face, as well.

A couple of times he looked up through slitted lids to see the girl, Stacey, standing a ways back from the three men assaulting him. She held her rifle under her arm, and Cuno could see a faint look of satisfaction stretching her pink lips as the fire's flames flickered across her dark eyes, beneath the brim of her man's cream Stetson.

Cuno tried to defend himself, but he felt as though he were rolling down a very steep, rocky hill with no way to break his plunge. And then he felt his clothes being ripped and torn from his body, and someone was pulling his boots off.

"No," he heard himself feebly cry, thrashing his arms futilely. "No . . . goddamnit . . . you *bastards* . . . !"

There was no way he could prevent himself from the final

humiliation—being stripped and left naked in his own camp. He'd never felt so helpless and enraged, and there was a point when someone was brusquely peeling his longhandles down his arms with such painful, raking, jerking movements that he wished they'd just get it over with, so that maybe the hammering of what felt like steel spikes into his brain plate would finally cease, and he could pass out.

Suddenly, he realized he *had* passed out. Now, as he opened his eyes, his tender brain was assaulted with buttery morning light. He squeezed them closed, wincing, hearing himself draw a sharp breath through gritted teeth.

"Christ!" he raked out, miserable, immediately aware that he was lying naked on the cold, bare ground.

His butt was cold. He could feel gravel and pebbles pressed taut against it, poking him. He lifted his head and tried to move his arms and legs, but they wouldn't budge. Opening his eyes again, he stared down the length of his body to see that he was indeed naked. Not only naked but bound spread-eagle on the ground.

Both wrists were tied to stout stakes. Both ankles were, as well. His torn clothes lay in twisted disarray around him.

Fury engulfed him, and, pulling at the stakes, he convulsed in a furious wail, tipping his head back, spittle flying from his lips to dribble down his chin and onto his chest. He continued to pull at the rawhide ties until he was so exhausted and the hammering in his head was so painful that he must have passed out again.

He found himself regaining consciousness again about an hour later, judging by the increased intensity of the light now bayoneting his eyeballs. He looked at each of the stakes to which he was tied.

His attackers must have chosen long stakes, which they'd sunk deep in the ground. Try as he might—and he was a strong, bulky young man in his early twenties—he couldn't budge them an inch. The rawhide was well braided around his wrists and ankles as well as around the corresponding stakes. When he pulled at them, they only drew tighter around each limb, stifling the blood flow, causing his hands and feet to turn blue and to burn.

Whoever had done the staking and braiding had done this before. They were damned efficient at it.

Cuno couldn't wait to find them and thank them for their handiwork.

If he could ever free himself of the bindings, that was. At the moment, as exhausted and miserable as he was, and as formidable as the bindings were, he seemed to be facing tall odds. He glanced down at his midsection and felt a jab of raw fear. He glanced at the sky arching over the pines jutting around him, knowing that he was as exposed to prey, including winged prey, as any man could be.

He'd heard of eagles swooping down on men in his situation, and tearing away vital parts.

One last time, he funneled his strength into his arms and legs, and, tipping his head back, cords of sinew standing out in his neck, he tried with all his considerable might to pull the stakes out of the ground. He heard the stakes and the rawhide creak. He heard himself yell with the effort.

He heard the yell echo around the forest between high, craggy ridges, and slowly die.

Feeling as though his heart was about to explode from his chest, and not sensing any movement in any of the stakes, he convulsed, relaxing, gritting his teeth at the burning pain in his blood-starved hands and feet.

Waves of nausea rolled over him. He turned his head to one side, and vomited. Then he nearly fainted. What kept him from going entirely out was a sound. He felt a faint vibration in the ground beneath him. He opened his eyes and looked around.

The thuds of horses rose in the north. Shadows moved in the trees. Two riders were moving toward him, following the same horse trail Cuno had been following near sundown the day before. They were trotting, holding their reins high. As they drew closer, Cuno could see that they were a man and a boy.

They were on course to skirt his camp on his left, the man riding ahead of the boy. Both stared straight ahead as they rode, and as they drew close enough that Cuno could make out their features beneath the wide brims of their Stetsons, he tried to hail them, but his voice was strained from his previous yells and wails.

He could only make a croaking sound. It was enough. The man turned toward him. He was lean-faced, with a ginger mustache, and he wore a chambray shirt beneath a light wool coat, and leather chaps and spurred boots.

He drew back on the reins of his claybank gelding, saying, "Whoa!"

The boy turned his head then, too, and his eyes widened when he found Cuno. The man clucked his horse off the trail, trotted into what remained of Cuno's camp, and drew rein beside him, staring down in surprise. The boy came, then, too, following the man's path through the brush near where Cuno had picketed Renegade.

Had picketed the stallion, which, he realized for the first time since regaining consciousness after the attack, was gone.

The bastards had stolen his horse, which didn't so much come as a shock as it kindled a new fire of rage within him.

"Help me," Cuno managed to rake out, gazing helplessly up at the man staring down at him. "Please . . . cut me loose."

The boy, twelve or thirteen, with a light spray of freckles across his sunburned cheeks, stared down at Cuno, hang-jawed.

"Who is he, Pa?"

The man studied Cuno for a time in dismay and then he looked around as though for the men who'd done this.

"They're gone," Cuno raked out again. "Help me. Please. Cut me loose."

The man jerked his rattled gaze back to Cuno, staring down at him in silence. Frustration burned through Cuno as he gritted his teeth and pulled at the ties.

"For chrissakes," Cuno said. "Cut me loose. *Please!*"

The boy turned to the man. He stared at him for a time before cutting his incredulous gaze back and forth between him and Cuno, his eyes remaining wide with befuddlement.

"Cut me loose!" Cuno pleaded, again straining at his bindings.

The boy turned to the older man. "You gonna cut him loose, Pa?"

The man's horse lowered its head to sniff at Cuno, and the man drew the reins up hard. The horse snorted. The man turned away, touched the claybank with his spurs, and angled the horse back toward the trail.

"No! Please!" Cuno urged.

"Ain't you gonna cut him loose, Pa?" the boy asked again, stunned by the man's behavior.

The man stopped, turning back to the boy. "That's Briggs's work. We want no part of it. Come on—we got work to do!" The man rode off, raising his elbows high as he booted his horse into a gallop.

"But, Pa!" the boy called, horrified.

The man stopped his horse abruptly and turned back toward the boy, his face dark with rage. "I said get your tail over here—we got beef to move!"

He started off again, kicking the horse hard, his hoof thuds dwindling quickly.

Cuno stared up at the boy. "Please," he said. "Come on, kid

. . . you gotta . . .”

"Who are you?" the boy asked.

"Cuno Massey."

"What'd you do to rile Briggs?"

Desperation was a cold wave washing through Cuno. He felt his life hanging by a thread. The man was gone. His only hope was the boy. "Not a damn thing, and that's the god's honest truth. Now, kindly cut me loose. *Please!*"

The boy stared down at Cuno, his light brown eyes entirely ringed with white. He jerked with a start when the man's voice boomed through the forest, "Hob, get your tail over here *now!* We want no *part* of that!"

The boy stared off in the direction of the man. He glanced down once more at Cuno, anguish showing in his young eyes, and then, biting his lower lip in frustration, he touched spurs to the horse's flanks and trotted back through the brush toward the trail.

"Nooo!" Cuno pleaded, his hoarse voice sounding frog-like. "Hob! *Nooo!*"

The boy glanced at Cuno once more, then whipped his head forward and galloped on down the trail, horse and rider quickly becoming a sun-dappled shadow that grew smaller and smaller, the horse thuds fainter and fainter.

When the sounds dwindled to silence, Cuno knew a hard moment of blind panic. His heart raced, beating so quickly that he was sure it would tear loose from its moorings. He could feel the throbs in his ears. His limbs tingled and grew icy, cold sweat popping out on his face and dribbling down his cheeks and into his eyes, stinging them.

He strained against the bindings until he could no longer feel anything but sharp pin pokes of pain in his hands and feet, and then warm darkness closed over him with merciful speed. Again, he was out. He woke to the afternoon sun blazing down on him. As he squinted against the brassy light filtering through the pine tops, his heart quickened again, and another wintery chill began washing up from the base of his spine.

He drew a deep breath, mentally calming himself, telling himself that it was over. So what if it was?

What kind of a life had he led, anyway?

Since Rolf Anderson and Sammy Spoon had murdered his father and stepmother, and he'd hunted them down and killed them, his life had been nothing except one long, violent chase. He'd met a young, half-Indian woman on the Bozeman Trail, when he'd been following Anderson and Spoon, and after his parents' killers were dead, he and July were married. They bought a small farm, and Cuno planted the seed of a child in his beloved's womb only to see her—and their unborn child—fall under a hail of bullets meant for him.

He'd discovered that killing only led to more killing.

More innocent people killed.

More running.

He'd even spent time in a federal prison for the murder of those two deputy U.S. marshals until a wild Mexican gal—one of the girls the marshals had intended to rape—had broken him out with the help of her brother's wild-assed bunch of Mexican *banditos* and *revolucionarios*.

It was off to Mexico for Cuno Massey, where he'd met a deputy U.S. marshal with a weak ticker, Spurr Morgan. He'd last seen Spurr in a town he and Cuno had helped save from marauders, and now he wished to god he'd run into the raggedy-heeled old lawman again. He wished Spurr would ride out of those pines, chuckle his wheezing chuckle, shake his head, then cut Cuno loose.

They'd build up a fire and cook some beans, share a bottle of whatever rotgut the old lawman was carrying. Over the past several years, Cuno had seemed destined to run into the old, whore-mongering reprobate in the unlikeliest of places. Why not here?

In his half-crazed state, Cuno looked around, half-expecting to see the wizened, potbellied old-timer come riding through the trees on his beloved stallion, Cochise.

Cuno actually found himself disappointed to see nothing but birds tittering among the pine boughs and the occasional cheeting of a squirrel angered by Cuno's presence here where the squirrel gathered its pine nuts and acorns in preparation for the coming mountain fall and winter.

Spurr . . .

"Where are you, you old bastard?" Cuno said, peeved that the old man was nowhere near.

He laughed at that. Laughed at the way his brain was turning to mush. He'd always considered himself brave, had always thought he'd confront death with a fateful, resigned eye. A stiff upper lip. He'd always hoped to see July and maybe even his baby again on the other side.

But here he was, keeping the wild, frightened stallion of his heart under a tight rein that was growing harder and harder to maintain.

He laughed again, trying to see the humor in his situation. Tied spread-eagle to the ground, his pecker lying slumped against his thigh—a gopher taking a nap half out of its hole.

A drunk gopher!

Fear-drunk, Cuno laughed at the image.

And then his brain seemed to switch off for a time. He lay there, limp against the ground, no longer fighting the rawhide bindings, staring up at the pines that swayed with the frequent, soft gusts of the summer breeze. The trunks creaked. Branches scraped together with ratcheting sounds. Occasionally, a cone dropped, tumbling out of the branches to plunk into the fragrant forest duff.

A nuthatch crawled along the underside of an aspen branch, hammering its stubby beak into the bark for insects and aphids. It didn't seem at all concerned about the naked man stretched out on the ground beneath it, likely only a few hours from death. When night closed down, the large predators of the forest would step out for their evening meal.

A hawk screeched.

That returned the wintery chill to Cuno's bones.

Chapter Three

He squinted up at the cobalt sky. The hawk was swooping in now from the east. It dropped into the forest canopy and disappeared for a second and then reappeared as it landed on a dead branch of a fir tree against which a dead aspen leaned. Maybe thirty yards away.

A rough-legged hawk.

The bird looked down at Cuno with its small, dark, round eyes in their shallow sockets above the hooked beak. A beak made for tearing flesh. The hawk's white-speckled brown feathers ruffled in the wind. It turned its head to peck at something beneath a wing and then let the wing drop back down to its side, and resumed its cold, impersonal stare at the man stretched out naked upon the ground.

Cuno scowled up at the bird of prey, feeling as though a cold hand had been placed upon his privates.

"Don't even think about it, pal," Cuno said.

But what could he do to prevent the bird from swooping down upon him?

He could yell and flex his knees and bob his head. That was about all. If he could work up the saliva, he could spit. Once or twice, that would likely frighten the raptor away. But hawks were smart. It would soon get the picture that the naked man was defenseless, and it would swoop down and, despite Cuno's yelling and screaming, would take whatever it wanted and probably return to the dead fir branch to dine.

Cuno's belly burned. He could imagine the hooked beak tearing into him.

He shook his head, trying to clear the thoughts from his horror-addled brain.

"Can't give into it," he told himself aloud. "Can't let 'em take my mind. They might have killed me, but I'm not going to go out wailing." He looked up at the bird and hardened his jaw, turning his fear to challenging rage as he yelled, "Come and get me, you bastard! Come on! What're you waiting for? Here I am! Take what you want!"

The bird stared coldly down at him.

For the next hour . . . maybe the next two hours, judging by the shadows revolving around Cuno's naked body . . . the bird remained on the dead limb, staring coldly down at its helpless prey. The bird was waiting for Cuno to die. It had the patience of stone.

Somehow, it reminded him of the girl, Stacey, who'd been with the men who'd done this to him. She'd had those same, cold, impersonal eyes that had stood out in sharp contrast to her otherwise comely features.

Suddenly, the bird opened its wings. It stretched its feathered legs and savage talons and leaped down off the limb and came swooping down toward Cuno through the columnar pines. He could hear the whooshing sound of its body cleaving the air above its shadow sliding along the ground; he could see the beak open as the bird gave its tooth-gnashing wail. Cuno steeled himself for the inevitable, seeing the bird's eyes flash in the sunlight as it continued dropping toward him, growing larger and larger before him.

The *eyes* growing larger and larger before him . . .

"Oh, shit," Cuno heard himself grunt, tensing every fiber in his body.

When the bird was maybe ten yards away, maybe five feet

directly above Cuno, the hawk suddenly flapped its large, ragged wings and darted upward after passing so close, Cuno could feel the wind of its body against his chest and face.

The raptor gave its ratcheting, mocking cry, and disappeared back into the forest canopy. The wings made a grating, sinewy sound as they flapped.

Cuno turned his head as much as he could to see the bird carom up into the blue, which quickly consumed it.

He drew a deep breath to calm his fluttering heart.

But the bird would be back. That's what its cold, coppery gaze and mocking cry had told Cuno just before it had swooped back skyward.

It would be back.

Maybe after the coyotes or the mountain lions had got what they'd wanted.

But, sometime soon, the hawk would be back to take what remained.

Hours passed.

Cuno dozed but did not sleep. His heart kept up a steady, insistent rhythm in his chest. He was too exhausted, too enervated to sleep, every ounce of his energy drained, his head continuing to throb from the blow of the rifle butt.

The light turned copper around him. It began to dim as the sun dropped down beneath the pines and teetered on the crest of a jutting, black ridge. From another, distant ridge, a coyote howled mournfully. Another coyote answered in a similar vein from a different ridge. The howling stopped for a time, during which apprehension crawled like a bug atop Cuno's flat belly.

Then the coyotes began yammering crazily and from nearer by. The two had come together now and had been joined by several others. They kicked up a din that sounded like a hundred mad witches calling to some black god residing in the smoking bowels of hell.

Cuno's heart beat faster.

With startling abruptness, the yammering stopped.

Dead silence except for the breeze and the occasional tumbling of a pinecone from a branch.

Cuno pricked his ears, listening for the sounds he knew would come.

Then they came.

The thudding of soft feet running along the forest floor. The thudding continued for a time, growing gradually louder, until the sounds of ragged panting joined them.

Cuno looked around. The forest was growing purple with closing night shadows. Against that purple, small shadows moved as the sounds of the panting and the running, padded feet continued to grow louder.

Shadows moved straight out away from him, several coyotes closing on him in a long line. One of the shadows slipped out from behind a fir tree maybe thirty yards away, and a shaft of vagrant, gray-purple light briefly shone on the dun-gray beast moving toward the camp.

The animal disappeared around an evergreen shrub, then moved out from behind it, and stopped.

Cuno sucked in a sharp breath and held it.

He stared straight out from between his spread legs at the coyote that was staring back at him, head down, ears pricked, mouth closed. Slowly, the coyote, which appeared to be a large, bushy male—nearly as large as a wolf—lifted its long snout and sniffed the breeze, half-closing its eyes as though mesmerized by what it was scenting.

The other coyotes were moving toward him, though no longer directly. They appeared to be zigzagging as they, too, sniffed the breeze, probably sniffing human now and wondering if they were being led into a trap. They'd likely smelled the scent of human before, but coyotes, like most predators, were also drawn by the smell of fear.

Cuno knew it was rare for coyotes to attack men unless their pups were threatened, but he'd heard of helpless men, lost in the forest or out on the prairie, who'd been devoured by a pack. To coyotes, food was food. They'd devour anything, *including* a man. Probably, fear was what had initially drawn the beasts his way.

Cuno could see the others now forming a semicircle around him, remaining back about thirty yards and milling around, working their black nostrils, sniffing the wind. The large one that had stopped continued toward Cuno now, gradually lowering its head as it approached.

"Go!" Cuno yelled. "Go on! Get out of here!"

He flexed his elbows and knees, trying to look as threatening as he could, trussed up as he was. The large coyote stopped. The others ran nervously this way and that, lowering their snouts to sniff the ground, mewling and whining. Cuno counted eight of them. No, nine, he saw now as another one came into his field of vision, staring at him from beneath a near fir, its dark eyes reflecting the last gray light.

"Go on!" Cuno cleared his throat, trying to raise his voice, to sound more menacing. "Get out of here, goddamnit! Get the hell out of here!"

The large, gray coyote came straight on slowly, lowering its snout, keeping its eyes on its prey.

"Get the hell out of here!" Cuno shouted again.

The beast stopped, turned, swung around, and for a hopeful second Cuno thought it was going to retreat. But, no. It merely turned in a complete circle and then, whining deep in its chest, it continued to pad toward Cuno, keeping its snout low to the ground.

Cuno flexed his body as much as he could, wincing at the pain in his wrists and ankles and at the nauseating throbbing in his head. "Go! Get! Get the hell out of here! I'm not a meal, goddamnit!"

He hated the brittle, quavering desperation he heard in his own voice.

Ten feet from Cuno, the coyote stopped. It raised its head, sniffing, sort of wrinkling its eyes, trying to discern whether or not its intended prey was dangerous. Something must have told it that the potential meal splayed out before it was helpless, for it gave another whine and then moved forward. The others came forward then, as well, and began circling Cuno, keeping their heads down, eyes riveted on their quarry.

A few hours ago, Cuno had thought he could never feel more helpless.

He'd been wrong.

The big, shaggy coyote ran in a complete circle around him, panting and whining. It and the others were all circling now, making quick, sharp, nervous movements. The large coyote stopped only four feet away, just to the right of Cuno's right hip, and showed its teeth. From deep in its throat it brought up a liquid growl.

Cuno tightened his body against the imminent attack.

"All right, you son of a bitch," he said through gritted teeth. "Come on! Be quick about it!"

The gray coyote jerked with a frightened start. Then, as though Cuno's shouts had enraged it, it showed its teeth again, raising its hackles and making a gurgling, growling sound before lunging toward him, opening its mouth to take the first bite.

Dirt and pine needles blew up in front of the beast. The coyote yipped with a start, pulling up sharply.

A half-second later came the hiccupping report of a rifle.

Chapter Four

As the crack of the rifle echoed through the forest, the coyote yipped, wheeled, and dashed off through the trees. The others stopped dead in their tracks, looking around and pricking their ears, sniffing, and then wheeled and ran off after their leader.

His heart still hammering his breastbone, every limb feeling as though it had turned to stone, Cuno swung his head this way and that, looking around. To his left rose the sound of two horses trotting toward him. He turned his head in that direction. The riders rode side by side, the smaller of the two holding a rifle butted against his left thigh. The other rider was a woman, her hair piled in a loose bun.

As they drew closer, Cuno recognized the boy, Hob.

Relief washed through Cuno like a soothing, warm wave of saltwater as the pair drew rein before him. Keeping her eyes on Cuno, the woman said, "Nice shooting, Hob."

The boy did not respond. He merely stared down at Cuno from beneath the brim of his hat, which was a size or two too large for him.

"That's him, Ma. That's the man there," the boy said, as if distinguishing Cuno from other men staked out in the forest.

"I guessed as much, Hob."

The woman scrutinized Cuno carefully, cautiously, frowning down at him from her perch atop a copper-bottom dun. The wind slid stray strands of light brown hair across her cheeks and nibbled at the hem of her long skirt. She wore a ruffled white blouse buttoned at her throat, and a spruce green shawl.

She was a fine-looking woman with a brown-eyed, heart-shaped face. Judging by the small crow's feet extending from the corners of her eyes, she was in her late twenties or early thirties.

Cuno was so exhausted that he could find no words. He merely stared back at the woman and the boy, resigning himself to the possibility that they might ride off, as the boy and the man had done before. He'd so steeled himself to die, had so prepared himself, that he found the appearance of the boy and the woman not so much a relief as an anticlimax.

Now he'd have to go through it all again. If not tonight or tomorrow, then sometime in the future. Next year, the year after that, in fifty years . . .

The woman tucked her bottom lip under her front teeth, narrowed her eyes in speculation, and then swung her right leg over the rump of the dun and dropped smoothly to the ground. Holding the horse's reins in one hand, she walked over to Cuno and stared skeptically down at him. He was stark naked, but he'd been through so many punishing emotions that something as frivolous as modesty was no longer in him.

The boy dismounted his strawberry roan and walked over to stand beside the woman. He glanced from Cuno to the woman, and said, "Shouldn't we cut him loose, Ma? It ain't right to leave a man to die out here . . . like this."

The woman gazed critically down at Cuno. "Who are you?" she asked.

"Cuno Massey."

"Did Briggs do this to you?"

"Yes."

"Because you ride with Jack Salmon." She hadn't made it a question but a cold statement of fact.

"No, that's not right. I don't ride with Jack Salmon. I don't ride with anyone. I'm just passin' through. But since I have no way to convince you of that, you'll either have to take my word for it or leave me here."

Cuno looked at the boy. "Ask Hob. Hob knows I'm not with Jack Salmon."

He sensed this to be true.

The woman looked at the boy, who met her gaze with a lucid one of his own. "I've seen Salmon's bunch, Ma. Seen 'em crossin' our range. I've seen 'em in camp." He shook his head slowly. "I've never seen this fella with 'em."

The woman turned to Cuno. She looked deeply troubled by the problem before her. She blinked, sighed, and then extended her hand to Hob. "All right. Give me your knife, son."

Hob pulled a folding Barlow knife from a sheath on his belt. He opened the knife and handed it over to the woman, who took it in her right hand and dropped to a knee beside Cuno. Staring skeptically into his eyes, she sawed away at the rawhide binding his left wrist to its corresponding stake.

The rawhide was strong; she had to work at it, hardening her jaws at times, more locks of her hair tumbling from the bun atop her head to dance across her cheeks and neck. As she worked, she glanced at the knife, but mostly she kept her gaze on Cuno, as though worried that once he was loose, he'd spring at her, like a wildcat freed from a trap.

When she'd finally sawed through the rawhide binding his left wrist, she sawed through the rawhide binding the right one.

She straightened, breathing hard, color having washed into her cheeks to betray what a beauty she really was. She had round, intelligent eyes where a wry tenderness lived, and a small, dark mole on the left side of her chin. Sliding several loose strands of hair back from her forehead, she extended the knife to the boy, and said, "All right—your turn, Hob. I'm played out."

The boy took the knife and went to work on Cuno's ankles.

Meanwhile, Cuno lay back against the ground, massaging the blood back into his hands and occasionally shaking them, gritting his teeth against the searing pain of the blood pouring into the starved flesh and awakening the half-dead nerves. The same pain visited first his right foot as Hob freed it from the stake, and then the left one as the boy stood and stepped back away from Cuno, tossing away the rawhide and closing the knife.

He, too, looked cautious, as if half-expecting Cuno to pounce on him.

Cuno sat up, rubbing the blood back into his feet, wincing and groaning and blinking against the throbbing in his battered head. He was dizzy, the darkening forest sliding uncertainly around him. The woman walked up to him. She'd gathered his torn and soiled clothes, and tossed them onto his lap, covering him.

"There you are, Mister Massey."

"Thanks, ma'am." Cuno looked up at her, relief swelling inside him and only just now managing to temper his physical agony. "I can't thank you enough."

"You can thank me by riding on out of here."

"I'll do that," Cuno said, watching the woman walk over to the horses, the reins of which Hob held in his hands. "Just as soon as I can track down my mount."

She stopped and turned to Cuno. "You don't have a horse?"

"Briggs took him."

The woman looked around, pensive. She shook her head and took the reins of her copper back from the boy. "At least you're alive," she said, and gave a little grunt as she toed a stirrup and swung up into her saddle.

"Yes, ma'am," he said, leaning back on his hands and extending his bare feet straight out before him. "At least I'm alive."

The woman stared down at him from atop her horse, and

canted her head slightly to one side. "Can you stand, Mister Massey?"

"Don't know yet. I haven't tried it."

"Well, why don't you try before we ride on?"

Cuno glanced at her, as did the boy, who'd swung up onto his own horse.

Cuno nodded. "All right."

Slowly, gingerly, holding his clothes against his crotch, his chagrin at his nakedness returning, he pushed up off his right hand and gained his feet with a grunt. The forest pitched violently, and he collapsed onto the log he'd been sitting on when Briggs's bunch had accosted him.

"I'm all right," Cuno said, drawing a deep breath, holding the clothes in his lap. "I'll make it."

He looked around and saw that his gear was still here. Briggs's bunch had scattered it, but all except his guns appeared to be here just the same, though it was maybe getting too dark for him to find and gather it all. He wasn't sure he had the strength to gather wood and build a fire.

The woman sat her mount beside the boy, staring stoically down at Cuno. He looked at her curiously, wondering why she didn't ride off.

The woman tossed her chin to indicate direction, and said, "We have a line shack atop that next ridge to the west. It's not far. If you can make it, you'll find wood and some canned goods. You can spend the night there. It has a comfortable bunk. I suggest you don't dally, however. My husband won't take kindly to finding you there."

Cuno studied the pretty woman. "What's your name?"

"You don't need to know that. Just know that the shack's there and you're welcome to it for a night."

She turned her horse, glancing commandingly at the boy, and said, "Come on, Hob. We'd best get back to the ranch before your father does."

The two heeled their horses back in the direction from which they'd come, leaving Cuno sitting there on the log, naked, his clothes in his lap, still too stiff and sore to move.

"Thanks again, ma'am," Cuno called raspily. "You, too, Hob. Many thanks," he added, knowing they probably couldn't hear now as their hoof thuds dwindled away in the darkness.

CHAPTER FIVE

Sam Chandler, tipped back in a Windsor chair, boots crossed on the roll-top desk in the San Juan Valley Stage Line office in Crow Mesa, jerked his head up from a nap at the rising thuds of hoof beats out on the main street. A big, bearded, middle-aged man clad in a weather-stained tan duster and low-crowned sombrero, Chandler dropped his feet to the floor and heaved his two hundred and twenty-five-plus pounds out of the complaining chair.

At first he thought the stage from San Lorenzo was rolling in but changed his mind when he didn't hear Burt Connor, the stage driver on that leg of the trail up from the railhead, yelling at his team. Instead, as the hoof thuds fells silent, he heard the voice of Lawton Briggs say, "Thanks for ridin' along, Stacey. You'd make a damned good deputy . . . if you ever care to change jobs."

Chandler stood at the office door, his hand on the knob but not turning it. He wanted to hear what Briggs and Stacey had to say to each other without them knowing he was present.

"Thanks for letting me ride along, Marshal. It makes me . . . well, it makes me feel like I'm doing something about bringing Dad's killers to justice. I can't stand sitting there in that office, just going over the books and schedules, knowing that Salmon's gang is out there, waiting to run down another gold or payroll shipment."

"I figured as much," Briggs said in his Irish brogue, above

the blowing and stomping of several horses just outside the door. "Anything to make you feel better."

"That mean I can go out again with you and your deputies?"

"Sure it does, sure it does," Briggs said. Chandler could hear the leer in the Irishman's voice. "Tell you what, why don't you join me over at the San Juan for a beer. Hot out on the trail today. Nothing like one of Pierce's cold ales to cut the dust."

Chandler gave a caustic grunt, jerked open the station's door, and stepped out onto the front gallery. Stacey sat her sorrel mare beside Briggs. The town marshal's three deputies, Travis Cole, Bonner McCallister, and Kiefer Lake, flanked them. Travis Cole's pants were charred, and his face was smudged by what looked like ash. He didn't appear to be in nearly the good mood that McCallister and Lake both were as they gazed with brash male interest at the stage line's female superintendent, Stacey Ramos.

Stacey had been about to respond to the marshal's offer, but both she and Briggs turned as Chandler walked out to the edge of the gallery, and hooked his thumbs behind his cartridge belt filled with both forty-five caliber bullets as well as paper wads of buckshot for his Richards sawed-off coach gun.

"Stage is due from Lorenzo any minute now, Briggs," Chandler said in his gravelly voice, thick and rough from all the cigarettes he smoked while riding shotgun on the stage line's coaches. "Otherwise, I'm sure Stacey would consider the offer."

Stacey scowled, coloring angrily, as she stared at Chandler.

Briggs gave a wooden smile as he held his reins up close against his broad chest. The deputies were smirking now and cutting expectant looks between Chandler and the marshal, who sat his steeldust gelding, regarding Chandler speculatively before saying, "You don't care for me too bloody much, do you, Sam?"

"Is it that obvious?"

"Sam!" Stacey said, gritting her teeth.

"No, no, no," Briggs said to her, keeping his flinty gaze on the shotgun messenger. "It's all right if he says it. I have nothing but respect for an honest man. Nothing worse than a bloke who hides his true opinions."

Briggs kept his gaze on Chandler a full ten more seconds before turning slowly toward Stacey and pinching his hat brim. "Maybe some other time—eh, Stacey?"

"Perhaps," Stacey said, the coldness of her response meant for Chandler.

"All right, then." Briggs turned once more to Chandler. "Good day, Sam. Good luck on the ride this afternoon."

Chandler didn't respond to that but only stood returning the town marshal's cold gaze. Finally, Briggs turned his horse away from the hitch rack and spurred it on up the street in the direction of the town marshal's office, his three deputies following like obedient dogs, the smirks slow to fade on their faces.

Stacey swung down from her saddle, slid her Winchester carbine from its sheath, tossed her reins over the hitch rack, and marched angrily up the gallery's front steps. She stopped in front of Chandler, her voice hard and admonishing. "What was that all about?"

"I don't like him," Chandler said mildly but giving an edge to his tone as he added, "And I don't like how he looks at you."

"What does it matter?"

"He's old enough to be your father."

Stacey chuckled. "Do you really think I'd have anything to do with that man?"

"No, I know," Chandler said. "I know what you're doing. You're doing to him what you do to those six town councilmen over yonder."

Stacey turned her head to follow his gaze to the six shopkeepers sitting out on the loafer's bench and wicker chairs fronting the land office, on the other side of the street. The broadcloth-clad businessmen sat together nearly every afternoon when business was slow, chinning in their bored, tired ways, nursing beers from the Bobcat Saloon and fanning themselves with their newspapers.

All six were aware of Stacey Ramos's presence here out front of the stage line office. They kept flicking their lusty gazes at her and shifting uncomfortably around on the bench beneath their bony asses, despite the fact that most were at least as old as Chandler and all were married.

"What're you talking about?" Stacey said in disgust.

"You bat your eyes at them and josh around with them just enough that they think in their blind male ways that you're actually interested. Or, at least that you're not *un*interested. That way you can order them around like well-broke horses.

"That's how you convinced the town council to hire Briggs, a gunman more than he is a lawman, and how you've convinced Briggs to leave no rock unturned in hunting down Jack Salmon. How you convinced Briggs to let you ride along with him and his deputies, and wreak holy hell on the countryside."

"Holy hell?" Stacey said, wrinkling her brows with incredulity. "What're you talking about, Sam? I'm looking for my father's killers. You know as well as I do they're on the lurk in this valley near the stage road. Salmon always sends at least one man ahead to sniff out information on the gold or payroll shipments."

"By the satisfied look in your eyes, I'd say you found one such man."

"We did." Stacey gave her chin a smug dip, smiling with satisfaction.

"I take it you used him to send Salmon another of your *messages*."

"Yes, we did that, too."

"Christ." Chandler shook his head darkly. "How do you know

your most recent victim was one of Salmon's men?"

"How do you know he wasn't, Sam?" Stacey said saucily.

She stepped around Chandler and went into the office, leaning over to scrutinize the edge of her roll-top desk. She brushed a hand at the fresh heel marks, and turned to arch an admonishing eyebrow at him. "You've been sleeping at my desk again."

"The back room's too hot."

Leaning in the doorway, Chandler watched her remove her hat and hook it on a rack, shake her hair out, and let it spill in honey waves across her shoulders. She pulled off her gloves and set them on a shelf above the hat rack.

"By god, you're a beautiful young woman, Stacey!"

She glanced at him wryly, then poured water from the pitcher into the basin atop the washstand. "You, too, Sam? I thought you were my lone holdout in Crow Mesa."

"Your pa was so proud of you—the way you built up this business and ran the hell out of it, grew up to be such a fine-lookin' woman. A real heartbreaker. Why, you're every bit the woman your ma was."

"Please, Sam," Stacey said, setting the pitcher back down on the shelf beneath the basin. "Don't start."

"I'm so sorry they're both not here to be with you. Your ma—hell, there was nothin' I could've done there. The influenza took her when you were still knee-high to a grasshopper. But, your pa, old Xavier . . ."

"You know I don't hold you responsible, Sam. You were Dad's best friend. Friends since you both came west after the war. If there was something you could have done, you would have." She tossed her hair back from her face and turned to him again. "Now it's my turn to do something."

Stacey lowered her head to the basin and sluiced water onto her face.

"You're going about it the wrong way, Stacey. Accosting every lone rider you and Briggs find in the valley, just assuming they're Salmon's men . . ." He let his voice trail away, and gave his head another dark wag. "It's going to lead to trouble. More than the trouble with Jack Salmon."

"How could there be more trouble?" she said, pausing as she continued to slap water to her cheeks, massaging the water into her pores, scrubbing away the trail dust. "My dad was a good man and a good driver, a man who could have kept drinking himself to death in the wake of my mother's death. But he didn't. He grabbed his second chance in life—"

"A chance that you yourself offered him once you'd built the stage line up," Chandler interjected.

She kept on going, as though Chandler hadn't said anything. "—only to be shot out of his driver's seat in cold blood." She gritted her teeth as she stared unseeing out the sashed window before her, water dribbling down her smooth, delicately sculpted cheeks. Her lips trembled with emotion. "Shot out of his seat and blown onto the trail where the coach's tires hammered the life out of him!"

Stacey's voice broke but she drew a deep breath, steeling herself. She whipped her rage-bright eyes to Chandler and said, "Jack Salmon and his entire gang must die, Sam. I won't rest until they're dead."

"What did this last guy you found look like?"

"What difference does it make?" Stacey laughed in exasperation. "You know his men come and go."

"Just because a man looks like he might ride with Salmon doesn't mean he really does, Stacey. If you and Briggs keep goin' after every lone rider packing iron out in the valley, trouble's gonna come to town in a big, big way. That's not something you can do and not pay the consequences for. It's vigilante justice. If your old man were here, he'd tell you.

"Him and me—why, we worked mining camps in Montana

and Wyoming where Judges Colt and Lynch were the only law. All that did was bring more violence, more killing. I tell you, it's not the way. We need a good lawman here in Crow Mesa. A *real* lawman. Not a hired gun. We need a man like Earp or Tilghman—or hell, a man like that old deputy marshal, Spurr Morgan—who'd follow the rule of law and bring the real culprits to justice."

"Ha!" Stacey laughed, scrubbing her cheeks with a towel. "Spurr Morgan is as old as the mountains, Sam." She turned a jeering but tender smile on the shotgun messenger still leaning in the doorway. "Older than you, even. He drank with Dad when he'd ride through here from time to time, back when I was young enough to sit on his lap, and he'd let me stick my tongue in his whiskey. He was old even then!"

"I know Morgan's no longer the man. Hell, I heard they retired him up in Denver. I'm just sayin', Stacey, that we need a real lawman here in Crow Mesa. An honest man who won't do more harm than good."

Stacey hung up the towel and swept her hair up onto the top of her head, dipping her chin slightly. "I beg to differ, Sam. I think Briggs is just the man we need here, just the man who'll help me bring the Salmon gang to justice."

Chandler watched the pretty young woman grab some pins off the shelf near the washstand and use them to secure her hair in a hastily built but businesslike bun. "You oughta be married by now—a girl as pretty as you."

She narrowed an eye at him. "Know anyone man enough?"

"No," Chandler said, chuckling. "No, Stacey, I really don't."

"Any sign of the stage?"

The shotgun messenger turned to the door. He stared to the east, up the valley, the direction from which the three o'clock stage would be rolling in any minute now from San Lorenzo. Here it would change drivers and shotgun messenger, gain or lose a passenger or two, then continue up around the west side of the Piños Altos, hitting all the mining camps before swinging back to Crow Mesa by late tomorrow.

The following day, it would head back to the railhead at San Lorenzo.

That was the loop. Mostly peaceful, it turned dangerous whenever one of the mines was either shipping gold out or payroll money in from the railhead.

"No sign of it yet," Chandler said.

"In that case," Stacey said, striding to the back of the room and through a curtained doorway, "I'll take a moment to say a few words to Dad. I didn't get a chance before I rode out with Briggs this morning."

Chandler stared at the curtain that was flopping back into place behind the girl. He walked to the doorway, slid the curtain aside, and walked on down the long hall to the back door, which Stacey was just now striding through, heading outside, leaving the door open behind her.

Chandler moved to the door and leaned against its frame. Beyond, Stacey strode along a path that wound up past the stage line's barns and corrals and windmill, toward the single, leaning cross that stood atop a low hill peppered with prickly pear and yucca, beneath the sagging branches of a lone cottonwood.

The girl climbed the hill, the sun shining brightly down on her, glistening in her hair.

When she got to the top of the hill, she dropped to her knees beside the mound of her father's grave, and the leaning cross, and she bowed her head. After a time, she raised her hands to her face. Even from this distance, Chandler thought he could see the young woman's shoulders convulse as she sobbed.

"I'm so sorry, Stacey," the old shotgunner said softly. "So, so damned sorry . . ."

A dark, ominous feeling touched him. It was a cold witch's hand laid upon the small of his back.

He turned his head to stare up at the cool, blue mountains where he knew that Briggs and his deputies and Stacey had ridden early yesterday and where something—maybe some sixth sensed acquired after all his hard years on the frontier—told him that an unseen storm might very well be brewing.

CHAPTER SIX

The night before, when Cuno Massey had managed to work up
some strength, however feeble, his body quivering in the growing chill of the descending night, he pulled on his torn and
filthy clothes. Stumbling around as though drunk, he shoved all
the strewn gear he could find back into his saddlebags, slung
the bags over his shoulder, and set out walking west.

A knot of hard rage burned just behind his eyes, aggravating
the throbbing in his battered head, as he moved up the gentle
slope of the western ridge. He had no weapons, no horse, and
his gear was a mess. All his limbs were as heavy as lead. Every
joint felt as though a nail had been hammered through it.

He had no idea how he was going to find the line shack in
the dark. The woman had said a trail led to it. The trail paral-
leled the top of the slope.

But how would he find the trail in the dark?

He probably should have built a fire in his original camp, but
he'd been too fatigued to gather wood and tend one. Besides,
he felt vulnerable out here without his weapons. There was a
chance that his assailants might return to the camp, to make
sure Cuno was still tied naked to the ground.

On any other night, that would have been just fine. He might
not have his weapons, but he had his fists, and he was confident
he could jump one of them and gets his hands on a weapon to
use on the others.

Tonight, however, no doing.

It was cold. He was battered nearly senseless, and exhausted. He needed shelter. If he could only find the line shack . . .

As he shambled up the ridge, following a crease cut by a narrow stream gurgling on his left, he shivered, bones clacking around in his body. His heart thudded heavily. His lungs felt the size of prunes. What kept him going, however, was the fire burning behind his eyes.

Sure enough, when he gained the crest of the ridge, he came to a trail—a meandering tan line in the darkness running from his right to his left. He followed the trail for a hundred yards along the lip of the ridge. He followed the trail's curve to the north, moving through a clearing lit by a star-dusted sky.

Ten minutes after leaving the crest of the ridge, he stopped. Just ahead lay the cabin—a box-like, dark shadow poking slightly out from a fringe of pines, starlight glistening dully on its shake-shingled roof.

"Hello the shack," he called wearily, not wanting to surprise anyone who might have holed up inside. After all he'd been through, getting shot by some stranger, possibly an owlhoot on the dodge, would be God's final laugh.

Save for the regular hooting of a distant owl, the night was silent. The cabin hunched darkly there at the edge of the pines, also silent.

Cuno continued forward. A worn path led to the front door, beside which sat an old chair constructed of pine saplings, with a seat comprised of thin, woven branches. A large washtub leaned against the front of the place, near the chair.

Cuno tipped an ear to the door, knocking once. "Hello?"
Nothing.

He grabbed the latch handle, turned it, felt the door ease in its frame, creaking, and opened it. Mad panting and the clattering of padded feet erupted from inside. There was a moan, and Cuno saw a shadow dashing toward him. Starlight glistened off two dark eyes.

Cuno gave a startled grunt as he jerked backward, but not before the beast—a young wolf or coyote—rammed into his left hip and sent him tumbling sideways and backward. He hit the ground hard, his tender bones feeling as fragile as holiday china.

"Christ!"

He rose onto an elbow and peered behind him. The beast's tan shadow loped off into the night.

Cuno turned to the dark door through which emanated the stale smell of pent-up air touched with the acrid odors of old fires.

"Any more of you in there?" he called.

He wasn't worried, only startled, his body aching from yet another assault. The frightened beast had likely climbed in through a broken window or under the floor and hadn't found its way out.

Cuno heaved himself to his feet, slung his saddlebags over his shoulder, shambled into the cabin, and fumbled around in the dark until he had a lantern lit and a fire going in the small, sheet-iron stove in a corner. There were several airtight tins on a shelf. He grabbed the nearest one, opened it with a knife, and gobbled up every pinto bean it contained.

Sated, feeling a little better, he fumbled out of his clothes, remaining in his longhandles and socks, and fed several split logs to the fire.

The shack was warm. It felt good. The warmth was leeching into his bones, soothing his aches and pains.

The seething knot behind his eyes, however, burned steadily. Hotly.

He sank back against the cot's sour pillow and drew the two wool blankets up to his chin. He laced his fingers together on his belly, and stared up at the ceiling.

He stared for a long time, his eyes and jaws hard. His cheeks were slightly flushed.

He wasn't seeing the ceiling. He was seeing the faces of each of the men and the young woman who'd stripped him naked and left him to die.

Jeston Taffly's voice reached into his wife's sleep, rousing her with: "Where were you yesterday afternoon?"

Olivia Taffly felt a slight rush of blood, but she kept her eyes closed, feigning a deeper sleep than she was actually in. She gave a faint, indignant grunt and rolled over, giving her husband her back. She squeezed her eyes closed and steadied her breathing, as though she were drifting back off.

Taffly placed his hand on her right arm, squeezing it gently. "You and Hob got home just before I did. I seen you from Coyote Ridge as I was ridin' back from the Soddermyers. You didn't mention bein' anywhere last night. I didn't ask because I figured it would come up, and you'd tell me."

Taffly squeezed Olivia's arm again, a little harder this time. "But you didn't." He paused. "How come?"

Olivia opened her eyes and stared at the red-papered wall before her—red with the gold of wheat stalks in gold-trimmed ovals—her heart quickening, her mind racing. Since he'd returned to the ranch only a little earlier than she and Hob had yesterday, she'd wondered if her husband had seen her and Hob returning from the west.

Well, she had her answer. And wasn't that just like him to not mention it, to wait for her to broach the subject, as though he were testing her. She supposed it was her own fault, though, for sneaking around behind his back. Sometimes she felt she had to, Jeston being the uncompromising man that he was.

And now, because he was who he was, she had to lie, because she was not strong enough to stand against him.

Olivia manufactured a smile and stretched her arms up above

Peter Brandvold

her head, moaning luxuriously as she said, "We walked down to the ravine to see if any of the raspberries were ripe. I wanted to treat us all to bowls of cream and raspberries for dessert."

"No, raspberries, huh?"

"Nope. Maybe next week."

Taffly yawned now, and rolled onto his back. Relief washed through Olivia. She thought the conversation was over, but then, a few seconds later as she tried to drift back to sleep, for only a little dawn light was touching the bedroom's single window, he said in an overly casual tone, "That's funny—I saw some ripe ones *last* week. Figured there'd be quite a few ripe ones *this* week."

Olivia opened her eyes again, tensely staring at the wall. "Really?"

"Yep."

"Hmm. I must've missed them."

"You *both* must've missed them."

Olivia drew a deep breath. "Yes, I guess we *both* must've missed them."

The bed creaked and swayed as Taffly rolled toward her once more. He scuttled closer, pressing himself up against her and sliding her nightgown up her leg. Olivia winced, then feigned another smile as she glanced at the man over her shoulder.

"Let me doze for another fifteen minutes or so . . . ?"

"Uh-uh," Jeston said, his breath warm against her ear as he slid Olivia's nightgown farther up her hips.

His hands were quick and rough. She could feel his desire pressing against her behind. "Got a long day ahead. Need a little satisfaction to get it started." He nuzzled her neck. "You don't mind, do ya? Hell, you might even enjoy it, if you give it half a chance."

He pressed his mustached mouth against the back of her neck as he shoved himself inside her. She winced again, sucking

242

a sharp breath against the pain. He grunted and slid himself farther inside her and then back out.

In again, back out.

The bed creaked and the headboard thudded against the wall. Olivia chewed her lower lip, embarrassment warming her ears. She wished he wasn't always so rough and loud about it. It was almost as though he were trying to awaken Hob. As though he were trying to prove to his adopted son how much he and Olivia loved each other. Or at least how much they enjoyed each other, though she'd rarely even come close to enjoying making love with the man.

Or maybe he was mocking the boy's disdain for him, Taffly, by coupling with his mother.

Could he be that cold? Olivia didn't want to think so, but she had her suspicions.

Taffly had adopted Hob two years ago, after he and Olivia were married, a year after her husband's death from a rattlesnake bite when he'd knelt on the ground to fix a wagon wheel.

Taffly stopped thrusting himself against her.

"Wait a minute," he said. "Hold on just one minute." He held himself inside her as he rose up to lean over her and scowl down into her face. "Hob didn't coax you into going back west and checking on that outlaw, did he?"

Olivia squeezed her eyes closed in dread.

"Oh, for Christ sakes!" Taffly yelled, thrusting against her so hard that Olivia went flying off the bed with a scream.

She hit the floor and rolled up against the wall and lay there, staring at the ceiling, dazed. Her ears rang from the assault of Taffly's shout. She saw him climb across the bed, tucking his dwindling manhood back inside his longhandles, gritting his teeth in anger.

"What did you do out there?"

He climbed off the bed and stood over Olivia, his chest rising and falling sharply. His eyes were nearly crossed, as they always did when he was in one of his rages. "You didn't turn him loose, did you?"

Olivia shoved her nightgown down her legs and heaved herself to a sitting position. "Jeston," she pleaded. "I'm convinced he wasn't one of Salmon's men."

"Oh?" Taffly's voice thundered loudly inside the small, puncheon-floored room. "And just how do you know that, Olivia?"

"I could tell," she said, knowing how feeble the explanation must sound to his ears.

Taffly jerked his longhandles up at his thighs and squatted down beside her, still looming over her, leaning toward her belligerently. "Do you have any idea what you've done?"

"I set an innocent man free, Jeston. I truly believe that."

She could hear Hob's footsteps outside the bedroom door, and called, "It's all right, Hob. Get dressed and start your chores!"

"It doesn't matter what you believe," Taffly said, his jaws so hard that Olivia thought they might snap. "Our ranch is the closest one to where that hardcase was stretched out. Briggs is gonna know it was one of us that freed him. You don't know what kind of a man Briggs is, but I do. I seen him at work in other towns. You get in his way, you do *anything* to set him off, he'll wipe you out. Hell, I got no doubt at all that him and his deputies will ride in here and burn us out for what you done."

He shoved an enraged arm and finger at the door. "What you and that disobedient brat of a son did!"

"He won't find out," Olivia said, half-heartedly. "He'll never know. The stranger is likely gone by now."

She hoped against hope that Jeston didn't think to check the line shack. She doubted it would occur to him, but she wasn't sure. For some reason, she found herself wanting very much for that handsome young stranger to shed this country unharmed. She wasn't sure why she did, but she did.

Cuno Massey might have been a big, tough-looking young man, but there'd been something in his eyes—a tenderness and even a vulnerability that went beyond yesterday's predicament—that had told Olivia he wasn't a bad person at all. That, in fact, he was a *good* person. A *kind* person. A man of integrity.

He'd just been in the wrong place at the wrong time.

Also, there'd been something haunted in his eyes.

Olivia Taffly herself knew something about inner demons . . . as well as outer ones, she thought, staring up at her husband's demonic, rage-sharp glare.

"Gone?" Taffly raged, slamming the back of his hand across Olivia's cheek. "*Gone?* You'd better hope he's not gone!"

Straightening, he picked her up by her arm and threw her across the bed, shouting, "You'd better hope he's not gone! If Briggs finds out he's still alive, you and that spoiled brat of yours as well as me—though I never did nothin' to deserve it— are gonna be burned out of our home!"

Olivia rolled wildly across the bed and, though trying to stop her momentum, hit the floor on the other side with a wail. She rolled across the floor, knocking over a night table and shattering a lamp.

Taffly grabbed his belt off a wall hook and stomped over to the door, bellowing, "Hob, get over here!"

"No!" Olivia cried, reaching for Taffly as though to stop him, but he was six feet away from her.

He flung the door open and stopped dead in his tracks, taking one step straight back. Beyond him, Hob stood in the open doorway holding his deceased father's old Civil War model Colt in both hands. He aimed the old piece at an upward slant, at Taffly's head.

Tears streamed down the boy's cheeks, and his lips trembled as he spat through gritted teeth, "Did you call me, you son of a bitch?"

CHAPTER SEVEN

Taffly stared down, aghast, at the normally mild-mannered child aiming the big pistol at him. Olivia saw the back of the man's neck and ears turn bright red.

He said, "Goddamn you, boy—don't you ever point a pistol at me! Haven't I taught you none better than that?"

Hob spat out, "You told me to never point a pistol at a man unless I intended to use it." He slid the barrel slightly left and gritted his teeth.

The old Colt roared, flames lapping from the barrel, the slug plunking into the ceiling and causing dust to rain down from the rafters. Taffly stumbled backward, holding his arms up around his head, cowering.

"Get out!" Hob shouted, more tears running down his cheeks as he clicked the pistol's hammer back. "Get out! Get out! Get out! No one ever hits my ma and lives to gloat about it!"

The boy's voice rose to a wailing shriek. "Get out now, and don't you ever come back!"

Olivia yelled, "Hob!" But she remained where she was, so shocked to see her twelve-year-old son acting this way—like a very angry and determined *man*—that she couldn't move a muscle but only watch, hang-jawed. Pride was a small bird flapping its wings in her chest.

"Give me the gun, boy," Taffly ordered, though he did not move toward the child but remained sort of leaning back against the bed. "Put it down. Now, I say!"

"No—*I* say," Hob said, giving no ground. He wagged the barrel toward the cabin's front door. "You get out of here. Go out to the barn and saddle a horse and ride the hell off of our place. This is my pa's and my ma's place. You're not my pa. You never were and you never will be. My real pa might be dead, but after what you done—and you done it before—he wouldn't want you anywhere near the ranch he built up from scratch. He'd want me to do just like I'm doin', and that's how it's gonna be. I'm running you off. You're worthless and no-good, and you're mean. If I ever see you within a mile of this ranch again, I'll shoot you in the head!"

Hob screeched out these last words again, his young voice cracking, spittle oozing over his trembling bottom lip.

"Easy, now," Taffly said, raising his hands, trying to placate the boy. "Hob, you're just riled. You don't mean what you're sayin'."

"Get out!" Hob stomped one bare foot down on the floor. "Get out now or I'll shoot you where you stand!"

He stepped back out of the doorway and to one side, narrowing one eye as he aimed up at Taffly's head.

"Christ!" Taffly exclaimed, his voice fearful. He glanced at Olivia. "Are just gonna kneel there and let him speak to me like this? Are you gonna let this crazy little polecat run me out of the house?"

Slowly, keeping her admiring eyes on her son, Olivia nodded her head. "Yes. Yes, I am, Jeston. You'd best leave now . . . while you still can."

"Go!" Hob railed.

"Ah, Jesus—you're both crazy!" Taffly exclaimed as he shuffled out the door, turning to face the boy, keeping his hands raised to his shoulders, palms out. "I never heard nothin' so crazy in all my days. Like mother like son, I reckon!"

"Get out!" Hob railed, following Taffly as the older man

shuffled backwards across the parlor's braided rug to the front door.

"Let me get dressed at least!"

"Out! Out! *Out!*" Hob screamed.

Red-faced, eyes now brighter with fear than with the rage they'd showed earlier, Taffly backed into the door and reached behind to fumble with the knob. "All right, I'm leavin'. Just take it easy with that thing. It's liable to go off!"

He managed to get the door open. As he stumbled out, drawing it closed, he yelled, "This ain't over, boy. Not by a long shot!"

He slammed the door and was gone.

Olivia, who'd walked out of the bedroom, heard Taffly's bare feet pad across the front stoop and into the yard as he ran for the barn.

Hob kept the big pistol aimed at the door. Olivia moved to his side, wrapping an arm around his shoulders. Only then did the boy lower his father's old revolver. He turned to his mother and loosed an enraged, horrified wail that quickly turned to sobs, the dam of his emotions breaking as he pressed his face against her side.

"This ain't over," Jeston Taffly snarled as he walked his clay-bank gelding up and over a low rise two miles east of his ranch.

His ranch, by god. It had become his when he'd married Olivia. He'd been working for Daniel Sherman when Daniel had died, but he'd saved some money, and he'd put it all into the Sherman Ranch, which was the Taffly Ranch now. Not only had he sunk his life savings into the ranch, he'd tried his damnedest to straighten out that kid, Hob.

Sullen little cuss . . . Who knew he had a devil inside him just waiting for its chance to show itself? This was the thanks Taffly got for taking over Daniel's thankless job of raising that polecat.

Taffly would be back for the ranch. And he'd be back to settle up with the boy and his mother, too!

Taffly winced as the horse stumbled in a wheel rut. He leaned forward and rose up in his saddle a bit, cupping his balls in his hand, cushioning them from the hard saddle. He'd been able to find no pants in the barn, only a rain slicker and an old battered Stetson of Daniel Sherman's. Riding was damned hard on a man's privates when he wasn't wearing pants but only wash-worn longhandles.

Not even any socks.

His feet were ice!

Taffly imagined wrapping his hands around Hob's throat, and smiled wickedly at the feeling of satisfaction the act itself would bring him. He wouldn't kill the kid, but he'd take him right to the edge, show him who really wore the pants in the family. And then he'd kick him out to the barn, where he'd remain for as long as he remained on the ranch.

Only Taffly and Olivia would live in the house from now on. If she wanted the kid fed, she could feed him out there with the other animals.

The clay rode up and over a pass between craggy peaks. As horse and rider started down into the next valley, Taffly saw the lights of the Soddermyer ranch house. He followed the trail down into the dark valley, shivering against the chill, flexing his toes to keep some feeling in them, and reined up in front of the cabin.

Steed Soddermyer was in his early sixties, but his hearing was still keen. He must have heard the horse approach, because his shadow moved in a window to the right of the cabin's front porch. The front door opened. The tall, stoop-shouldered Sod-dermyer ducked outside, a rifle in one hand, a hurricane lamp in the other.

Taffly could see Steed's wife, a half-breed named Wyoma,

standing in the doorway, peering over his shoulder. Taffly had been here only yesterday, returning Steed's seed bull, so they'd be surprised to see him here again so soon.

"Name yourself," Soddermyer said, setting the hurricane lamp on the porch rail to his left and taking the carbine in both hands, loudly cocking it as he sidled away from the light.

Humiliation burned Taffly's ears as he said, "Steed? Steed, it's me—Jeston."

Soddermyer came forward to stand at the top of the porch steps. "Jeston? By god, what're you doin' out so late? You got trouble?"

"Yeah," Taffly said, nodding dully, rage flashing behind his retinas.

Rage and humiliation.

He probably should have ridden to the line shack, but that would have doubled his distance, and he'd have been frozen solid by the time he'd reached it. Besides, he could get a hot meal and whiskey here. Steed always kept a bottle around, though Wyoma didn't like it much. Steed would also give him some clothes.

That would take the edge off his shame and embarrassment at having been run off his own place by a twelve-year-old kid wielding his father's old Civil War pistol.

"Yeah," Taffly said again, gritting his teeth and flaring his nostrils. "Yeah, Steed—I got trouble."

Cuno Massey woke with a start, lifting his head off his pillow and reaching for his Colt, wrapping his hand around only air. Then he remembered that the Colt and his rifle, and even the spare pistol he kept in his saddlebags, were gone.

He stared down across the end of his bed toward the shack's open door.

A tall man in a broad-brimmed hat and wool vest over a blue

calico shirt stood bathed in the buttery morning light pouring in around him. He aimed a pistol at Cuno, who steeled himself for the bullet, the fires of rage and frustration washing over him once more, remembering who had taken his guns and rendered him as defenseless as a newborn babe in the woods.

The man said nothing for several seconds.

Cuno couldn't see much of his face for the glare. Then he saw the man's lips stretch back from his teeth, as the man chuckled.

"No gun, eh?"

Cuno didn't respond to that. The man took two steps closer to the cot, and Cuno could see his unshaven face more clearly now. The man was grinning, his blue eyes bright beneath his hat. Long, red-brown hair curled onto his shoulders. He wore three holsters around his waist. The two on his hips were full. The one on his belly was empty. The gun in his fist was a Smith & Wesson Model 3 Schofield .44, silver-chased and walnut-gripped.

The barrel was aimed at Cuno's forehead.

The stranger looked around the cabin, then turned back to Cuno, frowning. "Where is it?"

"I don't have one."

The man studied him. Another grin stretched his mouth. "You don't say." He looked around again. "No rifle? No pistol?"

"That's right."

The man moved closer to Cuno and stared down at him, taking his measure. "You don't look too good. Nice-sized knot on your noggin there. You been roughed up some."

Cuno swung his feet to the floor, leaned forward, and took his head in his hands. The ache was still there, but it had abated some overnight. He'd managed to sleep fairly deeply, and he felt better for it, though he was still stiff and sore from the beating.

His hands and feet still tingled from the lack of blood.

"Who're you?"

"You first . . . since I'm the one with the gun an' all."

Cuno massaged the back of his neck. "Cuno Massey."

"Wayne Chisum."

"Well, Chisum, the place is occupied, and I'm not in the mood for company. If it's food you want, you're welcome to whatever you can find. Then kindly leave me be."

"You sure ain't very friendly."

"Nope."

"Think I'll stay for a cup of coffee, if you don't mind."

"I do mind. But, like you said, you're the one with the gun."

"That's right—I am." Chisum holstered the Schofield and walked over to the range. Keeping a cautious eye on Cuno, he opened the small stove's doors and poked around in the ashes with a stick from the woodbin. "And I got a little secret. I'll share it if you treat me nice."

Cuno narrowed an eye at the newcomer, who blew on the ashes inside the stove, coaxing several small flames to life. "You got a secret, do you?"

Chisum shoved a slender chunk of split pine onto the small flames, blew once more until the flames licked up around the new wood, and then turned to Cuno again. "You're gonna be mad."

"I'm gonna be mad?" Cuno was beginning to think this trail rider had been kicked in the head a few times too often. "What am I gonna be mad at? Maybe you're the one who's mad. Mad as a hatter."

Chisum chuckled and added a couple of more sticks of wood to the growing fire and then closed the door. He stood, grabbed a blue-speckled enamel coffee pot off a shelf, and set it on the stove. "I'm the one they was lookin' for—Briggs an' them. Briggs and that pretty Stacey Ramos and them raggedy-heeled deputies of Briggs."

Cuno looked at the man with renewed interest, glancing once more at the three pistols sheathed to the man's leather, brass-filled shell belt. "You're Salmon's scout."

Chisum laughed as he removed the cover from the coffee pot and set it on a wooden shelf. "Hold on," he said. "I'll be right back."

He went out and came back with a canteen. As he filled the coffee pot from his canteen, he said, "Yeah, I'm the scout they've been lookin' for. They killed one of Salmon's scouts a couple months back."

He chuckled delightedly again, a little girlishly for such a tall, otherwise masculine, and well-armed man, Cuno thought. "A man by the name of Ryker. Staked him out like they did you, and a mountain lion gutted him like a fish. I was the one that found Ryker. Didn't know a man had so many guts in him. I'll never forget how he looked after that lion got him, eatin' pretty much everything but his head and his bones."

He shook his head as he lidded the pot and positioned it in the center of the stove. He turned to Cuno and crossed his arms on his chest, letting his thumbs jut up across his shoulders.

He laughed again.

Cuno felt a familiar chill ripple up his spine at the images Chisum's story conjured. Images he himself had been conjuring only a few hours ago, when he'd been in Ryker's position.

"You found it funny?" Cuno said.

"No, no—not Ryker becomin' lion bait!" Chisum hurried to explain, raising his hands in supplication. "Hell, no—I got along fine with Ryker. He was never nothin' but straight with me, all the months we rode together in Salmon's gang. What I found amusing is that of all the men Briggs and them others have staked out naked as jaybirds, Ryker was the only one who really rode for Salmon."

"How many have they staked out?"

"Seven in all, I'm told."

Cuno considered that. Then he frowned at Chisum, who'd crossed his arms on his chest again. "How'd you know about me?"

"Oh, I heard 'em talkin' in town about you."

"What town?"

Chisum chuckled again in his needling way. "I think I'm gonna keep that under my hat. Don't want you ridin' in there until we've come to an agreement."

Cuno scowled, incredulous, and canted his head to one side. "What kind of agreement?"

Chapter Eight

Just then the coffee pot came to a boil. Chisum poked his hand into the Arbuckles sack on a shelf above the stove, and dropped a wad of coffee into the pot. He closed the lid and returned the pot to the center of the stove. Immediately, the pot began sighing loudly.

"Here's the deal," Chisum said, turning back to Cuno. "You throw in with us, but you stay here."

Cuno snorted. "Why would you need me to throw in with you? I'm nobody to you. Hell, I don't even have a gun."

"You won't need a gun for what you're gonna do."

"What am I gonna do?"

"Like I said, you stay here."

The coffee began boiling up out of the spout and around the lid. Chisum cursed and used a scrap of cloth to move it to the warming rack. Then he uncorked his canteen and dribbled in about a quarter cup of water. Returning the cork to the canteen and allowing the pot to sit while the grounds settled, he turned back to Cuno.

"You stay here until I come with a message from town. When I come, I'll bring you a horse and a gun. You might need a gun, after all. These is wild times, don't ya know?"

Chisum laughed at that in his girlish way. When Cuno only stared at him, befuddled, Chisum gave a rueful snort and brushed his fist across his mustache, coloring slightly.

An odd one, this Chisum, Cuno thought.

Chisum said, "When I come with a horse and a gun, I'll also come with a message. Your job will be to ride over Cavalry Peak and relay the message to Salmon. The plan was for me to do it myself, but the way it's turned out, it would look funny if I'm gone from town for that long. I sorta sunk a root there, don't ya know!"

He chuckled again.

"What town?"

"Only if you'll do it. Afterwards, you can do whatever you want, go wherever you want, do whatever you want to Briggs and Stacey and them deputies of Briggs. You don't look like a man who'd take what they did to you lyin' down, if you'll forgive the joke. Ha! But first, you take my message to Salmon and the rest of the gang."

Cuno thought it through. He knew it wouldn't be hard to figure out what town Briggs was marshal of, but he had some recovering to do. Also, he needed a horse and a gun. Normally, he didn't throw in with outlaws, but since he'd been mistaken for one, why not throw in with them?

Besides, someone had told him that the easiest way to learn about someone was to learn about his enemy.

Salmon's gang—at least one of the gang members—had been much more accommodating than Briggs had been. Besides, Briggs was no lawman. In fact, he was a man who rode around under the guise of a lawman while doing unlawful things.

Cuno had a feeling that Jack Salmon was probably the more honest of the two. Both probably needed killing, but as far as he was personally concerned, Briggs needed it worse.

Cuno shrugged. "Why not? I'm in no hurry to go anywhere . . . seein' as I don't have a horse or a gun."

"All right, then! Crow Mesa's the town."

"Crow Mesa," Cuno said, nodding slowly. He'd never heard of it, but there were lots of little towns in this neck of New

Mexico Territory he'd never heard of."

"What do you say we celebrate our partnership with a cup of hot mud?" Chisum said, gleefully filling a couple of blue-speckled tin cups.

When Chisum left, Cuno took a long nap. He was still deeply fatigued by the beating and the staking out. He woke in the late morning, got up, reheated the leftover coffee, poured himself a cup, and sat down at the table to drink the coffee and eat another tin of pinto beans.

The beans were good and nourishing, but they still left him unsatisfied.

He needed meat. Unfortunately, Chisum had refused to leave a gun with him, probably because the man wanted him to remain feeling vulnerable enough to follow through with their deal. Chisum had also not told him when he would come with the gun, the horse, and the message to relay to Salmon. He'd only said "soon."

Then he'd squeezed Cuno's shoulder, told him to get some rest, as he didn't look so good, and rode away.

Cuno looked around the cabin. There wasn't much here but a few necessities—the table, two rickety chairs, the cot, stove, a few shelves, some pots and pans, and maybe a dozen more airtight tins and a small bag of coffee. Cuno's belly growled at the prospect of having to rely solely on canned beans, tomatoes, and apricots for the next few days or until Chisum returned.

He'd probably be able to fashion a slingshot out of wood scrounged from the forest and rawhide from the cot. With that, he might be able to land a squirrel, at least. Maybe a sage hen. As a boy, he'd become handy with a slingshot as well as a bow and arrow, but he'd relied far too long on firearms. He'd be rusty.

He thought of his stolen guns again. He thought of Renegade.

Which one had appropriated the stallion? He felt a wry grin touch his mouth when he thought of anyone trying to ride the horse, as Cuno had taught the stallion to throw any stranger who tried to climb into the saddle. Of course, that could be broken out of a mount, but he felt a pinch of satisfaction at imagining Briggs's or one of his deputies' first attempt to step up into the hurricane deck.

Cuno would be glad to get back his guns and his horse. He and Renegade had been together since before his father and stepmother had been murdered, and they'd been through a lot together. They'd ridden many hard trails.

Cuno spied movement out the window to his left and instinctively slid his hand toward his right thigh, immediately remembering that the Colt was gone. Relief touched him when he saw the woman who'd ridden into his camp late yesterday afternoon.

She followed the trail through the sunlit meadow, coming at a slow curve from the east, wearing a cream blouse under a leather vest, and a green felt hat. Her skirt was the same color as the hat. Her hair was pulled into a loose horse tail curling down over her left shoulder.

A large sack hung from her saddle horn.

Cuno rose heavily, wincing as the throb kicked up in his head again, and opened the door. He stood in the doorway and watched the woman approach. She turned her head a little to one side, frowning, scrutinizing him critically.

She rode to within ten feet of the cabin and stopped the horse, continuing to regard him with curiosity as well as caution. Her lower lip was puffy on the right side. Dried blood glistened faintly in the sunlight sliding down between the pines that flanked the cabin.

"Hello," Cuno said, the first to speak.

The breeze brushed her bangs across her forehead. "Hello."

"What happened to your lip?"

Ignoring the question, she glanced down at the croaker sack hanging from her saddle horn. "I brought you a few supplies. I got to remembering there wasn't much here, and, figuring you'd need a few days to recover from your injuries, thought I'd bring over some things."

"I'm obliged." Cuno turned his head toward the cabin. "Won't you come in? The maid hasn't been here yet, but I can offer you a cup of coffee if you'll forgive the disorder."

He tried a smile on her, but she didn't respond. Stone-faced, she swung down from the saddle, unhooked the bag from the saddle horn, and walked up to Cuno, raising the sack by its neck. Her cool eyes probed his, as though she were looking for some secret message in them.

When he'd taken the sack, she said, "I could stand a cup of coffee before I head back."

Stepping aside for her, Cuno gestured at the doorway.

As she brushed past him, he enjoyed the female smell of her mingling with the sweat and the horse and leather smell from the ride over from her ranch. She moved to the table, removed her hat, hooked it on a spike in the wall, and sat in a chair.

"Still warm," Cuno said, placing his hand on the side of the coffee pot.

He filled the two cups and brought them over to the table, setting one down in front of her.

Then he sat down and said, "I don't know your name."

"Olivia Taffly."

Cuno sipped his coffee and regarded her from over the cup's rim. "What happened to your lip? Did he find out?"

"Yes."

Guilt was a sharp lance penetrating Cuno's side, twisting. He set the coffee cup down and ran a hand through his longish blond hair. "Shit!"

She looked at him strangely, as though surprised by the passion of his reaction.

"How 'bout the boy? Hob. Is he all right?"

"Hob is doing quite well." As though they'd known each other much longer than they had, she reached across the table and closed her hand over his. "It's not your fault. We had to free you. It was only right."

Cuno looked down at her hand on his.

She looked down at it then, too, as if she hadn't realized she'd placed it there. Color touching her cheeks, she slid her hand back over to her side of the table, and placed it on her coffee cup.

Then she looked up at him again with another question. "It was right, wasn't it? Turning you loose? You're a good man. You didn't deserve what they did to you. You have no involvement with Jack Salmon. Please tell me you don't."

The bayonet of guilt twisted once more, and he tried to not betray the pain with a wince. He looked down at his coffee. "It was right."

"I knew it was," she said, offering a rare, reassured smile.

"What happened with your husband?"

Olivia Taffly sighed, clearing her throat. "He saw Hob and me heading back to the ranch from the west. He was getting home about the same time we were. He figured it out. He's frightened of Briggs and the others. That was one of the reasons I rode over here, Mister Massey. I had to tell you that my husband knows we freed you. There's a chance that he'll come here, possibly looking for you, possibly because he'll want to hole up here for a while."

"Hole up here for a while?"

She paused, glanced out the window at a squirrel flickering around in a near pine, and then turned back to Cuno. With a dash of what could have only been pride and admiration, she said, "After he hit me, Hob ordered him out of the cabin at gunpoint."

"At gun—" Cuno cut himself off, grunting in surprise. "I never would have thought the boy had it in him."

"I didn't know he had it in him, either, and I'm his mother."

Cuno shook his head. She'd broken the ice between them with the same gesture earlier, so he reached across the table now to place his hand on hers, gently squeezing. "I'm very sorry for all the trouble, Olivia."

She looked down at his hand on hers. Suddenly, she squeezed her eyes closed as tears dribbled down her cheeks. Her mouth trembled.

She lifted her head, glancing desperately at the ceiling and saying in a quavering voice, "Oh, god, I just don't know what's going to happen now!"

CHAPTER NINE

Cuno rose from his chair and walked around the table to her. He dropped to a knee and, feeling awkward, always uncomfortable when trying to lend comfort, he placed his hand on her back.

She lurched in her chair with a start, and snapped a startled gaze at him.

He removed his hand, chagrined. "Sorry. I was . . ."

As she stared at him, her gaze softened. Her lips were rich and full. No more tears dribbled down her cheeks, but her wet face glistened in the light pushing through the window to her left.

"No," she said finally, in a hushed, raspy voice, her eyes boring into his. Slowly, whether unconsciously or not, she leaned slightly toward him, as though gravitating his way, needing him. Her lips opened.

Her breasts rose and fell slowly, heavily, behind her vest and blouse.

The heat of passion swept through Cuno, and he found himself leaning slowly toward her until their heads were a foot apart. They both held still for a moment, gazing into each other's eyes.

Then, as though by mutual consent, they slid their faces closer together until his mouth was on hers, his lips pressing gently against her lips, which gradually opened for him as she turned her head to one side and gave a soft groan of passion.

Suddenly, she pulled her head back. "No," she said, sucking her upper lip and shaking her head. "This can't happen."

She rose from her chair, walked resolutely around him to the door, and stopped. Cuno was still on one knee, watching her, his shoulders trembling a little with the excitement of his passion. She was beautiful and kind, and he sensed that she was as alone as he was, despite being married.

Standing just inside the doorway, she looked at him with troubled eyes, at war with herself. "I don't behave this way," she said softly, and then continued on through the doorway.

Cuno rose and followed her outside. She stood at the hitch rack, her back to him, her right hand on her horse's reins, looped around the age-silvered rack. She stared down at her hand on the reins. He could see she was trembling as though chilled.

Cuno walked to her, placed his hands on her shoulders, and turned her around brusquely, until she was facing him. He cupped her chin in his hand, and kissed her again—softly at first but then harder and harder until she opened her mouth for him, and her tongue welcomed his.

Cuno pulled his head away from hers, a thin strand of saliva stringing between their lips. "It's going to happen whether we like it or not," he whispered. "But if you really don't want it to, tell me so right now. And then climb up on your horse and ride the hell away, and stay away until I'm gone."

He heard the faint tremor in his own voice, felt the throbbing heat of raw lust down beneath his belly.

She stared up at him in shock, her eyes flicking between his own eyes, desperately probing him.

"Say it," he said, louder, startling her, so that she jerked her head back. "And then climb up on your horse and ride out of here."

"No," she said, slowly shaking her head, and placing the flat of her hand on his chest, leaning toward him. "No . . . I won't . . . I can't say it."

Cuno crouched, and, placing his left hand behind her thighs, his right hand behind her shoulders, swept her up off the ground.

"Oh!" she cried, but the look on her face was not one of dismay as she wrapped her arms around his neck.

It was a look of hunger, her eyes wide, lips parted, her swollen breasts rising and falling sharply, the pebbling nipples visible behind the fabric of her blouse and chemise. She stared up at him as he carried her into the cabin and laid her down on the cot.

They were both breathing hard now. Her hand began pulling at the buttons of her blouse, and he brushed them away. "Let me do it," he said, and went to work on the blouse.

When he had it open, he pulled the tails up out of her skirt and she lifted her shoulders off the cot as he pushed it off her shoulders. He tossed it onto a chair. She was not wearing a corset, but merely a chemise that was drawn back tight against her breasts, clearly delineating each, the nipples jutting. A strap of the chemise hung off her right, lightly freckled shoulder

He kissed her breasts through the chemise, and she ran her hand through his hair and over his ears, trailing her fingers along the sides of his face. Chuckling, she said, "I've never . . . I've never done anything like this before!"

"That's what they all say," he teased, kissing her right nipple through the chemise.

"No, it's true," she laughed, throwing her head back, enjoying his manipulations. "Never!"

He glanced up at her as he continued to suckle her nipple. "If you want me to stop . . ."

"Stop saying that," she ordered, sitting up suddenly and pulling the chemise up off her chest and over her head. As she tossed it onto the chair, her horse tail danced back down to hang over the side of the cot, and her breasts jostled.

They were rich and ripe and liberally freckled.

"Get out of your clothes," she ordered, whispering, her eyes on his bulging crotch. She cupped her breasts in her hands, squeezing. "Hurry!"

As Cuno kicked out of his boots and began shucking out of his clothes, she floundered around on the cot, grunting, kicking out of her riding boots, tugging off her stockings and getting out of her skirt and the rest of her underclothes. When Cuno peeled his longhandles off his legs and tossed them onto the table, he remembered the door.

He walked naked to it, glanced out to make sure they were alone, and then closed it.

He walked back to the cot, manhood swinging.

Olivia lay naked atop the cot, one bare leg bent toward the other one, partly concealing the tangle of light blond hair at the V between her thighs. She held a modest arm across her large, freckled breasts. The other was folded behind her head.

She stared at his midsection, smiling lustily. "Oh, my," she said.

Cuno climbed onto the cot, sandwiched her head between his forearms, and mounted her. He slid himself inside the warm wetness of her waiting portal, and held there, deep inside her, as she pressed her hands against his buttocks.

She wrapped her legs around him and kissed him, and then shoved her head slightly back away from his, gazing into his eyes the way she'd done before, taking his measure. Her eyes crossed bewitchingly.

"You are a good man, aren't you?" she asked, as though certain of the answer.

Cuno felt a tightness in his chest. He forced a smile as he

looked into her eyes, and said, "Yeah. Yeah, I'm a good man, Olivia."

"I knew you were," she said. "I knew Hob was right about you the very first time I saw you. That's why I set you free."

Again, Cuno felt that annoying tightness in his chest.

Ignoring it, he closed his mouth over hers and made love to her, unaware of the man moving through the woods toward the cabin from behind.

Jeston Taffly swung down from his claybank's back, tied the reins to a pine branch, and slid his Winchester from its saddle sheath. He stared hard through the trees toward the back of the cabin, where there was one window, on the right side, opposite of where he and Hob had stacked the wood they'd split last fall, when he and the boy had used the cabin during the fall gather.

He cursed and spat, his hands sweating as he gripped the Winchester in both hands. He'd been riding back to his ranch—*his* ranch, by god!—to take Olivia and her brat in hand, when he'd seen her ride out, heading west. Something had told him where she was heading, but he'd had to see for himself, so he'd followed her from a distance.

When it had become obvious that she'd been heading for the line shack, his hands had begun shaking. He'd known why she was heading there. She'd been heading there to see the man she'd released, probably to warn him that he, Jeston, knew.

Now as he began moving quietly through the trees toward the shack, his heart thudded heavily, determinedly. He'd recapture the man she'd freed and take him to Crow Mesa at gunpoint and turn him over to Briggs. That way, Briggs wouldn't come after Taffly and possibly burn the ranch.

The ranch, the woman, and even the boy, was all he had. He wasn't going to give them up. Not without one hell of a fight.

"Stupid bitch best thank me," Taffly muttered to himself as

he continued to close on the cabin, breathing quietly through his mouth, setting each foot down carefully so not to make any noise.

As he walked, he began to wonder what they were doing in there. From her backtrail, he'd watched Olivia ride up to the cabin a good thirty minutes ago. That's how long it had taken Taffly to leave the main trail, negotiate a creek fording, and ride around behind the shack, so he could approach with the slimmest chance of being seen. He'd half expected her to be gone once he himself reached the place.

How long did it take her to warn the man that her husband knew what she'd done?

Maybe she was doctoring him, he thought, sliding a sudden, nettling suspicion to the back of his brain.

He moved past the log he and Hob had used as a chopping block, past the single, leaning privy, and approached the cabin's rear wall, far left of the window. He'd meandered through the trees, trying to keep as many trees as possible between himself and that window, so he wouldn't be seen if the man inside . . . or Olivia . . . happened to glance through it.

Taffly drew within six feet of the cabin and walked along the rear wall, to the side with the window. He pressed his shoulder against the log wall and stopped suddenly when he heard a woman's laugh ebb through the window.

Then he heard a man's voice, muffled by the window and the stout log wall, as well.

"Oh!" the woman cried. "Oh! Oh! Oh!"

There was a thudding sound, like that of something solid banging a wall.

Taffly's heartbeat quickened, and his brows ridged as he frowned, horrified. His first thought was that the man she'd freed was killing her. But then she laughed again, and the regular thudding continued, and Taffly's ears began ringing with incomprehension.

The incomprehension was tempered with understanding.

A horrible understanding of what was going on inside the cabin.

He doffed his hat and slid his head across the frame of the window, peering into the line shack. Though he'd started to believe what his instincts told him was happening, his brain was slow to comprehend:

A naked woman bent forward across the eating table on the other side of the cabin.

A naked man, his back and bare buttocks facing Taffly, thrusting his hips against her from behind.

Taffly jerked back away from the window with a startled grunt, almost dropping his rifle. Then he spat a curse and ran around the corner of the cabin and up along the cabin's east wall.

"Bastard," he said as he ran, breathless, and pumped a cartridge into his rifle's chamber. *"Bastard!"*

He ran to the front door and reached for the handle.

Just before his fingers touched the handle, the door exploded outward and slammed into Taffly's face.

He grunted loudly and dropped his rifle as he stumbled backward, his nose throbbing and his eyes watering. The naked man bolted out of the cabin, and stooped to pick up the rifle while the woman—*Taffly's woman!*—stood back from the open doorway, her hair in disarray, clutching her blouse to her bare breasts.

CHAPTER TEN

As Taffly hit the ground on his butt, Cuno brushed dust from the man's rifle. Gritting his teeth, he moved away from the front door, and planted the rifle's sights on the man's head.

Taffly pushed up on his elbows, blood oozing from his nose and across his lips and chin. "You bastard," he said, spitting the fresh blood onto his chest. He looked past Cuno at Olivia standing just inside the doorway. "That's my wife you . . . you . . . *got* in there!"

"I'm no longer your wife," Olivia yelled in a quavering voice from the open door behind Cuno, holding her blouse to her breasts. "You hit me for the last time, Jeston. You're finished at the Quarter Circle Six!"

Taffly extended an arm and jutting finger at her. "I sunk money into that place! My own money! And I been breedin' up the stock with Soddermyer's bull!"

Ignoring the fact that he was naked, as he was getting all too accustomed to the condition of late, Cuno said, "You lost all that when you hit her. You lost your rifle here today. Now, get up and get out of here before I shoot you. You got three seconds!"

Taffly stared at the barrel of the rifle aimed at him. He looked at Olivia and then at Cuno, and scrambled to his feet, holding one hand to his broken nose. "This ain't finished by a long shot!" he yelled.

He ran stumbling around the corner of the cabin. The

crunching thuds of his footsteps dwindled.

Cuno walked over to the corner of the cabin and watched Taffly disappear into the trees, likely heading for his horse. Satisfied that the man was gone and would not be back, Cuno started back toward the cabin door.

Olivia was leaning in the doorway, still holding her blouse to her breasts. Her flushed cheeks betrayed her anxiety, but as she watched him move toward her, her expression softened. An ironic smile touched her lips. She'd taken her hair out of the horse tail, and now it hung messily down across her shoulders, still a little damp from the frenzy of their coupling.

Cuno stopped, looked down at his exposed and swaying manhood, threw his arms up, and shrugged. "Nothin' no more foolish-looking than a naked man."

Olivia chewed her thumbnail. "Some men look all right naked. You even got his rifle away from him, and you weren't wearing a stitch!" She started to laugh, but stopped. She sighed and shook her head. "I don't know whether to laugh or to cry. He would have shot us both if you hadn't seen him through the window."

Cuno walked up to her, placed his hands on the sides of her face, and brushed his thumbs across her cheeks. "But I did. He's gone, and unless he's got a pistol on his horse, he's unarmed."

Olivia shook her head. "He only carries the rifle. Jeston never liked pistols. His own father shot himself with one."

"Is Hob at the ranch?"

She shook her head again. "He's up in the higher ranges. I sent him there to get his mind off what happened last night. He's moving cattle around the summer pastures."

"Will Taffly go to the ranch? Will he wait for you there?"

"I don't think so." Olivia looked around, and Cuno could tell that thoughts and speculations were dancing around in her head.

"What are you thinking?"

Olivia looked at Cuno, frowning. "I'm thinking he's likely to head to Crow Mesa. He'll go to Briggs. He was very worried about Briggs finding out that I'd released you from their trap. I thought he *might* have gone to Briggs after last night. After today, I'm almost *sure* he will."

Cuno lowered his hands to her shoulders and pursed his lips, nodding. "That's all right."

"No, it's not all right. Cuno, you have to leave the county. If Briggs finds out you're still alive, he and his deputies will hunt you down."

"They can try. I'd like that."

She scowled, incredulous. "What?"

"Nothing."

Olivia placed her right hand on his left, atop her shoulder. "Cuno, you were planning on leaving here as soon as you could, weren't you? You weren't considering something as foolish as . . . I don't know . . . as riding into Crow Mesa? Looking for Briggs and his deputies . . . ?"

When Cuno didn't say anything, she said, "You were, weren't you? How did you think that would work?"

Cuno gave her a hard look. "If you let a man do something like what Briggs and the others did to me, if you let 'em get away with it, then they'll keep on doing it to whoever they want."

"You just want revenge."

"Of course, I want revenge. You bet I do. There's nothing wrong with evening the score. It may not be up to what's written in the Bible, but I've been to Bible school, and I've ridden the vengeance trail. Bible school didn't make much sense to me. Just words. Nice words, but words just the same. Riding the vengeance trail after my parents were murdered—that made sense."

"You obviously understand nothing about Lawton Briggs, Cuno."

"He doesn't understand much about me, either."

She gave a wry snort. "I asked if you were a good man. I guess I should have asked you if you were a *wise* man."

"Listen." Again, Cuno took the woman's head in his hands. He kissed her forehead. "I know my drifting through here has been a nightmare for you as well as for me."

"Not entirely," she interjected, pursing her lips lustily.

Cuno chuckled. "I know my drifting through here has been a nightmare for you as well as for me . . . aside from earlier today."

"Better."

"But I have unfinished business. I'm gonna finish that business before I go."

"You'll get nowhere but six feet under . . . if he takes the trouble to bury you, that is."

Cuno opened his mouth to respond, but Olivia placed two fingers on his lips. "Like I said, you understand nothing about Lawton Briggs. He may not look like much. And while I've heard he's not the best shootist the frontier has ever seen, he's probably the *meanest* the west has ever seen.

"When he finds out that you didn't die a slow death out there, he'll hunt you until he finds you. I know you're tough. I can sense that in you as well as your gentleness. And while I know little about your past, I know it was tragic. Your right thumb tells me you know your way around a gun, as well."

Cuno lifted the thumb in question, and saw the hard, yellow callus from several years of cocking the hammers of his Peacemaker and Winchester.

Olivia wrapped her hand around the thumb and lowered it, squeezing it. "But, like I said, while Briggs isn't necessarily a great shootist, he's mean. And he's cagey. Jeston told me he's tamed more than a half-dozen towns from Montana to Texas."

Again, Cuno opened his mouth to speak, and again she placed two fingers on his lips. She rose slightly on her tiptoes, sliding her face to within inches of his. "Cuno, if I bring you a horse from my ranch, will you promise to ride away from here and never come back . . . at least until Briggs is dead? Someone's likely to back-shoot him eventually. Despite how mean they are—or maybe because they're so mean—men like Briggs don't usually live that long."

"No," Cuno said. "But I'll take the horse." He smiled.

She frowned severely. "You're bound and determined to get yourself killed!"

"I'm worried about *you*," Cuno said. "How is this going to affect you? What if your husband . . . er, *ex*-husband . . . rides to town and tells Briggs what you did?"

"Briggs won't hurt me. He needs the backing of the town to keep his job, and I'm well-known in town. He knows that. He won't come after me, but he will come after you. The young woman who owns the stage line will make sure he's got plenty of help, as if he needed it. She's the one pulling Briggs's strings around Crow Mesa. The one who brought him here."

"Stacey?"

Olivia frowned. "You know about her?"

"She was with the men when they staked me out. And you're right, she was giving the quirt to ole Briggs, as if he needed it. What's got her drawers in such a twist?"

"Her father was killed on one of her coaches. He was a driver. A good one. He'd worked for a previous stage line and lost his job due to drink. Became the town's most notorious and laughable drunk, as a matter of fact. Stacey had been away at a teacher's college in Minnesota. After she graduated, she came back here to tend her father. She'd inherited money from her mother's side of the family.

"When the stage line went up for sale, she bought it—not only because it was a lucrative proposition in these parts, with all the various mountain mining camps needing a way to ship gold and payroll money—but because she wanted to give her father a second chance. Well, he got that chance. And one of Jack Salmon's men shot him in cold blood during a holdup."

"Shit," Cuno said, turning away from the doorway to walk slowly back through the cabin. He grabbed his longhandles and sat down on the cot. He'd intended to pull the underwear on, but now he found himself distracted by the girl's story.

Olivia rummaged through her clothes piled haphazardly on a kitchen chair. "She went a little crazy after that. Everyone in town thought so. She sent several regulators out to kill Jack Salmon. As though taunting her, Salmon sent each one of those killers back to Crow Mesa—belly down across his horse. After that, she sent for Briggs, and he hired deputies. None looks like much. They're from around here—ex-ranch hands—but they, too, are good with guns."

"Well, I know what that feels like," Cuno said, half-standing to shove a leg into his longhandles.

"What what feels like?" Olivia was dressing now, too.

"Having your father murdered in cold blood."

Olivia froze as she pulled a stocking up her leg, and looked up at him hopefully. "Does that mean you'll ride that horse I offered way, way away from here?"

Cuno shook his head. "It just means I know where her anger comes from. She misused it when she made sure that Briggs staked me out, naked as a jaybird. Left me out there to die slow. I'm sorry about what happened to her pa, but that gives her no right to torture innocent men drifting through the country."

"Don't tell me you're going to try to send her to the same place you'd like to send Briggs . . ."

"If she gets between me an' Briggs—sure enough, I will."
Cuno looked at Olivia, who sat down in a chair to pull her
other stocking on. "But, given what happened to her old man,
I'll give her the chance to step back out of the way. Hearing
what she's like, I doubt she'll take it."

Olivia turned her mouth corners down and nodded grimly. "I
doubt it, too."

"Olivia?"

"Yes, Cuno?"

"You and Hob best stay at your ranch for the next couple
days."

Olivia just stared at him.

"I got a feeling that after your husband gets to town—that
sounds like where he's headed, all right—there's gonna be
trouble out here in these mountains." Cuno stood and grabbed
his torn denims. "And it might be a while before it's over."

Olivia studied him sadly and with frustration. Quietly, she
said, "Ride over to the ranch with me. I'll give you a horse. No
strings attached."

"That's all right," Cuno said. "I got Taffly's rifle. For now,
that's all I need."

Guilt poked at him for the lie he'd just told this woman who
trusted him, who believed he was a good man. Actually, he
knew he had a horse on its way from town, and that he was going to ride that horse into Jack Salmon's camp, no doubt bearing information about the stage line.

He'd play both ends against the middle and hang around to
finish off the last man . . . or woman . . . standing.

Not a bad way to play it, he thought.

Even if it meant he was a low-down, dirty, rotten, lying
bastard. In this woman's eyes, anyway. She was the only one
around here he cared about.

And he cared what she thought of him.

CHAPTER ELEVEN

As he reached the ragged outskirts of Crow Mesa, Jeston Taffly's ears rang with humiliation and exasperation. A boy was playing with a dog behind the Bobcat Saloon. Both stopped and turned toward Taffly, who rode hunched low in his saddle, his mouth swollen where the line shack door had slammed into it.

Could the boy and the dog see his torn lips?

Could they see that his rifle scabbard was empty?

That the canvas trousers and wool shirt and even the hat he wore were not his?

In his half-crazed state, he wondered if the boy and the dog were somehow aware of his being kicked out of his house at gunpoint by his adopted son. Kicked out at gunpoint and in his underwear, so that he'd had to take refuge in Soddermyer's barn!

Taffly turned his head quickly forward and continued on down the broad main street of Crow Mesa. He passed the general store and the San Juan Valley Stage Line headquarters with its flanking barns on his left, and angled over toward the town marshal's office on the right side of the street, sandwiched between Howard's Drug Emporium and M.J. Vance's Tonsorial Parlor.

Smoke billowed low over the tonsorial parlor, as Vance usually had a steamer of hot water on the range for baths. Vance himself stood outside by his barber pole, leaning against his shop's open doorway, smoking his pipe. Taffly didn't look at the man directly, but he could feel Vance's eyes on him, studying him, probably scrutinizing the empty saddle scabbard and swollen lips.

"Jeston, what brings you to town in the middle of the week?" the barber asked.

Taffly kept his eyes on the marshal's office, which had a vacated look to it. There was no movement around the small, mud brick shack, and the front door was closed. No horses stood at the hitch rack fronting the place.

"Where's Briggs?"

"Him and his deputies rode out about an hour ago. Some kid from the Crown W came in yellin' about stolen horses, so they all went out, hopin' to cut 'em off before they cross the Rio, I reckon. Apaches or Mescins, most likely."

"Goddamnit!"

"What's wrong? Don't tell me you got hit by rustlers, too."

Taffly looked at Vance. "Uh . . . no, no. Leastways, it wasn't Apaches or Mescins."

He reined his horse away from the hitch rack.

"Who was it, then?" Vance, always the snoopy sort, wanted to know.

"Never mind. I'll talk to Briggs next week."

"I'll tell him you stopped by," Vance said as Taffly rode back in the direction he'd come.

"Mister Taffly?"

Taffly turned to his right. Stacey Ramos stood on the front stoop of the stage line office, holding a mess of papers against her chest and shading her eyes with her other hand. One of her two shotgun messengers, Sam Chandler, sat in one of the three chairs to the right of the door.

"What is it, Mister Taffly?" the pretty young woman asked him, frowning beneath her hand. She wore a plain, dark-colored cambric dress that hugged her comely figure enticingly. It had a white collar and white sleeves. Her gold-blond hair spilled across her shoulders. "You don't look so good, Mister Taffly. What happened to your face?"

Taffly was about to wave her off, his ears burning with shame. Since Briggs wasn't here, he just wanted to ride on out of town and go lick his wounds and sip some whiskey over in Soddermyer's barn while he pondered what his next step would be. The humiliation of his situation burned in his cheeks and made his smashed lips sting all the more agonizingly.

But then he remembered that Stacey Ramos was the headstrong gal here in Crow Mesa who was pulling Briggs's strings. She'd been the one to convince the town council to bring him here, to rid the valley of Jack Salmon. Some folks referred to her as Briggs's ramrod, though of course no one would ever refer to her that way in earshot of Briggs himself.

Taffly stopped his claybank and regarded the girl pensively. She stared at him gravely from beneath her hand. It couldn't hurt to tell her what he'd come to tell Briggs, he thought. She'd relay it to Briggs and, as bossy as she was said to be, might even insist that the marshal take action.

Taffly gigged the horse over to the office stoop, and glanced sheepishly at Vance still standing out front of the tonsorial parlor. A few other shopkeepers, some of them town councilmen, were out there now, as well. They'd likely been attracted to their stoops by Taffly's unexpected presence.

The rancher turned to Sam Chandler. He vaguely wondered, as outlandish as it seemed, if men could read another man's humiliation in his eyes, and, being able to read it, instinctively know that a woman's betrayal had caused it.

Not only a woman's, but a boy's, as well.

Taffly cleared his throat and straightened his shoulders, trying not to look so much like a truckling cur. No one needed to know all that had happened. In fact, no one needed to know *anything* of what had actually occurred. They only needed to know that the man who Briggs and Miss Ramos were after was loose and on the run.

"Had some trouble in the mountains earlier," he said. "Ran into a fella holed up in my line shack. The fella jumped me, tried to steal my horse. Managed to snatch my Winchester out of my saddle boot. While my horse was jumpin' around with me on its back, the fella threw a wild punch that somehow hit home!"

He chuckled as though at the improbability of his misfortune, and brushed his fingers across his mustache-mantled mouth. The mustache was crusted with dried blood.

"Since he had the rifle, I had no choice but to light a shuck. But I thought I'd head to town and inform Briggs. He should do somethin' about that fella. And I sure hope he can get my rifle back!"

He chuckled again, as though the situation wasn't half as tormenting as it actually was.

"Oh, well," Taffly said, starting to rein his horse away from the stage office's front gallery, "I'll maybe ride back into town next week, have a chat with Briggs."

Stacey Ramos said tightly, "What did this fella who attacked you look like, Mister Taffly?"

"What's that? What'd he look like? Oh, well . . . he was maybe just under six feet. Blond young fellow, hair sort of long. Big, stocky kid. Lots of muscle on him."

Again, Taffly chuckled and glanced at Chandler and then at Vance and the town councilmen, who were all out there now, and whom Taffly knew were listening intently to the conversation. "Damn near knocked over my horse when he was trying to wrestle me out of the saddle. I reckon I'm lucky he only got my rifle. Took me entirely by surprise, he did. Didn't look the sort when I first saw him!"

"Where's your line shack, Mister Taffly?" the girl wanted to know. Her expression was even darker than before.

She knew whom Taffly had just described, all right. She knew it was the man she and Briggs had staked out Apache-style. Taffly had pondered telling her that his wife, Olivia, had turned the young hardcase loose, but then they might suspect the other . . . and he didn't want anyone to ever know about the other . . .

He wasn't even going to relay that bit of ugliness and humiliation to his best friend in these parts, Steed Soddermyer.

Taffly told her where the shack was. He watched her draw a deep slow breath and turn her head a little, to stare off into the Palo Pintos rising spruce-green and jagged-topped to the west.

"Do you know the area?" asked Taffly.

She didn't answer for a few seconds. Then she muttered just loudly enough for Taffly to hear: "Yes, I know the area." She turned to him, lowering her hand and saying, "I'll let Marshal Briggs know. I'm sure he'll go out and find this man . . . who stole your rifle and holed up in your shack, Mister Taffly."

"Thank you, Miss Ramos. I'd appreciate that."

Taffly smiled and pinched his hat brim to Sam Chandler, who only stared at him darkly. Flushing a little with self-consciousness, wondering what the shotgun messenger's stony stare was all about, Taffly touched spurs to his horse's flanks and galloped on up the street and out of Crow Mesa, heading back into the mountains.

Stacey Ramos stared over the false façades lining the opposite side of the street from the stage line office, and into the mountains rising beyond them.

"I got me an ache," Sam Chandler said behind her.

"Oh, really?"

"Yeah. A bad one. I get it every time I see that hard set to your shoulders, and your voice gets kind of hard and low, like it just did when you were talking to Taffly."

"I know just the thing for such a pain, Sam."

"Ah, shit."

Stacey turned back to the bearded shotgun messenger, who sat back in his chair, one arm stretched out along the windowsill flanking him, one undershot boot hiked on a knee. "Don't you want to know what it is?"

Chandler looked away. "Nope."

"Well, I'll tell you, anyway. A nice ride into the mountains."

"I knew that's what you were going to say, and you're as wrong as snow in July!"

"Cooler up there. The air's lighter. That'll get rid of that ache right fast."

"You know, I never did care for that Jeston Taffly. He's got the smallest, flattest eyes of any man I've ever known, except for maybe Briggs."

Stacey turned to the bearded man again. "You think he's lying?"

"He was doing something, I'll guaran-damn-tee you that. And you are *not* going to go riding into those mountains after a man you damn near killed and who now probably has a sizable chip on his shoulder and is probably waiting for you to do just what you're considering. So I don't even have to *tell* you I'm not riding with you. Because you ain't going, see?

"Now, you might be my boss and can fire me at the drop of a hat, but as far as shotgun riders and drivers go, you only got me and Chisum, and since you got two rotations in the next week, you can't spare either one of us."

"You really have me over a barrel, Sam."

Stacey was looking at the mountains again, but she could hear the smile in the voice of the man behind her. "Don't I, though?"

She whipped around to him. "No, you don't. Because the men from the Slash Over K are in town. Leighton had to let them go. The bank is taking his ranch. They're over at the San Juan—a good dozen of them. Go over and pick out any that are sober enough to ride. Tell them I'll pay ten dollars a head. I'm going, and you're going, too, because you'd never let your best friend's daughter ride up into the Palo Pintos alone with a bunch of half-drunk, out-of-work punchers, and knowing there's likely a killer waiting for her up there.

"So you might as well get all your cussing and bucking out of your system, pull Leighton's men out of the San Juan, then go back to the barns and saddle us each a mount. I'm going to go over to the Bobcat and tell Chisum the office will be closed for the rest of the day, maybe through tomorrow morning. With any luck, we should be back by tomorrow afternoon."

"Stacey, goddamnit!"

"That's one down," Stacey said, dropping quickly down the porch steps and then striding up the street toward the Bobcat Saloon. "You have ten or twelve more to go. Why not finish them up while you walk over to the San Juan? Don't forget to make sure we each have a rifle, too, Sam!"

Behind her, Chandler cursed again.

As Stacey continued walking, she glanced again at the Palo Pintos.

How could the man who called himself Massey have got himself out of that trap? She'd watched Briggs and his men wrap the rawhide tightly about the man's wrists and ankles and sink the stakes deep into the ground.

Someone must have freed him.

Who?

The only people who lived in that section of the Palo Pintos were Taffly and his wife, the former Olivia Sherman, and her son, Hob. Of course, another drifter might have ridden through and freed him . . .

Or . . . could more of the Salmon gang be up there, certain that gold would be shipping soon?

Apprehension touched Stacey. She found herself slowing her pace as she continued to gaze into the blue-green haze of the Palo Pintos.

Did she really want to ride up there and confront Salmon? Even with Sam Chandler and a half-dozen of Leighton's men along to back her, it might not be much of a confrontation. Salmon rode with eleven of the toughest, meanest stagecoach robbers in the southwest. Several, including Salmon himself, were said to have ridden with Quantrill during the last years of the war.

Stacey picked up her pace. She had three days until the next stage came through. What was she supposed to do—wait for the man she and Briggs had left for dead ride down out of the mountains and shoot her from ambush?

No, she was going to ride up into those mountains and finish what she'd started. If she happened to run into Salmon himself, so be it. She'd prefer Briggs handle Salmon, but Briggs wasn't here. The fool had left with all of his deputies, leaving Stacey in the lurch at the worst possible time . . .

She had to take her chances. She thought it was worth the risk to wipe away the smug, self-satisfied grin likely adorning the face of the man who'd wriggled out of hers and Briggs's trap.

Also, he might be waiting around up there to find out which stage would be carrying the gold, and to relay the information to Salmon. One way or another, he had to die.

Stacey pushed through the Bobcat's batwing doors, and glanced around. The bartender, whom she'd recently hired to drive a coach for her, Neal Chaffee, stood behind his plank board bar, reading a newspaper spread open before him. A cup of coffee steamed beside the paper.

The only two customers were Doc Warren, sitting alone at the back, under a massive elk trophy and nursing a beer and a shot of whiskey, and the telegrapher, Pop Wade, whose office was just next door, close enough so that he could hear the key when it started clattering.

She nodded to Pop Wade, sitting by the window against the wall to Stacey's left, and then strode toward the bar. Chaffee was looking up at her now, still leaning over the newspaper. He worked a matchstick around between his lips.

"Now, ain't this a pleasant surprise?" Chaffee said in his unctuous way, letting his eyes flick across Stacey's chest. "What can I do you for, Miss Ramos?"

His reference letters had attested to his effectiveness at handling a stagecoach. That's why Stacey had hired him. Good drivers were few and far between. So she put up with the way the man always ogled her breasts and tried to spark her, as though he actually thought he might one day entice her into his bed in the lean-to hut off the back of the Bobcat from which the rankness of mouse urine ebbed into the main drinking hall.

"Sam and I are riding up into the mountains," Stacey told him. "I'd like you to keep an eye on the office. If anyone has a shipment or wants to buy a ticket, have them fill out one of the flimsies on my desk. I'll take their money before they board."

"You got it, Stacey."

"That's Miss Ramos, Chaffee. I'm your employer."

"Uh . . . of course." He grinned and rolled the matchstick around between his large, yellow teeth. "Miss Ramos, it is."

Stacey gave a disgusted sigh and headed back toward the batwings. Pop Wade beckoned her, and she walked over to his table. She glanced over her shoulder at Chaffee, and then leaned down, sliding her head up close to Wade's withered face, the man's upper lip mantled by a gray, pencil-thin mustache.

"News, Pop?"

Wade nodded. "I was gonna head over to the stage office to tell you, but I wanted to finish my beer. It just came in, not five minutes ago." Pop looked around to make sure no one was listening. Chaffee had gone back to reading his newspaper. Doc Warren stared with a bored air into his beer schooner, the handle of which he nudged in a slow circle.

"Thursday," Pop said, in a voice so low that Stacey had just barely heard him. "The Jim Dandy Mine's payroll, with back pay, is coming through from San Lorenzo on Thursday."

"The payroll." It was more of a quiet exclamation than a question. The Jim Dandy employed nearly fifty men. A payroll that size was a big risk for Stacey, as well as for the owners and superintendent of the Jim Dandy. They had a contract with the San Juan Valley Line, however, so Stacey had to ship it . . . and hope Salmon didn't pick that day to strike.

The problem was that even if she could find men willing to guard a coach knowing Jack Salmon's bunch was on the prowl, she couldn't afford to pay them what they'd want for such hazardous work. She was lucky to have Chandler and Chaffee. The former was here mostly out of loyalty to Stacey's dead father. Chaffee probably didn't know what he'd gotten himself in to.

The San Juan Line was teetering on the edge of bankruptcy. All because several months ago Jack Salmon had picked her line to prey on.

"Thanks, Pop."

Stacey glanced around the room again, making sure no one else had heard the private information. Since she couldn't provide more protection than that which she'd already hired, she had to make sure word of the shipment didn't get out. No one around here besides her, Wade, and Chandler must know what day the stage would be rolling "heavy."

Secrecy was her best weapon.

She thought of Salmon's man in the mountains. He was likely there to try to find out which stagecoach would be carrying gold. Stacey suspected that he might be "eavesdropping" on the telegraph wires, an easy-enough chore if you knew how to climb a telegraph pole and patch into the line with a portable telegraph box.

Or . . . perhaps Salmon had a spy here in town.

Stacey looked again at Pop Wade, who gazed levelly back at her. She trusted no one, but she thought if she *could* trust anyone, that man was Pop Wade.

On the other hand, the Jim Dandy would probably be shipping upwards of a hundred thousand dollars in gold coins.

"Keep it under your hat, Pop," Stacey said, smiling but filing her words to a slight, vaguely threatening edge.

She glanced once more at Chaffee, who was still absorbed in his newspaper, and then at Doc Warren, lifting his beer schooner to his lips.

Stacey swung around and left the Bobcat.

She did not see Pop Wade look at Chaffee, who had been gazing at Stacey's rump as she'd left the saloon.

Chaffee returned the telegrapher's look and grunted a clipped laugh before shaking his head and returning his eyes to his newspaper.

Chapter Twelve

Cuno had found his makings pouch among the belongings that had been strewn around his camp by Briggs's bunch. He'd shoveled them back into his saddlebags. Now, sitting in the rickety chair out front of the line shack, boots crossed on a log before him, he rolled the quirley between his lips, sealing it.

He struck a match to life on the side of the chair, touched the flame to the quirley, and sucked the smoke deep into his chest. He coughed a little when the astringent smoke hit his lungs. He'd never really taken to smoking, and hadn't wanted to. As a bare-knuckle fighter back in Nebraska, he'd known the value of good lungs.

When he smoked, it was mostly out of boredom, and that's what it was now.

He pulled the quirley out of his mouth and blew the smoke into the afternoon breeze. He was about to take another drag off the cylinder, but stopped his hand six inches from his mouth. He looked around. The birds and squirrels had fallen silent.

None were in sight. It was as though the forest had been abruptly deserted.

Immediately, he dropped the quirley on the ground and mashed it out with the heel of his boot. He reached back to grab the carbine he'd taken off of Jeston Taffly, and quietly pumped a cartridge into the chamber. He drew the cabin door closed and then stepped back around the left front corner, staring off toward the trail curving toward it from the clearing fifty yards beyond.

He could see nothing out there except the sun-sprayed mountain sage and wheat grass, and the tan curve of the trail itself curving into the trees, toward the cabin. Black flies hummed in the brush around him. That was the only sound.

Cuno pressed his back to the cabin wall.

He looked around, his eyes catching on the man in a Plainsman hat and red neckerchief aiming a rifle at him from beside an aspen roughly thirty feet away. Cuno jerked to his left just as the rifle cracked and flames lapped from the barrel.

The bullet slammed into the cabin's log wall with a loud, dull thud.

Cuno snapped his recently appropriated Winchester to his shoulder. He hadn't fired the strange rifle, to get the feel of it, because all the ammo he had were the nine rounds in its magazine. He fired now, aiming at the shooter's head, and watched the bullet punch through the man's throat, flinging blood and viscera and likely bits of spine out behind him to splatter onto the forest floor.

The man threw his head back, making choking, gurgling sounds as he dropped his rifle. As he staggered backward, falling, more rifles crackled in the woods, several bullets just now plunking into the cabin wall, to either side of Cuno. One clipped a log six inches above his head.

"Get him!" someone bellowed.

Calmly, Cuno dropped to a knee, took careful aim at a man standing beside a bullet-shaped boulder fifty feet away and to the left of where the first man had fired, and blew the man's hat off. He must have grazed him, to boot, because the man gave a yowl and tossed his head as though he'd been bitten in the ear by a blackfly.

Cuno pumped another round into the chamber, and shot the man again, in the small of the back as the man turned, throwing him straight forward and down with another yelp.

Rifles cracked loudly, echoing, bullets hammering the side of the cabin and throwing doggets of wood this way and that. Cuno turned toward the back of the cabin and took off running as fast as he could, pumping his arms and legs, wanting to get away from the cabin and into the brush where he'd at least have a fighting chance against the men who obviously outnumbered him.

How badly he was outnumbered, he didn't know. But his staying in the cabin would only have given them the option of burning him out or waiting until he was out of ammo, which wouldn't be long. Then they could shoot him out or drag him out.

As he ran out from the side of the cabin, shouting, the thunder of more rifles rose on his left, from the cabin's far side. They'd surrounded him, he could see now as puffs of smoke billowed in the tangled brush and secondary growth nearly straight out away from him, as well. He caught sight of one man ahead of him—a short man with a blond beard and wielding a Henry repeating rifle.

Cuno drew up behind a fir as the man fired the repeater into the opposite side of the tree. Cuno stepped out from behind the tree, aimed quickly, and shot the man with the Henry just as he was pulling back into a willow thicket.

The bullet tore into the man's left shoulder, spinning him around. He dropped the rifle. Cuno ran, hearing the crackle of rifle fire behind him now and to his left, while men cursed and shouted and a young woman's voice rose, distinct from the men's—"Get him, goddamnit! Don't let him get away!"

Stacey . . .

Cuno almost grinned at the girl's formidable, resolute anger that had compelled her to take to the mountains after him again. On the other hand, he knew the burning need to seek revenge.

A need that almost became a sickness at times, sometimes clouding your judgment.

He wondered if Briggs was here. Something told him he wasn't, or he'd have likely seen him or heard him by now . . .

The blond man was rolling on the ground behind the willows, clutching his shoulder. Cuno stood over him. The man glared up at him, rheumy-eyed, as though he were half-drunk. Cuno almost shot him but then, for some reason he wasn't sure of, maybe because he had nothing against this man personally, he eased his finger off the Winchester's trigger, picked up the Henry, and resumed running through the woods straight out away from the cabin.

"He's here!" the blond man shouted, his voice pinched with misery. "Here! He's here . . . runnin' north." He laughed miserably. "*Look* at the son of a bitch go!" He gave a yelp, then shouted, "Goddamnit—don't shoot *me*, you crazy bastards!"

Cuno traced a winding course through the woods, leaping deadfalls and ducking beneath low-hanging branches. Ahead, a ridge rose steeply toward rocky outcroppings studded with dwarf firs and cedars twisting up out of cracks in the bedrock. Cuno ran up the steep incline, angling toward the right, where sandstone poked like a thumb out of the slope, about forty feet up from the ridge's base.

He slipped behind the sandstone thumb, racked a fresh round into the Henry's chamber, and slid a glance down the incline where two men were just now running out of the woods toward the ridge. Cuno aimed, and fired. The man in a black hat and green neckerchief yelped and clutched his knee, falling and dropping his Winchester.

The other man dodged behind a fir bole.

Cuno held fire, not wanting to waste a shot. He'd gotten rid of the Winchester he'd appropriated from Taffly, because he'd known he had only a couple of more rounds in its magazine.

The Henry held sixteen shots. While he didn't know how many rounds its owner had snapped off, he thought there was a good chance he had more rounds at his disposal than he'd had with the Winchester.

Cuno looked behind him. A game path curved up the side of a bulging belly of dark, moss-spotted granite. Taking the Henry in one hand, he started up the steep incline. He was about to curve around behind the stone belly, when something hot ripped across the outside of his left thigh.

A rifle's bark followed a half a wink later, as Cuno's left knee buckled and hit the ground. Cursing as he rolled onto his side, he looked behind him and down through the corridor in the rock he'd just threaded, to see the girl, Stacey, standing beside a slender pine at the base of the ridge, calmly cocking another round into her Winchester's chamber and staring up at him coldly.

As the girl snapped her rifle to her shoulder once more, aiming up the ridge toward Cuno, he jerked his head back. The next bullet tore up dirt and gravel just above him.

The rifle's blast echoed wickedly around him.

The echoes hadn't finished chasing themselves around the ridge before he lurched to his feet, clutching his left leg with that hand, and began running as quickly as he could up the steep incline, dodging behind trees and boulders.

The girl's Winchester—at least, he assumed it was hers— barked quickly and wickedly, the slugs spanging shrilly off rock. As he ran, gritting his teeth against the searing pain in his leg, Cuno glanced behind him again. For the moment, he was out of danger, as the shoulder of the rocky slope was between him and the girl with the big chip on her shoulder.

Cuno continued climbing through the trees.

He heard men's voices behind him, but they weren't growing any louder. The girl must have called off the pack, knowing that

Cuno had the high ground and could pick them off easily as they climbed the slope beneath him. She was probably also hoping that since he was wounded, he'd go to ground out here and die up here among the rocks and gnarled cedars, with only the vaulting, impersonal sky for company.

When he could see the crest of the ridge through the taller pines above and beyond him, Cuno stopped and sat down on a large root humping up out of the ground. He stretched his left leg out and looked at the wound that had carved a nasty, bloody gash across the outside of that thigh.

"Bitch," he snarled through gritted teeth. "Goddamn little cold-hearted bitch!"

She didn't know a thing about him. Only that he'd been out here alone where Jack Salmon was known to send men to scout the stage trails and fish for information on gold shipments.

Easy pickings.

An easy target for her overzealous vengeance quest.

While he hated her with a blue fury whirling through his brain and setting his eyes on fire, he admired the girl, as well. She was out to avenge her father. She was going about it wrong, but anyone had to admire her selfless determination. Cuno knew something about that himself. The only difference: he'd have made damned sure he was after the right man.

That she hadn't, burned him no end. Removing his bandanna from around his neck, he threw his head far back and bellowed, "You fuckin' bitch—I'll see you in hell!"

The words echoed for a long time.

Then there was silence before the girl's voice rose, muted with distance but shrill, just the same: "I can't wait!"

". . . wait . . . wait . . . wait . . ." came the echoes.

Despite his fury, Cuno had to give a wry chuckle as he wrapped the bandanna around his leg and knotted it tight.

Something in him hoped he wouldn't have to kill her. But something in him also told him she wouldn't give him a choice.

CHAPTER THIRTEEN

Cuno dragged his wounded leg up the slope and then hunkered down at the crest, facing the downslope with the cocked Henry in his hands. He stared down through the rocks and trees, wondering if Stacey would send her men after him.

He wasn't sure how many she had left. He'd taken three, possibly four out of commission. He'd estimated that there were no more than seven or eight to begin with, which would leave no more than five.

As long as they didn't work around him and get behind him, he'd be all right. If they came up the slope, he'd pick them off one at a time. As long as he didn't run out of ammo, that was.

For a long time the only sounds were the breeze and the occasional peeping of a chickadee or the cawing of a hawk. Then, after a half hour at least, the low rumble of galloping hooves sounded in the far distance, back in the direction of the line shack.

Stacey and her attack dogs were retreating.

At least, they wanted him to believe they were.

Cuno used the Henry to hoist himself up off the ground and then, keeping his wounded left leg as stiff as he could, he negotiated the steep slope, having to take the descent at shallow angles to prevent gravity from hurling him straight down to the bottom. It took him twenty minutes to work his way back down to the base of the mountain, and by the time he did, the wound burned and blood oozed out from around the bandanna. Sucking air through his teeth, he retied it, then began shambling slowly back through the woods in the direction of the line shack.

He knew he shouldn't be in a hurry to return to the cabin. Stacey might have left a couple of men there, waiting for him. But he had to tend the wound or bleed to death. He had no choice.

Slowly, looking around carefully, he headed back through the trees. The only movement around him came from small birds and breeze-ruffled leaves. Finally, the cabin came into view. He paused to study it. It crouched there at the edge of the clearing, sun-dappled but with an air of menace now in the aftermath of the fusillade.

At least from the outside, it appeared vacant.

Cuno gritted his teeth as he continued forward. He moved around to the front of the shack. Finally, he went inside. The place was empty. He heaved a sigh of relief and slacked down onto the cot, his heart fluttering. He fell back against the pillow.

He had no intention of falling asleep, but that's what he did.

Hoof thuds woke him. He lifted his head, frowning, disoriented. A horse was galloping toward the line shack.

His heart quickening, Cuno grabbed the rifle from where it had fallen to the floor, and pumped a round into the chamber. Then he used the long gun to hoist himself up off the cot with a grunt. Before he could fully rise, however, the hoof thuds stopped just outside the shack. There was the squawk of tack leather as the rider dismounted.

Running footsteps, the sounds of strained breaths . . .

Then she stood in the doorway, breathless, staring at him, her wide eyes bright with fear.

"Cuno!"

Olivia Taffly moved toward him, her hair fluttering back behind her in the breeze. Cuno sighed and sagged back down onto the cot.

"Oh, Christ . . . I thought . . ." He looked at her as he sat there on the edge of the cot, extending his leg out at a stiff angle. "What're you doing here, Olivia? You shouldn't be here."

"I heard the shooting all the way back at the ranch. My god—it sounded like a war. I packed a few things and saddled a horse." Olivia turned and ran back outside, reappearing a moment later with a carpetbag in one hand, a burlap sack in the other. She slung the burlap sack onto the table, then dropped to her knees between Cuno's spread legs, setting the carpetbag down beside her.

"How bad are you hurt?"

"It's just a burn."

"Looks like more than just a burn to me."

"Only clipped the side of my leg. Bullet passed through." Cuno gritted his teeth. He felt as though a large, tender heart were beating in his thigh, just above the knee. "But it's barkin' like a son of a bitch!"

"Get out of your pants."

He looked at her as she began rummaging around in her carpetbag.

"Come on, come on!" she urged. "Get 'em off or I'll cut them off. We have to get the bleeding stopped, the wound cleaned, and stitched!"

"Shit, you think it needs stitches?" he said, unbuckling his belt.

"Most likely. I could cauterize it if I had a hot knife, but it would take too long to get a fire built up in the stove."

Cuno wrestled out of his torn and soiled denims. Olivia helped him. She glanced at the bloody leg of his one-piece underwear.

"You're going to have to get out of the longhandles, as well."

Again, he looked at her dubiously.

She gave him an ironic scowl. "It's not going to be the first time I've seen you naked. In fact, the first time I ever *saw* you, you were naked. Rather impressively so, I might add."

She bit her lower lip, eyes flashing up at him lustily as she pulled several flannel bandages out of the carpetbag, several small bottles and ointment tins spilling out onto the floor as she did.

"Yeah, I've been naked so much lately, reckon I should've got used to it."

She helped him peel the skintight, sweaty longhandles down his arms and chest and then down his legs. She mopped up the blood around the wound with the garment, rolled it into a bloody ball, and tossed it toward the door.

"Hey, that's the only longhandles I got!" Cuno protested.

"I'll fetch you a clean change of clothes from the ranch, once I've got you sewn up. My late husband was roughly your size."

Olivia took a swatch of flannel and laid it gently over the wound. Then she pulled a pint-sized whiskey bottle from the carpetbag, popped the cork, and dribbled whiskey onto the flannel until it was soaked.

A renewed, as well as an added, burn kicked up in the wound.

"Here," Olivia said, extending the bottle. "Take a drink. Better take a big one."

Cuno took the bottle and threw back a good third of the whiskey in it.

Soothing . . .

He drew a ragged breath and tensed, leaning his head back against the cot, as Olivia pressed the whiskey-soaked cloth deeper into the wound, soaking up the blood that had partially jelled, and sterilizing the cut. She continued to clean the wound with fresh swatches of whiskey-soaked flannel for another ten minutes, working gently.

As she did, Cuno felt a flush rise into his cheeks as he registered a warm stirring in his loins. He wasn't sure how it could be happening, but the woman's gentle hands, and even the burning in his thigh, had somehow stimulated him.

"My," Olivia commented. "I think you're going to live, after all."

"Ignore that," he said, staring up at the ceiling, embarrassed. "Don't know what gets into the fool thing sometimes."

"You're young and strong," Olivia said. Suddenly, he felt her warm lips on him, causing him to grow even harder. "And you like the touch of a woman's hand, even if it's to clean a wound. I'm flattered."

She briefly suckled the head of his manhood, teasing him, enjoying him. He wanted her to continue, but she stopped, frustrating him, and finished cleaning the wound with the whiskey.

When the blood was gone, Cuno looked down, disregarding his erection, to inspect the wound, which was a gouge across the front of his thigh, roughly the length and breadth of one of his index fingers. A clean trough with ragged edges, pink now after Olivia had cleaned the wound. A little blood welled up from inside it, but Olivia placed a dry swatch of flannel over it.

"Hold that there."

Cuno held the flannel in place. She removed a small, leather sewing kit from the carpetbag, threaded a needle with catgut, and then sterilized the needle with whiskey.

Chuckling, she glanced at his still-erect penis, and said, "Let's see what effect this has on your problem there."

As soon as she removed the flannel, pinched the wound closed, and poked the needle through small flaps of ragged skin, his erection dwindled. He lay back against the cot, gritting his teeth as she sutured him. He tried to keep his mind off the pain, but half-consciously he counted the sutures until she stopped at ten.

"There, that should do it," she said, gently dabbing Arnica

over the wound.

"Thanks," he said with a sigh, pushing up on his elbows and regarding the fresh stitches. The wound was as ugly as hell, and from past experience with bullet wounds, he knew it would ache and burn and then itch, and when the itching stopped, he could cut out the stitches.

He rolled onto his side and watched as she gathered her things and cleaned up, tossing the bloody bandages out on the ground by the door.

She came back into the cabin, turned to him, folded her arms on her chest, and leaned against the doorway, regarding him wistfully.

"Briggs?"

"Stacey."

Olivia frowned. Then she nodded. "Oh . . ."

"She's out to avenge her pa."

"Yes, she is. Rather headstrong in that regard," Olivia said. "Will she be back?"

"I don't think so. I think . . . at least, I hope . . . she assumes I'm dead. She knows she hit me, anyway. She doesn't know about you, so she probably assumes I bled to death. Not that I don't appreciate the help, but you'd best leave here, Olivia. Just in case she sends someone to see if I made it back to the cabin."

Olivia studied him darkly, her ripe figure silhouetted by the doorway. She wore a tan blouse and a long, burgundy skirt with black, side-button boots.

She moved forward, stood over the cot, staring down at him as though deeply troubled, and began unbuttoning her blouse. "I'd like to," she whispered. "I'd like to ride away from here and never think of you again, Cuno."

She shook her head as she let the blouse slip from her shoulders. She lifted her chemise up over her head, baring her breasts. "But I can't."

CHAPTER FOURTEEN

"Well, that was pretty," Sam Chandler said as he and Stacey Ramos, riding at the head of the pack of shot-up riders, rode into the outskirts of Crow Mesa.

"Shut up, Sam. Just shut up. I don't want to hear about it!"

He glanced back at the four men riding upright in their saddles. Three of the four were riding double, with a wounded rider mounted behind them, groaning or, in his case, cursing through taut jaws as he held a bloody hand to the side of his neck.

The fourth man was pulling two horses by their bridle reins, their dead riders slung belly down across their saddles. He was Dick Jurgens, former ramrod out at the Slash Over K before the ranch went belly up and he and the others were given their time and sent packing. They'd got as far as the San Juan Valley Saloon in Crow Mesa, and that's all the farther at least three were going to get.

The man with the neck wound would probably join the three dead men soon; he'd been bleeding so steadily as they'd ridden down out of the mountains, through the cloth he held to his neck, that Chandler thought he might have only a pint or two left in him.

The other three wounded would likely make it, as they'd mostly been winged. In a couple of cases, Chandler knew, they'd mistakenly shot each other as their quarry had unexpectedly run straight out behind the cabin and into the forest, so that the outlaws who'd surrounded the shack were shooting at each other as they'd fired on the man they'd been stalking.

Chandler chuckled darkly as he glanced at the dead and wounded behind him, and wagged his head.

"I said shut up, Sam," Stacey said tightly, her cheeks flushed with embarrassment and anger.

"I didn't say nothin'!"

"Good! Don't say any more!" She looked at Chandler. "I told you to rustle up the ones that were sober," she accused.

"Yeah, well, they all wanted to come . . . to impress the pretty Stacey Ramos, don't ya know. They were in no condition to take no for an answer." Chandler glanced back at Jurgens riding off the left hip of Chandler's speckle-gray. "Ain't that right, Dick?"

"They all wanted to come, all right," Jurgens said evenly, staring straight ahead. He was in little better mood than Stacey was. "It's their own damn fault." Now he looked at Stacey. "But I would have liked to have known what kind of man we were going after. You didn't say he was crafty."

"You knew he rode with Jack Salmon, and I told you he'd managed to get himself out of Briggs's bindings," Stacey spat at the man. "I didn't know I had to draw you a picture to get across he was *crafty.*"

Jurgens spat to one side in disgust.

As the pack pulled into Crow Mesa's main business district, Stacey saw Briggs and his three deputies just then riding into town from the opposite end, angling toward the town marshal's office. Like Stacey and her own raggedy-heeled pack of men, they were liberally coated in trail dust. Unlike Stacey's gang, however, none of Briggs's men appeared wounded.

As Stacey angled her horse over toward Doc Warren's office, which was housed in the second story of Hendrickson's Furniture Store, two doors away and on the near side of the marshal's office, Briggs saw her and rode toward her, his deputies following from several feet back, canting their heads with interest to appraise the motley men flanking her.

Briggs scowled dubiously from beneath the narrow brim of his bowler. Dust clung to his pewter brows and pewter muttonchops. His hollow-cheeked face was tomato red from fresh sunburn, his nose badly peeling.

"What in the hell do we have here, milady?" Briggs asked in his patronizing Irish brogue. "What on earth have you done to these poor boys? Why, they look like they've been through a hurricane spitting lead!"

As Jurgens dismounted to help the wounded down from the horses they were riding double on, Stacey narrowed her eyes at Briggs and said, "I had to find *someone* to go after the Salmon rider you left alive up in the Palo Pintos. He got out of your bindings and Jeston Taffly saw him holed up in his line shack. He stole Taffly's rifle and *tried* to steal his horse."

Briggs stared back at her mildly.

Stacey continued with: "Since you took all three of your deputies out after rustlers and left us high and dry here in Crow Mesa, I had to do *something*!"

She stopped. Briggs continued to stare mildly back at her. That seemed to annoy her.

"I hope you at least got your rustlers, Marshal Briggs . . . since you took the entire police force of Crow Mesa out after them. Shouldn't that be up to the county sheriff over in Socorro, anyway?"

Briggs shaped a slow smile. Several shopkeepers had come out onto their boardwalks to see what all the yelling was about. No one said anything. The only sound came from the horses shifting their feet and the groans of the wounded men being led by Jurgens and Doc Warren up the steps toward his office.

Jurgens stared warily back over his shoulder at Stacey and Briggs.

Chandler felt a burning in his belly.

"Well, you know your jurisdictional law right well, Miss Ramos," Briggs finally said, glancing around at the shopkeepers and then over at Sam Chandler sitting his horse beside Stacey. "The sheriff indeed would take care of things out in the county. But I think you know as well as I do that since Socorro is fifty miles from here, and the sheriff is not only old but a useless drunkard and it would take him nigh on three days just to ride from Socorro to Crow Mesa, I usually ride out when there's trouble—rustling trouble and *stage* trouble—near Crow Mesa."

Chandler turned to his feisty employer and said reasonably, softly, "You know that's how it's always been done, Stacey. Rustling can't go unchecked."

"No, but only because the ranchers hold so much power. All I have to say to you, Mr. Briggs," Stacey said, raising her voice again, cheeks flushed with anger, "is you'd best remember who brought you here. If you continue to prove yourself as ineffective as you've so far proven, I'm sure it won't take much convincing to get the city council to ask for your badge."

She glanced at the six city councilmen sitting where they usually sat this time of the day, on one of the boardwalks on the north side of the street. They all stared dubiously toward the hub of activity, the center of conflict. Now one of them slowly rose from his seat, glanced at the others, and slowly retreated into his shop, quietly closing the door behind him.

Stacey continued to glare at Briggs. The town marshal only gazed back at her with that weird, one-quarter smile on his mouth. His deputies glanced around at each other, darkly.

Finally, when Briggs didn't say anything more, Stacey chuffed in disgust and reined her horse toward the stage line office, ordering, "Stable my horse, Sam."

Chandler turned to Briggs, and offered a strained smile of his own. "She didn't mean it, Marshal. She's just high-strung, that girl. I'll see that she apologizes."

Chandler pinched his hat brim to the man, then rode over, grabbed the reins of Stacey's horse from the hitch rack, and led the mount around behind the stage line office toward the barns and stables.

Briggs glanced around at the shopkeepers eyeing him warily once more. Then he turned to his deputies and said mildly, "Let's get back to the office—shall we, gents?"

He turned his horse around and rode back over to the town marshal's office, the three deputies following without saying anything. A tense silence not only hung over them but the entire rest of the town.

Briggs reined up at the hitch rack and swung down from the saddle.

"Gentlemen," he said, "will one of you be kind enough to unsaddle and stable my horse for me?" He patted his horse's rump and smiled at Travis Cole, who regarded him skeptically. "Be sure to comb him out, too, will you, boyo? Especially his tail." He ran a gloved hand through the horse's tail. "Seems to have picked up quite a few burrs in those briar patches we rode through."

"Where, uh . . . where you goin', Marshal?" asked Cole with a tense smile.

Briggs stared toward the stage line office, and scratched his chin with his index finger. "I think I've, uh . . . done something to offend Miss Ramos. I'm going to go on over and see if I can't extend the old olive branch. Can't have the girl mad at us, now, can we, gents? Hold down the fort, buckos!"

He flashed a darkly pleasant smile and then carefully adjusted his hat and started walking down the street, angling toward the two-story stage line office. The deputies watched him in hushed, incredulous silence as he mounted the stage line office's front stoop, knocked on the door, and let himself inside.

"Miss Ramos?" he said quietly, looking around at the comfortably furnished front office—a roll-top desk on the right, a leather sofa and a rocking chair to the left, a cold stove in the corner. A large, framed map of the stage line's several forking routes hung on the wall above the desk.

Stacey Ramos was nowhere in sight.

Footsteps sounded in the rafters over the town marshal's head.

Briggs looked up at the ceiling. A nerve twitched high in his right cheek, and he brushed his hand slowly across the back of the Windsor chair fronting the desk as he made his way toward the back of the room, where a small door near another, curtained doorway led to a stairway that, he knew, would take him to Stacey Ramos's own private living quarters on the second floor.

He stopped when the office's front door opened behind him.

He turned, his hand instinctively going to the Colt holstered on his right thigh. He left the gun in its holster when he saw Sam Chandler walk in, ducking his head and doffing his hat, regarding Briggs with wary shadows behind his eyes.

The shotgun messenger closed the door, pegged his hat, hooked his thumbs behind his cartridge belt, and said, "Help you, Marshal?"

Briggs smiled. "I'm here to have a chat with our girl, Sam. Don't worry—I know the way."

He turned toward the rear door but stopped again when there was the *snick* of a gun being unholstered, and Chandler said, "Hold it, Marshal."

Briggs turned back to the grizzled, bearded man who appeared somehow too tall and bulky for the strength of his old bones, the shoulders sagging forward, back slouched, knees slightly bent.

"I can't let you go up there," Chandler said, aiming the long-barreled Smith & Wesson at Briggs's belly.

"Now, Sam," Briggs said, "I just want to have a chat with Little Miss, is all." He chuckled, but it sounded like a quarter-stroke of a whipsaw in green wood.

Chandler shook his head. "No. You take another step toward the door, I'll shoot you. I know what kind of a man you are, Briggs. I never wanted to bring you in here in the first place. I know she piss-burned you out on the street, and you're not accustomed to taking grief from a woman. So . . . you take another step toward that door, it'll be the last step you take."

"You're making a mistake, Sam."

"I've made 'em before. I'll make 'em again."

Briggs shrugged, and sighed. "All right."

He started toward the door. Chandler stepped to his right. He couldn't move far because of the desk chair. He narrowed a wary eye as he kept the S&W aimed at Briggs's belly. Briggs traced a straight course toward the door, holding his dark gaze on the taller, older man.

"Keep goin'," Chandler said as Briggs drew even with him.

"I'm goin'," Briggs said.

But then he stopped and made a swift chopping motion with his left hand, smashing the edge of that hand against Chandler's wrist, knocking the revolver from Chandler's grip. It hit the rug beneath the men's boots. Briggs swung his right fist against Chandler's left cheek, slamming the man back against the chair and the desk.

Chandler groaned, and tried to regain his feet, but Briggs was on him, smashing his face with another right cross. Then another . . . and another . . . and another . . . hammering away at the older, bearded man's face, his own jaws set hard, his eyes like flint, the left eye twitching at the corner.

Finally, Briggs stepped back. Chandler rolled down off the desk and hit the floor with a hard thud, groaning, writhing, only half-conscious. Blood dribbled onto the flowered rug from the cuts on his cheek and smashed lips.

Briggs heard footsteps on the stairs. The door at the back of the room opened. Stacey stood at the bottom of the stairs, her eyes growing wide as she saw Briggs standing over the groaning and writhing Sam Chandler.

"What in the hell is . . . ?"

Then she saw the dark look on Briggs's face. She wore a fur-trimmed housecoat, and her hair hung messily down across her shoulders, as though she'd been preparing herself for a bath. Briggs moved toward her. Stacey gasped, stepped back, and slammed the door.

Briggs could hear her quick, frightened feet hammering the stairs.

Briggs ran to the door, jerked it open, and fairly hurled himself up the narrow staircase. Near the top, he flung himself upward, and grabbed Stacey's bare left ankle just as she cleared the highest step.

The girl slammed to the floor with a scream.

"Help!" she cried. "Help me!"

Briggs gained the top of the stairs. Stacey tried to stand, but he grabbed the back of her neck, pulled her a little farther into the parlor of her private quarters, and slammed her back down onto the floor. He kicked the door closed, shot the bolt, and stood over Stacey, who was in a half-sitting position, gazing up at him with terrified eyes.

The robe was half-open. She wore only a camisole and white drawers. Her bare legs were pale and supple.

"Get out of here, Briggs! I'm warning you. Get out of here *now!*"

She tried to crawl away, toward where her gun belt hung

from a wall peg.

Briggs took three strides toward her, grabbed her right ankle, and pulled her back. Her face hit the hard wooden floor, and she screamed again.

"Help! Someone help me!"

Briggs threw himself onto her back, pinning her to the floor.

"Get off me, Briggs! Get off me now! I'm warning you!"

"You're warning me, huh? No, let this be a warning to *you.*"

He rose up a little and ripped the housecoat off her shoulders.

"Oh, god!" Stacey cried.

She writhed beneath him, tried to get away, but he pinned her head to the floor by placing his forearm against the back of her neck. She could only kick and buck as he reached down her waist with his gloved hand, and ripped off her drawers with two brutal, tearing jerks.

Stacey panted and grunted against the floor as Briggs ran his gloved hand between her pale buttocks. She winced at the brutal raking sensation of the man's glove, his fingers probing her most private area. "Oh, god, please . . . please!" she begged, the words catching in her throat.

Tears from the cold, sharp pain of the man's fingers dribbled down her cheeks.

"This is your warning, see, milady? This is your warning to never speak to Lawton Briggs in that tone of voice again, do you understand? You hurt my feelings out there on the street. And this is what happens when Lawton Briggs gets his feelings hurt."

Stacey could feel him rise up slightly onto one side, moving around on top of her. He was working the buttons on the fly of his pinstriped trousers and speaking with his lips only an inch away from her right ear. Spittle strung from his lips to dampen her hair hanging down over that ear.

She could feel the warm dampness of the man's saliva against her ear.

"Please, Briggs," Stacey almost sobbed, trying to keep her terror out of her voice as she spoke with her face pressed up hard against the floor. She didn't want to give in to her terror. She didn't want to give the man the satisfaction of knowing how horrified she was. "Don't do this, you bastard!"

"Bastard, eh?"

He fumbled around some more and then Stacey winced and gasped when she felt the firm warmth of his rod pressed against her buttocks. It felt like a dry, venomous snake, writhing against her.

Briggs pressed his tongue against her ear, probed around inside it, licking her. His breath was sour.

"Oh, god," Stacey said, squeezing her eyes closed. Then she realized she was sobbing, but she couldn't help it.

Pressing his throbbing rod against her butt, Briggs whispered into her ear: "Don't take it so hard, milady. You might even like it."

Then he gave a vicious grunt, and she felt the head of his shaft plunge into her.

"Ohh-Uhhhh!" Stacey cried against the floor, more tears oozing from her eyes as she felt the ripping and tearing sensation of the man's brutal penetration.

CHAPTER FIFTEEN

The sun-bleached skeleton was all dressed up and ready to ride.

It sat back against a boulder, bony legs extended, stovepipe cavalry boots crossed. It wore a battered blue campaign hat that the sun and weather had faded to something close to Confederate gray. It wore a yellow neckerchief, a gold-buttoned, sky-blue tunic, and dark-blue uniform trousers.

From its chest protruded an Apache arrow.

Someone had wedged a half-smoked cigar in one corner of the dead soldier's bony mouth, which boasted one silver-capped tooth. Very little parchment-like skin remained on the skeletal face and hands, which had been placed in the cadaver's lap, and the clothes were in tatters.

The empty eye sockets were as black as night.

The dead soldier appeared to be grinning around the cigar.

All dressed up and ready to ride. Only this soldier had already taken his last ride to his destination, wherever that was. Someone had had some fun with what the poor sergeant—he wore three gold chevrons on each sleeve—had left behind.

He sat here about twenty feet inside a narrow canyon, which Chaffee had indicated on the map he'd drawn for Cuno, the X on the map marking the position of Jack Salmon's hideout in the Desolados northeast of the Piños Altos. According to the map, Cuno was very near the hideout.

As if to verify the accuracy of Chaffee's map, a bullet spanged shrilly off the side of the boulder, six feet above the dead soldier's head. Cuno's horse, the pinto Chaffee had led out from town, lurched up and sideways as the rifle's bark echoed wildly around the canyon.

Cuno slapped his hand to the butt of the pistol on his right thigh—the gun and holster also a gift from Chaffee—but he left the gun in its sheath when a voice called out, "Go ahead and pull it, *amigo.* You'll be joining our friend there. That's all right—he's been wanting some company!"

The man had spoken with a thick Spanish accent.

Now his laughter chased the last echoes of his words around the canyon.

Cuno looked around, and picked out the brown face beneath a low-crowned, straw sombrero out of the rocks about forty feet up the canyon wall on his left. The man had a rifle aimed at him.

"Throw your hands up, *amigo!*"

Cuno raised his hands shoulder-high.

"Keep them there. You lower them an inch, and the sergeant won't be so lonely anymore!"

The sentry rose and came skipping and hopping along the rocks and boulders, tracing a serpentine course as he descended the canyon wall. Finally, he leaped onto a flat boulder just ahead and left of Cuno, and squatted there on his haunches, holding his old Spencer carbine in both gloved hands.

He wore a calico shirt, deerskin trousers ornamented with hammered silver disks, and knee-high, Apache-style moccasins. A leather makings sack dangled from a leather thong around his neck, which was wind-burned and sunburned a brick red; and he bore a large, pale, slashing scar on his right cheek, near the jawline.

Long, dark-brown hair dangled to his shoulders. He wore a silver spike in his right ear. His almond shaped eyes were long, long lashed, and his mouth was pursed with a mocking humor that dimpled his ruddy cheeks.

"Chaffee sent me," Cuno said.

"He did, did he?" The Mexican gave an exaggerated look of surprise. Then the grin returned, as mocking as before. "If so, what is the password?"

"Kiss my ass."

The Mexican threw his head back and roared, his mouth shaping a large, nearly perfect O. "Chaffee came up with that one himself."

"Good ole Chaffee. Barrel o' fun, ain't he?"

The Mexican straightened, turned to gaze up the canyon, and waved his rifle high above his head. Cuno saw a brief flicker of movement in the rocks high above the trail's right side, maybe a quarter mile beyond.

The Mexican turned back to Cuno. "Say, you don't have any tequila, do you?"

"No."

"Tobacco?"

"No," Cuno lied.

The Mexican scowled. "You could have brought a woman. That would have only been polite. Do you know how long we have been out here with the same three whores from Socorro?" He gave a frustrated grunt and then gestured with the rifle. "Ride on. But next time bring some tequila, some Mexican tobacco, and a *puta* or two, or—"

"Yeah, I know," Cuno said, touching spurs to the pinto's flanks and starting forward. "Or the sergeant won't be so lonely, anymore. I get your drift, *amigo*. See you on the way out."

"If they *let* you out, amigo!" the Mexican replied, and roared, his laughter echoing like the yammering of moon-crazed coyotes.

Ahead of Cuno, the canyon twisted and turned between its steep, rocky, boulder-strewn walls. The pinto's hoofs clacked off the uneven rocky floor littered with flood debris.

Glancing around, Cuno saw the sentry standing atop a flat boulder high above on his left. The man stood with his rifle cradled in his arms, staring nearly straight down at Cuno. He himself could have been made of stone. Aside from the slow turn of his head as he tracked the rider along the canyon floor, he didn't move, made no gesture at all.

The canyon walls leaned back away from Cuno. A sun-filled clearing lay dead ahead, fifty yards away and closing. Cuno could smell wood smoke and the succulent aromas of roasting meat.

He rode on into the clearing in which seven or eight *jacale*-like structures stood in a broad, ragged circle along the canyon's broad floor. Three or four small fires smoked among the brush huts. Beyond, ancient Indian cliff dwellings honeycombed the canyon's rear wall, jutting a good two thousand feet into the cobalt desert sky.

Small birds darted in and out of the dark openings, peeping.

The canyon was like an Apache encampment with a roped-off horse remuda lying far off to the right and at the edge of an aspen copse whose lime-green leaves flashed silver in the high country sunshine.

A creek shone in that direction, as well, glittering in tall grass. Two buxom, brown-skinned, black-haired young women in short, low-cut dresses were just now carrying wooden buckets of water toward the encampment, the high green grass dancing up around their bare knees.

A dozen or so men lounged around the smoky fires. One man rose from a rickety chair made of woven brush. He held a bottle in one hand. With his other hand, he grabbed his crotch as he yelled toward the women, "*Señorita* Loretta, please come quickly. My loins are heavy for you!"

The two young women glanced at each other skeptically. They were not thrilled to be here. They'd both probably had to work too hard on their backs to stay alive. They'd rather be back in Socorro.

Several of the other men chuckled. One threw an empty coffee cup at the man who'd yelled. He cursed, and said, "She's just playin' hard to get. Last night she said I was her favorite!"

A man with a rifle sat on a rock near where Cuno rode into the open canyon. He wasn't wearing a shirt, and his ancient broadcloth trousers were patched at the knees. He wore a battered Stetson over a mop of gray-brown curls, and a mustache of the same color mantled his small, mean mouth.

The man cocked the carbine in his hands, and rose, canting his head as he sized up the stranger on the pinto. "Company, Jack."

All heads turned toward the newcomer. A man sitting at the fire of the man who'd yelled, lowered a venison bone from his mouth, and, chewing, gained his feet heavily. He kicked an empty bottle as he tossed the bone down onto a tin plate, and then walked toward Cuno, stumbling a little, obviously drunk.

Jack Salmon was not at all as Cuno had pictured him. He was roughly Cuno's height, six feet, and a cap of dark, curly hair was set close to his skull. A potbelly bubbled out from behind his wash-worn longhandle top, so tight that Cuno could see the man's distended belly button. Suspenders dangled at his sides. He was sparrow-chested, round-faced, and his small, dark eyes were set close together atop a fleshy stump of a sun-blistered nose.

Jack Salmon had a rodent-like aspect. Cuno could smell him now as the man stopped before him. The stench was of rancid sweat and alcohol and sex. The man with the rifle had mean eyes. Salmon's eyes were meaner, darker, animalistic.

"What you got?" Salmon said, still chewing a mouthful of venison.

"Thursday."

Salmon studied him. So did the other man, who was a full head taller than Jack Salmon. They both eyed Cuno curiously, heads tipped toward each other as though in dubious, silent consultation.

"Thursday," said the bare-chested man with the rifle.

He nodded quickly, spat a wad of chaw to one side, and glanced at Salmon.

"Thursday," Salmon said, also nodding, as though working the information through his head. "All right. Thursday."

"Did Chaffee narrow it down any more than that?" asked the bare-chested man with the rifle. "Did he say morning . . . or afternoon . . . ?"

"Just Thursday," Cuno said, glancing around at the encampment once more, suddenly wishing he hadn't come here. Suddenly feeling dirty and a part of something he had no wish to be part of.

He'd made a bad decision, but he was here now, and there was nothing he could do about that.

As one of the two Mexican girls passed one of the fires, one of Salmon's men leaned out and grabbed a fistful of her dress. Laughing, he jerked the dress down off the girl's torso, baring her heavy, brown-tipped breasts.

The girl cried out, dropping her water bucket. The man laughed harder, pulled the girl down onto the ground, and then, shoving her forward onto her belly, he jerked the skirt of her dress up to her waist, baring the two round, brown swells of her naked bottom.

The man snickered through his teeth as he began fumbling with his fly buttons.

Then he mounted the girl, hammering against her roughly, holding her head by her hair. The girl moaned and sobbed as he rammed himself against her.

Cuno felt sick to his stomach. He looked at Salmon, who

leered at him. Cuno felt the almost uncontrollable desire to pull the Colt that Chaffee had given him, and shoot Jack Salmon in the face.

Right here and now.

But he'd never make it out alive.

All he could do was sit here and look around and hate himself for what he'd done.

Cuno had had enough. He pinched his hat brim to Salmon but kept his gaze hard and his mouth taut as he began turning his horse.

"What—you don't want to dine with us?" Salmon asked him. "Stay for a drink, at least!"

"No, thanks," Cuno said, touching spurs to the pinto's flanks and cantering back in the direction from which he'd come.

"Hey, kid—what's your name?" Salmon called.

But then the canyon walls closed around Cuno once more, and he was glad to be away from the camp. He put the pinto into a gallop, wanting to rid his nose of the stench of the place.

Of the stench of Jack Salmon himself.

CHAPTER SIXTEEN

Cuno slowed his pace as he retraced his path along the canyon's circuitous floor. The sun hammered brassily onto the canyon's western wall, on Cuno's right. Insects hummed. His nose was filled with the smell of the dry, peppery grass growing in sparse tufts between rocks.

He welcomed the smell, for it replaced the stench of the outlaw encampment.

Ten minutes after he'd left the camp, he saw the sentinel on the east ridge, sitting now on the flat-topped boulder he'd been standing on before, legs dangling down the side. He held his rifle barrel up on his right thigh. Cuno couldn't see the man's expression from this distance, but he thought he could see the white line of his teeth.

Was he grinning?

Cuno rode on. And then he realized that the man had, indeed, been grinning. And now Cuno realized what he'd been grinning at. There rose the sounds of a struggle—a woman struggling against a man who was grunting and laughing. There was a tearing of material, and then a shrill, horrified scream.

Cuno booted the pinto into a canter, reaching forward and sliding his rifle from its scabbard. Judging by the sounds, the commotion was occurring somewhere on the canyon floor. Cuno rounded a bend, spying movement to his right.

"Cuno!" a familiar voice cried.

Olivia Taffly broke free of the Mexican sentinel's grip, and came running toward Cuno, holding her blouse closed over her breasts. A saddled horse stood down the canyon a ways, switching its tail as it grazed on tufts of the wiry grass. Its bridle reins drooped to the ground.

"*Puta* bitch!" the Mexican cried, raising a rifle.

"No!" Cuno shouted, holding his own horse's reins taut as he raised his rifle in both hands but not before the Mexican's Spencer belched smoke and flames.

The bullet slammed into Olivia's back, throwing her brutally forward as she screamed, her head and arms snapping back. She fell and rolled, dust rising around her.

Cuno drew a bead on the Mexican, and squeezed the Winchester's trigger.

His bullet puffed dust from the Mexican's calico shirt as it plunged into his chest, throwing him straight backward with a clipped grunt. He landed under a lip of rock, half in and half out of the shade the lip laid down on the canyon floor.

"Olivia!" Cuno shouted, leaping from the saddle and running to drop to a knee beside the woman lying near a large rock and a tuft of Spanish bayonet, about ten yards off the trail.

She'd fallen on her back. She lay spread-eagle, blouse partway open to expose her chemise. Her breasts rose and fell sharply as she breathed. Blood oozed from her left side, about halfway between her waist and her shoulder.

"Olivia," Cuno said, cradling her head and shoulders against his knee.

She blinked, and gazed up at him, frowning as though seeing him for the first time. "How . . . could you?" she said.

"How could I what?"

Then he realized what she'd meant. She'd probably been on her way to visit him at the line shack when she'd seen him heading north. Curious about where he was going, she'd followed him . . . right into Jack Salmon's canyon, where the horny

Mexican sentinel had attacked her.

"How could you lie to me?" she asked, tears dribbling down her dusty cheeks. "You're . . . working for Salmon." She shook her head as though she couldn't believe what she was saying, though it all must have seemed so obvious to her now. "All along . . . you were working for Salmon."

There was no point in explaining. She knew enough to know that, for all intents and purposes, he'd lied to her. He had to get her out of the canyon before the other sentinel summoned the rest of the gang.

As though the second sentinel had been reading Cuno's mind, three quick rifle reports sounded from up the canyon. Then the sentinel shouted something Cuno couldn't make out, though he could hear the man's appeal echoing.

With the three gunshots, he'd been signaling Salmon and the rest of the gang.

Cuno unknotted his neckerchief. He reached into Olivia's torn blouse and pressed the wadded up cloth against the wound. It was a burn across the far left side of her rib cage. The bullet had passed on, thank god. She'd be sore for a while, but it was a wound much like his thigh wound. It wouldn't kill her.

Olivia jerked with a start, groaning, and lifted her head. "Oww!" she sobbed.

"Hold it there. I'm gonna get you on your horse!"

Olivia half-heartedly held the bandanna in place over the wound. Cuno ran over and retrieved Olivia's copper-bottom dun. He took the woman gently in his arms and lifted her up onto her saddle. She turned to give him a cold, accusing, bitter look.

"To think that I believed you. Everything you said. I was falling in *love* with you. And you were working for"—she glanced toward the dead Mexican—*"them!"*

"Not all the time." Cuno glanced up the canyon toward where

the Salmon riders would likely appear in a few minutes. "Not before Briggs staked me out and left me to die. Afterwards, I ran into one of Salmon's men from town who wanted me to get a message to Salmon."

He turned her horse to face down the canyon. Olivia held the bandanna against the wound with one hand; she wrapped her other hand around the saddle horn.

"It doesn't make a whole lot of difference," she said coldly. "You lied, just the same. You're not good. No good man would throw in with Jack Salmon."

"It was my way of getting back at Briggs."

"By throwing in with a man like Salmon." Olivia shook her head, pursing her lips. "What did you do up there, anyway? What did you ride in there for? What message did you give Salmon? When the next strongbox of gold would be shipped by the Ramos Line?"

Cuno's ears warmed with chagrin. He couldn't meet her bitter gaze. "We'll talk about it later. Pull your foot out of the stirrup."

"Why?"

"I'm going to climb up behind you."

"I can ride myself home, thank you. Give me the reins."

"You need me to help you. You might pass out."

"I won't pass out." Olivia jerked her gloved hand. "Give me the reins!"

Cuno sighed and handed her the reins. She gave him one last, cold look of disgust, then rammed the heels of her riding boots into the roan's flanks and lunged off down the canyon.

Cuno mounted his pinto and followed Olivia back across the bristling desert and up into the Palo Pintos. He wanted to make sure she didn't fall out of her saddle and die from blood loss along the trail.

As he rode, keeping about sixty, seventy yards behind the woman, he stopped several times to scan their backtrail. As far as he could tell, none of Salmon's riders was following him. They had bigger fish to fry than avenging the Mexican's death.

They were probably wondering who Cuno was and if the information he'd given them was genuine, but they'd assume it was. Most likely more than one of their riders had had a falling out with the other. Besides, the other sentinel had seen what the Mexican had been doing to Olivia. Salmon would chalk the killing up to a jealous rage over a woman. Nothing more.

They'd go after the gold on Thursday.

When Cuno and Olivia were deep in the Palo Pintos, he saw her swing off onto the trail that would take her the short distance more to her ranch. She was close enough to home now that she was out of danger.

Cuno paused to stare off at the intersecting trail, shame burning in him.

She'd been right. What he'd done had been wrong. Salmon's men were no better than Briggs and Stacey. What Briggs and the young woman had done to Cuno had been unforgivable. That said, it was possibly understandable, given what Salmon had done to the girl's father.

Salmon's men were worse even than Briggs. They were vermin.

The old saw was true: Two wrongs did not make a right. Somehow, Cuno had to atone.

He gigged the pinto on ahead and kept riding until he arrived at the line shack. He unsaddled the horse in the small lean-to stable and corral, rubbed it down, grained and watered it, and headed back into the cabin.

He started to throw the door closed, when a gun barked loudly, causing Cuno to jerk with a start. The slug tore into a ceiling support post behind him, as he swung around to see

Jeston Taffly standing back against the wall beside the door. He held a smoking Schofield in his right hand. A corked bottle jutted from a pocket of his wool jacket.

Smoke stinking like rotten eggs hung in the air around him.

He gritted his teeth as he took one step out away from the wall, and said, "The next one's goin' into your belly."

"Well, what are you waiting for?" Cuno said, more weary than frightened. "You got me dead to rights." He tossed Taffly's carbine onto the table and spread his open hands, indicating his belly.

"Uh-uh," Taffly said, grinning with menace. "I want you to wait for it. Dread it." The Schofield shook in his right hand. He wrapped his left hand around the bottle, removed it from his coat pocket, pulled the cork with his teeth, and took a pull.

He thrust the bottle at Cuno, gritting his teeth again with that drunken, enraged grin. "Want a sip?"

"No."

Taffly pulled the bottle back against him quickly, the whiskey sloshing loudly around inside the bottle. "Didn't mean it, anyway. I want you afraid."

"It's not going to work, Taffly. I can't say as I'm all that afraid to die. I've been so close enough times, I guess the fear got worn out of me."

Taffly waved the pistol at the chair on the far side of the table. "Sit down."

As Cuno stepped back toward the chair, Taffly grabbed his rifle off the table and leaned it against the wall by the door. Cuno sat down. Taffly set the bottle on the table and, keeping the quivering pistol aimed at Cuno's chest, pulled the near chair out from the table, and sat tensely down in it.

His eyes were red-rimmed and rheumy. From the stench and the way he slurred his words, he'd been drinking all day.

Working up the courage to kill in cold blood.

"I figured I'd find you both here," the man said when he'd taken another deep pull from the bottle. "Rode back to the ranch, she wasn't there. Rode over here."

"And then what were you going to do if you found us together? Shoot us?"

"Why not?"

"It wouldn't change anything."

Taffly took another pull from the bottle, wiping his mouth with the grimy sleeve of his jacket. "Maybe not. But it'd make me feel better."

"She doesn't love you. Seems to me you never gave her a chance to. You just moved into the house from the hired hand's shack when her husband died and started giving orders."

"I took her husband's place in that house, that's true. If it wasn't me, it would have been someone else." Taffly glared at Cuno from over the table, his pupils dilating visibly, ears turning red with mindless rage. "Now, what—you think *you're* gonna move in and take over?"

Cuno laughed. Not so much because he found anything funny in Taffly's words. He laughed at the man's bitter nonsense.

"Don't worry," Cuno said, sitting back in his chair. "I don't think she's any happier with me than she is with you right now. Whatever happened between us is over."

"Still leaves me out in the cold."

"We're all out in the cold. Why don't you get up and ride on out of here, Taffly? So far, you don't have any blood on your hands. Life is better that way, believe me. You can start again somewhere else. Fresh."

"Nah." Taffly shook his head and raised the cocked Schofield a little higher above the table. "I'm gonna kill you."

"All right. Have it your way."

Cuno had his hands on his knees. Now he slammed them up to the edge of the table, and, rising from his chair, lifted the table in front of him like a shield, pushing it back hard into Taffly.

The man screamed. The Schofield barked.

The slug plowed into a ceiling beam as Cuno continued to drive the table into Taffly. The man and his chair fell backward, hitting the floor with a thud.

Cuno saw the Schofield on the floor to his left. He kicked it away, then tossed the overturned table aside.

Taffly lay writhing on the floor, raging, fresh blood oozing through the reopened cuts in his lips. Cuno straddled the man, grabbed him by his coat lapel, and hammered his face three times with resolute right jabs.

Taffly fell back against the floor, stunned.

"Have you had enough?" Cuno asked him.

Taffly shook the cobwebs from his head, and glared up at Cuno. "I'm gonna kill you if it's the last thing I do!"

Cuno punched him again . . . again . . . and again.

Again, Taffly lay against the floor, blinking and groaning.

"How 'bout now?"

Taffly threw his right hand out as though searching for the Schofield.

Cuno hit him again—this time with a left uppercut that drove the man's head back hard against the floor. He was about to hit him again with the same fist, when Taffly, fear now sharp in his eyes, raised his hands in front of his face.

"Enough!" He was bleeding profusely from several lacerations, and his left eye was swelling. "Enough," he wailed, shrinking back against the floor.

Cuno pulled the man to his feet and led him outside. Taffly was dragging the toes of his boots, arms hanging slack at his sides. He was only half conscious. He unbuckled the man's cartridge belt and tossed it with its filled loops back through the cabin door. Cuno'd be needing all the ammunition he could get his hands on.

"Where's your horse?"

"Wha—huh . . . ?"

"Your horse?" Cuno said, louder. "Where is it?"

"B-back. Out back."

"Let's go find it."

He led Taffly around the line shack and into the woods. The man was staggering, drunk and beaten half-senseless. Finally, Cuno saw the man's horse. He helped Taffly into the saddle. The man groaned. Cuno gave him the bridle reins and then his hat, which he'd snatched off the line shack's floor.

"There you go—put that on. I'm doing you a favor, Taffly. One that you'll never have to repay. But don't thank me. Just get the hell away from here. A dynamite keg is about to explode around Crow Mesa. Believe me, you don't want to be anywhere near when it does."

Taffly looked around, his left eye swollen nearly shut. "Where . . . where in hell am I supposed to go?"

"Anywhere but here." Cuno slapped the rump of the man's horse, and watched it gallop east through the woods, heading toward the trail. "If I ever see you again—I mean *ever*—I'm going to kill you. No questions asked!"

The horse galloped through the trees, swerving around pockets of brush.

Gradually, the hoof thuds fell silent.

Taffly was gone.

Cuno went back into the line shack to load a rifle for a trip to town.

CHAPTER SEVENTEEN

Midmorning of the next day, Cuno rode down out of the mountains.

He'd spent enough time in the line shack. His body was well on the mend. In a few days, he'd be able to remove the stitches from his leg. He had a horse, a couple of guns, and enough ammo to retrieve his own weapons and his own horse, which he aimed to do sooner rather than later.

It was time he was reunited with the Colt Peacemaker the old outlaw, Charlie Dodge, had given him when he'd first set out on his journey to hunt down Rolf Anderson and Sammy Spoon. It was time he was reunited with the horse he'd set out on that journey on—his prized skewbald paint, Renegade.

It was time to finish what Briggs and Stacey had started . . .

He dropped down out of the pines and into the cactus-studded desert around noon A half hour later, the town appeared ahead of him, straddling the trail. He rode past the first adobe shacks and shanties and stock pens grown up with dusty brush and cactus, and on into the heart of the town.

He saw no reason to sneak around. He doubted that Briggs and his deputies and Stacey would be expecting him.

Stacey . . .

Maybe he'd see to her first, get her out of the way so that his path was clear to Briggs.

Cuno reined his horse to a stop in the middle of the street. The San Juan Valley Stage Line office lay on his left. The town marshal's office lay farther ahead, on his right. No one was in front of either place. In fact, there weren't many people on the street—only a few drifting in and out of the open shops that stood blazing in the intensifying heat and desert sunshine.

Six men dressed as shopkeepers sat out on one long bench and in a couple of chairs, in the deep shade of a roofed *galeria* to Cuno's right. They were flanked by a barbershop, a gun shop, a harness shop, and a land office. The men had been conversing among themselves as Cuno had ridden up, but now their eyes were on the stocky, blond stranger riding the dusty pinto.

Flies buzzed in the shade.

One of the shopkeepers had risen to get a drink from a clay *olla* hanging under the *galeria.* He paused now, the dripping gourd dipper held before his mustached lips. Frowning at the newcomer in the street, he lifted a hand to shoo a fly away from his face.

Cuno booted his horse up to the land office, dismounted, and tossed his reins over the hitch rack. The front door was open. A bearded man of late middle age sat at the roll-top desk just inside the door. He'd been asleep, leaning back in the chair, arms crossed on his chest, boots crossed on the desk. But now, as Cuno's boots thumped up the steps of the boardwalk, the man jerked in his chair, automatically reaching for the pistol on his hip.

He stayed the motion as Cuno entered the office, stepped to one side, and swung the door closed with a resolute click of the latch.

"Keep your hand away from your gun," Cuno said evenly.

The man dropped his feet to the floor and nudged the brim of his sombrero back up off his pale forehead, getting a better look at Cuno.

"Do we know each other?" the man said in a sleep-gravelly voice.

"Could be."

Cuno studied him for a moment. His face was puffy and discolored. One eye was badly bloodshot. Three stitches bristled from his split lower lip.

He'd recently taken a hammering. He didn't look well, but then, Cuno supposed no one would look well after such a beating.

"You're him, ain't ya?" the older man said with a fateful air, sitting back in the chair. He glanced at Cuno's leg, the one he moved tenderly on. The bulge of a bandage could be seen through the denim trouser leg. "You're . . . the one . . ."

"That's right."

"Christ."

"Who're you?"

"Chandler. Shotgun messenger. Friend of her pa's."

"Who did that to your face?"

The man stared at Cuno, pensive, apprehensive. "Briggs. He's runnin' off his leash." He paused. A muscle twitched in his age-spotted, sun-blistered face. "But then, I reckon you already know that . . ."

"Where's Stacey?"

"Why?"

"I just wanna talk to her . . . if she'll listen. I got news about Salmon."

The older man drew a deep breath and fingered an arm of his chair. "She's not good."

"How?"

"Briggs."

"Where is she?"

Chandler paused again, then gave another ragged sigh and raked a big, red hand down his face with an air of deep melancholy. "Upstairs." He glanced at a door at the back of the room, flanking a shelf displaying a miniature wooden stagecoach and four-horse team. "Like I said, she's in a bad way."

"Things get like that."

Cuno walked to the door, opened it, and started up the stairs. His boot thuds sounded inordinately loud in the tight canyon of the narrow stairway. A tintype hung on the right, papered wall— the photograph was of an older man, maybe Chandler's age, and Stacey.

The older man sat in a parlor chair. Owning vaguely Spanish features, he wore a bowler hat and suit too tight through the shoulders on him. Stacey stood behind him, one hand on his shoulder. Neither was smiling, as was the custom, but they both looked proud and happy to be posing for a photograph together.

Cuno paused at the door at the top of the stairs, and knocked twice.

There was no response, so he turned the knob and stepped into a quiet, shadowy parlor. Just beyond was a kitchen area with a small range and dry sink. A clock ticked woodenly on a wall.

The apartment was a small area, neat and clean, a rocking chair and a sofa being the only furniture in the parlor. A pipe sat in an ashtray on a small, round table beside the rocker, as though whoever had smoked it would return to it soon.

A door shone in the parlor's far wall.

Cuno walked to it, and knocked with the knuckle of his right index finger.

"I don't want anything to eat, Sam," came the girl's somber voice from the other side of the door.

Cuno opened the door, pushed it wide, and stepped into the doorway.

She lay on the bed that nearly filled the small room. She lay facing away from Cuno, sunlight from two windows blazing two large, golden rectangles on the bed, glittering in her hair fanned across her pillow.

"I'm not Sam."

She turned to him slowly, listlessly, rolling onto her side now to face him. There was a nasty cut on her chin, and her right cheek was bruised. A holstered gun hung from a bedpost. She made no move for it. She blinked once, slowly, and then her eyes studied Cuno for a long time. Her shoulders rose beneath the single sheet covering her, as she drew a deep breath.

She closed her eyes and wrinkled the skin above the bridge of her nose. "I'm sorry."

She squeezed her eyelids tighter.

Cuno hadn't been sure what he'd feel when he finally got close to her, but he was a little surprised to find himself feeling appalled by what had happened to her face. He no longer felt even half the rage he'd felt only yesterday.

In fact, he felt a strange sort of kinship with this girl. It was almost as though they were brother and sister. In spite of her hand in leaving him staked out to die, he found himself sympathizing with her plight. It wasn't all that far from his, after all.

Cuno said, "What'd he do?"

Stacey opened her eyes. She stared at him for a full fifteen seconds before her eyelids fluttered with emotion. A golden sheen of tears dripped down over her eyes, and she tried unsuccessfully to put some steel in her voice. "He showed me who was boss around here."

A fresh burn of anger rose up in Cuno.

"I told Salmon about the gold being shipped on Thursday. But I wasn't working for Salmon until a couple days ago, after you staked me out."

She stared at him with seemingly no thought or emotion.

"He has a spy in town relaying telegraph news. He gave me the news. I took it to Salmon."

"Who is this spy?"

"Never mind. I'll take care of him. But you'd better get out of that bed, because Briggs isn't gonna be much help to you on Thursday. You're gonna need every gun you got, including your own." He glanced at the Colt Lightning holstered on the bedpost.

Again, she just stared at Cuno. It was almost as though she'd only half-heard him.

Then she gave her head a slight shake, and pursed her lips. "Let them have it. I'm leaving here. I shouldn't have stayed after Pa died. There was nothing left for me here."

She turned around on the bed, giving her back to Cuno once more.

"I can't let them have the gold. Not now, after what I did. And you can't, either."

Cuno swung around and headed back across the parlor.

He heard the bedsprings squawk. "Where are you going?"

He stopped and turned back to her. She was half-sitting, staring toward him, her disheveled hair framing her pretty face. She held the bedcovers to her breasts.

"I'm gonna get my guns and my horse back from Briggs."

CHAPTER EIGHTEEN

Cuno went back downstairs. Chandler stood by the door, looking out into the street. He glanced at Cuno walking toward him.

"Something tells me Briggs got wind that a stranger's in town."

"What makes you think that?"

"The town council is no longer seated on the other side of the street. They're always there. All day ceptin' when one of 'em has a customer, which ain't very often."

"That's all right."

Cuno moved forward. Chandler partly blocked the doorway with his big, stooped frame. "You may regret goin' out there."

"Let's see."

Chandler shrugged and stepped aside. Cuno walked out onto the gallery and then down into the street. He shucked his Winchester from his saddle boot, and pumped a cartridge into the chamber.

As he began walking toward the town marshal's office, he stopped. Briggs was just then walking out of the office's front door and into the street. He kept walking straight out away from the office, and the three deputies followed him, spaced about ten feet apart—Travis Cole, Bonner McCallister, and Kiefer Lake.

Briggs stopped in the middle of the street.

Cole continued past him and stopped just beyond him, near

the street's far side. The other two, the bearded McCallister and stocky Lake, stopped between Briggs and the marshal's office, and turned to face Cuno. McCallister was grinning. They were all carrying rifles. They all, of course, had revolvers strapped to their hips or thighs.

Briggs glanced at the men to either side of him, and nodded.

They began walking slowly toward Cuno, holding their rifles up high across their chests.

Cuno started walking forward, then, too, holding his own rifle straight down by his right leg.

Cuno stopped walking when Briggs and his deputies stopped walking. There was a distance of about forty yards between Cuno and the lawmen.

Briggs stared hard at Cuno from beneath the brim of his bowler hat. The lawmen's long muttonchops twisted around in the hot, dry wind. The wind licked at the tails of his wool waistcoat and the sleeves of his striped shirt. He wore a pearl-gripped revolver in a holster over his belly button, the handle curving up against his gold watch chain.

Cuno's prized Colt was tucked behind the man's cartridge belt, near his left hip.

Briggs was smiling now, too—as though with delight.

The deputies narrowed their eyes as they sized up their opponent, the breeze nipping at their neckerchiefs. Kiefer Lake had been smoking a cigarette but now he let the quirley slip out of his mouth to the ground, where it sputtered and rolled before the wind grabbed it.

"I'll be taking my guns back, Briggs," Cuno said. "I trust my horse is safe and sound?"

"He wouldn't let anybody ride him, boyo," Briggs said. "He ain't much bloody good if he can't be ridden—now, is he . . . boyo? I was fixin' to shoot him, and I will, just as soon as I've shot you. Toss you both in the same ravine."

It was Cuno's turn to grin. "Talk's cheap. Proof is in the pudding. Now, are you assholes going to aim those rifles, or are you just gonna stand there, rattling your spurs and looking stupid?"

Cole, the string bean whom Cuno had thrown into the fire, opened his mouth to howl like an Apache as he snapped his Winchester to his shoulder. Because he was the first one to move, he was the first one to take a bullet, Cuno snapping up the barrel of his borrowed Winchester and sending one through the man's belly.

As the others commenced firing, Cuno threw himself forward, racking another round into the Winchester's chamber. He hit the ground on his stomach, propping himself on his elbows as the first barrage screamed over his head.

Aiming hastily, he triggered a round into the knee of McCallister, and then another round into Lake's lumpy chest. Lake stumbled backward, dropping his rifle and staring down in wide-eyed horror at the blood geysering from the hole in his chest.

He hit the ground as though he'd been punched in the face, still looking at the blood issuing from his chest, and screaming.

Briggs drilled three rounds into the dirt around Cuno. All three rounds missed because the man was sidestepping toward the boardwalk, apparently wanting cover. Cuno rolled to his right as Briggs sent another two rounds into the street, dangerously close.

He rolled up onto his belly, raising his Winchester and aiming toward Briggs, who just then lowered his own rifle and slipped into a break between buildings, running off toward the buildings' rear.

Cuno shouted, "Don't run away from me, you son of a bitch!"

He flinched as a rifle cracked in front of him. The bullet carved a cold line across the side of his neck. He turned to where McCallister lay sprawled in the street, fumbling another round into his carbine's breech, grimacing against the pain in his right, bloody knee, the leg of which formed a precarious angle in the street before him.

Cuno swung his Winchester toward McCallister. The man screamed in horror, knowing he couldn't get his own rifle to his shoulder in time to save himself. He was right. Cuno's next bullet punched through his chest, just beneath his neck, snapping the man's bearded head back and forward.

He dropped his rifle with a grunt of pain, blinking bewilderedly at Cuno, and then rolled his eyes back into his head and flopped backward, jerking as he died.

Cuno turned back toward where Briggs had fled.

He looked up and down the street, expecting to see Briggs's rifle poke out from behind a rain barrel near another alley mouth. Slowly, warily, Cuno gained his feet, quickly brushing his hand across the back of his neck. It came away bloody, but not bad. Just a burn.

Slowly, Cuno moved back down the street, in the direction of the stage line office. Holding his rifle out from his right side, he slid the barrel from left to right and back again, looking for his target.

The street was deserted. The sun blasted down on the butterscotch-colored amalgam of dirt and ground horseshit. A small dust devil spun near the empty chairs of the town council. It died as it hit the covered gallery, pelting the boards lightly with dirt.

Cuno mounted the gallery where the sun glare wasn't so bright. Slowly, he moved down along the front of the eerily silent shops, his boots thumping softly along the boards. As he continued to cast his gaze up and down the street, he glimpsed movement ahead on his right.

A hatted head and a rifle barrel poked out from around the far corner of a drugstore. Cuno threw himself through a large, sashed window on his left as the rifle began belching wickedly, bullets plunking into the front of the shops where Cuno had been standing a second ago. Screeching glass rained down around him.

Cuno winced as several glass shards bit into him. He heaved himself to his feet as Briggs's rifle continued to bark on the other side of the street, throwing lead through the front wood frame wall of the land office. Cuno ran forward, dropping to a knee by another window.

He could see Briggs kneeling at the corner of the drugstore, tipping his rifle barrel up as he cocked the weapon.

Cuno aimed through the window and ground his teeth as he blew out the glass. Through his wafting powder smoke and shattering glass, he watched Briggs fling his rifle into the air as he bounded up off his knee and stumbled backward, yelling.

Cuno jerked open the land office door and stepped out onto the gallery, kicking one of the town councilmen's chairs out of the way. He watched Briggs writhing in the alley mouth off the corner of the drugstore. Stepping down off the gallery, he headed toward the lawman.

He stopped suddenly at the raspy bark of a rifle being cocked to his left.

He swung around to see Neal Chaffee step out through the batwings of the Bobcat Saloon. Chaffee aimed a cocked carbine straight out from his right shoulder.

"Double-crossin' son of a bi—"

KA-BOOMMMM!

Chaffee was blasted up off his feet and thrown forward off the narrow stoop of the Bobcat. He hit the street and rolled, leaving a bloody path in the dust behind him. He stopped rolling about six feet to Cuno's left. He lay on his back, gritting his teeth as he glared up at Cuno.

He grunted, writhed, and then his body fell slack. His eyelids dropped halfway down over his eyes, and he was dead.

A boot thudded inside the Bobcat. A man's tall, stooped, bearded figure pushed through the batwings. Sam Chandler stood on the Bobcat's stoop, both barrels of his sawed-off, double-barreled shotgun smoking in his hands.

"Had me a feelin' about him," Chandler said. "Him bein' new and takin' a job so close to the telegraph office when he was also drivin' a coach for Miss Stacey."

Chandler spat a wad of chaw into the street and brushed a fist across his mouth.

Cuno said, "You got it right. Thanks for backin' me."

He continued toward Briggs who lay breathing like a landed fish and cursing loudly.

"Bastard!" Briggs bellowed. "Bloody goddamn son of a bitch!" He glared up at Cuno staring down at him. "Who in the hell are you, and where the hell did you come from, boyo?"

The marshal was pressing one gloved hand to the bloody wound in his upper right thigh and another to the wound in his left side, just above his rib cage. His face was a sweaty, red mask of pain against which his pewter muttonchops stood out in contrast.

His eyes were a devil's slanted gray eyes tinged with yellow.

"I'm the traveler you shouldn't have waylaid, Briggs."

He bent down and slid his prized Peacemaker out from behind Briggs's cartridge belt. He ran an appreciative hand over the gun, spun the cylinder, and slid it down behind his cartridge belt.

Briggs turned his gaze to Chandler. "Sam, get me to a doctor. I'm the marshal of this town, and—"

"Shut up, Briggs," the shotgunner growled.

Cuno glanced at Chandler. "Help me, will you?"

He reached down and grabbed a fistful of Briggs's shirt collar. Chandler grabbed a fistful of the marshal's vest, and they dragged Briggs through the dust and deposited him in the street out front of the marshal's office.

Cuno turned to Chandler. "Can you find four good, long stakes and a sledgehammer?"

Briggs bellowed and kicked. "Don't you . . . don't you think about it, boyo!"

Chandler grinned. "Sure, I reckon I can find some picket pins over to the livery barn."

He turned and strode off toward the town's lone livery barn. Cuno went into the marshal's office and found four sets of handcuffs in a couple of drawers of Briggs's desk. He walked out of the office and closed one bracelet of each cuff around Briggs's wrists and ankles.

"Don't worry," he told the lawman, bellowing curses at him. "I'm not gonna strip you like you stripped me. I wouldn't put the town through it, Briggs. This will do."

When Chandler returned with the four picket pins, Cuno knocked them into the ground with the sledgehammer while Briggs bellowed and writhed and demanded that the doctor tend him. Doc Warren came out of his office, but he stood halfway down the stairs running up the side of the furniture store, and merely stared incredulously toward the scene of the loud, grisly commotion.

The town council had scuttled out of their shops, and they, too, stood staring dubiously toward Cuno, Briggs, and Chandler, who sat on the marshal's office front steps, rolling and smoking a quirley.

When Cuno had all four pins driven into the street, he cuffed Briggs's wrists and ankles to the pins. The pins were spaced out far enough that Briggs couldn't lift the bracelets up and over the pins.

He was stretched out in the street like some grisly, bloody, bawling angel.

Cuno straightened and stared down at the raging lawman.

Briggs glared up at him, his eyes a pulsating yellow-gray. "You bastard," he rasped through gritted teeth. "You goddamn bloody bastard!"

"Yeah, that was my sentiment about you, when you had me in a similar situation. The only difference here, Briggs, is you're gonna die where you are. No one's gonna get you out of this. Anyone tries, they'll get the same."

He'd raised his voice and looked around as he'd vowed that last statement.

He was sure that enough had heard him and that the threat would spread.

Cuno spied movement in the stage line office door. Stacey stepped out onto the gallery. She wore a plain blouse and skirt, and she'd brushed her hair. Her face was drawn and pale around the cuts and bruises.

She dropped off the steps and walked out into the street to stand over Briggs, who stared up at her without saying anything. The look on his face was one of regret, chagrin, humiliation. He looked away from the girl staring stonily down at him.

She said, "I came out to join your send-off, Briggs. Enjoy your slow ride to hell, you sick son of a bitch."

The marshal snapped his pain-racked eyes at her. "You go ahead and see what Salmon does to your stage line now, you bloody little bitch!"

Stacey spat in his face.

Briggs jerked his head to one side. The saliva ran down his cheek.

Cuno looked at Stacey and glanced down the street at where Neal Chaffee lay in front of the Bobcat Saloon. "You're gonna need a driver."

"Can you drive a team?"

Cuno nodded.

Stacey nodded, then, too. "The stage from San Lorenzo should pull through here around noon tomorrow. Here is where we switch drivers and shotgun messengers. The pull to the west, into the mountains, is where Salmon will hit us."

Briggs laughed bizarrely, pulling at the picket pins. "Oh, he's going to hit you tomorrow, little miss." He laughed again. It was half-laughter, half-sobbing at the misery in his stretched-out body. "He's going to hit you *hard*!"

CHAPTER NINETEEN

"Comin' up on a damn good place for Salmon to hit us," Chandler said the next afternoon, around three. "Keep your eyes peeled."

Leaning forward in the driver's box, the ribbons loose in his hands, strung between his fingers so that he could control each horse separately, Cuno said, "Don't worry—they're peeled."

He'd never driven a stagecoach before, but he'd driven dozens of four- and six-horse hitches of mules. This was roughly the same thing.

Cuno looked around. It was damned rugged country—a giant red dinosaur's mouth of sun-blasted rock and crumbling canyons to the left, down a steep slope. A towering sandstone ridge studded with gnarled cedars and cactus loomed on the right. The trail curved sometimes precariously between the badlands and the ridge, making fast travel impossible.

If Salmon hit them in here, there would be no getting away from him.

Cuno looked down at the badlands. A hot breath wafted out of that dinosaur's mouth at him, smelling like rock and pine resin. The sun reflecting off all that red sand and rock was blinding. The sun hammered down, but it was so hot that Cuno's sweat evaporated before it could soak into his shirt, which Olivia Taffly had given him from a trunk she'd kept of her first husband's possibles.

Olivia . . .

Shame burned at him. He shook his head, clearing the emotion. He couldn't afford the distraction of regrets over the past.

He looked at Chandler. The man held his double-barrel Greener straight up from his right thigh. His head was turned as he inspected the towering ridge, knowing that men could be hiding in any one of those cracks and niches, preparing to step out on a pinnacle of rock and fire down at them.

"Why do you keep doing this?" Cuno asked the man. "After getting hit so many times by Salmon, on a damned impossible route into the mountains. Why don't you just take your pay and hightail it to Albuquerque?"

Chandler turned to him, hiking a shoulder. "I was friends with Stacey's pa. Since she's too stubborn to close up shop, I reckon I gotta stay and see what I can do to help the fool girl." He frowned. "Why in hell are you doin' this? You're young, got your whole life ahead of you. Stacey and Briggs abused you in a way no man should ever abuse another. Still, you're here, tryin' to save this line. It's so damn crazy I almost don't trust you."

Cuno smiled as he stared out over the team's bobbing heads. "You think I'm still in with Salmon?"

"Nah. I don't think you're in with Salmon. After seein' you take down Briggs and his deputies, I think you're too good, too cagey, to be in with Salmon. He's all about greed and brute killin', just like Briggs himself." Again, Chandler shook his head, thoroughly baffled. "You're a puzzle."

"I can't say as I know for sure myself," Cuno said, frowning out over the team as they began climbing up through pines, the badlands slipping out and away from them on his left. "I reckon I'm just trying to make amends."

"Amends for what?"

"For letting the need for revenge get away from me, so I lost my sense of what's right and what's wrong. We all need to hold on to that, you know. It might sound stupid, but in this world, it really is all we have. Without it we're lost."

Chandler nodded and squeezed the double barrels of the Greener in his gloved hands, looking around warily. "Yeah . . . I think Stacey mighta learned that lesson, too. The hard way." He paused, chuffing wryly. "Who knows—maybe Briggs learned, there at the end."

Early that morning, Cuno had found Briggs lying dead between the picket pins, in the middle of Crow Mesa's main street. The man had died with an expression of raw horror still ablaze in his wide eyes and wide-open mouth, as though he'd watched the devil in the form of a stinking, red-eyed, ragged-winged bird swoop down out of the sky sometime during the man's long, last night to pluck out his soul and fly it to hell.

Cuno had to admit a pang of disappointment upon finding the "town tamer's" body. He'd wanted him to suffer longer. Blood loss had probably contributed to Briggs's demise. Blood loss and the humiliation of his ironic fate.

"Up ahead there," Chandler said. "That's where Stacey'll be."

Cuno followed the older man's gaze toward a sandstone shelf humping up out of the ground, on the trail's left side. Above it was a slope carpeted in heavy pines and cedars. As the stage approached the outcropping, Cuno saw Stacey step out between two trees, at the very top of the abruptly shelving bench.

Cuno drew back on the team's ribbons, "Whoa, team. Whoa."

He looked around, for Salmon could hit them anywhere in here. There was a better chance he'd hit them farther on, where the country was even more rugged and where there was a good southern trail toward the border. They were about halfway between Crow Mesa and the Jim Dandy Mine, which was another good ten miles farther on from here.

But no one knew what Salmon would do. A lifelong outlaw, he'd proven to be unpredictable.

Cuno set the brake, locking the wooden blocks against the front wheel, and handed the reins to Chandler, who'd set his Greener on the floor near his feet.

"You got it?" Cuno asked.

"I ain't no driver—don't like the idea of driving this damned contraption—but I seen how ole Xavier done it, like he was born doin' it—so I reckon I can drive 'em a piece. It's slow country through here, anyways."

"If you hear or see anything, just stop 'em and set the brake. That's all you can do. If all goes as planned, I'll be along shortly."

"If all goes as planned . . ." the shotgunner-turned-temporary-jehu said with a sigh, situating the ribbons in his hands. He glanced behind him and down at the coach roof. "I hope our boys perform when the chips are down."

"They will," Cuno assured the man, as he stepped off the side of the coach and onto the ledge, where Stacey waited, the reins of Cuno's skewbald paint, Renegade, in her hand.

Stacey glanced at the horse. Renegade was eagerly sniffing Cuno's ear. "You were right—he took to me."

"He'll let others ride him as long as I show him it's all right."

"You two must have quite the relationship."

"We've been together long enough." Cuno patted the stallion's neck. "You'd best get along. Don't want Salmon to ride up on us while we're making the switch."

Stacey wrapped her hand around Cuno's forearm, and kissed his cheek. "Thank you."

"Don't thank me. This little plan of mine might just get us all killed. And then we'll lose the gold, to boot."

"We had to do something. There was no other way."

Stacey stepped down off the shelf and into the coach's driver's boot. She stepped over Chandler's knees, sat on the seat beside the old man, and scooped his shotgun up off the floor, brushing dust from the stock.

Cuno pinched his hat brim to her. "I'll be close."

Stacey nodded. Chandler released the brake handle with a grating thud, and then, taking the ribbons unconfidently in his big, gloved hands, whipped them lightly against the team's back, clucking.

"Get up now, you mangy old cayuses," he urged.

As the coach lurched on up the trail, Stacey glanced at Chandler, and smiled, likely because Chandler was merely repeating what her father had called the team, doubtless with no little affection.

As the coach rattled on up the hill, Cuno hitched his Peacemaker and cartridge belt higher on his hips, and swung up onto Renegade's back. He put the horse on up the steep slope, which ran generally parallel with the trail. The plan had been for Cuno to drive the team the first half of the trip, and for Chandler to ride shotgun, and then for Cuno to switch places with Stacey at the halfway point.

The skills of an experienced driver weren't as much in demand on the latter half of the journey; because of the terrain, the team would have to be held to a fast walk. Almost anybody could do that. Now what was needed more than a driver was an experienced gunman to ride parallel with the trail, keeping an eye on the coach here where Salmon was most likely to hit it.

If . . . or when . . . Salmon held up the coach, Cuno hoped to be in position to foil the robbery and to kill Salmon if none of the others. Of course, if all went as planned, Salmon's entire gang would be wiped out by the end of the day. But that was going to take some luck, Cuno speculated as he glanced to his right now to see the stagecoach lurching along the trail about two hundred and fifty feet below.

They were getting into higher, cooler country now. The sweat was beginning to linger on Cuno's back, turning cold when the breeze kicked up.

He followed the lip of the ridge, occasionally swerving around natural formations and then having to find his way back to the edge of the canyon. Below, the stage bounced and jerked over the chuckhole-peppered trail following the cut of an ancient river that had once roared down the side of this mountain, forming the badlands below.

Several times he got far enough ahead of the coach that he was able to stop and survey the terrain ahead of it for any sign of Salmon's men. Finding himself once more ahead of the stage following a broad horseshoe bulge in the canyon wall—a bulge which the terrain prevented Cuno himself from following—he stopped Renegade, swung down from the saddle, and looped the reins over a pine branch.

He shucked his Winchester, which he'd retrieved from the town marshal's office back in Crow Mesa, and started down the boulder-littered slope, heading in the direction of the ancient river trail below. He couldn't hear or see the stage from this vantage, but he could see the bottom of the canyon where the stage would likely be in a minute or two, once it had made its way around the bulge.

He weaved his way down the steep slope, avoiding large rocks, boulders, and cedars. He moved, crouching, holding his rifle in both hands, knowing this would be as good a place as any in the canyon to affect an ambush.

Something thudded behind him.

Cuno whipped around, heart quickening. A pinecone, freshly fallen from a breeze-nudged branch, rolled toward him.

Cuno exhaled slowly, lightened his grip on his rifle, and turned back toward the canyon floor. He took two steps forward. A spur chinged faintly behind him. Before he could do anything more than tense again, there was the metallic rasp of a rifle behind cocked.

The cold, round maw of the barrel was pressed against the

back of his neck.

"Well, hello there," said the man behind him.

CHAPTER TWENTY

The man behind Cuno said, "Suppose you toss that rifle down. Then you can go ahead and drop that Peacemaker, too." He pressed the rifle barrel harder against the back of Cuno's neck, and drew his voice taut. "Do it slow. If you move too fast, I'm gonna blow a hole through your neck!"

Cuno lowered the rifle, stepped forward, and set it on a flat-topped rock. Slowly, he slid the Peacemaker from its holster and set it on the rock beside the rifle.

"Get your hands up!"

Raising his hands shoulder-high, palms out, Cuno turned around to see an unshaven, sandy-haired young man in a slouch hat and yellow neckerchief standing behind him. The kid couldn't have been much over nineteen. He was short and fair-skinned, his hair closely cropped. His little, brown eyes were nervous. One of his front teeth was chipped, giving him a scruffy, naïve look.

Cuno remembered seeing him around one of the fires in Jack Salmon's hideout canyon. Probably occupying a lower rung in the Salmon bunch's hierarchy, he was likely up here keeping an eye on the gang's horses, tethered nearby. That meant the others were likely below, waiting for the stage.

"Hey, I remember you," the kid said, narrowing his little eyes, puzzled. "You rode into camp the other day. What're you doin', sneakin' around out here . . . ?"

"I have to talk to Salmon," Cuno said, thinking fast. "There's been a change of plans."

"What kind of a change of plans?"

"I gotta talk to Salmon, kid."

He let his voice trail off when he heard the stage's distant clattering echoing up from the bottom of the canyon.

The kid shifted his gaze toward the canyon below and behind Cuno.

Cuno lunged toward him, reaching for the kid's rifle.

The kid was too quick. He jerked back, swinging his rifle wide, then bringing it to bear on Cuno once more, his jaws hard, face flushed.

Cuno stopped, resetting his feet on the gravelly slope.

The kid crouched over the rifle's barrel. "You make one more move like that, and you're wolf bait, pard!"

In the canyon below, someone whistled.

Cuno swung back around to face the canyon floor. He could now see a half-dozen or so men hunkered down behind rocks and tufts of shrubs near the bottom of his own slope as well as near the bottom of the opposite ridge.

The stagecoach was just now coming into sight from Cuno's right. As it did, the men on both slopes rose from behind their covering rocks, and Chandler pulled back on the teams' reins.

Cuno now saw how vulnerable the stage was here in this canyon.

If someone wanted to hold it up, there wasn't much the driver or even the shotgun messenger could do. If they didn't stop the stage, they'd both be shot out of the driver's box and the team would be easily overtaken and stopped.

As planned, neither Chandler nor Stacey gave any resistance. As the man who could only be Salmon himself walked out to the edge of a large boulder looming over the trail and began shouting and gesturing with his aimed rifle, Stacey raised the shotgun and her free hand above her head. Chandler raised both his hands, as well.

Stacey tossed the shotgun away.

Salmon shouted, "Now, the brake!"

Chandler spat to one side and pulled the brake lever back.

Behind Cuno, the kid chuckled.

Cuno's heart beat heavily, steadily, as Salmon and the other men made their leisurely way down the ridges, hopscotching rocks, one man sliding and falling momentarily to one knee when his boots hit slide-rock. One of the stage's lead horses, sensing trouble, whinnied and pitched.

"Settle that horse down, Chandler!" Salmon ordered as he leaped down off a rock to the canyon floor, pointing at the troublesome leader.

Cuno slid his gaze around the men descending on the canyon. He looked at the coach itself. He could see no movement behind the windows.

Good, he thought. *Easy, now. Hold on.*

Don't get in a hurry, fellas . . .

As he approached the coach, Salmon laughed mockingly, pointing at Chandler and Stacey, bending back at the waist as his mocking laughter echoed around the canyon.

"Hey, purty girl," Salmon said, "why don't you climb up on the coach roof and roll that strongbox off? Would you do that for me, please?"

All dozen outlaws were moving up to both sides of the coach now. They weren't worried. They had the situation in hand. They'd done this before, and every time had been as easy as walking into a mercantile and buying a bag of chopped tobacco. They had the situation in hand.

Everyone knew the stage line had no money for armed guards beyond its gray-bearded shotgun messenger. The line was essentially at the mercy of anyone wanting to rob it, as well as the terrain it had to traverse in getting gold or payroll coins in or out of the mountain mining camps.

Stacey stood, cursing Salmon, who laughed at the girl's vinegar, and then climbed up onto the coach roof.

As she did, Cuno slid his gaze back to the coach.

Easy, easy . . .

He glanced back at the kid standing six feet behind him, holding the rifle on him.

"Ain't a damn thing you can do," the kid mocked around his chip-toothed grin. "So just rest easy less'n you want a bullet in the back."

Cuno turned his head forward. "I reckon you got us again," he said with a feigned air of defeat.

The outlaws continued to gather around the coach. Jack Salmon walked up to stand by the near front wheel, tipping his head back to watch Stacey maneuver the strongbox. He'd rested his rifle barrel on his shoulder. Cuno slid his gaze from Stacey to the coach's near door and back again.

Meanwhile, Chandler stared down at the outlaws, holding his hands shoulder-high, palms out. He didn't say anything.

As the outlaws continued to close on the coach, Salmon said, "Who're your passengers today, Miss Stacey? Anyone we might like to meet?" He glanced at one of the other outlaws. "Pull 'em outta there, J.C.!"

Stacey glanced up the ridge toward Cuno. She paused.

It's all right, Cuno told her silently. *Don't mind me. Keep goin' . . .*

"Come on outta there!" ordered the man who'd reached for the handle of the near door.

At the same time, Stacey flipped open the strongbox's lid. She pulled out a sawed-off shotgun, which she tossed to Chandler, who caught it one-handed. Just as the outlaw jerked the coach's door open, Stacey pulled a second coach gun out of the strongbox.

Chandler fired first, blowing a head of one of the outlaws gathered below him clean off the man's shoulders. Stacey whipped the second coach gun up over the strongbox's open lid, and sent ten-gauge buckshot hurling into Salmon and a handful of the others who stood gaping up at her, so shocked by what they were seeing that they were slow to react.

Three rifle barrels bristled from the coach's near windows.

The rifles roared, belching red flames and white smoke.

The kid behind Cuno said, "What . . . in . . . the . . . ?"

Cuno lurched forward, gripped his revolver, and continued hurling himself over the top of the rock he'd set the Colt on. The kid triggered three rounds at him, all three screaming shrilly off the top of the rock.

Cuno landed on his butt on the rock's other side. He raised his Colt, aimed up at a slant, and sent three slugs slamming into the kid's chest, shredding his pinstriped shirt and throwing the kid backward with a clipped yowl.

The echoing thunder in the canyon sounded like a small war being fought. Men howled and screamed. The coach team whinnied.

As Cuno heaved himself to his feet and reached for his rifle, he saw three horses bucking in the coach's traces. Chandler was standing on the floor of the driver's boot, firing a six-shooter he'd hidden under the seat, howling like a banshee. Stacey knelt on one knee atop the coach, pivoting at the waist as she triggered a carbine, causing the Salmon bunch to dance around, screaming and triggering their own rifles or pistols wide, as bullets punched through them.

The strongbox atop the coach hadn't been carrying any gold coins, but only the two shotguns. The strongbox containing the coins was inside the coach, along with the six town councilmen whom Cuno and Stacey had convinced to ride in the coach,

It had taken some convincing, but the town councilmen had known that a town without a stage line was a town on its last legs. So they'd agreed to fight in Stacey's army for that reason, but also because it was damned hard to refuse such a pretty and bewitching young lady, as they'd already known when she'd convinced them to hire Lawton Briggs.

Briggs had been a mistake. This idea, however, had proven to be a good one. As this was the height of the ranching season, there was no one else in town to help except for the town councilmen themselves.

Now as the remainder of the Salmon bunch howled his last and the shooting grew more and more sporadic, both coach doors opened and the six council members spilled out, three through each door, each holding a smoking rifle in his hands and looking damned proud of himself.

Cuno glanced at the dead kid, then started down the hill.

He stopped when a figure moved before him—Jack Salmon himself, peppered with buckshot, trying to crawl his way up the steep slope to safety. Salmon stopped when Cuno's shadow slid over him. The man, one eye socket a bloody pulp, looked up at Cuno, his lower jaw sagging. Even his lips were bloody.

Salmon held a Colt in one hand. As he started to raise it, snarling like a gut-shot coyote, Cuno extended his Winchester one-handed, and sent a final round through the man's brain plate.

Cuno looked over Salmon's quivering body toward the canyon floor.

The councilmen were spread out, staring up at Cuno.

So were Chandler and Stacey. There was no more shooting. The bad men were dead, the stage line saved.

At least for now . . .

Cuno stepped around Salmon and continued making his way

354

down the slope. He stopped suddenly. What was the point? His horse was at the top of the ridge behind him. Besides, there was another woman in these parts he had to see and settle up with, if there was a way to do that.

He'd feel better for trying. Then he'd move on and try to stay ahead of the law until that amnesty came through, if it ever did. Maybe he'd head up to Denver and try to locate Spurr Morgan.

Cuno stared down the canyon at Stacey Ramos staring up at him. She held the barrel of her double-barrel Greener on her shoulder. Her face was shaded by her hat brim.

Cuno pinched his own hat brim to her, waved his rifle, then turned around and headed back up the ridge to his horse.

ABOUT THE AUTHOR

Western novelist **Peter Brandvold** was born and raised in North Dakota. He has penned over ninety fast-action westerns under his own name and several pen names, including Frank Leslie. He wrote thirty books in the popular, long-running *Longarm* series for Berkley. He is the author of the ever-popular .45-Caliber books featuring Cuno Massey, as well as the Lou Prophet and Yakima Henry novels. The Ben Stillman books are a long-running series with previous volumes available as e-books. Head honcho at "Mean Pete Publishing," publisher of lightning-fast western e-books, he has lived all over the American West but currently lives in western Minnesota with his dog. Visit his website at www.peterbrandvold.com. Follow his blog at: www.peterbrandvold.blogspot.com.

The employees of Five Star Publishing hope you have enjoyed this book.

Our Five Star novels explore little-known chapters from America's history, stories told from unique perspectives that will entertain a broad range of readers.

Other Five Star books are available at your local library, bookstore, all major book distributors, and directly from Five Star/Gale.

Connect with Five Star Publishing

Visit us on Facebook:
   https://www.facebook.com/FiveStarCengage

Email:
   FiveStar@cengage.com

For information about titles and placing orders:
   (800) 223-1244
   gale.orders@cengage.com

To share your comments, write to us:
   Five Star Publishing
   Attn: Publisher
   10 Water St., Suite 310
   Waterville, ME 04901